R.A. Salvatore's
WAR OF THE SPIDER QUEEN BOOK 1

Dissolution

RICHARD LEE BYERS

R . A . S A L V A T O R E ' S
War of the Spider Queen Book 1: Dissolution

Cover art by Brom

US ISBN: 0-7869-2714-3
UK ISBN: 0-7869-2733-X
620-88554-001-EN

U.S., CANADA,
ASIA, PACIFIC, & LATIN AMERICA
Wizards of the Coast, Inc.
P.O. Box 707
Renton, WA 98057-0707
+1-800-324-6496

EUROPEAN HEADQUARTERS
Wizards of the Coast, Belgium
P.B. 2031
2600 Berchem
Belgium
+32-70-23-32-77

FORGOTTEN REALMS®

R.A. Salvatore's

WAR OF THE SPIDER QUEEN

For Ann

Acknowledgments

*Thanks to Phil Athans, my editor,
and to Bob Salvatore for overseeing this project.*

It was a flicker of clarity in the foggy realm of shadowy chaos, where nothing was quite what it seemed, and everything was inevitably more treacherous and dangerous. But this, the crystalline glimmer of a single silken strand, shone brightly, caught her eye, and showed her all that it was and all that would soon be, and all that she was and all that she would soon be.

The glimmer of light in the dark Abyss promised renewal and greater glory and made that promise all the sweeter with its hints of danger, mortal danger for a creature immortal by nature. That, too, was the allure, was, in truth, the greatest joy of the growth. The mother of chaos was fear, not evil, and the enjoyment of chaos was the continual fear of the unknown, the shifting foundation of everything, the knowledge that every twist and turn could lead to disaster.

It was something the drow had never come to fully understand and appreciate, and she preferred that ignorance. To the drow, the chaos was a means for personal gain; there were no straight ladders in the tumult of drow life for one to climb. But the beauty was not the ascent, she knew, if they did not. The beauty was the moment, every moment, of living in the swirl of the unknown, the whirlpool of true chaos.

So this, then, was a movement forward, but within that movement, it was a gamble, a risk that could launch the chaos of her world to greater heights and surprises. She wished she could remain more fully conscious to witness it all, to bask in it all.

But no matter. Even within, she would feel the pleasure of their fear, the hunger of their ambition.

That glimmer of the silk edge, cutting the gray perpetual fog of the swirling plane, brought a singular purpose to this creature of shifting whims and reminded her that it was time, was past time.

Never taking her gaze off that glimmer, the creature turned slowly, winding herself in the single strand. The first strand of millions.

The start of the metamorphosis, the promise.

Gromph Baenre, Archmage of Menzoberranzan, flicked a long, obsidian-skinned finger. His office door, a black marble rectangle incised all over with lines of tiny runes, swung noiselessly shut and locked itself.

At least certain that no one could see him, the drow wizard rose from the white bone desk, faced the back wall, and swirled his hands in a complex pattern. A second doorway opened in the stippled calcite surface.

His dark elf vision unimpaired by the lack of light, Gromph stepped into the blackness beyond the new exit. There was no floor there to receive his tread, and for a moment he fell, then he invoked the power of levitation granted by the House Baenre insignia brooch that he was never without. He began to rise, floating up a featureless shaft. The cool air tingled and prickled against his skin as it always did, and it also carried a rank, unpleasant smell. Evidently one of the creatures native to this peculiar pseudoplane of existence had been nosing around the conduit.

Sure enough, something rattled above his head. The rank smell was suddenly stronger, pungent enough to make his scarlet eyes water and sting his nose.

Gromph looked up. At first he saw nothing, but then he discerned a vague ovoid shape in the darkness.

The archmage wondered how the beast had gotten inside the shaft. Nothing ever had before. Had it torn a hole in the wall, oozed through like a ghost, or done something stranger still? Perhaps—

It plummeted at him, putting an end to his speculations.

Gromph could have effortlessly blasted the creature with one of his wands, but he preferred to conserve their power for genuine threats. Instead, he coolly dismissed the force of levitation lifting his body and allowed himself to drop back down the shaft. The fall would keep him away from the beast for long enough to cast a spell, and he didn't have to worry about hitting the ground. In this reality, there was no ground.

The bejeweled and sigil-adorned Robes of the Archmage flapping around him, he snatched a vial of venom from his pocket, set it alight with a spurt of flame from his fingertip, and recited an incantation. On the final syllable, he thrust his arm at the creature, and a glob of black, burning liquid erupted from his fingertips.

Propelled by magic, the blazing fluid hurtled straight up the shaft to splash against the descending predator. The creature emitted a piercing buzz that was likely a cry of pain. It floundered in the air, bouncing back and forth against the walls as it fell. Its body sizzled and bubbled as the spattered acid ate into it, but it resumed diving in a controlled manner.

Gromph was mildly impressed. A venom bolt would kill most creatures, certainly most of the petty vermin one encountered in the empty places between the worlds.

Manipulating an empty cocoon, he cast another spell. The beast's body crumpled and folded into itself, and for a heartbeat, it was a helplessly tumbling mouse—then it swelled and rippled back into its natural form.

All right, thought Gromph, then I'll cut you up.

He prepared to conjure a hail of blades, but at that moment, the creature accelerated.

Gromph had no idea the creature could descend any faster than it had hitherto, and he wasn't prepared for the sudden burst of speed. The creature closed the distance between them in an instant, until it was hovering right in his face.

It had the melted or unfinished look common to many such beings. Rows of blank little eyes and a writhing proboscis sat off center in its bump of a head, only vaguely differentiated from its rubbery blob of a body. The monster possessed no wings, but it was flying—the goddess only knew how. Its legs were the most articulate part of it. Ten thin, segmented members terminated in barbed hooks, which lashed at Gromph again and again and again.

As he expected, the frenzied scratching failed to harm him. The enchantments woven into Gromph's *piwafwi*—not to mention a ring and an amulet—armored him at least as well as a suit of plate. Still, it irked him that he had allowed the beast to get so close, and he felt more irritated still when he noticed that the creature's exertions were flinging tiny smoking droplets of his own conjured acid onto his person.

He growled a final spell and snatched hold of the malodorous predator, seizing handfuls of the blubber on its torso. Instantly the magic began its work. Strength and vitality flowed into him, and he cried out at the shocking pleasure of it.

He was drinking his adversary's very life, much as a vampire might have done. The flying creature buzzed, thrashed, and became still. It withered, cracked, and rotted in his grasp. Finally, when he was certain he'd sucked out every vestige of life, he shoved it away.

Focusing his will, he arrested his fall and drifted upward again. After a few minutes, he spied the opening at the top of the shaft. He floated through, grabbed a convenient handrail, pulled himself over onto the floor of the workroom, then allowed his weight to return. His vestments rustled as they settled around him.

The large circular chamber was in most respects a part of the tower of Sorcere—the school of wizardry over which the Archmage presided—but Gromph was reasonably certain that none of the masters of Sorcere suspected its existence, accustomed to secret and magical architecture though they were. The place, lit by everlasting candles like the office below, was well nigh undetectable, even unguessable, because its tenant had set it a little apart from normal space and conventional time. In some subtle respects it existed in the distant past, in the days of Menzoberra the Kinless, founder of the city, and in another way, in the remote and unknowable future. Yet on the level of gross mortal existence, it sat firmly in the present, and Gromph could work his most clandestine magic there secure in the knowledge that it would affect the Menzoberranzan of today. It was a neat trick, and sometimes he almost regretted killing the seven prisoners, master mages all, who had helped him build the place in exchange, they imagined, for their freedom. They had been genuine artists, but there was no point in creating a hidden refuge unless one ensured it would remain hidden.

Dusting a few specks and smears of the flying vermin from his nimble hands, Gromph moved to the section of the room containing an extensive collection of wizard's tools. Humming, he selected a spiral-carved ebony staff from a wyvern's-foot stand, an onyx-studded iron amulet from its velvet-lined box, and a wickedly curved athame from a rack of similar ritual knives. He sniffed several ceramic pots of incense before finally selecting, as he often did, the essence of black lotus.

As he murmured a invocation to the Abyssal powers and lit a brazen censor with the tame little flame he could conjure at will, he hesitated. To his surprise, he found himself wondering if he truly wanted to proceed.

Menzoberranzan was in desperate straits, even though most of her citizens hadn't yet realized it. In Gromph's place, many another wizard would embrace the situation as an unparalleled opportunity to enhance his own power, but the archmage saw deeper. The city had experienced too many shocks and setbacks in recent years. Another upheaval could cripple or even destroy it, and he didn't fancy life in a Menzoberranzan that was merely a broken mockery of its former glory. Nor did he see himself as a homeless wanderer begging sanctuary and employment from the indifferent rulers of some foreign realm. He had resolved to correct the current problem, not exploit it.

Except I am about to exploit it in at least a limited way, aren't I? he thought. Give in to temptation and seize the advantage, even if so doing further destabilizes the already precarious status quo.

Gromph snorted his momentary and uncharacteristic misgivings away. The drow were children of chaos—of paradox, contradiction, and perhaps even perversity. It was the source of their strength. So yes, curse it, why not walk in two opposite directions at the same time? When would he get another chance to so alter his circumstances?

He moved to one of the complex pentacles inlaid in gold on the marble floor and traced the tip of the black staff along its curves and angles, sealing it. That done, he swept the athame in ritual passes and chanted a rhyme that returned to its own beginning like a serpent swallowing its tail. The cloying sweetness of black lotus hung in the air, and he could feel the narcotic vapors lifting his consciousness into a state of almost painful concentration and lucidity.

He lost all track of time, had no idea whether he'd been reciting for ten minutes or an hour, but the moment finally came when he'd recited long enough. The netherspirit Beradax appeared in the center of the pentacle, seeming to jerk up out of the floor like a fish at the end of an angler's line.

His centuries of wizardry had rendered Gromph about as indifferent to ugliness and grotesquerie as a member of his callous race could get, yet even he found Beradax an unpleasant spectacle. The creature wore the approximate shape of a dark elf female or perhaps a human woman, but her body was made of soft, wet, glistening eyeballs adhering together. About half of them had the crimson irises characteristic of the drow, while the rest were blue, brown, green, gray—a miscellany of the colors commonly found in lesser races.

Her body flowing, her shape warping, Beradax flung herself at her summoner. Fortunately, she couldn't pass beyond the edge of the pentacle. She slammed into an unseen barrier with a wet, slapping sound, then rebounded.

Undeterred, she lunged a second time with the same lack of success. Her resentment and malice infinite, she would spring a million times if left to her own devices. Gromph had caught her, trapped her, but something more was needed if they were to converse. He shoved the ritual dagger into his belly.

Beradax reeled. The eyeballs comprising her own stomach churned and shuddered. A few fell away from the central mass to fade and vanish in the air.

"*Kill you!*" she screamed, her shrill voice unnaturally loud, her gaping mouth affording a shadowy glimpse of the eyeball bumps lining the interior. "I'll kill you, wizard!"

"No, slave, you will not," Gromph said. He realized the chanting and incense had parched his throat, and he swallowed the dryness away. "You'll serve me. You'll calm yourself and submit, unless you want another taste of the blade."

"Kill you!"

Beradax sprang at him again and kept springing while he pulled the athame back and forth through his abdomen. Finally she collapsed to her knees.

"I submit," she growled

"Good." Gromph extracted the athame. It didn't leave a tear in his robes or in his flesh, which was to say, the knife's enchantments had worked precisely as expected, hurting the demon rather than him.

Beradax's belly stopped heaving and shaking.

"What do you want, drow?" the creature asked. "Information? Tell me, so I can discharge my errand and depart."

"Not information," the dark elf said. He'd summoned scores of netherspirits over the past month, and none had been able to tell him what he wished to know. He was certain Beradax was no wiser than the rest. "I want you to kill my sister Quenthel."

Gromph had hated Quenthel for a long time. She always treated him like some retainer, even though he too was a Baenre, a noble of the First House of Menzoberranzan, and the city's greatest wizard besides. In her eyes, he thought, only high priestesses deserved respect.

His antipathy only intensified as the two of them attempted to advise their mother, Matron Mother Baenre, the uncrowned queen of Menzoberranzan. Predictably, they'd disagreed on every matter of policy from trade to war to mining and had vexed one another no end.

Gromph's animus intensified still further when Quenthel became Mistress of Arach-Tinilith, the school for priestesses. The mistress governed the entire Academy, Sorcere included, and thus Gromph had found himself obliged to contend with her—indeed, to suffer her oversight—in this one-time haven as well.

Still, he might have endured Quenthel's arrogance and meddling indefinitely, if not for their mother's sudden and unexpected death.

Counseling the former matron mother had been more an honor than a treat. She generally ignored advice, and her deputies were lucky if she let it go at that. Often enough, she responded to their suggestions with a torrent of abuse.

But Triel, Gromph's other sister and the new head of House Baenre, had, over time, proved to be a different sort of sovereign. Indecisive, overwhelmed by the responsibilities of her new office, she relied heavily on the opinions of her siblings.

That meant the archmage, though a "mere male," could theoretically rule Menzoberranzan from behind the throne, and at long last order all things to please himself. But only if he disposed of the matron's other counselor, the damnably persuasive Quenthel, who continued to oppose him on virtually every matter. He'd been contemplating her assassination for a long time, until the present situation afforded him an irresistible opportunity.

"You send me to my death!" Beradax protested.

"Your life or death are of no importance," Gromph replied, "only my will matters. Still, you may survive. Arach-Tinilith has changed, as you know very well."

"Even now, the Academy is warded by all the old enchantments."

"I'll dissolve the barriers for you."

"I won't go!"

"Nonsense. You've submitted and must obey. Stop blathering before I lose my patience."

He hefted the athame, and Beradax seemed to slump.

"Very well, wizard, send me and be damned. I'll kill her as I will one day butcher you."

"You can't go quite yet. For all your bluster, you're the lowliest kind of netherspirit, a grub crawling on the floor of Hell, but tonight you'll wear the form of a genuine demon, to make the proper impression on the residents of the temple."

"*No!*"

Gromph lifted his staff in both hands and shouted words of power. Beradax howled in agony as her mass of eyeballs flowed and humped into something quite different.

Afterward, Gromph descended to his office. He had an appointment with a different kind of agent.

As Pharaun Mizzrym and Ryld Argith strolled through the cool air, fresher than that pent up in Melee-Magthere, the latter looked about Tier Breche, realized he hadn't bothered to set foot outside in days, and rather wondered why, for the view was as spectacular as ever.

Tier Breche, home to the Academy since that institution's founding, was a large cavern where the labor of countless spellcasters, artisans, and slaves had turned enormous stalagmites and other masses of rocks into three extraordinary citadels. To the east rose pyramidal Melee-Magthere, where Ryld and others like him turned callow young drow into warriors. By the western wall stood the many-spired tower of Sorcere, where Pharaun and his colleagues taught wizardry, while to the north crouched the largest and most imposing school of all, Arach-Tinilith, a temple built in the eight-limbed shape of a spider. Inside, the priestesses of Lolth, goddess of arachnids, chaos, assassins, and the drow race, trained dark elf maidens to serve the deity in their turn.

And yet, magnificent as was Tier Breche, considered in the proper context, it was only a detail in a scene of far greater splendor. The Academy sat in a side cavern, a mere nook opening partway up the wall of a truly prodigious vault. The primary chamber was two miles wide and a thousand feet high, and filling all that space was Menzoberranzan.

On the cavern floor, castles, hewn like the Academy from natural protrusions of calcite, shone blue, green, and violet amid the darkness. The phosphorescent mansions served to delineate the plateau of Qu'ellarz'orl, where the Baenre and those Houses nearly as powerful made their homes; the West Wall district, where lesser but still well-established noble families schemed how to supplant the dwellers on Qu'ellarz'orl; and Narbondellyn, where parvenus plotted to replace the inhabitants of West Wall. Still other palaces, cut from stalactites, hung from the lofty ceiling.

The nobles of Menzoberranzan had set their homes glowing to display their immensity, their graceful lines, and the ornamentation sculpted about their walls. Most of the carvings featured spiders and webs, scarcely surprising, Ryld supposed, in a realm where Lolth was the only deity anyone worshiped, and her clergy ruled in the temporal sense as well as the spiritual one.

For some reason, Ryld found the persistence of the motif vaguely oppressive, so he shifted his attention to other details. If a drow had good eyes, he could make out the frigid depths of the lake called Donigarten at the narrow eastern end of the vault. Cattle-like beasts called rothé and the goblin slaves who herded them lived on an island in the center of the lake.

And there was Narbondel itself, of course. It was the only piece of unworked stone remaining on the cavern floor, a thick, irregular column extending all the way to the ceiling. At the start of every day, the Archmage of Menzoberranzan cast a spell into the base of it, heating it until the rock glowed. Since the radiance rose through the stone at a constant rate, its progress enabled the residents of the city to tell the time.

In their way, the Master of Melee-Magthere supposed, he and Pharaun were, if nowhere near as grand a sight as the vista before them, at least a peculiar one by virtue of the contrasts between them. With his slender build, graceful manner, foppish, elegant attire, and intricate coiffure, the Mizzrym mage epitomized what a sophisticated noble and wizard should be. Ryld, on the other hand was an oddity. He was huge for a member of his sex, bigger than many females, with a burly, broad-shouldered frame better suited to a brutish human than a dark elf. He compounded his strangeness by wearing a dwarven breastplate and vambraces in preference to light, supple mail. The armor sometimes caused others to eye him askance, but he'd found that it maximized his effectiveness as a warrior, and that, he'd always believed, was what really mattered.

Ryld and Pharaun walked to the edge of Tier Breche and sat down with their legs dangling over the sheer drop-off. They were only a few yards from the head of the staircase that connected the Academy with the city below, and at the top of those steps, beside the twin pillars, a pair of sentries—last-year students of Melee-Magthere—stood watch. Ryld thought that he and Pharaun were distant enough for privacy if they kept their voices low.

Low, but not silent, curse it. Ever the sensualist, the mage sat savoring the panorama below him, obviously prolonging his contemplation well past the point where Ryld's mouth had begun to tighten with impatience, and never mind that on the walk up, he'd admired the view himself.

"We drow don't love one another, except in the carnal sense," Pharaun remarked at last, "but I think one could almost love Menzoberranzan itself, don't you? Or at least take a profound pride in it."

Ryld shrugged. "If you say so."

"You sound less than rhapsodic. Feeling morose again today?"

"I'm all right. Better, at least, now that I see you still alive."

"You assumed Gromph had executed me? Does my offense seem so grievous, then? Have you never annihilated a single specimen of our tender young cadets?"

"That depends on how you look at it," Ryld replied. "Combat training is inherently dangerous. Accidents happen, but no one has ever questioned that they *were* accidents occurring during the course of Melee-Magthere's legitimate business. The goddess knows, I never lost seven in a single hour, two of them from Houses with seats on the Council. How does such a thing happen?"

"I needed seven assistants with a degree of magical expertise to help me perform the summoning ritual. Had I called upon full-fledged wizards, they would have joined the experiment as equal partners. They would have emerged from the ritual possessed of the same newly discovered secrets as myself, equally able to conjure and control the Sarthos demon. Naturally I wished to avoid such a sharing, so I opted to use apprentices instead."

Pharaun grinned and continued, "In retrospect, I must admit that it may not have been a good idea. The fiend didn't even require seven heartbeats to smash them all."

An updraft wafted past Ryld's face, carrying the constant murmur of the metropolis below. He caught its scent as well, a complex odor made of cooking smoke, incense, perfume, the stink of unwashed thralls, and a thousand other things.

"Why perform such a dangerous ritual in the first place?" he asked.

Pharaun smiled as if it was a silly question. Perhaps it was.

"To become more powerful, of course," the wizard answered. "At present, I'm one of the thirty most puissant mages in the city. If I controlled the Sarthos demon, I'd be one of the five. Perhaps even the first, mightier than dreary old Gromph himself."

"I see."

Ambition was an essential part of the drow character, and Ryld sometimes envied Pharaun his still-passionate investment in the struggle for status. The warrior supposed that he himself had achieved the pinnacle of his ambitions when he became one of the lesser masters of Melee-Magthere, for certainly he, born a commoner, could never climb any higher. From that day forward, he'd stopped peering hungrily upward and concentrated on looking down, to guard against all those who wished to kill him in hopes of ascending to his position.

Pharaun was a Master of Sorcere as Ryld was a Master of Melee-Magthere, but perhaps, being of noble blood, Pharaun really did aspire to assassinate the formidable Gromph Baenre and seize his office. Even if he didn't, wizards, by the nature of their intricate and clandestine art, maintained a rivalry that encompassed more than who was a master, who was chief wizard in a great House, and who was neither. They also cared about such things as who could know the most esoteric secrets, could conjure the deadliest specter, or see most clearly into the future. In fact, they cared so deeply that they occasionally sought to murder each other and plunder one another's spellbooks even when such hostilities ran counter to the interests of their Houses, severing an alliance or disrupting a negotiation.

"Now," Pharaun said, reaching inside the elegant folds of his *piwafwi* and producing a silver flask, "I'll have to turn my back on the Sarthos demon for a while. I hope the poor behemoth won't be lonely without me."

He unscrewed the bottle, took a sip, and passed the container to Ryld.

Ryld hoped the flask didn't contain wine or an exotic liqueur. Pharaun was forever pressing such libations on him and insisting that he try to recognize all the elements that allegedly blended together to create the taste, even though Ryld had demonstrated time and again that his palate was incapable of such a dissection.

He drank and was pleased to find that for a change, the flask contained simple brandy, probably imported at some expense from the inhospitable world that lay like a rind atop the Underdark, baking in the excruciating sunlight. The liquor burned his mouth and kindled a warm glow in his stomach.

He handed the brandy back to Pharaun and said, "I assume Gromph told you to leave the entity alone."

"In effect. He assigned me another task to occupy my time. Should I succeed, the archmage will forgive me my transgressions. Should I fail . . . well, I'll hope for a nice beheading or garroting, but I'm not so unrealistic as to expect anything that quick."

"What task?"

"A number of males have eloped from their families, and not to a merchant clan or Bregan D'aerthe either but to an unknown destination. I'm supposed to find them."

Pharaun took another sip, then offered the flask again.

"What did they steal?" asked Ryld, waving off the drink.

Pharaun smiled and said, "That's a good guess, but you're wrong. As far as I know, no one walked off with anything important. You see, it isn't just a few fellows from one particular House. It's a bunch of them from any number of homes, noble and common alike."

"All right, but so what? Why does the Archmage of Menzoberranzan care?"

"I don't know. He offered some vague excuse of an explanation, but there's something—several somethings, belike—that he's not telling me."

"That's not going to make your job any easier."

"How true. The old tyrant did condescend to say that he isn't the only one interested in the fugitives' whereabouts. The priestesses are equally concerned, but that emphatically did not make them want to join forces with Gromph. Matron Mother Baenre herself ordered him to drop the matter."

"Matron Baenre," said Ryld. "I like this less with every word you speak."

"Oh, I don't know. Just because Triel Baenre rules all Menzoberranzan, and I'm about to flout her express wishes . . . Anyway, the archmage says he can no longer investigate the disappearances himself. Seems the ladies have their eyes on him, but, lucky me, I am not so burdened."

"That doesn't mean you're going to find the missing males. If they fled the city, they could be anywhere in the Underdark by now."

"Please," said Pharaun with a grin, "you don't have to try to cheer me up. Actually, I'm going to start looking in Eastmyr and the Braeryn. Apparently some of the runaways were last sighted in those déclassé vicinities, and perhaps they linger there still. Even if they do intend to depart Menzoberranzan, they may still be making preparations for the journey."

"If they've already decamped," Ryld said, "you might at least find a witness who can at tell you what tunnel they took. It's a sensible plan, but I can think of another. It's reckless to gamble your life when you don't even understand the game. You could flee Menzoberranzan yourself. With your wizardry, you're one of the few people capable of undertaking such a dangerous trek alone."

"I could try," Pharaun said, "but I suspect Gromph would track me down. Even if he didn't, I would have lost my home and forfeited the rank I worked my whole life to earn. Would you give up being a master just to avoid a spot of danger?"

"No."

"Then you understand my predicament. I imagine you've also figured out why I called on you today."

"I think so."

"Of course you have. Whatever it is that's truly transpiring, my chances of survival improve if I have a comrade to watch my back."

Ryld scowled. "You mean, a comrade willing to defy the express will of Matron Mother Baenre and risk running afoul of the Archmage of Menzoberranzan as well."

"Quite, and by a happy coincidence you have the look of a drow in need of a break from his daily routine. You know you're bored to death. It's painful to watch you grouch your way through the day."

Ryld pondered for a moment, then said, "All right. Maybe we'll find out something we can turn to our advantage."

"Thank you, my friend. I owe you." Pharaun took a drink and held out the flask again. "Have the rest. There's only a swallow left. We seem to have guzzled the whole pint in just a few minutes, though that scarcely seems possible, refined, genteel fellows that we—"

Something crackled and sizzled above their heads. Waves of pressure beat down on them. Ryld looked up, cursed, scrambled to his feet, and drew a dagger, meanwhile wishing he'd strapped on his weapons before stepping outside Melee-Magthere.

Pharaun rose in a more leisurely fashion.

"Well," he said, "this is interesting."

chapter

TWO

Scourge of vipers writhing in her hand, soft, thin gown whispering, Quenthel Baenre, Mistress of Arach-Tinilith, prowled about, glaring at the younger females standing huddled in the center of the candlelit, marble-paneled room. She always had a knack for striking fear into the hearts of those who displeased her, and these students were no exception. Some trembled or appeared to be biting back tears, and even the sullen, fractious ones refused to look her in the eye.

Enjoying their apprehension, Quenthel prolonged her silent inspection until it was surely on the verge of becoming unbearable, then she cracked the whip. Some of her startled pupils gasped and jumped.

As the five long black- and crimson-banded vipers that comprised the lashes of the whip rose twisting and probing from the adamantine handle, Quenthel said, "All your lives, your mothers have told you that when a student ascends to Tier Breche, she remains here, sequestered from the city below, for ten years. On the day you entered the Academy, I told you the same thing."

She stalked up to one of the students trapped at the front of the group, Gaussra Kenafin, slightly plump and round-faced, with teeth as black as her skin. Responding to Quenthel's unspoken will, the whip snakes explored the novice's body, gliding over its contours, tongues flickering. The Mistress of Arach-Tinilith could see Gaussra straining mightily not to recoil for fear that it would provoke the reptiles into striking.

"So you did know," Quenthel purred, "didn't you?"

"Yes," Gaussra gasped. "I'm sorry. Please, take the snakes away!"

"How impertinent of you. You and these others have forfeited the right to ask me for anything. You may kiss her."

The last statement was addressed to the serpents, and they responded instantly, driving their long fangs into cheek, throat, shoulder, and breast. Gaussra collapsed—fully expecting to fall into a seizure, mouth foaming, her own blackened incisors chewing her purple tongue.

Shaking from the sting of the bites, Gaussra sat on the floor, very much alive; her terror was apparent, her humiliation complete.

"You will return to your House," Quenthel said, relishing the look on Gaussra's face as the true meaning of that statement sank in. "If you come that close to my scourge again, the vipers will allow their venom to flow."

Quenthel stepped away from Gaussra, who scrambled to her feet and ran from the chamber.

"You all knew what was expected of you," she said to the rest of the novices, "but you tried to sneak home anyway. In so doing, you have offered an affront to the Academy, to your own families, to Menzoberranzan, and to Lolth herself!"

"We just wanted to go for a little while," said Halavin Symryvvin, who seemed to carry half of her insignificant House's paltry wealth in the form of the gaudy, gold ornaments hanging about her person. "We would have come back."

"Liar!" shouted Quenthel, eliciting a flinch.

Rearing, the whip vipers echoed the cry.

"Liar!"

"Liar!"

"Liar!"

In other circumstances, Quenthel might have smiled, for she was proud of her weapon. Many priestesses possessed a whip of fangs, but hers was something special. The snakes were venomous and likewise possessed a demonic intelligence and the power of speech. It was the last magical tool she'd crafted before everything turned to dung.

"Oh, you would have returned," she continued, "but only because your mothers would have sent you back or else killed you for shaming them. They have sense enough to cleave to the sacred traditions of Menzoberranzan even if their degenerate offspring do not.

"Your mothers wouldn't mind if I slaughtered you, either. They'd thank me for wiping clean the honor of their Houses. But Lolth desires new priestesses, and, despite all appearances to the contrary, it is remotely possible that one or two of you are worthy to serve. Therefore I will give you one more chance. You won't die today. Instead you will sever a finger from each of your hands and burn them before the altar of the goddess to beg her forgiveness. I'll ring for a cleaver and a chopping block."

Quenthel surveyed their stricken faces, enjoying the sickly, shrinking fear. She would enjoy watching the actual mutilations as well. The most amusing part might be when a novice had already cut one hand, and had to employ it, throbbing and streaming blood, to maim the other. . . .

"No!"

Surprised by the outburst, Quenthel peered to see who had spoken. The mass of would-be truants obliged her by dividing in the center, opening a lane to the willowy female standing in the back. It was Drisinil Barrison Del'Armgo, she of the sharp nose and green eyes, whom Quenthel had from the first suspected of instigating the mass elopement. Somehow the long-legged novice had smuggled a sizable dagger, more of a short sword really, into the disciplinary session. She held it ready in a low guard.

Quenthel reacted as would any dark elf in the same situation. She yearned to accept the challenge and kill the other female, felt the need like a sensual tension pressing for an explosive release. Either responding to her surge of emotion or else themselves vexed by Drisinil's temerity, the whip vipers reared and hissed.

The problem was that, despite Quenthel's assertions to the contrary, the students were not altogether devoid of importance. They were the raw but valuable ore sent to the Academy to be refined and hammered into useful implements. No one would fret over a few amputated pinkies, but the matron mothers did expect that, for the most part, their children would survive their education, an assumption the idiot Mizzrym renegade had already called into question. True, Pharaun had only lost males, but still, by any sensible reckoning, he had used up the school's quota of allowable deaths for several years to come.

At this juncture it would be a poor idea for Quenthel to kill any student, certainly a scion of the powerful Barrison Del'Armgo. Quenthel didn't want to stir up discord between the Academy and the noble Houses when Menzoberranzan already perched on the brink of dissolution.

Besides, she was a bit concerned that the other failed runaways might take it into their heads to jump into the fight on their ringleader's side.

Quenthel quieted the vipers with a thought, fixed Drisinil with her steeliest stare, and said, "Think."

"I have thought," Drisinil retorted. "I've thought, why should we spend ten years of our lives cooped up on Tier Breche when there's nothing for us here?"

"There is everything for you here," said Quenthel, maintaining the pressure of her gaze. "This is where you learn to be all that a lady of Menzoberranzan must be."

"What? What am I learning?"

"At the moment, patience and submission."

"That's not what I came for."

"Evidently not. Consider this, then. All the priestesses of Menzoberranzan are currently playing a game, and the object of the game is to convince others that nothing is amiss. If a student leaves Arach-Tinilith prematurely, as none has ever done since the founding of the city, that will seem peculiar, a hint that all is not as it ought to be."

"Perhaps I don't care about the game."

"Your mother does. She plays as diligently as the rest of us. Do you think she will welcome you home if you jeopardize her efforts?"

Drisinil's emerald eyes blinked, the first sign that Quenthel's stare was unsettling her. "I . . . yes, certainly she would!"

"You, a traitor to your House, your city, your sex, and the goddess herself?"

"The goddess—"

"Don't say it!" Quenthel snapped. "Or your life ends, and your soul is bound to torment forevermore. I speak not only as Mistress of Arach-

Tinilith, but as a Baenre. You remember Baenre, Barrison Del'Armgo? We are the First House, and you, merely the Second. Even if you should succeed in departing Arach-Tinilith, even if your gross and uncouth dam should be so unwise as to accept you back into that hovel you Del'Armgo call a home, you will not survive the month. My sister Triel, Matron Mother Baenre, will personally attend to your destruction."

It was no less than the truth. There was no love lost between the two Baenre sisters, but when it came to maintaining the supremacy of their House, they supported one another absolutely.

Drisinil swallowed and lowered her eyes a hair. "Mistress, I mean no disrespect. I just don't want to mutilate myself."

"But you will, novice, and without any further delay. You really have no other option . . . and isn't it convenient, you already have a knife in your grasp."

Drisinil swallowed again, and, her dagger hand shaking a little, brought the blade into position to saw at her little finger. Quenthel thought the procedure might go easier if the novice walked a few steps and braced her pinkie atop the nearby table, but apparently she was taking "without any further delay" quite literally, and that was fine with the high priestess. In her imagination, she was already savoring the first slice when a blare like a sour note blasted from a hundred glaur horns split the air.

For an instant, Quenthel faltered, not frightened but disoriented. She had been told what this ugly noise was but had expected never to actually hear it. To the best of her knowledge, no one ever had.

The priestesses of Menzoberranzan enjoyed a complex relationship with the inhabitants of the Abyss. Some infernal entities were the knights or handmaidens of Lolth, and during worship were venerated as such, but on other occasions the clerics did not scruple to snare spirits with their summoning spells and compel them to do their bidding. Sometimes the creatures stalked the physical plane of their own volition, slaughtering any mortal who crossed their path, not excepting the drow, who were by some accounts their kindred.

The founders of the Academy had shielded Tier Breche in general and Arach-Tinilith in particular with enchantments devised to keep out any spirit save those the occupants saw fit to welcome. Countless generations of priestesses had deemed those wards impregnable, but if the ear-splitting alarm told true, the barriers were falling one by one.

The blare seemed to be coming from the south. The pleasures of chastisement forgotten, Quenthel ran in that direction past countless chapels, altars, and icons of Lolth in both her dark elf and spider forms; past the classrooms where the faculty gave instruction in dogma, ritual, divine magic, torture, sacrifice, and all the other arts the novices needed to learn. Their books, chalkboards, and whimpering, half-dissected slave victims forgotten, some of the teachers and students appeared on the brink of venturing out to investigate the alarm, while others still looked startled and confused.

The blaring stopped. Either the demon had given up attempting to force its way in, or else it had breached every single ward. Quenthel suspected the latter was the case, and when the screaming started, she knew she was right.

"Do you know what's breaking through?" she panted.

"No," hissed Yngoth, perhaps the wisest of the whip vipers. "The intruder has shielded itself from the Sight."

"Wonderful."

The echoing cries led Quenthel into a spacious candlelit hall filled with towering black marble sculptures of spiders, set there to make the temple's entryway as impressive as possible. The battered valves of the great adamantine double door in the curved south wall gaped crookedly, half off their hinges, affording a glimpse of the plateau outside. Several priestesses lay battered and insensible on the floor. For a moment, Quenthel couldn't make out what had caused the mess, then the culprit scuttled across her field of vision toward another hapless servant of Lolth.

The intruder was a gigantic spider bearing a close resemblance to the gleaming black effigies around it, and upon seeing it, Quenthel scowled at an unfamiliar and unwelcome pang of doubt.

On the one hand, the demon, if that was what it truly was, was attacking her pupils and staff, but on the other, it was a kind of spider, sacred to Lolth. Perhaps it was even her emissary, sent to punish the weak and heretical. Maybe Quenthel should simply step aside and permit it to continue its rampage.

It sensed her somehow, turned, and rushed toward her as if it had been looking for her all along.

Though many spiders possessed several eyes, this one, she observed, was exceptional beyond the point of deformity. The head behind the jagged mandibles was virtually nothing but a mass of bulging eyes, and a scatter of others opened here and there about the creature's shiny black bulb of a body.

Its peculiarities notwithstanding, the spider's manifest hostile intent resolved Quenthel's uncertainty in an instant. She would kill the freakish thing.

The question was, how? She did not feel weak—she never had and never would—but she knew it was scarcely the optimal time for her to fight such a battle. On top of any other disadvantages, she wasn't even wearing her mail tunic or *piwafwi*. She rarely did within the walls of Arach-Tinilith. For the most part, her minions feared her too much to attempt an assassination, and she had always been confident that she wouldn't need armor to disappoint any who did not.

As she backed away from the charging spider, her slim, gleaming obsidian hands opened the pouch at her belt, extracted a roll of vellum, and unrolled it for her scrutiny, all with practiced ease and likewise with a certain annoyance, for the magical scroll was a treasure, and she was about to use it up. But it was necessary, and the parchment was scarcely the only magical implement hoarded within those walls.

Rapidly, but with perfect rhythm and pronunciation, she read the verses, the golden characters vanishing from the page as she spoke the words. Dark, heatless flame leaped from the vellum to the floor and shot across that polished surface faster than a wildfire propagating itself across a stand of dead, dry fungus, defining a path that led from herself to the demon.

The black conflagration washed over the demon's dainty bladed feet. It should also have driven the many-eyed creature helplessly backward, but it didn't. The arachnid kept coming nimbly as before, which was to say, considerably faster than the best effort of a drow.

"The spirit has defenses against the magic!" cried K'Sothra, perhaps the least intelligent of the whip vipers and certainly the one most inclined to belabor the obvious.

Quenthel wouldn't have time to attempt another spell before the spider reached her, nor could she outrun it. She would have to outmaneuver it instead. Dropping the useless sheet of parchment, she turned and dived beneath the belly of one of the statues. Unless it had the power to shrink or shapeshift, the invader wouldn't be able to negotiate the same low space.

She slid on the floor, rubbing her elbows hot. One of the snakes cursed foully when its scaly, wedge-shaped head rapped against the stone. She rolled over and saw that she had only bought herself a moment. No, the demon couldn't slip under the statue but, clustered eyes glaring, it was rapidly clambering over the top of it. Up close, it had a foul, carrion smell.

Quenthel knew that if she permitted the spider to pounce down on her, the monster would hold her down and snip her apart with its mandibles. She sprang to her feet and swung her whip.

The vipers twisted in flight to bring their fangs to bear. Those poisonous spikes plunged deep and ripped downward, tearing gashes in some of the demon's bulging, clustered eyes before yanking free. The organs gushed fluid and collapsed, and the serpents thrashed in joy.

Quenthel could feel their exultation through the psionic link they shared, but she knew it was premature. The spider had plenty of other eyes, and the stroke had only balked it for an instant. It was still going to spring.

Though caught without certain of her protections, Quenthel was at least wearing the necklace of dull black pearls. She reached up, slipped one of the enchanted beads from the specially crafted fine gold chain, and threw it at the spider.

White light blazed around her, seemingly emanating from all directions at once. Thanks be to Lolth, this time her magic had an effect. The spider slipped and floundered. Encased in an invisible sphere of magical force it thrashed about in panic. The explosion had opened horrid sores that speckled the creature's body. Unfortunately, it seemed able to ignore whatever pain those wounds caused it and continued scratching at the restraining sphere. Blue-white sparks flashed at the tips of its feet, and Quenthel knew it was using more than brute force and panic to break free.

Speak to me, Quenthel thought, sure the words would be heard in the spider's mind. She felt a connection, but a tenuous one, perhaps attenuated by the sphere of force.

The sphere faded as Quenthel swung the whip again, trying to smash through the creature's hideous visage and into the brain that presumably lay behind it.

The spider sprang away as explosively as one of its tiny jumping cousins, arcing high and landing at the far end of the chamber behind a rank of sculptures. The spirit scuttled through the shadows, and even though Quenthel was watching intently, in another second she lost track of it.

Where are you? she sent.

The reply was a burst of anger from the creature no mere words could convey. Quenthel gave up trying to communicate with it, though if it was a servant of Lolth, it should respond to her.

"You could get out now, Mistress," said Hsiv, the first imp Quenthel had bound inside a whip viper. "From over there, it couldn't reach you before you run out the door."

"Nonsense!" she snapped. "The brute disrupted my Academy, threatened my person, and I will have my vengeance."

Infected with her anger, the banded vipers reared and hissed until she silenced them with a mental command.

One of the priestesses sprawled on the floor was moaning in pain. Quenthel stalked over to the spider's victim and kicked her in the head, silencing her instantly.

The drow high priestess had eliminated all extraneous sounds, but it didn't help her locate the spider. Save for the soft hiss of her own breathing, the chamber was silent.

Turning slowly, heart pounding, she inspected the arachnid effigies all around her. Did that jointed spindle of a leg just twitch? Did that head, coyly turned just enough that she couldn't quite get an adequate look at it, possess too many eyes? Had the figure on the right shifted a hair closer when she wasn't looking?

No, no, and no. It was just her imagination, trying to supply what observation had not.

She sniffed repeatedly, but that was no help, either. The spider's stink hung in the air, but it seemed no stronger in one direction than another.

Curse it, the demon had to be somewhere!

Yes, she realized, but it didn't have to still be on the floor, not if it could skitter up vertical surfaces like its smaller kindred.

Assuming the demon was clinging to the upper walls or ceiling it might have taken it a moment to shake off the shock of the flare and its ugly wounds, but surely it was creeping into the best position from which to leap down on its adversary.

Quenthel peered upward. The artists had decorated the shadowy highest reaches of the chamber as well. The ceiling was an octagonal web acrawl with painted spiders, providing splendid camouflage for the creature. If it was in fact crouching in their midst, she couldn't see it.

Still scanning the ceiling, the whip vipers keeping watch as well, she backed to one of the wall sconces and read the trigger phrase from another scroll, whereupon the candle flame leaped up and turned a roiling black. She put her arm into the darkfire, and her flowing gossamer sleeve caught instantly.

Though they were at the end of what was, thus far, the non-burning arm, the serpents hissed and coiled in alarm. Quenthel brought them to heel with a brutal thrust of her will. Feeling naught but a pleasant warmth, she silently commanded the darkfire. A portion of the magical stuff flowed down her arm and congealed into a soft, semisolid ball in her palm. She threw it, and her magic shot it up like a sling bullet to strike the ceiling fresco where it splashed into a great gout of murky flame.

Quenthel followed that first missile with a steady barrage. Where the darkfire had kissed it, the fresco began to burn with ordinary yellow flame, suffusing the air with eye-stinging smoke and a vile stink that was also a sickening, throat-clenching taste at the back of her mouth.

She was throwing blindly, but with the blaze above spreading, it shouldn't matter. Surely the spider wouldn't simply sit still and allow itself to burn. The fire ought to spur it into motion and thus into visibility.

Unless, of course, the spider wasn't really on the ceiling, which was a real possibility. Maybe it was actually hiding elsewhere. It might even be creeping up on her while she stared at the burning painting and the nervous vipers worried more about their proximity to a darkfire than about keeping watch.

No, her intuition had pointed her in the right direction. She spotted the spider as it gathered itself to spring down at her, and having flushed it out, she need only survive its renewed attack.

She dived from beneath its plummeting form and rolled, leaving a trail of black, burning scraps of cloth behind on the floor. The creature with its tattered, oozing eyes landed with a thump, its eight legs flexing to absorb the impact.

Quenthel scrambled up and backed away from it. Her whole gown was aflame, nearly her entire body shrouded in darkfire. She threw another ball of the stuff, which spattered on the demon's back and streamed down its flanks. To her delight, her magic affected it again. The spider too wore a mantle of shadowy flame, the heat rippling the air above it.

That meant it ought to drop, didn't it, or at least flounder about in helpless agony? The fire was surely damaging it, for Quenthel could smell its flesh charring even through the omnipresent reek of burning paint, but the demon turned and scuttled after her.

She aimed the next burning missile at the cluster of eyes that seemed in some indefinable way to constitute the very core of the thing. The spider did lurch and falter when the burning darkness splashed over the orbs, but only for a second, and it kept coming.

Unable to outrun it, hoping she'd at least softened it up a little, Quenthel shouted her goddess's name and lunged to meet it. Sheathed in darkfire, her whole body was a weapon and would burn the spider wherever it touched. Where the black flame on the monster's limbs was giving way to yellow, it could burn her, too, but not if she didn't let it. Their natural savagery overcoming their fear of fire, the whip vipers lashed and struck in a frenzy of bloodlust.

At first, swinging the whip, ducking and dodging, she kept herself clear of the spider's mandibles. She shifted left when she should have jumped right, and the razor-sharp pincers snapped shut around her.

They stopped short of piercing her flesh. Loath to clasp her blazing body and be seared thereby, the spider faltered for just an instant. Before it could muster the will to proceed, Quenthel struck a final blow.

The ophidian lashes crashed through the demon's charred and tattered visage and bit into what lay beneath. The spider jerked, froze, twitched two of its legs in a purposeless way, and the burning hulk of it slowly sank to the floor, just as Quenthel's spell elapsed and all the darkfire still crackling in the chamber winked out of existence.

She shouted in exultation. Equally ecstatic, only a little singed, the vipers danced at the end of the scourge. Everyone's good mood lasted just as long as it took for the Baenre priestess, clad primarily in smoke and ash, to turn toward the door.

Though she'd been far too busy to notice hitherto, at some point a number of teachers and students had evidently crowded into the space to watch the battle. They were watching Quenthel still, eyes wide, faces uncertain.

"It was a desecration," said Quenthel. "A mockery."

She stared at them with haughty expectation.

They peered back at her for a moment, then folded their hands and bowed their heads in obeisance.

T H R E E

Tall and lithe, the left side of her otherwise handsome face creased with an old battle scar of which, she recognized, she was rather foolishly proud, Greyanna Mizzrym entered her mother's presence dirty, sweaty, and still clad in her mail shirt. Greyanna knew Mother didn't like for her daughters and other chattels to come to meet with her fully armed, but she had an excuse. She'd just returned from an inspection tour of Mizzrym operations in Bauthwaf—"around-cloak," as the dangerous network of tunnels immediately surrounding Menzoberranzan was called—only to hear from a frantic functionary bearing the fresh marks of a whip of fangs that the matron mother wished to see her as soon as possible.

Actually, even knowing the articles likely wouldn't save her if things went horribly wrong, Greyanna rather liked having a justification to walk in on her parent with her mace in her hand and her shield on her arm. She couldn't think of any reason why Mother would have decided to kill her at this particular point in time, but one could never be altogether sure, could one?

Certainly not with Miz'ri Mizzrym, a female regarded even by other dark elves as excessively and capriciously cruel. She sat enthroned in her temple with all of *her* weapons and protections ready to hand, the six-headed whip and the purple rod of tentacles, the enchanted rings gleaming on her fingers. She might have been considered comely even by the exacting standards of her exquisite race, except that her mouth drew down in an ugly and all but perpetual scowl. She regarded her daughter's martial appointments coldly but without comment.

Greyanna lowered her head and spread her hands, offering the proper obeisance, and said, "Matron Mother. You wished to see me?"

"I wished to see you yesterday."

"I was off conducting family business." Of course, Mother knew that as well as she did. "We have to keep up with our duties even now. Especially now—as you yourself have observed on more than one occasion."

"Watch your insolent tongue!"

Greyanna sighed. "Yes, Mother. I apologize. I didn't mean to speak out of turn."

"See that you refrain from doing so again."

Miz'ri fell silent, perhaps to gather her thoughts, perhaps simply in an effort to rattle her daughter's nerves. Such petty, pointless attempts at intimidation were virtually a reflex with her.

Greyanna wondered if a servant had been instructed to fetch her a chair for the remainder of the interview. It didn't look like it. That was typical of her mother as well.

"Your brother Pharaun . . ." Miz'ri said at last.

Greyanna's eyes opened wide. "Yes?"

"I think it might finally be time for the two of you to get reacquainted."

The younger female held her scarred features calm and composed. It was rarely a good idea to show strong emotion to anyone, particularly Mother. If you showed her that something mattered to you, she would find a way to hurt you with it. Even so, Greyanna couldn't quite suppress a shiver of anticipation.

She and her twin sister Sabal had loathed one another from the cradle onward. Of course, in the noble Houses of Menzoberranzan, rivalry between sisters was expected and encouraged. Certainly Miz'ri encouraged it, perhaps simply for her own amusement. But for some reason—perhaps it had something to do with the fact that outwardly, they were identical—her daughters' enmity far transcended even her expectations. It was more bitter and more personal. Each yearned to injure and thwart the other for its own sake at least as much as to improve her own relative standing in the family.

All but choking on their loathing of one another, they fought a duel that lasted decades and encompassed every facet of their existence, and gradually, on every battlefield, Greyanna began to prevail. She sabotaged many of Sabal's plans to enhance the fortunes of House Mizzrym and found ways to take credit for those that succeeded. By secretly tainting some of the sacred articles in this very shrine, she ensured that her twin's public rituals would fail to produce even the feeblest sign that the Spider Queen found her worship acceptable. She sowed doubt about Sabal's competence and loyalty in the ears of everyone who would listen.

Over time, Greyanna rose to become her mother's most valued aide, while Sabal was seen as a dolt fit only for the simplest of tasks. She was forbidden the use of her family's more powerful magical artifacts, lest she break them or turn them to some ill-conceived purpose. From kin to slave warriors, any member of the household who might once have supported her aspirations shunned her as if she were diseased. At that point, Greyanna could have killed her easily, and she expected she'd get around to it eventually, but Sabal's misery was so satisfying that she put it off.

Put if off until Pharaun came home from Sorcere.

Before her little brother departed to Tier Breche, Greyanna had barely noticed him. Of course, you didn't pay attention to young males unless you were unlucky enough to be put in charge of them. They were the silent little shadows creeping about the house, cleaning, ever cleaning, straining to master their inherent magical abilities, and learning their subordinate place in the world, all under the impatient eyes—and whips—of their minders. As far as she could remember, Pharaun had been as cowed and pathetic as the rest.

The Academy transformed him into something considerably more interesting, though, to say nothing of dangerous. Perhaps it was mastering the formidable powers of wizardry, or maybe it was immersion in an enclave comprised entirely of males, but somehow he emerged from his schooling polished, clever, and bold, possessed of a sharp wit and glib tongue that frequently danced him up to the brink of chastisement and safely back again.

Amazingly, he threw in with Sabal, who had all but abandoned hope of ever climbing higher than her current degraded estate. To this day, Greyanna could only explain his decision by positing a perverse and unnatural bond between them, but whatever his reasons, with the help of Pharaun's ideas, advocacy, and magic, Sabal essayed new ventures, succeeded brilliantly, and began to scale the ladder of status once more. She did so more quickly than Greyanna could have imagined, and the family came once more to regard the twins as peers, equal in merit and promise. Accordingly, their private war resumed, even more vicious and murderous than before, but this time Sabal—say Pharaun, rather—proved a match for her.

Greyanna tried to break the stalemate by convincing Pharaun to change sides. She expected it to work, for after all, she and Sabal looked exactly alike and shared precisely the same prospects. Why, then, should the wizard not throw in with the stronger, shrewder sister who had risen to the top of House Mizzrym without his help? Think of the triumphs they could accomplish together! Though inwardly sickened by the prospect, she even smiled lasciviously and offered him the inducement she believed Sabal had given him.

Her brother laughed at her. It was at that instant that Greyanna came to hate him just as savagely as she did her sister.

Perhaps she owed him a debt for his cutting mockery. Conceivably, it goaded her to new heights of ingenuity, for it was shortly afterward that she hit on the stratagem that would destroy Sabal.

A band of gray dwarves had been raiding in the tunnels southeast of the city, and Sabal was leading the force endeavoring to hunt the bandits down. Taking extraordinary measures, driving her agents, whether mortal, elemental, or demonic, relentlessly, Greyanna located the duergar in advance of her twin. Then came the hard part. She and her helpers had to abduct one of the slate-colored little males without the knowledge of his fellows, equip him with a platinum amulet that her subordinate clerics, mages, and her personal jeweler had created in an amazingly brief time, bind the marauder with spells of forgetfulness and persuasion, and slip him back among his friends.

Sabal found the duergar two days later. After her troops exterminated the brigands, they looted the bodies and found the brooch, which was valuable, beautiful, and, as those wizards who were present soon discovered, conferred several useful magical abilities. It never occurred to Sabal that a treasure plundered from a dead dwarf might constitute a trap laid by a sister dark elf, and she happily laid claim to that portion of the spoils.

From that day forward, Sabal slowly, subtly sickened in body, mind, and spirit, meanwhile struggling pathetically to hide any appearance of weakness from all who might discern it and decide to exploit it to kill her, torment her, or strip her of her rank. Which, of course, was pretty much everyone in Menzoberranzan.

Pharaun probably recognized her deterioration, but he was unable to arrest it. Perhaps he didn't even know she was constantly carrying an unusual new magical device about her person. The curse that was poisoning her, that lay insidiously threaded among all the benign enchantments, made her cling to the amulet with an obsessive fascination and fear that others would steal it if she didn't keep it hidden.

During the several months of Sabal's malaise, Greyanna sometimes wondered if Pharaun would ally himself with her if asked again. She didn't. She just watched and waited for her chance to finish Sabal off. She'd learned her lesson. No matter how unlikely the possibility seemed, she would not leave her twin alive to recoup her fortunes yet again.

One night, Pharaun left the castle, either on some errand or simply because he was finding the situation inside oppressive. Later on, the suspicious, insomniac Sabal somehow slipped away from her guards and servants and began aimlessly wandering the citadel on her own.

Greyanna and half a dozen of her minions confronted Sabal in the fungus garden, where the topiarist had trimmed the phosphorescent growths into fanciful shapes, fertilized in some cases with the ripe, diced remains of expired slaves. Sabal's final moments might have seemed pitiful, had Greyanna been susceptible to that crippling emotion. Her addled, desperate twin tried to use the platinum amulet against its maker, but Greyanna dispelled its powers with a thought. Then Sabal endeavored to cast a spell, but she couldn't recite the lines with the proper cadence or execute the gestures with the necessary precision.

Laughing, Greyanna and the other waylayers closed in on their victim, and they didn't even have to strike a blow. Their mere proximity made Sabal wail, clutch at her heart, and fall over dead as a stone. Weak to the last.

For a second, Greyanna felt a bit cheated, but she shook the feeling off. Sabal was dead, that was the main thing, and with a bit of luck, she would still have Pharaun to torture.

Chanting words that sent a cold, charnel breeze moaning through the garden, she reanimated Sabal's corpse. She had use for it, first as a lure then as an instrument of humiliation. She hoped that before his extermination, her brother might be induced to spend one more tender interlude with it.

When Pharaun returned to House Mizzrym an hour later, his hair and garments were as immaculate as ever, but he reeked of wine and walked with a slightly weaving and excessively careful tread. Evidently he'd been drinking his troubles away. Perfect.

As it had been instructed, the zombie stepped out of a doorway at the other end of the hall. Its arms were extended in a beseeching gesture.

Pharaun took a few steps toward it and faltered. Drunk or not, he had finally noticed that, despite Greyanna's efforts to keep it warm, it was moving stiffly, awkwardly, as Sabal, even in the throes of her illness, never had. But he'd spotted the anomaly too late. He'd already advanced to the very center of the trap.

Greyanna whispered a spell of paralysis. Pharaun staggered as his muscles all clenched at once. The fighters swarmed out of their hiding places, surrounded him, clubbed him repeatedly, and threw him down beneath them.

She laughed with delight. Then her henchmen, more or less clumped in a pile on the floor, cried out in surprise and consternation. They started to stand up, and she saw that Pharaun did not lie crushed, bloody, and helpless on the floor beneath them. Impossible as it seemed, somehow he'd resisted the paralysis, then used his wizardry to extricate himself from the midst of his attackers.

Knowing that Sabal was dead, Pharaun must likewise assume that without the aegis of a high priestess he could no longer survive in House Mizzrym. Certainly he couldn't count on his vicious mother, who hadn't bestirred herself to save one daughter from another, to do more for a paltry son. He was surely running back toward the exit.

"That way! Fast!" Greyanna shouted, pointing, goading her agents into motion.

When they rounded a corner, they saw Pharaun sprinting along ahead of them, his *piwafwi* billowing out behind him. He wasn't weaving or stumbling—evidently desperation had cured his intoxication—but he was clutching his head, and leaving a trail of bloody drops on the polished floor. Evidently all the bludgeoning had done at least a little good.

Greyanna's minions shot their hand crossbows, but the darts bounced off the wizard's cloak, which had obviously been enchanted to serve as armor. She stopped running long enough to conjure a blaze of fire under Pharaun's feet. Her assassins cried out and shielded their eyes against the glare. Though surely burned, her brother stayed on his feet and kept going. The flames winked out behind him as suddenly as they'd appeared.

The chase rounded another corner. Ahead of Pharaun was an adamantine double door, which swung open seemingly of its own accord. In reality, Greyanna knew, the wizard had used his silver-and-jet Mizzrym House token to open it. She tried to use her own insignia to slam it shut again, but she was just out of range.

Pharaun plunged through the exit. He was on the landing, a sort of balcony from which the occupants of the stalactite castle that was House Mizzrym could look down on the city. As was the custom, a company of guards stood watch there, and Greyanna screamed for them to stop the mage.

They no doubt intended to be obey. She was a high priestess and he, a mere male, and manifestly trying to run away to boot. But alas, since their primary function was to look for miscreants trying to *enter* the castle, Pharaun had taken them by surprise. He had time to conjure some sort of hindering spell and dash on.

When Greyanna made it to the door, she saw what manner of hindrance the fugitive had chosen. The guards were all bewildered, some standing stupefied or milling aimlessly, a couple fighting with each other.

A clattering, followed a split second later by grunts and cries of pain, snapped her head around to the right. At the far end of the landing, a second contingent of sentries also looked at least temporarily incapacitated, these because Pharaun had pelted them with a conjured barrage of ice. He disappeared down the exit they'd been guarding, the winding crystal staircase, gorgeous with magical luminescence, which connected House Mizzrym with the cave floor below.

Greyanna felt a twinge of annoyance, but only that. Apparently she wasn't going to get a chance to torture Pharaun, but he was unquestionably going to die. He really had nowhere to run, and if the wretch weren't mired in a blind panic, he'd know it.

At least she could deliver the stroke that would seal his doom. She hurried to the edge of the landing, saw that the blistered, bloody-headed fool was better than halfway down the radiant diamond steps, and pronounced, as quickly as possible, the long, awkward arcane word that would make the staircase vanish. That alone wouldn't kill him unless he lost his head. The ability to levitate granted by the same brooch that allowed him to pass through the House's doors would keep him from falling. Limited to strictly vertical movement, however, he ought to make an easy mark for spells and arrows.

She spoke the final syllable. Just as the steps seemed to pop like a bubble, Pharaun leaped, his long legs making him look like a pair of scissors spread to the maximum possible width. He barely made it onto the flattened apex of the gigantic stalagmite that served as the stair's lower terminus.

Greyanna was impressed. That jump was an impressive display of athleticism for a battered scholar of hedonistic habits. Not that it would do him any good. He really had run to the end of his race. She leaned out and shouted for the foulwings to kill him. Winded, still stumbling off-balance from hurdling across the empty space, Pharaun surely couldn't fend off both of them at once.

Grotesque winged predators that commonly reeked of their caustic ammonia breath, the foulwings bespoke the Mizzrym's power and magical prowess and lent the first step on the path to their citadel a certain style that mere soldiers could not match They also made terrifying watchbeasts. With a snap of their clawed, batlike wings, in no wise hindered by their lack of legs, they spun their long-necked bodies around to loom over Pharaun. Forked snouts with fanged jaws at the end of either branch came questing hungrily down. From her perch, Greyanna looked on with a rapacity no less keen than theirs, albeit a rapacity of the soul.

Pharaun shouted something. Greyanna couldn't quite make it out, but it didn't seem to be a magical word, just a cry of fear or a desperate plea for mercy—a plea the giant beasts would not heed.

Except that they did. They hesitated, and he lifted his hands. Their deadly jaws played delicately about his fingers, taking in his scent.

She cried again for the brutes to kill him. They twisted their heads around to look at her, but he spoke to them once more, and they ignored her command.

Greyanna stared in amazement. Pharaun had no doubt had some limited contact with the foulwings, for after all, he lived in the same castle with them, but she knew he'd never ridden one. Only the females of House Mizzrym enjoyed that privilege, and it was only by riding that you established genuine mastery over the creatures. How, then, could he possibly enjoy a rapport with them deeper than her own?

Pharaun scrambled onto a foulwing's back, and both it and its fellow sprang into the air. Obviously her brother had managed to dissolve the enchantment that made the beasts want to sit contentedly at their post.

The wizard managed his mount more deftly than Greyanna herself could have done without benefit of saddle, bridle, and goad. He shot her a mocking grin as he turned to flee. The other, riderless foulwing soared and swooped aimlessly, enjoying its liberty.

Greyanna shook off her stunned disbelief. She still desperately wanted to know how Pharaun had learned to ride the creatures—probably Sabal had taught him, but how had they managed it without anyone else finding out?—but she wasn't going to stand there pondering the question. The answer was less important than the kill.

She turned and looked around. Those guards whom Pharaun had addled were disoriented still, but some of the soldiers he'd battered with hailstones appeared to have regained their composure.

"Shoot him!" she shouted, pointing at the rapidly receding target. "Shoot!"

With commendable haste, they obeyed. They took up their crossbows, aimed, and the bolts leaped forth in a ragged clatter.

Pharaun's foulwing lurched, then plummeted down and down and down, crashing to earth somewhere amid the hollowed stalagmite edifices of the city.

"Got him," said the captain of the guard.

Bigger and stronger than he, Greyanna had no difficulty knocking the male to the floor.

"You got the foulwing," she said. "We don't know that you hit Pharaun at all. We don't know that he didn't use his wizardry or his levitation to cushion his fall. We don't know that he isn't down there alive and well laughing at us. I need to see his corpse, and one way or the other, you will fetch it for me. Turn out every available priestess, wizard, and warrior— drow or slave. *Jump!*"

Jump he did. It was the last bit of satisfaction that was to come her way.

Her mortal agents flooded the streets, while she remained in her personal sanctum in House Mizzrym, summoning spirits and casting divinations to aid the search. Astonishingly, maddeningly, it was all to no avail. When light flowered in the base of Narbondel, signaling the advent of the new day, she was forced to admit that at least for the time being, Pharaun had eluded her.

A month later, she learned that her brother had somehow made his way all the way up to Tier Breche and begged the Archmage of Menzoberranzan himself for a place in Sorcere, and, remembering the wizardly talent the younger male had demonstrated throughout his training, Gromph had seen fit to take him in.

The news came as a considerable relief. She'd feared her brother had fled Menzoberranzan and placed himself permanently beyond her reach. Instead, he'd simply hopped up on a shelf above the city. He was bound to hop down again eventually, and she would have him.

Or so she thought, until her mother sent for her. Possessed of the same intelligence concerning her fugitive son's whereabouts, Miz'ri had formed a very different idea of what ought to be done about it: Nothing.

Even though they were only males, the Masters of Sorcere possessed both a degree of practical autonomy and an abundance of mystical power, and, always weaving her labyrinthine schemes to elevate the status of House Mizzrym, Mother had decided not to unnecessarily provoke the wizards. Which was to say, as Pharaun had obtained a place in that cloistered, many-spired tower, he was more significant in exile than he had ever been at home, and Greyanna would have to let him live. She had achieved what ought to have been her primary goal, preeminence among her sisters and cousins, but her vengeance would remain unfinished.

Through all the decades that followed, it galled her. A hundred times she planned to defy her mother's command and kill Pharaun anyway, only to abandon her stratagems just short of implementation. As fiercely as she hated him, she feared Miz'ri's displeasure even more.

Was it possible that at long last the matron mother had changed her mind? Or was this some new cruelty, was Miz'ri perhaps going to somehow force Greyanna into an odious proximity with a brother who was still untouchable?

"It might be nice to see Pharaun again," the younger female said in the blandest tone she could muster.

Miz'ri laughed. "Oh, I daresay it would, to see him and kill him, isn't that the way of it?"

"If you say so. You know our history. We played out the whole *sava* game under your nose." *I imagine you relished every minute of it,* she thought.

"Yes, you did, and so I know this will interest you. Sadly, a problem has arisen that even supercedes my desire to get along with the mages of the Academy. While you were away, males continued to desert—"

"Pharaun ran off from Sorcere?" Greyanna interrupted, her eyes narrowed. "Were they finally going to punish him for getting those novices killed?"

"No, and no! Shut your mouth, let me tell the tale, and we'll come to your little obsession in a moment."

"Yes, Mother."

"Males continue to elope, and despite our warning him off, Gromph still intends to investigate the matter. Hoping to escape our notice and displeasure, he decided to do so by proxy, and summoned a suitable agent to his office to discuss the matter. Happily, we members of the Council possess a scrying crystal with which we recently managed to pierce the obscuring enchantments shrouding the room. Some of them, anyway. We still can't see in, but we can hear what goes on, and that sufficed to reveal the archmage's plan as well as the identity of his minion. Now, if you must, you may excitedly babble your brother's name."

"I imagine Gromph told him this is his one big chance to redeem himself."

"Exactly. The question is, how shall we priestesses respond?"

"I gather there's a reason you don't just tell Gromph you're on to his plan."

"Of course, several. For one, our first confrontation with him was courteous and mild, but who knows, a second might be less so. As things stand, we hesitate to push him very hard. For another, we don't want him to know we can eavesdrop on him. He'd either block us out or hatch his plots elsewhere. It's better all around simply to take his pawn out of play. Given that Pharaun is a *secret* operative, whatever may befall him, the archmage can hardly take exception to it. The catch being that dealing with your brother is a formidable undertaking, arguably on any occasion but certainly at the moment."

Greyanna nodded. "Because he's a wizard, and we are . . . what we are."

"So where, the Council wondered, can we find a priestess so bold, so motivated, that even now she'll be eager to hunt the male when he descends to the city. I told the others I thought I knew of a candidate."

"You were right."

"The beauty of it is that you do have a personal score to settle. If people see you do something unpleasant to Pharaun, they won't have to wonder what the reason is."

"Yes, I see that. May I draw on all the resources of our House to aid me in my efforts?"

"I can only give you a few helpers. If people saw you descend on the city with House Mizzrym's entire army at your back, they wouldn't assume it's a personal matter. You can have your pick of magic weapons from the armory. Don't waste them, though. Expend only what you need."

Greyanna inclined her head. "I'll start preparing right away."

Miz'ri finally smiled, and somehow, in defiance of any reasonable expectation, it made her face more threatening, not less.

chapter

FOUR

The Silken Rack was not, as visitors to Menzoberranzan sometimes assumed, a fine cloth emporium. It was, technically, a massage parlor, but only a vulgarian would call it that. Rather, it was a palace of delight, where the most skilled body servants in the Underdark provided what many dark elves considered to be most exquisite of all pleasures.

Waerva Baenre was herself of that opinion. She had already soaked her pampered, voluptuous form in warm, scented oil, and she would have liked nothing better to lose herself utterly in the touch of her masseur.

But that, alas, was not possible. She'd come to this shrine of the senses on business, business that could be conducted far more safely and discreetly there than in the Baenre citadel or the ambassador's residence in West Wall. That was why she, by nature gregarious, had hired a cozy private room containing only two contoured couches and a pair of hulking deaf-mute human masseurs in preference to her supremely gifted Tluth.

Happily, the tongueless slave she'd chosen for herself was also highly competent. He kneaded her neck muscles in a way that was pain and bliss at the same time, wringing a groan of sweet release out of her. Naturally, it was at this somewhat undignified moment that Umrae came though the door.

Not that Waerva's momentary discomposure made Umrae smile. The Baenre couldn't imagine what it would take to accomplish that. A rather gaunt, homely female, her skin the unhealthy dull gray-black color of charcoal, the cut of her nondescript garments subtly divergent from the styles of Menzoberranzan, Umrae always arrived at these clandestine meetings stiff and awkward with nervous tension. Waerva supposed that was the difference between commoners and nobles. No matter how perilous the situation, an aristocrat always managed a certain grace.

"She's looking at maps!" declared Umrae. Her voice matched her appearance. There was no music in it.

"I'm not surprised," Waerva replied. "Your mistress is reasonably clever. I never thought she would remain complacent forever." The body servant dug his fingertips into Waerva's upper back, and she shivered. "We'll talk about it, but first, please, set my mind at ease. Tell me that no one who matters saw you enter this particular room."

Umrae scowled, apparently irked by the very suggestion. "No, of course not."

"Then for pity's sake, take off your clothes. You supposedly came here for a deepstroke, and you want to look as if you've had one when you get back home. Besides, these fellows are worth the rent."

Still frowning as if she suspected Waerva was perpetrating some sort of joke at her expense, Umrae gestured brusquely to the human, slightly smaller and less muscular than his compatriot, whom the Baenre had left for her use. Careful not to make eye contact, the slave began to undress her and hang her garments on the hooks set in the wall.

"So what are we going to do?" the commoner asked. "She's guarded. Even with the resource you gave me, I'm not sure I could kill her and escape, but surely you have skilled assassins at your disposal."

"Of course." Waerva had to close her slanted ruby eyes as her body servant squeezed and rubbed another clenched muscle into warm, limp submission. It was remarkable how she didn't even realize they were tight until the masseur got his hands on them. "Murder would have its advantages. It would take her off the *sava* board for good and all."

"Then we're agreed?" Umrae asked as she lay down on her couch. Her body servant gently spread her mane of coarse white hair to expose the flesh beneath.

Waerva grinned. "You sound so eager."

"I admit I'm not fond of her." Umrae's human opened a white porcelain bottle of unguent, and a sweet scent tinged the air. "That's not the point. The point is to shield us all for as long as we need it."

"I quite agree," said Waerva, "and my concern is that an assassination could prove counterproductive. Might it not call attention to your mistress's suspicions? Might it not lend weight to them? Does she not have a deputy of like mind ready to take over in the event of her demise?"

Umrae scowled, pondering the questions, plainly not enjoying it much. Her slave spread a thin coat of amber oil onto her back.

From elsewhere in the building echoed the faint, distorted sounds of shouting, laughter, and splashing. Waerva guessed it must be males amusing themselves in one of the bathing pools. The females of the city were scarcely in the mood for boisterous horseplay.

At last Umrae said, "All right, what do you want to do?"

"Counter the threat in a subtler way. She can't injure us if she's never afforded the chance to confirm her suspicions."

"How will you ensure that?" Umrae's voice quavered as her thrall began to lightly pummel her gleaming back with the bottoms of his fists.

Good luck loosening up those petrified limbs, Waerva thought. "I am a priestess of the Baenre, am I not?"

"The least of them."

"How insolent of you to say so." Waerva tensed with annoyance until her masseur's hands rebuked her.

"I only meant—"

"I know what you meant, and I don't deny it. It's why I'm here, after all. Yet consider this: My aunt Triel has always depended on the advice of two people, Gromph and Quenthel. She can't really talk to Gromph anymore because she's keeping him in the dark with the rest of the males. I doubt she'll see much of Quenthel for a while, either. The tiny she-demon will stay busy contending with her own problems. She's endured some sort of mishap up on Tier Breche."

Umrae twisted her head around to look at her sister conspirator and said, "I've heard rumors about that. What actually happened?"

"I don't know—" Though I wish to the goddess I did, she thought—"but whatever it was, it works to our advantage. We want Triel to suffer a dearth of counselors."

"What about her magical new son? They say he accompanies her everywhere."

Waerva smiled. "Jeggred's not a factor. He's a magnificent specimen but scarcely a font of sage advice. I assure you poor, uncertain Triel will be absolutely frantic for plausible insights from other Baenre priestesses, even the lowlier ones like me. I will buy our friends the time they need to work free of outside interference."

"You will if Triel trusts you."

"In this, she will. We Baenre are proud. It will be inconceivable to Triel that one of our females would wish to abandon the First House in favor of a new life elsewhere. Of course, she wasn't born at the absolute bottom of the internal hierarchy, was she, with dozens of older sisters and cousins taking precedence over her and holding all the important offices. Even if I started recklessly trying to pick them off whenever one lowers her guard even slightly, it could still take me centuries to ascend to a position of genuine power within the family."

"All right, that makes sense. What will you tell her?"

"The obvious." Waerva sighed shakily as her human went to work on her sacroiliac. "For all we know, it may even be the truth."

"I suppose."

Umrae lapsed into a sullen silence. Her body servant's hands made slapping and sucking sounds as they played about her slick, moist, bony back.

"By the six hundred and sixty-six layers of the Abyss," said Waerva, "what ails you? If you're having seconds thoughts, the time for that is well past."

"I'm not. I want to be something better than milady's secretary. I want a surname. I want to be a high priestess and a noble."

"And you will. When your cabal crushes the established order, they'll reward me for my help by making me matron mother of a new but exalted House, whereupon I will adopt you as my daughter. Why, then, do you appear so morose?"

"I just wonder. This silence . . . is it really a boon for us, or a calamity? Are we seizing a great opportunity or madly rushing to our doom?"

How much better I'd rest if only I knew, thought Waerva.

"Let me ask a question," the Baenre priestess said. "Deep down in your heart of hearts, did you serve out of reverence or fear?"

"I served for power."

"Come to think of it," said Waerva, "I did, too. So let us seize the power that still sparkles within our reach."

"I—" Umrae moaned and curled her toes as her human finally managed to send a thrill of pleasure singing along her nerves.

Waerva thought it was a good sign.

Pharaun drank in the spectacle of the Bazaar. Born and raised a Menzoberranyr, he had of course visited this bustling place countless times before, but after several tendays of house arrest spent wondering if his life was at an end, it seemed rather wonderful to him.

Many of the stalls shone with light, be it phosphorescent fungus positioned to flatter the vendor's wares, magical illumination cast for the same purpose, or merely the incidental fallout of some other enchantment. The gleaming was never so fierce as to offend a dark elf's eyes, though. The citizens of the city wended their way through the aisles in the nurturing darkness that was their natural habitat, and what an interesting lot those citizens were.

A high priestess, from House Fey-Branche judging from the livery of her retainers, emerged from her curtained litter to inspect riding lizards with an eye as knowledgeable and a hand as steady as any groom's. A somewhat seedy looking boy, perhaps a disfavored son from one of the lesser Houses, engaged a cobbler in conversation while a confederate opened his voluminous mantle to slip an expensive pair of snakeskin boots inside. Male commoners, obliged to lower their eyes to every female and step aside for every noble of either gender, compensated by sneering and swaggering their way among the creatures less exalted than any drow. These latter were a motley assortment of beings—gray dwarves, the goggle-eyed fish-men called kuo-toas, and even a huge, horned ogre mage from the World Above—bold enough to trade or even dwell in a dark elf city. Lowliest of all, at least as numerous as the free but in their utter insignificance far easier to overlook, were the slaves. Orc, gnoll, and bugbear warriors guarded their masters and mistresses, harried, starveling goblins fetched and carried for the merchants, and little reptilian kobolds collected litter and hauled it away.

Pharaun knew from occasional errands there that if this hub of commerce had existed in one of the lands that saw the sky, it would have been exceptionally noisy. But the Menzoberranyr, to keep their cavern from roaring with a constant echoing clamor, had laid subtle enchantments about the smooth stone floor. Sounds close at hand were as audible as was natural, but those farther away faded and blended to the faint drone he and Ryld had heard while sitting on the brink of Tier Breche.

In the Bazaar, several of the magical buffers operated in close proximity to one another. To newcomers, the effect could be a little disconcerting as a single step sufficed to carry them from whispering quiet to raucous noise, the full volume of an auctioneer's shout or a piper's skirling.

Happily, no such enchantments existed to suppress the smells of the marketplace, a glorious olfactory tapestry redolent of spice, exotic produce imported from the surface world and, alas, a little past its prime, mulled wine, leather, burned frying oil, rothé dung, freshly spilled blood, and a thousand other things. Pharaun closed his eyes and breathed in the scent.

"This is always grand, isn't it?"

"I suppose," answered Ryld.

For his excursion away from Tier Breche, Ryld had tossed a *piwafwi* around his burly shoulders. The cloak covered his dwarf-made armor and short sword, and its cowl obscured his features, but no garment could have hidden the enormous weapon sheathed across his back. Ryld called the greatsword Splitter, and while Pharaun deplored the name as ugly and prosaic, he had to admit that it was apt. In his friend's capable hands, the enchanted weapon could with a single swing cleave almost anything in two.

Ryld looked entirely relaxed, but the wizard knew the appearance was in one sense deceptive. The Master of Melee-Magthere was reflexively scrutinizing their surroundings for signs of danger with a facility that even Pharaun, who regarded himself as considerably more observant than most, could never match.

"You suppose," Pharaun repeated. "Is that just your usual glumness speaking, or do you find something lacking?"

"I do," said Ryld. He waved his hand in a gesture that took in the diverse throng, the stalls, and the maze of paths snaking among them. "I think the Bazaar could use some order."

Pharaun grinned and said, "Careful, or I'll have to report you for blasphemy. It's chaos that made us, and made us what we are."

"Right. Chaos is life. Chaos is creativity. Chaos makes us strong. I remember the creed, but as a practical matter, don't you see that all this confusion could serve as a mask for the city's enemies? They could use it to smuggle their spies and assassins in and to smuggle stolen secrets and treasure out."

"I'm sure they do. That's certainly the way our agents operate in marketplaces elsewhere in the Underdark."

An orc female came scurrying through the crowd with her head down and a parchment clutched in her hand. Perhaps her master had threatened her with a whipping if she didn't deliver a message quickly. She tried to dodge through the narrow space between Pharaun and another pedestrian, misstepped, and bumped into the wizard.

The pig-faced slave looked up and saw that she'd just jostled an elegantly and expensively dressed dark elf. Her mouth with its prominent lower canines fell open in terror. With a flick of his fingers, Pharaun bade her begone. She turned and ran.

"Then the Council should control the Bazaar properly," said Ryld. "Don't just send the occasional patrol marching through to discourage thievery. License the merchants. Conduct routine searches of their pack animals, tents, and kiosks."

"From what I understand," said Pharaun, "it's been tried, and every time it was, the Bazaar became less profitable and wound up pouring fewer coins into the coffers of the matron mothers. I daresay the same thing would happen today. Regulation would also inconvenience all the Houses who are themselves running illicit operations hereabouts. I assure you, a goodly number of them do."

Pharaun should know. Before his exile from his own family, he and Sabal had played a substantial role in House Mizzrym's covert and highly illegal trade with the deep gnomes, or svirfneblin, arguably the deadliest of the dark elves' many foes.

"If you say so," said Ryld. "Not being a noble, I wouldn't know about things like that."

The wizard sighed. It was true, his friend was about as humbly born as a dark elf could be, but during his climb to his present eminence, he had perforce become fully acquainted with the ways of the aristocracy. It was just that at odd moments he took an obscure satisfaction in pretending to a peasantlike ignorance.

"Well, I rejoice that you remain so close to your roots," Pharaun said. "I'm counting on your familiarity with the slums to see me safely through my encounters with the lower orders."

"I've been wondering when that's going to happen. Shouldn't we have gone to Eastmyr or the Braeryn straightaway?"

"No point going there blind if we can acquire some intelligence first."

Pharaun supposed that in fact, they'd better collect it quickly, but it was a pity. He could have used some idle time drifting through emporia like, for instance, Daelein Shimmerdark's Decanter with its astonishing collection of wines, liquors, and, for those who knew how to ask, potions and poisons from all over the world. Perhaps it would clear his head.

Or maybe it would only give him another enigma to ponder, for though there was still plenty to buy, it seemed to him the Bazaar as a whole was offering fewer goods than usual. Why was that? Could it possibly have anything to do with the runaway males?

And what about the demon spider that had materialized above him and Ryld on the plateau and proceeded to break into Arach-Tinilith? Did that tie in, or was it simply a gambit in one of Menzoberranzan's innumerable secret feuds that had nothing at all to do with his concerns?

He had to grin. He knew so little, and what little he had gleaned was scarcely a source of reassurance.

"There it is," said Ryld.

"Indeed."

Carved from a long, relatively low protrusion of stone, the Jewel Box sat just inches beyond what custom decreed to be the limits of the Bazaar, where all traders were required to shift their stalls to a different spot every sixty-six days. Despite its lack of a signboard or other external advertisement, the establishment had always attracted a steady trickle of shoppers and merchants, and when the two masters descended the stair that ran from street level to the limestone door, Pharaun could hear considerably more sounds of revelry that usual. There was laughter, animated conversation, and a longhorn, yarting, and hand-drum trio playing a lively tune. The third string of the yarting was a little flat.

Ryld knocked with the brass knocker, whereupon a little panel slid open in the center of the door. A pair of eyes peered out, then disappeared. The portal swung open.

Pharaun grinned. In all his visits there, he had never seen anyone turned away, and he suspected the business with the peephole was just an agreeable bit of nonsense intended to make a visit to the Jewel Box seem even more piquantly criminal. Perhaps the doorman actually would attempt to dissuade a female if one had sought admittance.

The low-ceilinged room beyond the threshold smelled of a sweet and mildly intoxicating incense. The three musicians had crowded themselves onto a tiny platform against the west wall. A few of the patrons were attending to the performance, but most had elected to focus on other pleasures. At one table, half a dozen disheveled fellows tossed back their liquor simultaneously in what appeared to be a drinking contest. Other males threw daggers at the target on the wall with a blithe disregard for the safety of those standing in the immediate vicinity of their mark. Dice clattered, cards rustled and slapped, and coins scraped across tabletops as the luckier gamblers raked in their winnings.

Ryld studied his surroundings with his customary unobtrusive vigilance, surreptitiously cataloging every potential threat. Still, Pharaun was amused to see that his friend's eyes lingered on the web-shaped *sava* boards for an instant, which was likely all the time he required to analyze the four contests in progress.

Sava was an intricate game representing a war between two noble Houses—at least that was what it currently represented. Pharaun had seen an antique set that recapitulated in miniature the drow's eternal struggle with another race, but such pieces had gone out of fashion long before his birth, probably because no player had wanted to be the dwarves.

With its gridlike board regulating movement and its playing pieces of varying capacities, *sava* resembled games devised by many cultures, but celebrating the chaos in their blood the drow had found a way to introduce an element of randomness into what would otherwise unfold with a mechanical precision. Once per game, each player could forgo his normal move to throw the *sava* dice. If the spider came up on each, he could move one of his opponent's pieces to eliminate any man of its own color within its normal reach, a rule that acknowledged the dark elves' propensity for doing down their kin even in the face of a serious external threat.

Pharaun, who privately considered himself cleverer than Ryld, had always been a little chagrinned that he couldn't defeat the weapons master at *sava*, but alas, his friend wielded mother, priestess, wizard, warrior, orc slave soldier, and dice as brilliantly as he did a sword. Indeed, he claimed that fighting and *sava* were the same thing, though Pharaun had never quite understood what the assertion meant.

The wizard clapped Ryld on the shoulder and said, "Play. Amuse yourself. Win their gold. Just remember to make conversation while you're at it. See what you can learn. Meanwhile, I'll try my luck in the cellar."

Ryld nodded.

Pharaun navigated his way across the crowded room to the bar. Behind it on a stool sat wizened, one-legged Nym, an elderly male who for sheer surly, unwavering misanthropy rivaled any demon the Master of Sorcere had ever conjured. The old retired battle mage was happily engaged in snarling threats, obscenities, and orders at the goblin thralls pouring drinks, but he grudgingly suspended the harassment long enough to accept a handful of gold. In return, he tendered a worn, numbered leather tab with several keys attached.

Thus equipped, Pharaun walked through the arch beside the bar and down another flight of steps. At the bottom waited the real business of the Jewel Box and the reason Nym had not seen fit to hang a placard outside.

In Menzoberranzan, where a goddess and her priestesses reigned supreme, few female dark elves ever found it necessary to sell their bodies. Only a handful of the sick and infirm, dwelling in the most abject need, had ever stooped to such a degradation. Accordingly, one might assume that any male wishing to purchase intimate companionship would find his choice limited to these rare unappealing specimens or the females of one of the inferior species.

But that wasn't quite the case, at least not if a male had a heavy purse. The reason was that, while they generally devoted their military efforts to fighting cloakers, svirfneblin, and other competing civilizations of the

Underdark, drow cities on rare occasions waged war on one another. Once in a while, such conflicts yielded female prisoners.

The prudent, legitimate thing to do with such potentially dangerous captives was interrogate, torture, and kill them. That fact notwithstanding, Nym had on several occasions managed to bribe officers to give him their prisoners, whom he then smuggled into Menzoberranzan and down to the cellar of the Jewel Box.

Nym had gone to all this trouble based on the shrewd and well-proven assumption that a goodly number of Menzoberranyr males would pay handsomely for the privilege of dominating a female, and in his establishment, one could do anything one wanted with a captive. Nym would even provide a customer with a bastinado, a brazier of coals, thumbscrews . . . his only stipulation being that one must pay a surcharge if one left a permanent mark.

Since the brothel's existence was an open secret, Pharaun wasn't sure why the matron mothers hadn't shut it down. On the face of it, it certainly seemed to encourage disrespect for the ruling gender. Perhaps they felt that if a male had a refuge in which to act out his resentments, it would make him all the more deferential to the females in his home. More likely, Nym was slipping them a substantial portion of the take.

At any rate, the Jewel Box seemed a reasonable place to seek information concerning rogue males, especially if one had a spy in place. Pharaun wasn't confident that he did anymore, but one never knew.

The stairs emptied into a hallway of numbered doors. Moans of passions and grunts of pain sounded faintly from behind several of them. It was busier than usual.

The mage strolled down the passage until he found number fourteen. He hesitated for an instant, then scowled and turned the largest of his keys in the lock. The door swung open.

Seated on the bed, shackles clutching her wrists and ankles, Pellanistra looked much as he remembered, the same powerful, shapely limbs and heart-shaped face, with only a few more scars where one or another of her visitors had pressed down two hard, as well as a split lip and closed, puffy eye where a more recent caller had beaten her.

She lifted her face, saw him, and charged with her long-nailed hands outstretched. Then she staggered as one of her governing enchantments riddled her body with pain, and an instant later hit the end of the chains securing her to the wall. She lost her balance and fell on her rump.

"Hello, Pellanistra," Pharaun said.

She spat at him, then screwed up her face at another flare of punishment. The gobbet of saliva fell well short of the wizard's soft, high boots.

"Much as I dislike descending to the obvious," Pharaun said, "I feel compelled to observe that you're only hurting yourself." He stepped forward and extended his hand. "Come on, let's sit and have a talk, just like in the old days. I'll even remove the shackles if you wish."

"We had a bargain!" she said.

"I refuse to have an extended conversation with someone sitting on the floor. It compromises my dignity as much as it does yours. Come on, be sensible. Take my hand."

She didn't do that, but, chains clinking, she did clamber to her bare feet unassisted. He caught a whiff of some flowery scent that Nym had forced her to wear.

"Now, isn't that better?" he asked. "Do you want the manacles off?"

"We had a compact, and I was holding up my end."

"I wish you'd invite me to sit down."

"You abandoned me!"

Pharaun spread his slender, long-fingered hands and said, "All right, priestess. If you think it necessary, we'll belabor the self-evident a bit longer. Yes, I recruited you into my service. Yes, you were doing splendidly—well on your way to earning your liberation—but my circumstances changed. Surely you heard something about it."

"Yes. You backed the wrong sister, and Greyanna made a fool of you. She killed her twin, and you were powerless to stop it. If you hadn't turned tail and run away to Sorcere, she would have slain you, too."

Pharaun smiled crookedly. "I don't think I'll encourage the bards to put it quite that way when they compose the epic story of my life."

"But after you established yourself up on Tier Breche, after you were free to come and go as you pleased, you could have returned here."

"I have, on occasion, just not to call on you. I thought it might be a little awkward."

"I could have helped you the same as before."

"Alas, no. After my withdrawal from House Mizzrym, I no longer had a stake in the power struggles within my family or among the noble Houses, either. I no longer needed intelligence about such matters. The only rivalry that concerned me was the one among wizards, and even if you number the foremost practitioners of my art among your guests, I doubt they whisper the esoterica of their newly invented spells in your ears. When it comes to our discoveries, we wizards are a closemouthed breed."

"You don't know what it was like for me . . . *is* like for me, abused and degraded by my inferiors, constrained in body, mind, and soul, unable to commune with Lolth. . . ."

Pharaun raised his hand. "Please, you're embarrassing yourself. You sound like a whining human, or one of our foul cousins in the World Above. Cease this tirade, take a breath, and think, then you will realize, enemy of Menzoberranzan, that my concern for your well-being has always been, at best, limited. How could it be otherwise? Sentiment certainly wasn't strong enough to make me spend a fortune buying you free of Nym, or, if he and I couldn't strike a deal, break you out of here. Not when you hadn't fulfilled the terms of our covenant. As you no doubt recall, you were supposed to provide me useful information over the full course of twenty years. I admit it wasn't your fault that you couldn't, but still, that's just the way things fell out."

"Fine," she gritted. "You're right, I'm being ridiculous. In forsaking me, you simply behaved as any sensible drow would. Now what in the name of the Demonweb do you want?"

He nodded at the other end of the room and said, "May we . . . ?"

She gave a curt nod, and they seated themselves, she on the mattress of her wide octagonal bed and he on a cushioned granite chair.

"This is much nicer," he said. "Would you like me to send for some wine?"

"Just get on with it."

"Very well. I imagine my plight will amuse you. After the goddess knows how many years breathing the rarefied and dispassionate air of scholarship, imparting knowledge to eager young minds, advancing the frontiers of the mystic arts—"

"Murdering other wizards for their talismans and grimoires."

He grinned. "Well, that was implied, of course. Anyway, after all that, I find myself again embroiled in the more mundane aspects of life in our noble metropolis. There's a puzzle I must solve on pain of the archmage's severe displeasure, and I will be grateful unto death and beyond if you help me unravel it."

"How would I do that?"

"Don't be disingenuous. It doesn't suit you. The same way as always. I assume foolish boys still sometimes gossip and boast to their hired females, even though if they stopped to think about it, they'd remember you loathe them and wish them only ill. I likewise imagine that you still sometimes find yourself obliged to entertain at gatherings where such idiots, unmindful of your presence, discuss their most secret affairs with one another."

"In other words, you wish to resume our old arrangement. Which still had four years to run. If I assist you with your current problem, will you continue to concern yourself with 'mundane' affairs, or will you lock yourself away in your tower once more?"

He considered lying, but his instincts told him she'd see through it.

"I'm not entirely sure what will become of me," he said. "As far as I know, if I'm successful, I ought to wind up reestablished in Sorcere with all my transgressions forgiven, but for some murky reason, I wonder. I'm caught up in something I don't yet understand, and only the dark powers know where it will lead."

"Then if you want my help, you'll have to set me free . . . *today*."

"Impossible, I don't have the requisite funds on my person, nor the leisure to dicker with Nym, for that matter. You know he'd stretch any negotiation out for days, just to be annoying. Nor do I have time to arrange an escape."

She only stared at him, and he understood.

"Ah," he said.

"Is it a bargain?"

"It is if you actually give me some help. My problem is this: An unusual number of males have run away from home of late."

"That's your errand? To find some rogues? What makes it important enough to send a Master of Sorcere?"

He smiled. "I have no idea. Do you know anything about it?"

She shook her head. "Not much."

"Frankly, any crumb of genuine information will put me ahead of where I am now."

"Well, I've heard only the vaguest hints, but they suggest this isn't just a case of an unusual number of males deciding independently to elope. They all ran to the same place for the same reason, whatever that reason may be."

"I thought as much," said Pharaun. "Otherwise, why would Gromph be interested? But it's reassuring to hear that your own agile mind has arrived at the same conclusion."

She sneered.

Pharaun absently ran his fingertip along one of the swirling lines woven into his robe.

"I doubt a threat would suffice to draw so many boys away from home," he said. "Some would have the courage to defy the threatener or the sense to appeal to their kin for protection. Nor would a hypnotic charm do the trick. Aside from the natural resistance to such effects that all we dark elves possess, some of the males would have carried wards in the form of amulets and such. No, I think we have to assume the rogues sneaked away of their own volition to accomplish some positive end. But what?"

"They're organizing a new merchant clan?"

"I thought of that, but Gromph says no, and I'm sure he's correct. For if that were the case, then why the secrecy? Since trade is important to all Menzoberranzan, people don't generally object when a male becomes a merchant. It's one of the two or three legitimate ways to distance oneself from Mother's harsh and arbitrary hand." He grinned. "No offense. I'm sure that in happier times, the males under your authority had no reason to complain of you."

"You can bet I would give them reason now."

"Given your more recent experiences, that's understandable. So, if the rogues aren't putting together a caravan, what are they doing? Preparing to flee Menzoberranzan for good and all? Or, goddess forbid, have they slipped away already?"

"I don't think so. I can't tell you precisely where they are, but I believe they're still somewhere in the city proper, the Mantle, or conceivably out in the Bauthwaf."

"Now that truly is good news. I wasn't keen on a hunt through the wilds of the Underdark. Not only is there a general lack of amenities, the wine-makers are uncorking the new vintages the tenday after next."

Pellanistra shook her head. "You haven't changed."

"Thank you, I'll take that as a compliment. Now, let's get down to the crux of the matter, shall we? I require names. Which of your visitors dropped these 'vaguest hints' which you have so sagaciously interpreted?"

She gave him a smile radiant with spite. "Alton Vandree and Vuzlyn Freth."

"Who themselves subsequently disappeared and are thus unavailable for questioning. It makes sense, I suppose, but it's unfortunate all the same."

"I've given you everything I have," she said. "Now fulfill your end of the deal."

The wizard frowned and said, "My dear collaborator, it would devastate me to disappoint you. Yet I stipulated that you'd have to offer me information of some significance, and frankly, I'm not sure you've delivered. I really know little more than I did before."

"Do it, or I'll tell every soul who comes into this cell that you're looking for the runaways. Perhaps that will have some 'significance' for your mission. I assume it is supposed to be a secret. Things usually are where you're involved, and you haven't mentioned a legion of assistants following you about."

Pharaun laughed. "Well played. I surrender. How shall we do this?"

"I don't care. Burn me with your magic. Stick a dagger in me. Break my neck with those long, clever fingers."

"Interesting suggestions all, but I'd just as soon that Nym didn't bill me for your demise. If we can make it look as if your heart just stopped of its own accord sometime after I take my leave, I'll have a chance."

He cast about, noticed the thick, fluffy pillow on the bed, picked it up, and experimentally gripped it at both ends. It felt good in his hands.

"This ought to work," he said. "Perhaps you could oblige me by lying down?"

chapter

F I V E

Ryld sipped his chilled, tart wine with a sense of satisfaction, secure in the knowledge that the game, though technically still in progress, was already won. In three more moves, his onyx wizard and orc would trap and mate his opponent's carnelian mother.

As usual, he had accomplished his victory without recourse to the dice. Truth to tell, those clattering ivory cubes with the magically warmed images incised on the faces were the one aspect of *sava* he didn't like. They interjected blind luck into what should be a contest of pure cunning.

Ryld's adversary, a scrawny young merchant clansman with an uncouth habit of letting drops of liquor slide from the corners of his mouth as he guzzled, had thrown the dice early on and gloated when chance allowed him to eliminate one of the older male's priestesses.

Shoulders hunched, brow sweaty, he stared at the board as if the fate of his soul were being decided thereupon. A truly competent player would have recognized almost instantly that there was only one move he could make. Indeed, he would have foreseen the inevitable mate just three moves hence and resigned.

Mindful of his true purpose for visiting the Jewel Box, Ryld, doing his best to sound only casually interested, took up the thread of the conversation that he and the slightly tipsy trader had been carrying on in fits and starts.

"Did your cousin give you any warning that he was going to run away?"

"No," the clansman answered curtly. "Why would he? We despised each other. Now shut up! You're trying to break my concentration."

Ryld sighed and settled back in his spindly, flimsy-looking limestone chair. From the corner of his eye he glimpsed something that made him sit up straighter, double-check the precise position of Splitter leaning against the wall, and stealthily loosen his short sword in its oiled sheath on his belt.

He himself didn't quite know what had alerted him. These weren't the first circle of revelers he'd watched rise from their seats and draw their weapons, either to play at fencing or to settle a quarrel that had nothing at all to do with the hooded male defeating all comers at *sava*. Indeed, within the confines of the Jewel Box, blades rasped from their scabbards with a certain regularity. Superficially, this new quartet was no different, but somehow Ryld knew that they were. Sure enough, they stalked straight toward him and his oblivious opponent through the fragrant haze of incense. Other patrons, likewise sensing the swordsmen's intent, made haste to clear the way.

A blade with a glowing redness—an imprisoned spirit perhaps—oozing inside the adamantine, flicked in a horizontal sweep at the tabletop. Ryld caught the weapon and pushed it away before it could upset the *sava* pieces or his neatly stacked winnings. The long sword was as sharp as only an enchanted weapon could be, but he managed the grab without cutting his hand. Finally startled from his reverie, the scrawny boy looked wildly about.

"May we help you?" asked Ryld.

"We've been listening to you," said the owner of the long sword.

Though not so big as Ryld, he was nonetheless husky and tall for a drow male, and the points of his prominent ears seemed to reach above the top of his head like a bat's. He was the best dressed and plainly the leader of the foursome, even though his broad, sullen face bore the mottled bruises of a beating. The weapons master assumed that some noble female must have seen fit to give the male a pummeling. His companions would think none the less of him for that.

Especially since, Ryld noted, two of them were hurt as well, moving a trifle stiffly or slightly favoring one leg. Perhaps they were all kinsmen, and one of the priestesses in their House had gone on a regular tear.

"You've been asking a lot of questions about runaways," the swordsman continued in a threatening drawl.

"Have I?" Ryld replied.

He reflected that it was too bad the three musicians had left the stage a few minutes back. He doubted that anyone had managed to eavesdrop on his conversations while the longhorn was shrilling away.

The other male scowled and asked, "Why?"

"Just making conversation. Do you know something about the rogues?"

"No, but I know that in the Jewel Box we don't like it when people are too curious. We don't like them hunting runaways. We don't like them listening to every private thing we say and reporting back to the Mothers."

"I'm not a spy."

Maybe he was, but he had no intention of confessing it to this fool.

"Ha!" the swordsman scoffed. "If you were, you wouldn't admit it."

"Be that as it may, I suggest you and your friends return to your table and let this boy and I finish our game."

The male with the red sword swelled like an inflated bladder on the verge of bursting. "You're trying to dismiss me like a servant? Do you have any idea who I am?"

"Of course, Tathlyn Godeep. I trained you. Do you remember me?"

Ryld pushed back his cowl, exposing his hitherto shadowed features.

Tathlyn and his friends goggled at their former teacher as if he had just revealed himself to be some ancient and legendary dragon.

"I see you do. So I'll bid you good day."

Tathlyn looked as if he was groping for a comment that would allow him to terminate this confrontation with his dignity intact, but the onlookers started to laugh. His fear less compelling than his pride, he screwed the sneer back onto his face.

"Yes," he said, his voice raised to cut through the laughter, "I know you,

Master Argith, but you don't know me, not the person I have become. Today I am the weapons master of House Godeep."

House Godeep was one of the petty Houses of Narbondellyn, whose frantic rivalries on the very bottom rungs of the ladder of status were almost beneath the notice of the nobles farther up. Ryld doubted the Godeeps would rise much higher with Tathlyn leading their warriors. During his training, the boy had learned to swing a sword with reasonable skill, but he had always demonstrated extraordinary recklessness and general poor judgment when placed in command of a squad.

"Congratulations," said Ryld.

"Perhaps if you'd known I would rise to such an eminence, you wouldn't have taken such delight in smashing my knuckles and beating my shoulder to pulp."

"I didn't do it for sport. It was to teach you to close the outside line and to stand up straight. I tried simply telling you to make the adjustments, but you didn't heed me.

"Now," Ryld continued, "I've explained I have no intention of tattling to the matrons about anything I might happen to learn in this place. Is my word good enough for you? If so, we should have no quarrel."

"That's what you say."

"Lad—excuse me . . . Weapons Master, pause, breathe, and reflect. I sense you're feeling angry over your aches and bruises. Perhaps you want to take it out on someone, but I'm not the person who administered the beating."

Tathlyn stood silent for an instant, then he said, "No, you're not, and I suppose all the punishment during training was for my own good. No hard feelings, Weapons Master. Enjoy your match."

He started to turn away, then whirled back around. The point of the red long sword streaked at Ryld's neck.

Before the four companions had even reached the *sava* table, Ryld had inconspicuously centered his weight and planted his feet in a manner that would allow him to get out of his chair quickly. He simultaneously sprang up and brushed the blade aside with a sweep of his arm, but he didn't strike it at quite the proper angle. The wicked edge of the red sword drew a little blood.

Ryld realized that this was his first real fight in the better part of a year. He'd intended to go out with one of the companies patrolling Bauthwaf, slaughter himself a few of the predators that were always wandering in from the caverns farther out, but somehow he had never bestirred himself to do it.

That was no problem. He had no fear that he was rusty. It was just that, looking back, he was surprised at his lack of motivation.

All these thoughts flashed through his mind in an instant and without slowing his reactions in the slightest.

Tathlyn jumped back out of reach, but one of his companions was lunging at Ryld. It looked like they all intended to fight, which probably meant they were all the weapons master's kin and subordinates. Otherwise, one or more of them might have stayed out of the quarrel.

Ryld twitched himself out of the way of his attacker's wild head cut, drew his leaf-bladed short sword, and thrust. The onrushing Godeep's momentum, Ryld's strength and skill, and the magical keenness of his point served to bury the weapon deep in the crook of his assailant's fighting arm. Though not his favored weapon, the short sword—enchanted to wound even incorporeal spirits—was a fine blade. Blood started from the puncture, and, staggering, the Godeep dropped his falchion. It would actually have been easier to kill the dolt than merely incapacitate him, but Ryld was on a secret mission, and outright homicide was far more likely to attract attention than a simple tavern brawl.

Tathlyn and his other two friends saw their chance and rushed in. Ryld knew that he didn't have time to pull the embedded short sword out of his victim's flesh. If he tried, his other enemies would have him. He cloaked the wounded Godeep in a ragged bulb of darkness and shoved him at the others.

Ryld couldn't see through the obscuring field any more than his adversaries could, but, peering around the edges of it, he saw the wounded Godeep reel into his fellows and stagger them, startle them, too, with the sudden, unexpected impediment to their sight. That gave the weapons master the time he needed to whirl, take in the obstructive clutter of furniture and gawking *sava* players before him, and leap up onto the table where his own game sat waiting. His racing feet annihilated the snare he'd so cunningly laid for the merchant, hurling the pieces rattling across the board and onto the floor.

He jumped down on the other side, grabbed Splitter, and spun back around to face his enemies. In one smooth blur of motion, he yanked this most trusted of all his weapons from its scabbard and came on guard. Despite its hugeness, the greatsword was so perfectly balanced that it felt as light as a dagger in his grasp.

He noticed that the noncombatants in the taproom had begun shouting encouragement and insults at the fighters. A couple quick-thinking gamblers were giving odds.

Ryld's three remaining adversaries manhandled their shadow-shrouded kinsman out of their way and stalked forward, manifestly hoping to pin the fencing teacher against the wall. The one on the left hung back a bit, none too eager, but he didn't look as if he'd actually turn and run unless Tathlyn told him to, or else he saw the weapons master himself go down under Splitter's razor edge.

Ryld had no intention of letting himself be trapped. He moved away from the wall the same way he'd moved up to it, springing onto the table and charging across.

When he reached the far edge, he discovered a rapier poised to skewer him in the vitals when he plunged off. The Godeep on the other end of the blade—the bolder of Tathlyn's two kinsmen—was quick, and he'd conceived a pretty good tactic. Ryld's impetus was such that he probably wouldn't have been able to stop himself from hurtling right onto the Godeep's point.

But he could whirl Splitter through a sweeping low-line parry. The greatsword clanked into the other male's lighter blade and snapped the last six inches off.

Ryld jumped down almost on top of the rapier fighter, so close it would require a moment to bring Splitter's blade to bear, a moment that the other Godeeps might turn to good advantage. Instead, the weapons master bashed the greatsword's heavy steel ball of a pommel into the center of the rapier-wielder's forehead. The impact thudded, and the male fell backward.

Something clacked hard but harmlessly against Ryld's breastplate. He glanced down and saw that one of the spectators, someone who'd bet on his opponents, perhaps, had shot a hand crossbow at him—but the weapons master didn't have time to look for the culprit. He had to pivot to fend off his fellow swordsmen.

Predictably, Tathlyn was in the lead. Ryld cut at the weapons master's head, and his erstwhile student instantly backpedaled, retreating just far enough to avoid the stroke. He'd learned good footwork somewhere along the way, better than Ryld remembered.

Slipping in and out of the distance, Tathlyn feinted and invited, putting on a show. Meanwhile, the other Godeep, the wary one, circled, trying to get behind Ryld.

The weapons master allowed the boy to creep part way round to his flank, then he sprang at Tathlyn and cut wildly, seemingly off-balance and overcommitted to the attack.

The other Godeep had Ryld's back, at a moment when the teacher looked entirely incapable of turning and defending. Reluctant or not, the boy couldn't pass up such an opportunity. He charged.

Ryld whirled, bringing Splitter around in a sweeping horizontal stroke. The greatsword with its superior length struck one step before the Godeep would have initiated his own attack. Thanks to Ryld's deftness, the huge, preternaturally sharp blade merely gashed the boy's wrist instead of lopping off his hand. The petty noble dropped his broadsword, then had the bad judgment to reach for his dagger. The weapons master slashed his leg, tumbling him to the floor.

Ryld knew that by spinning to attack the one Godeep, he had given his back to Tathlyn, who was surely driving in to kill him. The teacher whirled back around. Sure enough, Tathlyn had rushed into the distance and was cutting at his head. Ryld parried with Splitter's edge, hoping to snap the Godeep weapons master's long sword as he had the rapier. The crimson blade struck the greatsword on the forte, just above the parrying hook, rang, and rebounded, still in one piece. It was made of good metal, Ryld thought, well forged, with strengthening enchantments woven in.

But its virtues alone couldn't save its master. Ryld feinted low to draw the red sword down, then cut high. Splitter sliced Tathlyn's brow, and blood poured into the Godeep weapons master's eyes. He reeled backward.

Ryld could tell that none of his adversaries had any fight left in them. He turned once more, surveying the room. Whoever had shot him, the fellow had prudently put his hand crossbow away.

"Nicely done," said Pharaun, lounging, goblet in hand, by the bar.

"How long have you been there?" Ryld replied, walking to retrieve his short sword. Its victim had pulled it free and left it on the floor. "You could have helped me."

"I was too busy wagering on you." The wizard held out his purse, and grumbling losers dropped coins into it. "I knew you wouldn't need help against a couple drunks."

Ryld grunted, wiped his weapons on a handy bar rag, and asked, "Do you want that red sword? It's a good weapon. Maybe a Godeep family heirloom."

Pharaun grinned. "Which would mean they acquired it when, last tenday? No, thank you anyway, but what would a spellcaster do with it? Besides, I wouldn't want the weight to stretch and chafe my clothes."

"Suit yourself."

The Master of Sorcere sauntered up to Ryld, then spoke far more softly. "Are you about ready to go? I'd just as soon take my leave before Nym wanders downstairs."

Ryld wondered what mischief his friend had committed. "Almost," he said. "Give Nym something to pay for the cleanup."

The warrior walked to the *sava* tables, retrieved Splitter's scabbard and his own winnings, then looked around for the trader. The boy had made a hasty withdrawal from the table the instant the fight began, but he hadn't gone far. Most every drow had a taste for blood sport.

Ryld tossed him a gold coin with the Baenre emblem stamped on it. "Here are your winnings."

The young merchant looked puzzled. Perhaps the drink was to blame.

"If a player disturbs the arrangement of the board, he loses," Ryld explained. "It's in the rules."

"It was gratifying to come upstairs and observe you handling our confidential inquiries with your usual light touch," Pharaun said.

He paused to let a floatchest, attended by a dark elf merchant and six hulking bugbear slaves, drift across the lane. The stone box looked like a sarcophagus. Maybe it was. In the Bazaar, a shopper could purchase nearly anything, including cadavers and mummies once embalmed with strange spices and laid to rest with mystic rites. Indeed, such wares were available either whole or by the desiccated piece.

"It wasn't my fault," Ryld replied. "I did nothing to provoke that fight." He hesitated. "Well, perhaps I was a bit brusque when the Godeeps first stalked up to the table."

"You? Never!"

"Spare me your japes. Why do we have to question people anyway?" The Master of Melee-Magthere ducked beneath the corner of a low-hanging rothé-hide awning and added, "You ought to be able to look in a scrying pool and find the runaways."

Pharaun smiled. "Where would be the fun in that? Now seriously, why did the Godeeps take exception to your no doubt impeccably subtle questions in the first place? Were they in league with the rogues?"

"I don't think they knew anything. I think they were merely sympathetic to the idea of eloping and generally in a foul mood. It looked as if one of the females in House Godeep had disciplined them with her fists or a cudgel, and they only needed an excuse to try and take their resentment out on someone."

"This hypothetical priestess beat the House *weapons master* as if he were a thrall, or at best, the least useful of her male kin? Doesn't that strike you as odd?"

"Now that you mention it, somewhat."

"The Jewel Box was unusually crowded today as well."

Pharaun noticed a blindfolded orc juggling daggers for the amusement of the crowd and paused for a moment to watch the show. Ryld heaved a sigh, signaling his impatience at the interruption in their deliberations.

The wizard counted five sharp knives, which the slave's scarred hands caught and tossed with flawless accuracy. A laudable performance, even if it lacked a certain elan. Pharaun tossed a coin to the orc's owner, then strolled on. Ryld tramped along beside him.

"So," said the weapons master, "Tathlyn gets a thrashing, the brothel enjoys a glut of patrons, and you see a connection. What?"

"What if all those boys endured a beating, or at least some sort of unpleasantness, at the hands of their female relations? What if that's the reason they flocked to their sad little sanctuary, to lie low, lick their wounds, and kick around one of Nym's captives in their turn?"

Ryld frowned, pondering the notion. "You're guessing that priestesses in a diversity of Houses have grown more harsh and unreasonable. Obviously, that could provoke a spate of runaway males, but what could make the dispositions of all those priestesses curdle in unison?"

"I have a hunch that when we figure that out, we'll be getting somewhere."

The two masters circled around a colossal snail pulling a dozen-wheeled cart. The creature's mouth opened into an O and Pharaun—who had once only narrowly survived an encounter with such a giant mollusk in the wild—nearly sacrificed his dignity by flinching, even though he knew this particular specimen had undoubtedly been divested of its ability to spew a caustic sludge. Sure enough, nothing flew from the draft creature's maw except a few clear, harmless droplets. The wagoner lashed the hostile snail with his long-handled whip.

"What did you learn downstairs?" asked Ryld.

"Nothing, really," said Pharaun, "nothing we hadn't already inferred. Still, I was able to oblige an old comrade. That was pleasant in its own way."

"If neither of us discovered anything substantial, our visit to the Jewel Box was a waste of time."

"Not a bit of it. The bloodshed perked you up, didn't it? You've pretty much been smiling ever since."

"Don't be ridiculous. I admit it was an interesting little scuffle . . ."

Ryld began to recount the battle one action at a time, with comprehensive analysis of the alternative options and underlying strategy. Pharaun nodded and did his best to look interested.

Triel, Matron Mother of House Baenre and a diminutive ebony doll of a dark elf, marched briskly down the corridor, covering ground rapidly despite her short stride. Eight feet tall, his two goatlike legs more nimble even than most drow's, Jeggred had no difficulty keeping up with his mother. The scurrying, frazzled drow secretary, though, looked as if she was in imminent danger of dropping her armload of parchment.

When Triel heard voices conversing a few yards ahead, she wanted to move faster still. Only a sense that a female in her august position ought not to compromise her dignity by running held the impulse in check.

"I think it's a test," said one soft female voice.

"I worry it's a sign of disfavor," answered the other, a hair deeper and a bit nasal. "Perhaps we've done something to offend—"

Triel and her companions rounded a corner. There before them loitered a pair of her cousins. Their mouths fell open when they saw her.

Triel looked up at her son's face, which, with its slightly elongated muzzle, mouthful of long, pointed fangs, slanted eyes, and pointed ears, seemed a blend of drow and wolf. That wordless glance sufficed to convey her will.

Jeggred pounced, his long, coarse mane streaming out behind him. With each of his huge, clawed fighting hands, he grabbed a cousin by the throat and hoisted her up against the calcite wall. His two smaller, drow-like hands flexed as if they too wished to get in on the violence.

Perhaps they did.

Triel had conceived a child in a ritual coupling with the glabrezu demon Belshazu. The result was Jeggred, a half-fiend known as a draegloth, a precious gift of the Spider Queen. His mother was quite prepared to believe that cruelty and bloodlust burned in every mote and particle of his being. Only his reflexive subservience, tendered not because Triel had borne him but because she was first among the priestesses of Lolth, kept him from immediately slaughtering his prisoners, or, indeed, pretty much anyone else with whom he came in contact.

Occasionally Triel's lack of height was an advantage. It didn't feel awkward or claustrophobic to step inside the circle of Jeggred's two longer arms and stand before the cousins. Up close, she could smell the sweat of their fear just as easily as she could hear the little choking sounds they were making or the thuds as their heels bumped against the carved surface behind them.

"I forbade you to speak of the situation in public," she snarled.

The cousin on the left started making more noise, a tortured gargling. Perhaps she was trying to say that she and the other one had been alone.

"This is a public part of the castle," Triel said. "Anyone, any *male* might have come along and overheard you."

She swung her whip of fangs, aiming low to ensure she didn't accidentally lash Jeggred's hands or arms. The five writhing adders gashed their targets but not enough to satisfy their mistress. She struck again and again. Her anger rose and rose until it became a kind of rapture, a sweet simplicity in which nothing existed but the cousins' thrashing, the smell and feel of their blood spattering her face, and the pleasant exertion of her snapping arm.

She never knew what brought her out of that joyous condition. Perhaps it was simply that she was winded, but when she came to her senses, the two babblers were dangling limp and silent in Jeggred's grip.

Both the draegloth and the scribe were smiling. They'd thoroughly enjoyed the cousins' excruciating torture, but there were things still to be done, and she'd wasted time losing her temper.

Which was bad. Matron Mother Baenre, de facto ruler of the entire city of Menzoberranzan, should be able to govern herself as well.

Triel's emotional volatility was of comparatively recent origin. She'd been calm and competent all the while she served as Mistress of Arach-Tinilith. That role, arguably second only to her mother's in prestige, had suited her well, and she'd never aspired to anything more.

Nor had she truly believed that more was even possible. Her mother seemed immortal. Indestructible. But then, suddenly, she was gone, and the ambition that at one time or another goaded every dark elf awoke in Triel's breast. How could she *not* strive to ascend to her mother's throne? How could she let Quenthel or one of her other kin climb over her head to order her about forever after?

She managed to claim the title of Matron Mother, and though she soon came to feel somewhat overwhelmed by the scope and intricacies of the position, at first it wasn't so bad. Things were relatively normal and didn't require some dramatic intervention from on high to set them right.

Moreover, she had Quenthel and Gromph to advise her. True, her sister and brother invariably disagreed, but Triel could review their competing proposals and pick the one that suited her. It was considerably easier than having to come up with the ideas herself.

But she had a crisis to manage, perhaps the greatest crisis in the long history of the dark elves, and apparently she would have to do it alone. She obviously couldn't confide in Gromph, and insolent Quenthel claimed she had to attend to the security of Tier Breche before she could focus on anything else.

Triel gave her head a shake, trying to dislodge her doubts and worries.

"Let them down."

Jeggred obeyed, and she turned to the secretary.

"When you get a chance," she said, raising her voice over the choking gasps of the two cousins, "have somebody haul them out to Arach-Tinilith to be patched back together, and have someone wash away the blood. But for now, we'd best get moving. I think we're late."

The trio moved on. A final turn brought them to the door. Behind it was the dais overlooking the largest audience chamber in House Baenre. A pair of sentries guarded the entry to ensure that no one would sneak through to stab the matron mother in the back. They snapped to attention when they saw her coming.

Triel swept on through the entry with Jeggred and the clerk in tow. The hall on the other side glowed with soft magical light to facilitate the examination of documents. A sweet perfume scented the air, and a fresco of Lolth adorned the ceiling. The guards along the walls—dark elves near the dais, ogre and minotaur slaves farther down—saluted, while the supplicants and petitioners made the obeisance proper to their stations, anything from a dignified inclination of the head and spreading of the hands to an abject grovel flat on the floor.

Looking down on them from the elevated platform, Triel reflected that it was astonishing just how many such folk turned up each and every tenday. She'd thought people were always demanding her attention when she ruled the Academy, but she'd had no conception of the hordes of idiots who constantly sought Matron Baenre's ear, often to resolve trivial if not nonsensical concerns.

She sat down on her mother's throne, an empress's ransom in gold with a flaring back shaped to resemble an arc of spiderweb. Her predecessor had been a relatively large female, and her successor always felt a bit childlike and lost in the chair. She had enough of a sense of irony to comprehend the accidental symbolism.

She surveyed the waiting throng and discovered Faeryl Zauvirr at the very front with some long, bulky rolled papers tucked under her arm. The matron mother smiled, for at least she knew how to deal with this one particular petitioner. For a blessed change, Waerva, one of the lesser fe-males of her House, had made herself useful. She'd come up with some significant information and a sensible idea of what to do about it.

Triel decided she might as well start out feeling dominant and shrewd. Perhaps it would set the tone for the rest of the session. She waited for the herald to conclude the ceremonials and the crowd to rise. Then, still spat-tered with blood, and with Jeggred looming reassuringly behind her throne, she motioned for Faeryl to step forward.

c h a p t e r

S I X

Faeryl was pleased to be chosen first. In retrospect, she thought the same thing would have occurred even if she hadn't made sure of a position immediately in front of the dais. The haughty Menzoberranyr often feigned disinterest in their client city, but she knew they understood the importance of Ched Nasad.

It was hard not to hurry, but she forced herself to approach the throne with a stately tread consonant with the dignity of her position, the stature of her House, and the grandeur of her homeland. It was also difficult to offer a second graceful obeisance without dropping her roll of maps, but she accomplished that as well.

"Ambassador," said Triel without any extraordinary warmth. Perhaps she considered Faeryl's presence inappropriate.

"Matron Mother," Faeryl replied. Tall, broad-shouldered and thick-waisted by the standards of her slender race, she would have dwarfed the Baenre had the two of them been standing side by side. "I know we sometimes meet in private, but after tendays of deliberation I arrived at a conclusion, one that compelled me to confer with you at the earliest opportunity."

"What conclusion?" Triel asked.

She still seemed unconcerned if not downright cold. Perhaps she was preoccupied with her affliction.

Faeryl had of course fallen prey to the same malaise, but to her own surprise, she'd discovered she was at least as worried about something else: the well-being of House Zauvirr and the magnificent city in which it amassed its wealth, fought its covert battles, and worked its magic.

"I keep track of the caravans arriving from Ched Nasad," the ambassador said. "For the past six tendays, none has. None. As the Matron Mother is undoubtedly aware, several major trade routes converge in the City of Shimmering Webs, which then funnels the merchants on to Menzoberranzan. At least half the goods that reach your cavern come through us. Except that now, they aren't reaching you. The steady flow has dried up. Except in time of war, that's unprecedented."

"It's an odd coincidence, certainly, all the merchant clansmen choosing other destinations, but I'm sure they'll decide to head for Menzoberranzan next trip, or the trip after that."

Faeryl had to make a conscious effort to compose her features. Otherwise she would have scowled. If she hadn't known better, she would have thought Triel was being deliberately obtuse.

"I suspect it may be more than a coincidence," the ambassador said. "A thousand thousand dangers haunt the Underdark, and the philosophers tell us new ones are spawning all the time. What if something has cut the route between Menzoberranzan and Ched Nasad? What if it's killing everyone who tries to pass through?"

"More than one tunnel connects the cities," rumbled the draegloth unexpectedly, and despite the perfume wafting through the air, Faeryl caught a whiff of the creature's putrid breath. "Is that not so?"

"Exactly!" Triel reached back around the edge of her golden chair and gave the half-fiend an approving pat on the leg. "Your theory doesn't stand up, Ambassador."

Not for the first time, Faeryl wished that Triel's mother was still leading House Baenre. The greedy, vicious old autocrat could be hard to contend with, but though she would have cherished a draegloth as a mark of Lolth's approval and delighted in the demidemon's gift for slaughter, she wouldn't have tolerated it speaking unbidden at a formal conference, any more than she would have borne such disrespect from anyone else.

"If the threat consists of more than one beast," the emissary said, "or more than one manifestation of a phenomenon, it could cut more than one passage."

Triel shrugged. "If you say so."

"I hesitate to mention it," said Faeryl, "lest I be thought an alarmist, but it's even possible that some misfortune has befallen Ched Nasad itself."

"A misfortune so abrupt and all-encompassing that your folk never even had a chance to dispatch a messenger to Menzoberranzan?" Triel replied. "Nonsense. Even Golothaer, home of our ancestors, didn't perish in an hour. Besides, I am personally aware of several communiqués having reached here from Ched Nasad in only the past few days."

"I have received some of those sendings myself, Matron Mother, and find their excuses suspicious at best. In any case, the dearth of traffic from Ched Nasad warrants investigation, and as my city's representative in Menzoberranzan, the task is my responsibility."

"No one has charged you with it."

"Then I take it upon myself. Yet I'm reluctant to venture across the Underdark with merely my own little entourage for protection. Traders guard their caravans very well. Anything that could destroy all those merchant trains would likely put a quick end to me, too, in which case, Matron Mother, the priestesses of Menzoberranzan would know no more about the new menace beyond their borders than they do now. Accordingly, I ask you to provide me with a sizable escort. I'll march it to Ched Nasad and back again and see what befalls me along the way."

"You have an enterprising nature," said Triel "It does you credit. Alas, Menzoberranzan can't spare any troops. Not at this time. Our forces are engaged in training exercises."

Faeryl fancied she knew the real reason the Baenre was at present reluctant to divest herself of any portion of her military strength. Her caution made perfect sense on its own terms, but surely it must yield to the gravity of the envoy's concerns!

"Matron Mother, if trade with Ched Nasad does not resume, the people of Menzoberranzan will find themselves bereft of countless amenities.

Some of your craftsmen will lack the raw materials they need for their work. Your own merchant clans will endeavor to send caravans to my city, and those expeditions will probably not return."

"I imagine some clever male will import the same goods via a different route if he can reap a profit thereby."

Faeryl was beginning to feel as if she were mired in some lunatic dream.

"Matron, you can't be serious. Ched Nasad is the single greatest source of wealth your people possess."

Demons of the Web, it was in fact half again as populous as Menzoberranzan itself. The two realms had long been equals, and it was only a comparatively recent happenstance that had reduced the once independent City of Shimmering Webs to vassalage.

Triel spread her dainty, obsidian hands in a gesture of helpless resignation and said, "Wealth that is as much ours when stored in our trading costers in Ched Nasad as in our own vaults here."

Faeryl didn't know what else to say. No argument, however cogent, seemed capable of piercing Triel's shield of bland, almost mocking complacency.

"Very well," the ambassador said through gritted teeth, struggling to keep a grip on her temper. "If I must, I'll manage without your help. It will exhaust my purse, but perhaps I can hire some of the sellswords of Bregan D'aerthe."

Triel smiled. "No, my dear, that won't be necessary."

"I don't understand."

"I cannot give you leave to depart so precipitously. Who then would speak on behalf of your people? Even more importantly, I believe you may be right. Some new peril may be lurking in the Underdark and massacring drow left and right. I don't want it to kill you as well. I hold you in too high an esteem, and I certainly wouldn't want the other nobles of Ched Nasad to think that I blithely sent you to your doom. They might infer that I have little regard for even the most exalted officers of your splendid city, when of course, nothing could be farther from the truth."

"You honor me. Yet considering what's at stake—"

"Nothing is more important than your safety. *Anything* could happen if you attempt to traverse the tunnels at this unsettled time. You might not even make it out of Bauthwaf. Why, one of Menzoberranzan's own patrols, weary from too much duty, imagining a dwarf crouched behind every stalagmite, might mistake your band for a hostile force and loose a volley of poison darts at you. You might die an agonizing death at the hands of your own friends, in which case I would never forgive myself."

A chill crept up Faeryl's spine, because she understood what Triel had really said. The matron mother had just forbidden her to leave the city, on pain of death.

But why? What accounted for Matron Baenre's sudden hostility? Faeryl had no idea until she happened to glance up at the draegloth's face. Somehow the half-fiend's leer suggested an explanation.

Triel had decided Faeryl was less diplomat than spy, an agent for some power inimical to Menzoberranzan, who'd concocted this business of missing traders to provide herself with a good excuse to leave the city and report to her superiors.

Matron Baenre couldn't allow it, couldn't permit a spy to pass along the tale of Menzoberranzan's newfound weakness. She didn't dare, because it was entirely possible that not all dark elf enclaves had suffered the same calamity, and even if they had, perhaps the dwarves, duergar, deep gnomes, and illithids had not.

What remained unclear was why Triel believed as she did. Who had put the idea in her head, and what did that person have to gain by holding Faeryl in the city?

Jaw tight, the emissary stifled the impulse to confront Triel about the latter's true concerns. She knew she wouldn't be able to draw the Baenre into an genuine consideration of the allegations against her. Taking a malicious pleasure in the play-acting, Triel would simply feign shock that Faeryl doubted her trust and good will.

Indeed, if Faeryl wanted to avoid further humiliation, all she could do was go along with the pretense.

She smiled and said, "As I said before, Matron Mother, your concern honors me, and I will of course obey you. I'll remain in the City of Spiders and savor its many delights."

"Good," said Triel, and Faeryl imagined the words that remained unspoken: We'll know where to find you when it's time for your arrest.

"May I have your permission to withdraw? I see there are many others seeking the benefit of your wisdom."

"Go, with my blessing."

Faeryl offered her obeisance, exited the hall, and walked through the great mound that was the Baenre citadel until she found herself alone and unobserved in a short connecting passageway. She took the rolled maps of the Underdark, the charts she had imagined that she and Triel might consult together, from beneath her arm. Teeth bared in a snarl, she smashed them repeatedly against the wall until the stiff parchment cylinder flopped limp and battered in her hands.

Gromph and Quenthel strolled about the plateau watching the apprentices and masters of Sorcere perform the rituals. The sound of chanting and the pungent scent of incense filled the air, along with various conjured phenomena: flashes of light, dancing shadows, demonic faces appearing and disappearing, moaning and crackling. All to lay a new set of wards about Tier Breche.

Gromph was mildly impressed. By and large, his minions were doing a good job of it, though they weren't laying any enchantments he couldn't pierce. In fact, since he was supervising them at their labors, getting past the wards would be easy.

"I wonder if all this will actually protect us," said Quenthel, scowling, her long skirt rippling in the stray breeze kicked up by someone's incantation.

Gromph was surprised that even after Beradax's attack, she hadn't donned a suit of mail. Perhaps she thought her frightened novices and priestesses required a show of confidence.

"It didn't protect us before," hissed one of the annoyingly vocal snakes comprising the whip on her belt.

Four of them were twisting this way and that, watching for danger. The fifth kept its cold eyes staring at Gromph, not, the archmage was convinced, because his sister suspected him of trying to murder her. Or rather she did, but not specifically. She simply had too many viable suspects. There were subordinates who aspired to be Mistress of Arach-Tinilith, and the myriad foes of House Baenre. Perhaps it was even Triel seeking to forestall the all but inevitable day when Quenthel would challenge her for preeminence.

"Enchantments can attenuate with time," said Gromph, honestly enough.

"The new ones will be stronger. Strong enough, I trust, to keep you safe in Arach-Tinilith."

"It isn't just the temple at risk," Quenthel snapped. "Next time, a demon could attack Sorcere or Melee-Magthere."

Don't count on it, Gromph thought, but he said, "I understand."

"I've seen enough for now," said the mistress, her scowl deepening. "Don't let your males slack off. I want the defenses complete before you leave to cast your spell into Narbondel."

"Consider it done."

Quenthel turned and walked back toward Arach-Tinilith. The primary entrance to the imposing spider-shaped temple had become merely an odd-looking hole. The artisans hadn't yet finished repairing the crumpled adamantine leaves of the gate. Gromph smiled to think how that must annoy his sister. Knowing her as he did, he was fairly certain the unfortunate metalworkers had already felt the weight of her displeasure.

Well, perhaps they wouldn't have to bear it for much longer. He fingered a small ornament, a black stone clasped in a silver claw dangling over his heart.

Quenthel hadn't asked about the trinket, nor had Gromph expected her to. He always wore his amulet of eternal youth and the brooch that helped him imbue Narbondel with radiant warmth. Beyond those two staples, he tended to adorn the Robes of the Archmage with a constantly changing array of charms and talismans, depending on his whim and the particular magical tasks he expected to perform that day. His sister had had no reason to suspect that this particular trinket was of any particular significance, certainly not to herself.

If she had noticed it at all, she probably assumed the stone was onyx, ebony, or jet. In actuality, it was polished ivory cut from a unicorn's horn after Gromph slew the magical equine—sacred to the despicable elves of the World Above—in a necromantic rite. The orb was only black because of the entity he had placed inside it only two hours before.

"That was her," he murmured, too softly for any of the spellcasters bustling about him to overhear. "Did you take her scent?"

Yes, the demon answered, its silent voice like a nail scratching the inside of Gromph's head. *Though it was unnecessary. I may not possess the power of sight, but that has never hindered me as I sought my prey.*

"I was just making sure. Now, can you succeed where Beradax failed?"

Of course. No one of your world has ever escaped me. Afterward, I will feast on Quenthel's soul, one tiny morsel at a time.

Most likely the netherspirit would do exactly that, and if it failed, Gromph had six more waiting in line to pick up where it left off. Perhaps it wouldn't even come to that. He had, after all, manipulated events in such a way as to inspire more mundane assassins.

A third-year student came scurrying up with a stubby chalcedony wand in his hand. Recalled to more immediate concerns, Gromph sighed and prepared to teach the youth how the device worked.

Pretending to take an interest in an itinerant vendor's rack of cheaply forged and poorly balanced daggers, Ryld turned and surreptitiously surveyed the intersection.

A fellow with what the weapons master suspected were self-inflicted sores on his legs chanted for alms and shook a ceramic bowl. Since it was a rare if not demented dark elf who ever felt the tug of pity, the beggar sat near the entrance to a shabby boarding house catering to non-drow.

A female hurried by with a hooked and pointed pole—virtually a pike, when one really looked at it—on her shoulder and a giant weasel on a leash. She was plainly an exterminator headed out to rid a household of some substantial infestation.

A snarling noble from House Hunzrin drew his rapier and lashed a commoner with the flat, evidently because the latter had been a trifle slow stepping out of his way. The Hunzrins were notorious for their virulent arrogance. Perhaps it stemmed from the fact that they controlled the greater part of Menzoberranzan's agriculture. Or maybe they were compensating for the fact that, for all their wealth, they were stuck living in "mere East."

Any number of other rather drab and hungry-looking souls rushed on about their business.

"Reliving childhood memories?" the wizard asked.

"You forget," Ryld replied, "I was born in the Braeryn. I had to work my way up to get to Eastmyr."

"I daresay you took one look around, then kept right on climbing."

"You're right. Just now, I was checking to see if someone's tailing us. No one is."

"What a pity. I was hoping that if we asked enough questions in diverse male gatherings, some more friends of the runaways would try to murder us, or at least seek to learn what we're about. Perhaps the rogues are too canny for that."

"What do we do now?"

"Visit the next vile tavern, I suppose."

They started walking, and Pharaun continued, "Say, did I ever tell you how, two days into my first mission to the World Above, I wound up having to tail a human mage while the sun was blazing in the sky? I was blind with the glare, my eyes—"

"Enough," Ryld said. "You've told this a thousand times."

"Well, it's a good story. I know you'll enjoy hearing it again. There I was, blind with the glare . . ."

As the two masters strolled on, they passed a doorway sealed with a curtain of spiderweb. Forbidden by sacred law to disturb the silken trap until such time as its builder ceased to occupy it, the luckless occupant of the house had placed a box beneath his front window to serve as a makeshift step.

Across the way, a ragged half-breed child, part dark elf, part human by the look of her, brushed past a drunken laborer, then quickened her pace a trifle. Ryld hadn't actually seen her lift the tosspot's purse, but he was fairly certain she had.

Pharaun came to a sudden halt. "Look at this," he said.

Ryld turned, the long, comfortable weight of Splitter shifting ever so slightly across his back. On a wall at the mouth of an alley, someone had clumsily daubed a rudimentary picture of a clawed hand surrounded by flames. Though it was small and smeared in paint that barely contrasted with the stone behind it, Ryld was slightly chagrined that Pharaun had noticed it and he hadn't, but he supposed wizards had a nose for glyphs.

"Do you know what this is?" asked Pharaun.

"An emblem of the Skortchclaw horde, one of the larger tribes of orcs. I've been to the Realms that See the Sun a time or two myself, remember?"

"Good, I'm glad you confirm my identification. Now, what is it doing here?"

Ryld took a reflexive glance around, searching for potential threats, and said, "I assume some orc painted it."

"That would be my supposition, too, but have you ever known a thrall to do such a thing?"

"No."

"Of course not. What slave would dare deface the city, knowing that each and every drow takes pride in its perfection?"

"A crazy one. We've all seen them go mad under the lash."

"Whereupon they attack their handlers. They don't creep about scrawling on walls. I'd like to questions the people in these houses on either side. Perhaps someone can shed some light on this occurrence."

"You get curious about the strangest things," Ryld said, shaking his head. "Sometimes I think you're a little mad yourself."

"Genius is so often misperceived."

"Look, I know this puzzle is going to nag at you, but we're right in the middle of trying to find the runaways and so save your life. Let's stick to that."

The tall, thin wizard smiled and said, "Yes, of course."

They walked on.

"But eventually," Pharaun said after a moment, "when we've located the rogues and covered ourselves in glory—or at least convinced Gromph to let me continue breathing—I am going to inquire into this."

They traveled another block, then a column of roaring yellow fire fell from the sky, engulfing Pharaun's body. Wings beat the air, and an arrow streaked at Ryld.

The netherspirit couldn't see the new enchantments surrounding Tier Breche, but as the uttermost attenuated projection of its substance washed over them, it could feel them.

Metaphorically speaking, the wards were not unlike a castle. There was the motte, the steep slopes of which would slow an enemy's approach while the defenders rained missiles down on him. Atop that loomed the thick, high walls, virtually unbreachable and unclimbable. Amid those was the recessed gate, defensible by spears and arrows loosed from three directions.

Within the passage itself, murder holes gaped in the ceiling to rain burning oil on the invaders' heads, while beyond it rose a gatehouse with battlements at the top, another barrier to enclose the first section of the courtyard and turn it into a killing pit.

Gromph's first countermagic, the one that had admitted the late and unlamented Beradax to the temple, had stormed the fortress like a rampaging army equipped with catapults, rams, and siege towers. The archmage's second effort resembled a mine sappers had excavated to pass unobtrusively beneath the walls. Except that this hole ran though extradimensional space.

As the netherspirit understood it, this method of egress was arranged by the Baenre eldermale so that the occupants of Arach-Tinilith would experience another kind of terror. They had already discovered the dread of a screaming alarm, and they would learn the fear that came when death slipped into their midst without any warning at all.

Pulling in the longer tendrils of its ectoplasmic substance, the entity—it and its kind had no names, an advantage in that most wizards therefore lacked the ability to summon them—poured its formless form into the tunnel, albeit not without a measure of trepidation. If Gromph's magic was unable to neutralize the conjurations of his minions, this was where the spirit would discover it in some unpleasant way.

As it crept down the mine, it sensed the wards poised above and around it, enchantments like hanging axes, precariously balanced and eager to fall, or taut tripwires attached to crossbows, or caltrops strewn lavishly underfoot. The constructs of mystical force fairly quivered like living things with their compulsion to slay, but none of them detected the intruder.

The other end of the tunnel, which would not exist for mortal eyes unless they were magically augmented, opened on a corridor. The netherspirit climbed out and took its bearings. It was inside one of the spider leg annexes of Arach-Tinilith, some distance from Quenthel's suite, but that was all right. It was confident that nothing could bar its path to its target.

The intruder hunched and drifted around a corner and saw a novice standing watch. Happily, the dark elf female didn't notice it, though that was scarcely a surprise. For some reason it didn't fully understand, Gromph had given it the guise of a demon of darkness, and it was all but indistinguishable from the ordinary, empty gloom behind it.

The netherspirit yearned to kill the mortal, but Gromph had forbidden it to do harm to anyone but Quenthel unless she was fool enough to stand between it and its appointed prey. With a pang of regret, it slipped past the sentry and on down the corridor. Soon it came upon a row of cells. Within the square little rooms, students recited their devotions.

So eager for bloodshed was the entity that the hall seemed to last forever. Soon enough, though, the spirit reached the spider's cephalothorax. This was the round, firelit heart of the temple, home to the grandest chapels, the holiest of altars, and the quarters of the temple's senior priestesses.

The intruder flowed into a spacious and largely empty octagonal chamber, where the air was perceptibly cooler than in the surrounding rooms and hallways. Statues of Lolth stood between the eight open rectangular doorways, and inlaid lines and curves of gold defined a complex magical sigil on the floor, a pentacle seemingly focused on a nexus of power at the exact center of the room. The same figure adorned the lofty ceiling, reinforcing the enchantment.

The netherspirit had no particular desire to discover what that enchantment was. It crawled along the walls, making sure not to touch the edge of the design.

Waves of power beat from the middle of the figure as something woke or became more real in the center of the chamber. A sharpness tore into the top of the spirit's vaporlike body, stunning it for an instant with a burst of unexpected pain.

Something jerked the living darkness toward the middle of the chamber. It realized that despite its lack of solidity, something had caught it with the equivalent of a hook and line. It also understood that simply avoiding the pentacle hadn't been good enough. Apparently when one entered the room, one was supposed to say a password or something.

The pulling ended abruptly, and the pain diminished. Shaking off its shock and disorientation, the darkness cast about and discerned the being crouching over it. The attacker was nearly as amorphous as itself, but the essence of it was fixed, hard, a mass of knobs and angles.

The attacker extruded additional lengths of itself to transfix the darkness. The piercings burned, made the spirit shake uncontrollably, and seemed to be leeching out its strength.

This, Gromph's agent realized with a kind of wonder, was the cold that could extinguish a mortal life in a heartbeat. The intruder had never felt the sensation before—not in a painful way—and shouldn't have been feeling it at all, but the prisoner of the pentacle wasn't just cold. It was the *essence* of cold, the pure *idea* of cold given life, just as the netherspirit to some degree embodied the concept of darkness.

Bits of the assassin began to clot, to gum, and to harden to a brittle rigidity, at which point they broke away. It wasn't truly injured as yet, but if it wanted to keep it that way, it knew it had better strike back at its assailant.

It washed its leading edge over the spirit of cold and discovered stress points, hairline cracks, imperfect junctures. Of course—the prisoner's structure resembled a mass of ice.

Gromph's agent materialized members like hammers, which pounded at the weak spots. It slid thin planes of itself into the fissures, then thickened them, forcing the edges apart.

The cold spirit snatched its frigid claws out of its foe. Its mind babbled a psionic offer of surrender. The cloud of darkness ignored it and continued the attack.

The freezing prisoner of the sigil exploded into motes of frost. They peppered the spirit of darkness for a second then they were gone.

Pleased with itself, the victor turned, inspecting each of the doorways in turn, trying to see if the battle had attracted anyone's attention. Apparently not, and actually, that made sense. The struggle had been relatively quiet, conducted largely on another level of existence.

The darkness reached the entrance to Quenthel's suite without further incident. Another sentry waited there, a spiked mace all but crackling with mystic force in her hand. Left to her own devices, she might hear her superior's distress and try to intervene, and the spirit decided to prevent such an occurrence. It rose around the priestess, blinding her, thickened a length of itself, and whipped it around her neck.

The female thrashed a little, then passed out for want of air. Her assailant laid her down and slid beneath the door.

Scores of costly icons decorated Quenthel's private rooms, so many that the place seemed a temple of Lolth in its own right. Beyond that, however, the suite was sparsely furnished, albeit with exquisite pieces, as if the Mistress of Arach-Tinilith practiced an asceticism at odds with the habits of the average sybaritic Menzoberranyr.

The darkness sent an intangible ripple of itself probing ahead. At once it discovered an element of Quenthel's personal defenses. It was not, as the spirit might have expected, a hidden mantrap woven of potent divine magic but a simple set of crystal wind chimes rendered invisible and hung at a point where any oblivious intruder would be sure to bump his head on them. Apparently the Baenre priestess believed that so long as an assassin gave her a second's warning, she would be able to handle the threat herself.

Maybe she could. The netherspirit would never know, because it had no intention of informing her of its coming. It took a certain ironic amusement in sliding its smokelike form directly through the dangling crystals without disturbing them in the slightest.

Eyes closed, in Reverie no doubt, Quenthel sat straight-backed and cross-legged on a rug. Along the back wall, pulses of mystical force throbbed from a pair of iron chests and from behind a theoretically secret door. The high priestess had invoked some formidable magic to protect her valuables. It was too bad she wasn't similarly careful with her life.

Gromph's agent flowed forward, and something reared hissing atop a round little table. It was the five vipers comprising an enchanted whip. Distracted by the magical power blazing at the back of the chamber, the netherspirit had missed feeling the lesser emanations of the vipers.

Fortunately, it didn't matter. The animate darkness had skulked too close to its prey for anything to balk it. It solidified a twisting strand of itself and slapped the table over, sending the whip flying. At the same time it darted, stretching, to pounce on Quenthel.

Her slanted eyes opened but of course saw only blackness. She opened her mouth to speak or shout, and the demon shoved a tendril inside.

chapter

S E U E N

For an instant, the world blazed bright and hot, searing Pharaun's skin. However, when the flame was gone it left little more than a tactile memory of pain. Gasping, the wizard took stock of himself. Except for a blister or two, he was all right. Some combination of the protective enchantments woven into both his vest and *piwafwi*, his innate drow resistance to hostile magic, and the silver ring he wore bearing the insignia of Sorcere, had saved him from fatal burns.

Ryld had drawn Splitter. An arrow whizzed down from a rooftop across the street, and the burly swordsman batted it out of the air. A huge flying mount wheeled overhead, vanishing from view before Pharaun could get a good look at it.

"Are you all right?" Ryld asked.

"Just singed a little," Pharaun replied.

"Here are your rogues, not so canny after all. We'll either have to rise into the air after them or pull them down to the street."

"We'll do neither. Follow me."

"Run?" the weapons master asked, swatting away another arrow. "I thought we wanted to catch one of them."

"Just follow."

Pharaun began moving down the street, meanwhile peering upward, looking for his attackers. Ryld scowled but trailed along behind him.

The Master of Sorcere glimpsed a swirling motion from the corner of his eye. He pivoted. Crouched on the edge of a roof, a spellcaster spun his hands in fluid mystic passes.

Gesturing, speaking rapidly, Pharaun rattled off his own incantation. He was racing the other mage, and he finished his magic first. Five darts of azure light leaped from his fingertips, shot at the spellcaster, and plunged into his chest. From that distance, he couldn't tell how badly he'd hurt his colleague, but at the least his foe flailed his arms in pain. The Academician's attack had disrupted his spell.

Ryld knocked another arrow away, and only then did Pharaun realize that this time, the shaft had been hurtling at him. An instant later, a studded mace seemingly made of shadow flew out of nowhere and swung itself at his head. Splitter flicked over and tapped that manifestation. As conjured objects often did, the war club vanished at the greatsword's touch.

"In here," Pharaun said.

The two masters ran to the arched sandstone door of one of the modest houses on the street. Pharaun suspected that the tenants had locked it at the first sign of trouble, and evidently Ryld agreed, because he didn't bother trying the handle. He simply booted the door and broke the latch. The weapons master scrambled inside.

The front room of the home was crowded. Pharaun might have expected that. The population of the city had grown considerably since its founding but the number of stalagmite buildings was of necessity fixed. The poor had to squeeze in wherever they could.

Thus, an abundance of paupers lived in the hovel, and a goodly number of them had gathered in this common space, either to relax or to dip rothé stew from the iron caldron on the trestle table. Surprisingly, the simple meal actually smelled appetizing. The aroma made Pharaun's mouth water and reminded him that he hadn't dined in several hours.

Ryld brandished Splitter at the occupants of the house with a flashy facility calculated to quell aggressive impulses.

"We apologize for the intrusion," Pharaun said.

The weapons master glowered at him. "*Why* are we running?"

"That pillar of fire was divine magic, not arcane." Pharaun lifted his hand, displaying the silver Sorcere ring and reminding his friend of its power to identify, not just protect him from, magic. "It's priestesses attacking us. Killing them would call attention to us, make the Council even more eager to put a stop to our inquiry. It might even make them want to kill us irrespective of how our mission turns out or of what Gromph decides."

Pharaun grinned and added, "I know I promised you glorious mayhem, but that will have to wait."

Ryld replied, "It's a difficult thing to sneak away from foes who hold the high ground."

"I'm an inexhaustible font of tricks, haven't you noticed?" Pharaun beamed at the assembled paupers and said, "How would you all like to assist two masters of the Academy engaged in a mission of vital importance? I assure you, Archmage Baenre himself will wax giddy with gratitude when I inform him of your aid."

His audience stared back at him, fear in their eyes. One of the female commoners produced a bone-handled, granite-headed mallet and threw it. Ryld caught it and hurled it back. The makeshift weapon thudded into the center of the laborer's forehead, and she collapsed.

"Would anyone else care to express a reservation of any sort?" Pharaun asked. He waited a beat. "Splendid, then just stand still. I assure you, this won't hurt."

The Master of Sorcere pulled a wisp of fleece from a pocket and recited an incantation. With a soft hissing, a wave of magical force shimmered through the room. When it touched the paupers, they changed, each into a facsimile of Ryld or Pharaun himself. Only a single child remained unaffected.

"Excellent," said Pharaun. "Now all you have to do is go outside, at which point, I recommend you scatter. With luck, many, if not all of you, will survive."

"No!" cried one of Ryld's doubles in a high, agitated voice. "You can't make us—"

"But we can," said Pharaun. "I can fill the house with a poisonous vapor, my friend can start chopping you to pieces. . . . So please, be sensible, go now. If the enemy breaks in here, your chances will be significantly worse."

They looked sullenly back at him. He smiled and shrugged, and Ryld hefted Splitter. The commoners began to scurry toward the door.

The two masters fell in at the back of the crowd, prepared to chivvy folk along as necessary.

"Shadows of the Pit," murmured Pharaun, "I wasn't at all sure they would actually do it. I am a persuasive devil, aren't I? It must be my honest face."

"Decoys aren't a bad idea," said Ryld, "but now that I think of it, why not just turn us invisible?"

Pharaun snorted. "Do I tell you which end of the sword to grip? Invisibility's too common a trick. I'm sure our foes are prepared to counter it. Whereas the illusion may work. It's one of my personal, private spells, and we Mizzrym are famously deft with phantasmata. Now, when we get outside, don't lose track of me. You don't want to go skipping off with the wrong Pharaun."

Most of the commoners had vacated the house. Pharaun drew a deep breath, steadying himself, and he and Ryld plunged out into the open.

The commoners were scattering as directed. As far as Pharaun could tell, no one had attacked any of them. Perhaps, as he'd hoped, the enemy was entirely flummoxed.

The masters, fleeing like the rest, turned one corner and another. Pharaun was beginning to feel the smugness that comes from outwitting an adversary when something rattled and rustled above his head. He looked up in time for it to slam him in the face and knock him down. Dropped from a fair height, the thick, coarse strands of rope comprising the net struck with the force of a club.

Also trapped, Ryld cursed, the language vulgar enough to make the Braeryn proud.

Pharaun needed a second to shake off the shock of the impact, and he realized his current situation was even more unfortunate than he'd initially thought. The net, woven in a spiderweb pattern, was animate. Scraping his skin, striving to render him completely immobile, the heavy mesh shifted and tightened around him.

A foulwing landed on the street. In the saddle sat an otherwise handsome priestess with a scarred face—a Mizzrym face, lean, intelligent, and sardonic. Strangely, she wore a domino mask, and Pharaun suspected he knew why.

Grinning, the female said, "I knew you'd try to trick me with illusions, Pharaun. That's why I brought a talisman of true seeing."

Though he wasn't sure she could see it from outside the net, Pharaun made it a point to smile back when he said, "And you were correct. Hello, Greyanna."

Quenthel was immune to fear. She did not, could not, panic. Or so she had always believed, and in fact, she wasn't panicking, but she was as desperate and bewildered as any ill-wisher could desire.

She wasn't certain, but she believed the vipers' hissing and a bump and clatter had roused her from her trancelike state of repose. She'd opened her eyes and seen nothing. Evidently someone had conjured a patch of darkness around her, or worse, cursed her with a blindness spell. She opened her mouth to speak to the whip snakes, and something cold and thick jammed itself inside.

Her throat clogged, she was suffocating. Meanwhile, something else, something that felt like the cool, dexterous tip of a demon's tentacle, slid around her wrist.

She yanked her hand away just before the unseen member could lock around it and thrashed to keep her limbs free of the other tendrils that began to grope after them. None of it helped her breathe.

She battered furiously at the space around her. Logic told her that her attacker had to be there, but her fists merely swept through empty space. Her chest ached with the need for air, and she felt unconsciousness nibbling at her mind.

She did the only thing left. She bit down.

At first, she couldn't penetrate the mass, but she strained, snarled in her throat with effort, and her teeth sank into something leathery and oily.

In an instant, it vanished. It didn't yank itself free, it just melted away.

Quenthel's teeth snapped together with a clack.

Scrambling to her knees, she sucked in a couple deep breaths, then called, "Whip!"

"Here!" Yngoth cried from somewhere on the floor. "We didn't see the demon until the last second. It *is* the darkness!"

"I understand."

At least she wasn't blind. She'd heard of demons made of darkness itself, though she had never had occasion to summon one. They were said to be hard to catch and even harder to bind.

"Guard!" she called.

This time she didn't hear an answer and wasn't surprised. The invader's presence suggested the sentry was either a traitor or dead.

Quenthel sensed something rushing at her. She flung herself sideways, and something crashed against the patch of wall immediately behind the space she'd just vacated. The stone floor chilled her through her gauzy wisp of a chemise.

As planned, she fetched up against the stand where she kept certain small pieces of her regalia. She leaped up and groped about the rectangular stone tabletop. To her disgust, a couple items rattled to the floor, but then her fingers closed on a medallion of beautifully cut glass.

Squinting, she invoked the trinket's power. A dazzling glare blazed through the room. Quenthel had to shield her own eyes, hoping the terrible light would destroy a living darkness altogether.

The magic light and the equally supernatural darkness made for a split second when the lighting in the room was as it was before the creature had entered. At least Quenthel could open her eyes.

Her assailant, seemingly unaffected by the light, was a ragged central blot with long, tattered arms snaking throughout the room, ubiquitous as smoke. Drinking in all the glow, reflecting none, it was dead black and deceptively flat-looking. It thrust a long, thin probe at the medallion and Quenthel jerked the token aside. The shaft of blackness veered, compensating, and struck the medallion hard enough to knock it out of her hand. The light died instantly when the glass medallion shattered on the floor.

Fortunately, the illumination had lasted long enough for her to note the locations of several other objects on the stand. She instinctively ducked, the tentacle swept over her head and tousled her hair, and she grabbed a scroll. As before, she would regret expending any of the spells contained therein, but she'd regret dying even more.

Conversant with the contents of the parchment, she didn't need to see the trigger phrase to "read" it. She recited the words, and a shaft of yellow flame roared down from the ceiling through the spot where the core of the demon had been floating. The firelight showed that it was still there. The blaze passed right through it, and all its arms and streamers of murk convulsed.

The column of flame vanished after a moment, leaving, despite the care the drow had taken to shield her eyes, a haze of afterimage bisecting her vision. It took her a second to realize that dull, wavering stripe was the only thing she could see. The darkness had survived. It had clotted its essence around her to seal her eyes once more.

You're a tough one, she thought, sending the unspoken words to the mind of the demon as she, a divine emissary of Lolth, was trained to do.

There was no response, and Quenthel felt no connection made between her mind and the consciousness of the demon. This was no servant of Lolth's.

Alive and impossible to command, it would surely grab or strike at her, and this time intuition was failing her. She had no idea from where the attack would come, so she didn't know which way to dodge to evade it. She simply had to guess, jump somewhere and not let blindness and indecision delay her. She pivoted, and something struck her shoulder.

At first it was just a startling jolt, then pain burned at the point of impact, and wet blood flowed. Either the darkness could harden its members into claws or else it had picked up a blade from somewhere in the chamber.

Quenthel was glad her teachers had taught her to suffer a wound without the shock of it freezing her in her tracks, helpless to avert her adversary's follow-up attack. She kept moving, making herself, she hoped, a more difficult target.

Something hissed. The source of the sound was almost under her feet. Evidently, dragging the whip handle behind them, her vipers had been slithering about endeavoring to locate her in the dark. She stooped, fumbled about their cool, sinuous lengths for a moment, achieved the proper grip, and lifted the weapon.

The serpents reared, hissed, and peered, each in a different direction. Quenthel realized they could see what she could not. The darkness was preparing to attack.

The priestess deepened her psionic link with her snake-demon servants. She still couldn't see where her adversary's tentacles were poised, but she had a sense of them. That would have to do.

The darkness reached for her, and, turning and turning, she swung the whip repeatedly. Her aim was inexact, but the vipers twisted in the air to correct it.

Toward the end, she was breathing harder, and her actions were getting bigger, slower, and wilder, as any combatant's will if she performs too many without a pause. Then something long and pointed plunged into the back of her thigh.

Quenthel knew at once from the flare of pain and the gush of blood that this puncture wound was worse than the gash in her shoulder. She staggered a step, and her leg began to fold. The whip vipers hissed in alarm.

She shouted to focus her will and quell the agony, to force the limb to obey. Throbbing, it straightened.

She spun and struck at the tentacle that had stabbed her, lashing it to pieces before it could do the same again. At that same instant, her serpent familiars detected hands reaching for her neck. She spun, destroyed those as well, and at last the shadow stopped attacking.

Feeling the blood stream down her leg to pool on the floor, her mind racing, Quenthel considered her situation. She must be causing the demon pain—if not it would attack relentlessly, never faltering until she fell—but that didn't necessarily mean she was well on her way to killing it. From what she knew of such entities, it seemed entirely possible that she would have to do more harm to the nucleus at the end of the tendrils to accomplish that. Assuming she could reach or even locate it amid the obfuscating gloom.

It might be better not to try, to take advantage of this momentary respite and make a run for it, but she knew that if she moved the demon would move with her, which would mean she'd still be scurrying sightlessly along. In her suite, that wasn't an enormous problem—she knew every inch of the space by heart—but outside, she could easily take a hard, incapacitating fall. If that happened or if her leg gave out before she found help, her foe would have little difficulty finishing her off.

No, she would kill the cursed thing by herself, quickly, while she was still on her feet. The only question was, how?

One of the weapons in her hidden closet might do the trick, but she had no way of reaching them. The demon would slay her while she fumbled in the dark to manipulate the hidden lock. She would have to make do with the resources in her hands, which meant using another scroll spell and taking a gamble as well.

The demon renewed the attack. Quenthel struck and deflected a tentacle with sawlike teeth on the edge. Next came an arm terminating in a studded bulb like the head of a mace. Poised to beat her skull in, that one was no use either. She sidestepped the blow, the vipers tore into the limb, and the living darkness snatched it back.

A simple tentacle, with no blades or bludgeons sprouting from its end, snaked toward her. It seemed as if it was going to try to grab and restrain her weapon arm. She pretended she didn't notice.

The strand of shadow dipped to the floor, hooked around Quenthel's ankle, and jerked her good leg out from under her. The change of target caught her by surprise, and she fell hard on her back, banging her head and shooting pain through her wounded limbs.

It took her an instant to shake off the shock. When she did, she sensed the fiend's other limbs poised to slash and pound. She was almost out of time to recite the trigger phrase.

But not quite.

She rattled off the three words, and power seethed and tingled inside her flesh. She discharged it into the living darkness, an easy task since the demon was holding onto her. She held her breath, waiting to see what would happen.

Like allowing her adversary to seize her, this too was a part of the gamble. The magic she had just unleashed would weaken a dark elf or pretty much any other mortal being to the point of death. However, depending on its precise nature, the demon—or whatever it was—might simply shrug it off. It might even feed on the blast of force and grow stronger than before.

The ploy worked. The fiend was susceptible, at least to some degree. She knew it when the entity's limbs flailed and thrashed in spasms, the one on her ankle releasing her to twist and flop about. The ambient darkness blinked out of existence for a second as the creature's grip on its surroundings wavered.

One instant of vision was all Quenthel needed to mark where her enemy's ragged core was floating. She scrambled up, charged it, and found that she was hobbling, every other stride triggering a jolt of pain. She didn't let the discomfort slow her down.

The creature of darkness was recovering. Two tendrils squirmed at Quenthel. She ducked one and lashed the other, which flinched back.

After two more steps, she judged, hoped, that she'd limped within striking distance of the entity's formless heart. She swung the whip, and shouted in satisfaction when she felt the vipers' fangs rip something more resistant than empty air.

She struck as hard and as fast as she could, grunting with every stroke. Her snakes warned her of tendrils looping around behind her, and she ignored the threat. If she left off attacking the center of the darkness, she might not get another chance.

The darkness obscuring the room started rapidly oscillating between presence and absence. Quenthel's motions looked oddly jerky in the disjointed moments of vision.

Tentacles grabbed and dragged her backward. She shouted in rage and frustration. As if responding to her cry, the arms dissolved, dumping her back on the floor.

Quenthel raised her head and peered about. There was no longer any impediment to sight. The murderous darkness was gone. Her last blow must have been mortal. It had just taken the creature another second or two to succumb.

"It's dead!" hissed Hsiv. "What now, Mistress?"

"First . . . I'm going to sit . . . and tend my wounds, then we're going to look . . . for my sentry," panted Quenthel, attenuating her rapport with the vipers. In too deep and prolonged a communion, shades of identity could bleed in one direction or the other. "If she's lucky, she's already dead."

She wished she were as undaunted as she was trying to sound, but it appeared that demonic assassins were going to keep coming for her. She'd hoped that the appearance of the spider demon might be an isolated incident. She'd thought that if any more such fiends did appear, the renewed wards would keep them out. Plainly, she'd been too optimistic.

At least Arach-Tinilith was the seat of her power. There, she could deploy a small army of retainers and a hoard of magical devices in her own defense, but those resources hadn't helped her against the darkness, and she couldn't help wondering how many hostile visitations a priestess in her condition could hope to survive.

c h a p t e r

E I G H T

Greyanna's henchmen came floating down around her. Two were warriors, one a wizard, and the third was another priestess. All wore the half masks of true seeing, giving them the deceptively foolish look of actors in a pantomime.

Pharaun tried to levitate, but the net was too heavy. He willed his animate rapier into existence. The steel ring vanished from his finger, and the long, slim sword materialized outside the net. The blade started slicing at the thick ropes, but to little effect. A rapier was a thrusting weapon and not suited to sawing. Tensing his muscles against the remorseless pressure of the tightening web, he turned the floating sword around to threaten his fellow representatives of House Mizzrym.

Greyanna laughed. "Is that one little bodkin supposed to hold us all at bay?"

"Possibly not," said Pharaun, straining to work his fingers closer to one of his pockets. "That's why I instructed it to kill you first."

"Did you, now?"

His sister motioned her warriors forward. Twin brothers possessed of the same slightly yellowish hair and deeply cleft chin, they carried pale bone longbows slung over their backs in preference to the more common crossbows.

Greyanna herself remained on her mount and produced a scroll from within her *piwafwi*. Thanks to his remaining ring, Pharaun could see from the complex corona of magical force shining around the rolled parchment that it contained, among others, a spell to disrupt the other fellow's magic. Perhaps she intended to use it to render the dancing rapier inert long enough for her minions to break or immobilize it.

The wretched ropes were digging into the wizard's flesh like knives. He would hardly have been surprised if they drew blood. They were certainly cutting off his circulation and numbing his extremities. Trembling with effort, he shifted his fingers another inch.

"My companion is Ryld Argith," he said, "a Master of Melee-Magthere. He's never done anything to you, and you will place yourself in debt to the warriors of the pyramid by killing him."

Entangled as he was, Pharaun couldn't even turn his head to look at his friend anymore, but he could hear Ryld grunting and swearing and feel him shaking the net. The swordsman was plainly trying to free himself, but it seemed unlikely that even his extraordinary strength would be enough if he was unable to bring one of his blades to bear, and apparently such was the case.

"I've kept tabs on you through the years." Greyanna said. "I know Master Argith is your most valued comrade. I don't need him trying to liberate or avenge you. Our mother will handle Melee-Magthere."

On further inspection, Pharaun observed that the subordinate priestess had readied a scroll as well. That struck him as vaguely odd, but he supposed this was hardly the time to ponder the possible significance.

The warriors were approaching steadily but warily, and not merely, he suspected, because of the hovering rapier. Greyanna could neutralize the weapon, but they feared that Pharaun would work some terrible magic that only required speech, not gestures or a focal object. He was sorry to disappoint them. He did have one or two such spells in his memory but none that could annihilate all five of these unpleasant folk at a single stroke, and he knew that once he conjured some devastating attack, they would abandon any intention of taking him alive for a demise by torture. They would strike back as fast and murderously as possible, and immobilized in the mesh, he would have little hope of defending against their efforts.

"Actually, you ought to think twice about harming either of us," he said, hoping that further conversation would slow the fighters' advance, even if only for a second.

Greyanna chuckled. "Be assured, I've thought of it a thousand thousand times."

"The archmage won't like it."

"I'm acting on behalf of the Council. I doubt he'll deem it politic to retaliate . . . any more than Melee-Magthere will."

"Well, Gromph won't sign his name to your cadaver, but someday . . ."

Pharaun's fingers finally jerked into the pocket and closed around a small but sturdy leather glove. With the net still tightening every second, it was just as hard to withdraw the article as it had been to reach it. He experimented to see if he could possibly fumble it through the proper mystical pass.

Such a cramped, tiny motion was neither easy nor natural for him. He was accustomed to conjure with a certain flair, making sweeping, dramatic gestures. Yet he had on occasion practiced making the signs as small as possible. It was good for his control and had a few times allowed him to cast a spell without an adversary realizing what he was about. So he had some hope of properly manipulating the glove. If only the web wasn't so constrictive or his hand so dead and awkward.

"Excuse me," Greyanna said, then suspended the conversation to read from her scroll.

It was of course divine magic, not arcane, and Pharaun didn't recognize all the words. The effect, however, was unmistakable. The rapier jerked and fell to the ground with a clank. The masked wizard stepped forward and scooped it up. Pharaun was content at least with the fact that the rapier's peculiar enchantment would make it impossible for Greyanna's henchman to turn the weapon on him—at least not for an hour or so.

Pharaun recognized the mage, whose high, wide forehead and small, pointed chin were unmistakable. Pharaun had always thought they made the other mage's head look like an egg. He was Relonor Vrinn, an able wizard and longtime Mizzrym retainer. He was still wearing his silk sash with the spell foci tucked inside and an eight-pointed gold brooch securing it.

Scimitars in hand, the warriors approached the net. Judging from their smiles, they'd decided there was nothing to fear and were looking forward to beating the two prisoners unconscious.

Pharaun was not yet satisfied with his employment of the glove, but he was rather clearly out of time. He would just have to try the pass and see if it worked. He shifted the focus one more time, meanwhile reciting an incantation under his breath.

A giant hand, radiant and translucent, appeared beneath the net. The instantaneous addition of another object lodged inside jerked the mesh even tighter. Pharaun knew the jolt was coming, but he cried out anyway.

The pain only intensified when, responding to the wizard's unspoken command, the hand hurtled twenty-five feet into the air, carrying the net and its prisoners along. For a moment, Pharaun feared he would black out, but the pressure eased. As he'd hoped, and despite the best sliding, bunching efforts of the web of ropes, his own weight was dragging him free. He shoved and thrashed to speed the process along.

When he was able, he looked over at Ryld. The hulking warrior was wrestling free of the net as well, though he lost hold of Splitter doing it. The greatsword fell point first, narrowly missed plunging through one of the Mizzrym warriors, and stuck pommel up in the smooth stone surface of the street.

"We have to fall," said Ryld. "If we just float here, they'll shoot and magic us to pieces."

"Let's go," Pharaun replied.

The masters released their holds and plummeted. One of the soldiers hit Ryld with an arrow, but the missile failed to penetrate his armor. A ball of flame exploded in the air, but Relonor had aimed too high, and the blast only made his targets flinch. Pharaun used his House insignia to slow his descent just a little. He thought that otherwise he'd break his legs.

As a result, he saw Ryld—who possessed a similar levitating talisman, his bearing the sigil of Melee-Magthere—reach the ground a moment ahead of him. The Master of Melee-Magthere tucked into a ball, rolled, sprang up with short sword in hand, and lunged at the soldier who'd loosed the arrow. The masked male leaped backward, dropped his bow, and whipped his scimitar out of its scabbard again. While he was so engaged, Ryld yanked Splitter out of the ground.

Pharaun landed. Despite his attempt to cushion the impact, it slammed up his legs and sent him staggering. As he fought to recover his balance, he noticed Relonor swirling his hands in a star-shaped pattern.

As the Master of Sorcere lurched upright, the other mage completed his incantation. A long, angular reptilian thing sprang from the palms of the older drow's outstretched hands as if they were the doorway to another world. Wreathed in flowing blue flame, the monster charged Pharaun.

Relonor was a gifted mage but no marvel as a tactician. In the excitement of the moment, he'd reflexively cast his favorite spell, and characteristically for a Mizzrym retainer, it was an illusion. He'd forgotten that his foe, born in the same House, might well recognize the sequence of mystic passes. Of course, even if Pharaun hadn't, his silver ring would have shown him what sort of magic the other male was creating.

He ignored the phantasm and reached into a pocket to snatch a tiny crystal and commence a spell. He ignored the apparition even when it lunged so close he felt the imaginary but searing heat of its halo of flame.

An intense coldness, visible in the fan of drifting ice crystals it instantly created, exploded from his hand. It passed right through the reptile, dissipating the illusion in the process, and washed over Relonor. It painted him with rime, and he fell backward.

Pharaun grinned. Greyanna was a fool to accost him with so few retainers in her train. Didn't she realize that two masters of Tier Breche were more than equal to the worst that she and her four dolts could do?

The foulwing flapped its batlike wings and hopped closer to the melee. As its legless body pounded down on the ground, Greyanna opened a leather bag and flung a handful of its contents into the air.

The falling motes flared with greenish light when they struck the ground. Each seethed and sparkled upward like a spore instantaneously growing into a fungus. In an instant, a number of animate skeletons stood upon the street. They carried a miscellany of weapons and shields but shared a common purpose. As one, they oriented on the masters and advanced.

Shifting back and forth, Ryld cut the undead creatures down. Pharaun took momentary shelter behind his friend, then the swordsman cried out, staggered, and dropped his guard. The skeletons surged forward, and the twins, who'd been hovering at the periphery of the fight, darted in as well.

Caught by surprise, Pharaun only just had time to conjure a dazzling, crackling fork of lightning. The power held the enemy back for a moment, and Ryld recovered his balance.

"All right?" asked the Master of Sorcere.

"Yes." Ryld chopped a spear-wielding skeleton's legs out from under it. "Something was trying to tamper with my mind, but it's gone now."

"It won't stay gone unless I confront the spellcasters."

Pharaun floated up into the air, beyond the skeletons' reach, making sure he would have a clear shot at Greyanna and the others. In his absence, the creatures would likely be able to surround Ryld, but that couldn't be helped.

Surveying the scene, he saw that Relonor was still lying motionless on his back. Positioned beyond the melee, Greyanna and her sister priestess were reading from scrolls.

For a moment, Pharaun's thoughts exploded into a terrifying madness, but reason quickly reasserted itself. He sucked in a deep breath, trying to quell the residual fear, and a second assault wracked his body. He cried out, and the agony passed. Somehow he'd weathered both spells.

He threw a seething ball of lighting at Greyanna, but it winked out of existence halfway to the target, unmade by the priestess's defenses. She and the other cleric employed their scrolls again.

A dazzling, searing beam of light erupted from Greyanna's hand. It slashed across Pharaun's face, and he closed his eyes just in time to keep it from blinding him. It was painful nonetheless, but his own defenses kept it from burning his face off.

The other priestess flailed at him with a sizzling bolt of lightning. As it was one of his own favorite forces to command, it hardly seemed fair. He stiffened with the shock for a moment or two, and the magic lost its grip on him.

He feared the spasm had cost him precious time. By the time it passed, he thought the priestesses were surely in the process of casting new spells, but when he looked at the lesser of the two she wasn't creating any magic. She'd dropped her suddenly blank scroll on the ground and was rooting in her leather pouch, presumably for another means of magical attack.

Clasping a bit of coal and a tiny dried eyeball held in a little vial, Pharaun created an effect. Power sighed and rippled through the air, and a mass of darkness appeared around the female's head, blinding her.

The wizard's thoughts flew apart once more, then reassembled themselves. He rounded on Greyanna. She was still clutching her scroll, evidently still casting from it. He began to conjure, and she, evidently uncertain of the parchment's power to protect her, tore open the bag.

It had occurred to Pharaun that the sack might have more spores in it, but he'd assumed they would produce more skeletons. This time, though, the glittering motes burst in midair, swelling into ugly little beasts resembling a cross between a bat and a mosquito.

The stirges swirled around him, jabbing at him with their proboscises, striving to drink his blood. They interfered with the motion of his hands and so spoiled his conjuration. He restored his weight and fell back to the ground, where Ryld, beset by clinking skeletons on all sides, beheaded one with a sudden cut. One of the twins edged toward him but balked when the big male pivoted in his direction.

Pharaun slammed down on the street. Trailing chattering stirges, he sprinted toward the fallen Relonor. A couple skeletons turned to hack at him, but most of them were too intent on killing Ryld to notice him. Up close, the things stank. Pharaun thought they must still have some scraps of rotting flesh about them somewhere.

Just as he reached the unconscious wizard, Greyanna's foulwing landed on the other side of the body with a ground-shaking thump. Pharaun roared out a painfully loud magical shout, and the beast recoiled, carrying its rider with it.

Pharaun stooped, ripped the brooch off Relonor's sash, turned, and ran. Greyanna screamed in rage. The foulwing roared its strange double roar, and two sets of jaws clashed shut behind the fleeing male.

A stirge's proboscis jabbed him in the back, staggering him, but was unable to penetrate his *piwafwi*. Another spell rattled his mind but with no permanent ill effects. A skeleton appeared on his flank, swinging a notched, rusty axe at his head. Splitter flashed in an arc and smashed the undead thing into tiny pieces.

Pharaun caught hold of the hem of Ryld's *piwafwi* and glanced around at Greyanna.

Her face a mask of fury, she tossed away her scroll, which was likely blank, and held her hands high to receive the long staff materializing from some extradimensional storage. He could see why she wanted the instrument. It blazed with mystic power, but it was also slow in attaining tangibility. Some chance interaction of the magical energies playing about the battleground was retarding its transition to the physical plane.

Why, then, didn't she leave off summoning it and attack in some other manner? Why—

In a flash of inspiration, the answer came to him, and it was astonishing.

But he was scarcely in a place conducive to contemplation of his discovery, and it was time to remedy that. He peered at the brooch he'd taken from Relonor, found the trigger word implicit in the kaleidoscopic pattern shining around it, and spoke.

Greyanna regarded the open space in the middle of the ring of aimlessly milling skeletons, and the stirges swooping and wheeling above. A moment before, Pharaun and his hulking accomplice had been standing there, but they were gone. If her eyes had not deceived her, her brother had flashed her that old familiar mocking grin as he vanished. How dare he smirk at her like that when it was she who had driven him from House Mizzrym!

She regarded her iron staff, taller than she was, square in cross-section, graven with hundreds of tiny runes, and warm as blood to the touch. The weapon had failed her. She trembled with the impulse to swing it over her head and smash it against the stone beneath her feet until it was defaced, deformed, and useless.

She didn't, because she knew Pharaun's escape was really her fault, not the staff's. She should have summoned the weapon sooner. She should have been more aggressive with the sack. Damn this degrading and inexplicable season! Because of its vicissitudes, her mother had instructed her to play the miser with every personal resource, even though she was fighting for the welfare of House Mizzrym and all Menzoberranzan.

Well, she wouldn't make the same mistake next time. It was her responsibility to look after her troops and return them to the castle. She dismounted, squared her shoulders, put on a calm, commanding expression, and proceeded with the business at hand.

Neither of the twins were hurt, and her cousin Aunrae merely needed the ball of darkness around her head dispelled. It was Relonor who concerned Greyanna, but fortunately the mage was still alive. A healing potion mended him sufficiently to stand, clutching his sash so it wouldn't slip off and shrugging out of his ice-encrusted cloak.

While the twins helped Relonor hobble about and so restore his circulation, Aunrae came sidling up to Greyanna. To her cousin's admittedly jaundiced eye, in Aunrae the usual Mizzrym tendency to leanness had run to a grotesque extreme. The younger female resembled a stick insect.

"My commiseration on your failure," Aunrae said.

Her expression was grave, but she wasn't really trying to hide the smile lurking underneath.

"I didn't realize just how powerful Pharaun has become," Greyanna admitted. "Before his exile, he was quite competent but nothing extraordinary. It was his cunning that made him so dangerous. I see that all the decades in Tier Breche have turned him into one of the most formidable wizards in the city. That complicates things, but I'll manage."

"I hope the matron will forgive you your ignorance," Aunrae said. "You've wasted so much magic to no effect."

The conjured skeletons and stirges began to wink out of existence, leaving a residue of magic energy. The air seemed to tingle and buzz, though if a person stopped and listened, it really wasn't.

"Is that how you see it?" Greyanna asked.

Aunrae shrugged. "I'm just worried she'll feel you bungled things, that your hatred of Pharaun made you blind and clumsy. She might even decide someone else is more deserving of the preeminence you currently possess. Of course, I hope not! You know I wish you well. My plan for my future has always been to support you and prosper as your aide."

"Cousin, your words move me," Greyanna said as she lifted the staff.

No one could heave such a long, heavy implement into a fighting position without giving the opponent an instant's warning, so Aunrae was able to come on guard. It didn't matter. Not bothering to unleash any of the magic within her weapon, wielding it like an ordinary quarterstaff, Greyanna bashed the mace from the younger priestess's fingers, knocked her flat with a ringing blow to her armored shoulder, and dug the tip of the iron rod into her throat.

"I'd like to confer on one or two matters," said Greyanna. "Do you have a moment?"

Aunrae made a liquid, strangling sound.

"Excellent. Listen and grow wise. Today's little fracas was not in vain. It proved that Relonor can locate Pharaun with his divinations. Even more importantly, the battle enabled me to take our brother's measure. When we track him down again, we'll crush him. Now, do you see that I have this venture well in hand?"

Deprived of her voice, Aunrae nodded enthusiastically. Her chin bumped against the butt of the staff.

"What a sensible girl you are. You must also bear in mind that we aren't hunting Pharaun simply for my own personal gratification. It's for the benefit of all, including yourself. Therefore, this isn't an ideal time to seek to discredit and supplant one of your betters. It's a time for us to swallow our mutual distaste and work together until the threat is gone. Do you think you can remember that?"

Aunrae kept nodding. She was shaking, too, and her eyes were wide with terror. Small wonder; she must have been running short of breath. Still, she had the sense not to try to grab the staff and jerk it away from her neck. She knew what would happen if she tried.

Greyanna was tempted to make it happen anyway. Aunrae's submission was a small pleasure beside the fierce satisfaction that would come from ramming the staff into the helpless female's windpipe. The urge was a hot tightness in her hands and a throbbing in the scar across her face.

But she needed minions to catch the relative she truly hated, and, annoying as she was, Aunrae was game, and wielded magic with a certain facility. It would be more practical to murder her another day. Greyanna was sure she could manage it whenever she chose. Despite her ambitions, Aunrae was no threat. She lacked the intelligence.

Feeling a strange pang of nostalgia for Sabal, who had at least been a rival worth destroying, Greyanna lifted the staff away from her cousin's throat.

"You will whisper no poison words in Mother's ears," the First Daughter of House Mizzrym said. "For the time being, you will leave off plotting against me or anyone else. You will devote your every thought to finding our truant brother. Otherwise, I'll put an end to you."

Ryld had never experienced instantaneous travel before. To his surprise, he was conscious of the split second of teleportation, and he found it rather unpleasant. It didn't feel as if he were speeding through the world but as if the world were hurtling at and through him, albeit painlessly.

Then it was over. He'd unconsciously braced himself to compensate for the jolt of a sudden stop, and the absence of any such sensation rocked him on his feet.

By the time he recovered his balance, he knew more or less where he was. A whiff of dung told him. He looked around and confirmed the suspicion.

Pharaun had dropped the two of them in a disused sentry post on a natural balcony. The ledge overlooked Donigarten with its moss fields, grove of giant mushrooms, and fungus farms fertilized with night soil from the city. Hordes of orc and goblin slaves either tended the malodorous croplands or speared fish from rafts on the lake, while rothé lowed from the island in the center of the water. Overseers and an armed patrol wandered the fields to keep the thralls in line. Additional guards looked down from other high perches about the cavern wall.

Ryld knew Pharaun had transported them about as far as was possible. In the Realms that See the Sun, teleportation could carry folk around the world, but in the Underdark, the disruptive radiance of certain elements present in the rock limited the range to about half a mile—far enough to throw Greyanna and her pack off the scent.

Pharaun held the pilfered golden ornament up, inspecting it.

"It only holds one teleportation at a time," he said after a moment. Even after all his exertions, he wasn't panting as hard as he might have been; not bad for such a sybarite, thought Ryld as he set down his bloody greatsword. "It's useless now, and I lost my dancing rapier, curse it, but I'm not too disconsol—"

Ryld grabbed Pharaun by the arm and flipped him, laying him down hard.

The wizard blinked, sat up, and brushed a strand of his sculpted hair back into place.

"If you'd told me you craved more fighting," Pharaun said, "I could have left you behind with my kin."

"The hunters, you mean," Ryld growled, "who found us quickly."

"Well, we asked a fair number of questions in a fair number of places. We even *wanted* someone to find us, just not that lot." Pharaun stood back up and brushed at his garments, adding, "Now, I have something extraordinary to tell you."

"Save it," Ryld replied. "Back there in the net, when you and Greyanna were chatting, I got the strong impression that the priestesses weren't just hunting some faceless agent. They knew from the start their target was you, and you knew they knew."

Pharaun sighed. "I didn't know the matrons would choose Greyanna to discourage our efforts. That was a somewhat disconcerting surprise. But the rest of it? Yes."

"How?"

"Gromph has invisible glyphs scribed on the walls of his office. Invisible to most people, anyway. They protect him in various ways. One, a black sigil shaped a little like a bat, is supposed to keep scryers and spellcasters from eavesdropping on his private conversations, but when he and I spoke, it was drawn imperfectly. It still would have balked many a spy, but not someone with the resources and expertise of, oh, say, his sisters . . . or the Council."

Ryld frowned. "Gromph botched it?"

"Of course not," Pharaun snorted. "Do you think the Archmage of Menzoberranzan incompetent? He drew it precisely as he wanted it. He knew the high priestesses were trying to spy on him—they surely always have and doubtless always will—and he intended them to overhear."

"He was setting you up."

"Now you're getting it. While the clerics stay busy seeking me, the decoy, my illustrious chief will undertake another, more discreet inquiry undisturbed, by performing divinations and interrogating demons, probably."

"You knew, and you undertook the mission anyway."

"Because knowing doesn't change my fundamental circumstances. If I want to retain my rank and quite possibly my life, I still have to complete the task the archwizard set me, even though he was playing me for a fool, even with Greyanna striving to hinder the process." Pharaun grinned and added, "Besides, where *did* all those runaways go, and why do the greatest folk in Menzoberranzan care? It's a fascinating puzzle, even more so now that I've inferred a portion of the answer. Did I leave it unsolved, it would haunt me forevermore."

"You played me for a fool," said Ryld. "Granted, you warned me the priestesses might interfere with us, but you greatly understated the danger. You didn't tell me you were marked before we even descended from Tier Breche. Why not? Did you think I'd refuse to accompany you?"

Most uncharacteristically, the glib wizard hesitated. Far below the shelf, a whip snapped and a goblin screamed.

"No," said Pharaun eventually, "not really. I suppose it's just that dark elves are jealous of their secrets. So are the nobly born. So are wizards. And I'm all three! Will you pardon me? It isn't as if you've never kept a secret from me."

"When?"

"During the first three years of our acquaintance, whenever we fraternized, you kept a dagger specially charmed for the killing of mages ever close to your hand. You suspected I was only seeking your company because one of your rivals in Melee-Magthere had engaged me to murder you as soon as the opportunity arose."

"How did you discover that? Never mind, I suppose it was your silver ring. I didn't know what it was back then. Anyway, that's not the same kind of secret."

"You're right, it isn't, and I regret my reticence but I do propose to make up for it by sharing the most astonishing confidence you've ever heard."

Ryld stared into Pharaun's eyes. "I'll pardon you. With the understanding that if you withhold any other pertinent information, I'll knock you over the head and deliver you to your bitch sister myself."

"Point taken. Shall we sit?" Pharaun pointed to a bench hewn from the limestone wall at the back of the ledge. "My discourse may take a little time, and I daresay we could use a rest after our exertions."

As he turned away from the molded rock rampart, Ryld noticed that the cracking of the whip had stopped. When he glanced down, two goblins were carrying the corpse of a third, hauling it somewhere to be chopped apart and the pieces turned to some useful purpose. Possibly chow for other thralls.

The fencing teacher sat down and removed a cloth, a whetstone, and a vial of oil from the pockets of his garments. He unfastened his short sword from his belt, pulled on the hilt, and made a little spitting sound of displeasure when the blade, which he had been forced to put away bloody, stuck in the scabbard. He yanked more forcefully, and it came free.

He looked over at Pharaun, who was regarding with him with a sort of quizzical exasperation.

"Talk," the warrior said. "I can care for my gear and listen at the same time."

"Is this how you attend to mind-boggling revelations? I suppose I'm lucky you don't have to use the jakes. All right, here it is . . . Lolth is gone. Well, maybe not *gone*, but unavailable at least in the sense that it's no longer possible for her Menzoberranyr clerics to receive spells from her."

For a moment, Ryld thought he'd misheard the words. "I guess that's a joke?" he asked. "I'm glad you didn't make it while we were in the middle of a crowd. There's no point compounding our crimes with blasphemy."

"Blasphemy or not, it's the truth."

Rag in hand, Ryld scrubbed tacky blood off the short sword.

"What are you suggesting," the weapons master asked, "another Time of Troubles? Could there be two such upheavals?"

Pharaun grinned and said, "Possibly, but I think not. When the gods were forced to inhabit the mortal world, the arcane forces we wizards command fluctuated unpredictably. One day, we could mold the world like clay. The next, we couldn't turn ice to water. That isn't happening now. My powers remain constant as ever, from which I tentatively infer this is not the Time of Troubles come again but a different sort of occurrence."

"What sort?"

"Oh, am I supposed to know that already? I thought I was doing rather well to detect the occurrence at all."

"Only if it's really happening."

Ryld inspected the point of the short stabbing blade, then took the hone to it. Bemused by Pharaun's contention, he wondered how his canny friend could credit such a ludicrous idea.

"I want you to think back over the confrontation from which we just emerged," said the Master of Sorcere. "Did you even once see Greyanna or the other priestess cast divine magic from her own mind and inner strength as opposed to off a scroll or out of some device?"

"I was fighting the skeletons."

"You keep track of every foe on the battleground. I know you do. So, did you see them casting spells out of their own innate power?"

Ryld thought that of course he had . . . then realized he hadn't.

"What does that suggest?" Pharaun asked. "They have no spells left in their heads, or only a few, which they're hoarding desperately because they can't solicit new ones from their goddess. Lolth has withdrawn her favor from Menzoberranzan, or . . . something."

"Why would she do that?"

"Would she need a reason—or at any rate, one her mortal children can comprehend? She is a deity of chaos. Perhaps she's testing us somehow, or else she's angry and deems us unworthy of her patronage.

"Or, as I suggested before, the cause of her silence, if in fact she is mute when her clerics pray to her and not just uncooperative, may be something else altogether. Perhaps even another happenstance involving all the gods. Since we have only one faith and clergy in Menzoberranzan, it's difficult to judge."

"Wait," Ryld said. He unstoppered his little bottle of oil. The sharp smell provided a welcome counterpoint to the moist stink of the dung fields. "I admit, I didn't see Greyanna or any of the lesser priestesses working magic, but didn't you yourself once tell me that in the turmoil of battle, it's often easier and more reliable to cast your effects from a wand or parchment?"

"I suppose I did. Still, under normal circumstances, would you expect a pair of spellcasters to conjure every single manifestation that way? Just before our exit, I saw Greyanna groping in the ether for a weapon that was slow in coming to her hand. The sister I remember would have said to the Hells with it and dumped some other magic on our heads. That is, unless something had circumscribed her options."

"I see what you mean," Ryld conceded, "but when the clerics lost their powers in the Time of Troubles, it destabilized the balance of power among the noble Houses. Those who believed the change made them stronger in relative terms struck hard to supplant their rivals. As far as I can see, that isn't happening now, just the usual level of controlled enmity."

He laid the short sword aside and picked up Splitter.

Pharaun nodded and said, "You'll recall that none of the Houses attempting to exploit the Time of Troubles ultimately profited thereby. To the contrary, the Baenre and others punished them for their temerity. Perhaps the matron mothers took the lesson to heart."

"So instead of hatching schemes to topple one another, they . . . what? Enlisted every single priestess in a grand conspiracy to conceal their fall from grace? If your mad idea is right, that's what they must have done."

"Why is that implausible? Picture the day—a few tendays past?—when they lost the ability to draw power from their goddess. Clerics of Lolth routinely collaborate in magical rituals, so they would have discovered fairly quickly that they were all similarly afflicted. Apprised of the scope of the situation, Triel Baenre, possibly in hurried consultation with our esteemed Mistress Quenthel and the matrons of the Council, might well have decided to conceal the priesthood's debility and sent the word round in time to keep anyone from blabbing."

"The word would have to pass pretty damn quickly," said Ryld, examining Splitter's edge. As he'd expected, despite all the bone it had just bitten through, it was as preternaturally keen and free of notches and chips as ever.

"Oh, I don't know," the wizard said. "If you lost the strength of your arms, would you be eager to announce it, knowing the news would find its way to everyone who'd ever taken a dislike to you? Anyway, since this is the first we've learned of the problem, the deception obviously did organize in time."

"Or else everything is as it always was, and the plot exists only in your imagination."

"Oh, it's real. I'm sure Triel deemed the ruse necessary to make sure no visitor would discern Menzoberranzan's sudden weakness." He grinned and added, "And to fix it so we poor males wouldn't swoon with terror upon learning that our betters had lost a measure of their ability to guide and protect us."

"Well, it's an amusing fancy."

"Fire and glare, you're a hard boy to convince, and I'll be cursed if I know why. You've already lived through the Time of Troubles, the previous Matron Baenre's death, and the defeat of Menzoberranzan by a gaggle of wretched dwarves. Why do you assume our world cannot have altered in some fundamental way when you've watched it change so many times before? Open your mind, and you'll see my hypothesis makes sense of all that has puzzled us."

"What do you mean?"

"Whatever they're up to, how is it that for the past month an unusual number of males have dared to elope from their families? Because they somehow tumbled to the fact that a priestess's wrath now constitutes less of a threat."

"While the clerics," said Ryld, catching the thread of the argument, "are eager to catch them because they want to know how the males know about the Silence, if we're going to call it that. Hells, if all those males had the nerve to run away, maybe they even know more about the problem than the females do."

"Conceivably," said Pharaun. "The priestesses can't rule it out until they strap a few of them to torture racks, can they? But they don't want Gromph involved with capturing the rogues because . . . ?"

"They don't want him to find out what the runaways know."

"Very good, apprentice. We'll make a logician of you yet."

"Do you think the archmage already knows the divines have lost their magic?"

"I'd bet your left eye on it, but he's in the same cart as the high priestesses. He posits that the fugitives might know even more."

Ryld nodded. "In a war, or any crisis, you have to cover every possibility."

"The notion of the Silence even explains why the Jewel Box was so crowded, and why some of the patrons were in a belligerent humor or even bruised and battered. Females divested of their magic might well feel weak and vulnerable. Consciously or otherwise, they'd worry about losing control of the folk in their household and compensate by instituting a harsher discipline than usual."

"I see that," said Ryld.

"Of course you do. As I said, the one hypothesis accounts for every anomaly. That's why we can be confident the idea is valid."

"How does it account for the relative paucity of goods in the Bazaar?"

Pharaun blinked, narrowed his eyes in thought, and finally laughed. "You know, it's difficult for genius to soar in the face of these carping little irrelevancies. Actually, you're right. At first glance, the Silence doesn't explain the marketplace, but it explains so much else that I still believe the idea correct. Have I persuaded you?"

"I . . . maybe. You do make a kind of twisted sense. It's just that it's a hard idea to take in. The one truth our people have never questioned is that Menzoberranzan belongs to Lolth. Everything in the cavern is as it is because she willed it so, and the might of her priestesses is the primary force maintaining all that we have and are. If she's turned her face from the entire city, or is lost to us in some other way. . . ." Ryld spread his hands.

"It is unsettling, but perhaps, just perhaps, it affords us an opportunity as well."

Ryld extended a telescoping metal probe, attached a cloth to the hook on the end, and started swamping out the blood-clogged scabbard.

The warrior asked, "What do you mean?"

"Just for fun, let's make the same leap of faith—or fear—that Gromph and the Council did. Assume the rogue males can explain the cessation of Lolth's beneficence. Assume you and I will find them and extract the information. Finally, assume we can somehow employ it to restore the status quo."

"That's a lot of assuming."

"It is. Obviously, I'm letting my imagination run amok. Yet I have a hunch—only a hunch, but still—that if two masters of the Academy could accomplish such a triumph, they might thereby win enough power to make my friend the Sarthos demon look like small beer. You wanted to find something to our advantage, as I recall."

"Your sister may find us first. She tracked us once. Do you still think we shouldn't kill her, or her vassals either?"

"That's a good question," Pharaun sighed. "They're attacking us with potent magic. I suspect that leather bag holds nine sets of servant creatures, each deadlier than the one before."

"In that case, why didn't she chuck them all at us?"

"Perhaps, in the absence of her innate powers, she was trying to conserve her other resources. Alas, she may not be so parsimonious next time."

"So what do we do?"

"Well, you know, I truly do want to kill Greyanna. I always have, but I suppose the prudent course is to avoid our hunters if possible. If not, we'll do what we must to survive. I may at least make a point of disposing of Relonor. I suspect he located us with divinatory magic. He was always good at that."

"Can you shield us?"

"Perhaps. I intend to try. Stay right where you are, and don't speak."

Pharaun rose and reached into one of his pockets. Out in the lake, something big jumped. Noticing the splash, an orc on a raft grunted to his fellows, and they readied their barb-headed lances.

chapter

NINE

As Drisinil took hold of the door handle, the stump of her little finger throbbed beneath its dressing. The novice still found it difficult to believe that, after fighting for her life against the demon spider, Mistress Quenthel had immediately returned to the matter of the would-be truants and their self-inflicted punishment. It bespoke a calm and meticulous nature. Drisinil admired those qualities, but it didn't make her hate their exemplar any less.

She took a final glance around the deserted corridor. No one was about, and no one was supposed to be, not in that length of that particular wing of Arach-Tinilith at that hour of the night.

She slipped through the sandstone door and pulled it shut behind her. Unlike much of the temple, no lamps, torches, or candles burned in the room beyond the threshold. That was by design, to keep a telltale gleam from leaking out under the door.

Drisinil's sister conspirators awaited her. Some were novices with bandaged hands, just like herself. Others were instructors. Those high priestesses, hampered by their dignity, were having some difficulty making themselves comfortable among the haphazardly stacked boxes and tangles of furniture littering the half-forgotten storeroom. Of course, it didn't help that they hesitated to clear away the shrouds of filthy cobwebs dangling everywhere for fear a living spider remained within.

Drisinil wondered if that particular prohibition made sense any longer. Perhaps spiders were no longer sacred.

Then, angry at herself, she pushed the blasphemous thought away. Lolth abided, beyond any question, and was likely to chastise those who even for a moment imagined otherwise.

Once she wrenched her mind back to immediate concerns, Drisinil was momentarily nonplussed to find the company regarding her expectantly. Did they expect her to preside over the meeting?

But then again, why not? She might be a novice, but she was Barrison Del'Armgo as well, and breeding mattered, perhaps more than ever when even the most powerful priestesses were running out of magic. Besides, the secret gathering had been her idea.

"Good evening," she said. "Thank you all for attending,"—she smiled wryly—"and for not reporting me to Quenthel Baenre."

"We still could," said Vlondril Tuin'Tarl, a strange smile on her wrinkled lips. "Your task is to convince us we shouldn't."

The teacher was so old that she had begun to wither like a human crone. Most folk believed her mystical contemplations of ultimate chaos had left her a little mad. No one, not even another instructor, had opted to sit in her immediate vicinity.

"With respect, Holy Mother," Drisinil said, "isn't that self-evident? The goddess, who nurtured and exalted our city since its founding, has turned her back on us."

Once again, Drisinil couldn't help thinking of other possibilities, but even if she'd seen a point to it, she wouldn't have dared to mention them. No one would, not in her present company.

"And Quenthel is to blame," added Molvayas Barrison Del'Armgo.

Though stockier and shorter than Drisinil, her aunt had the same sort of sharp nose and uncommon green eyes. Richly clad, the elder scion of the House carried an enemy's soul imprisoned in a jade ring, and at quiet moments one could occasionally hear the spirit weeping and pleading for release. Second to Quenthel as Barrison Del'Armgo was ever second to

Baenre, Molvayas had helped her niece pass word of the meeting, and her support lent it a certain credibility.

"How do you know that?" asked T'risstree T'orgh.

Deceptively slender, a fully trained warrior as well as a priestess, she was notorious for carrying a naked falchion about in preference to the usual mace or whip of fangs, and gashing the exposed flesh of any student who displeased her with a fast but precisely controlled cut to the face. The short, curved blade lay across her knees.

Drisinil waited a beat to make sure Molvayas intended her to answer the question. Apparently she did, and rightly so, since it was the younger female who had actually conceived the argument.

"When Triel was mistress here," said the novice, "all was well. Shortly after Quenthel assumed the office, Lolth rejected us."

" 'Shortly' being a relative term," said a sardonic voice from somewhere in the back of the room.

"Shortly enough," Drisinil retorted. "Perhaps the goddess gave us time to rectify the error. We failed to do so, so now she's punishing us."

"She's afflicting all Menzoberranzan," T'risstree said, "not just Tier Breche."

"Surely," said Drisinil, "you didn't expect her to be *fair*. I hope a priestess knows Lolth's ways better than that. Her wrath is as boundless as her might. Besides which, Arach-Tinilith is the repository of the deepest mysteries and thus the mystic heart of Menzoberranzan. It makes perfect sense that whatever befalls us here should touch the city as a whole.

"In any case," the novice continued, "Lolth has shown us her intent. Despite our safeguards, two spirits invaded the temple, the first in the guise of a spider, the second a living darkness. Spider and darkness, reflections of the essence of the goddess. The demons injured those who got in their way. They bruised them and broke their bones, but they didn't try to kill any of us, did they? They were plainly seeking Quenthel, and they sought to kill her and her alone."

Some of the other priestesses frowned or nodded thoughtfully.

"It did seem that way," said Vlondril, "but what do you think is unacceptable about Quenthel? Isn't she doing all the same things Triel did?"

"We don't know everything she does," said Drisinil, "and we don't know what she thinks. Lolth does."

"But you don't know she sent the demons," T'risstree said. Born a commoner but risen to a level of power and prestige, she had evidently shed the habit of deference to the aristocracy. "Perhaps one of Quenthel's mortal enemies sent them."

"What mortal possesses a magic potent and cunning enough to penetrate the temple wards?" Drisinil replied.

"The archmage?" Vlondril offered, picking at the skin on the back of her hand. Her tone was light, as if she spoke in jest.

"Even if he does," Drisinil said, "Gromph is a Baenre, too, and Quenthel serving as mistress strengthens his House. He has no reason to kill her, and if it isn't he, then who? Who but the goddess?"

"Quenthel is still alive," said a priestess from House Xorlarrin. She'd worn a long veil to the conclave, apparently so anyone who noticed her walking the halls would assume she was engaged in a certain necromantic meditation. "Do we think Lolth tried to kill her and failed?"

"Perhaps," Drisinil said. Some of her audience scowled or stiffened at what could be construed as blasphemy. "She is all-powerful, but her agents are not. However, I think she intended the first two assassins to fail. She's giving her priestesses a chance to ponder what's happening. To comprehend her will, perform our appointed task, and earn her favor once more."

Vlondril smiled. "And we do that by murdering Quenthel ourselves? Oh, good, child, very good."

"We kill her ourselves," Drisinil agreed, "or, if that isn't feasible, we at least assist the next demonic assassin in whatever way we can."

T'risstree shook her head. "This is sheer speculation. You don't know the mistress's death will bring Lolth back."

"It's worth a chance," Drisinil said. "At the very least, if we give the demons what they want, they'll stop invading Arach-Tinilith. They haven't slain any of us yet, but if we don't help them, and Quenthel lives on, they may decide to eliminate us, too, for after all, it's a demon's nature to kill."

"The demons may be less dangerous than House Baenre," T'risstree said.

"The Baenre won't know who facilitated Quenthel's demise," Drisinil said. "So what will they do, wreak their vengeance on every priestess in Arach-Tinilith? They can't. They need us to educate their daughters and perform the secret rites."

"If Quenthel dies," said a priestess leaning against the wall, "Molvayas has a fair chance of becoming Mistress of Arach-Tinilith—but how do the rest of us stand to gain?"

"My niece has explained," said Molvayas, "that we'll all renew our bond with the goddess and replenish our magic. Beyond that, I promise that if I become mistress, I'll remember those who lifted me up. High priestesses, you will be my lieutenants, ranking higher than any other instructor. Novices, your time at Arach-Tinilith will be spent far more pleasantly than is the rule. You, too, will exercise authority over your peers. You'll enjoy luxuries. I'll excuse you from the more onerous ordeals and teach you secrets most pupils never learn."

"We'll hold you to that," said another voice from the back, "and expose you if you renege."

"Exactly," said Molvayas. "You'll always be in a position to inform House Baenre of my guilt. Your numbers are too great for me to murder all of you, and so you know you can trust me to keep my pledge. Even if it were otherwise, I'd be stupid to play you false, considering that I'll always need loyal supporters."

"It's tempting," the veiled Xorlarrin said. "I'd take almost any chance to win my magic back. Still, we're talking about the Baenre."

"Damn the Baenre!" Drisinil spat. "Perhaps killing Quenthel is the first rumble of the cave-in that will bury the entire clan."

"What cave-in?" T'risstree asked.

"I don't know, exactly," Drisinil admitted. "Still, consider this: Houses rise and fall. It's the way of Menzoberranzan and the will of Lolth. Thus far, House Baenre has been the exception, perching on the top of the heap for century after century. Perhaps, with the old matron mother's death, the family has finally forfeited the goddess's regard. Why not . . . everyone knows Triel is out of her depth. Perhaps it's time at last for House Baenre to honor the universal law. If so, wouldn't it be glorious to commence the decline in their fortunes here, now, this very minute in this very room?"

"Yes," T'risstree declared.

Surprised, Drisinil turned to face her. "You agree?"

Setting her razor-edged falchion aside, T'risstree rose and said, "I was dubious, but you convinced me." For an instant, she grinned. "I don't like

Quenthel anyway. So yes, we'll usher her into her tomb, regain the goddess's approval, and run the academy as we please."

She extended her hands. Drisinil smiled and clasped them despite the twin shooting pains the pressure produced, then she turned to the other females and said, "What about the rest of you? Are you with us?"

They tendered a ragged chorus of assent. She guessed that those who doubted she had hit on the way to propitiate Lolth were nonetheless eager to move up in the temple hierarchy, or at least disliked Quenthel. Maybe they were simply indulging the innate dark elf taste for bloodshed and betrayal.

Drisinil herself truly did believe she'd contrived the proper metaphysical remedy for their woes but deep down, she was even more excited at the prospect of avenging herself on her torturer. How could it be otherwise? For the rest of her life, her self-mutilated hands would announce to any who looked that someone had once defeated and humiliated her.

"I thank you," she said to the other clerics. "Now, let's put our heads together. We have much to plan and only a little time before others will start to miss us."

And plan they did, whispering, bickering, occasionally grinning at some particularly inventive and vicious suggestion. Drisinil knew that some if not all of the scheming would come to nothing—it was too contingent on Quenthel's doing precisely what the plotters wanted exactly when and where they wanted it done—but the effort served to cement their commitment to the conspiracy and to limn at least the bare bones of a strategy.

Finally it was done. The priestesses started to slip out the way they'd come, one and two at a time. The more restless stood in a clump around the exit, awaiting their turns. T'risstree was among them.

Drisinil crossed the floor in as relaxed and casual a manner as she could affect. She didn't want someone to realize her intent, and, surprised, react in some audible way.

No one did. All dark elves were actors in that they were liars, and perhaps she was a better dissembler than most. She sauntered within arm's reach of T'risstree, took hold of the dirk concealed inside her long, fringed shawl, and drove the blade into the high priestess's spine. This time, for whatever reason, the stumps of her severed pinkies didn't hurt a bit.

T'risstree's back arched in a spasm of agony, and, to Drisinil's surprise, her teacher tried to flounder around to face her. Her arm shaking, T'risstree lifted the falchion.

Drisinil turned along with the high priestess, keeping behind her. She grabbed hold of T'risstree's hair, jerked her head back, and sliced open her throat. The instructor collapsed. The sword slipped from her fingers and clanked on the floor.

The onlookers gawked.

"T'risstree T'orgh meant to betray us," Drisinil said. "I saw it in her eyes when I took her hands. We can leave the carcass here for the time being. With luck, no one will discover it until after Quenthel's death."

Either the other conspirators believed her explanation, or, more likely, didn't care that she'd murdered the teacher. A few congratulated her on her finesse, and, utterly indifferent to the corpse sprawled in their midst, resumed their departures.

Drisinil picked up and examined the fallen falchion. Once Quenthel was slain, it ought to look nice on her wall.

Faeryl prowled the rounded, treacherous surfaces at the apex of the ambassadorial residence. She was trying to monitor all four sides of her home, which entailed clambering about with a certain celerity. Yet she was also trying to hide from anyone who might be peering from the window of a neighboring mansion or up from one of the quiet residential boulevards of prosperous West Wall, and the faster she moved, the more problematic stealth became. She'd sneaked up there two hours ago, when everyone else thought she was bundling or burning documents, and she still wasn't sure she'd struck the proper balance between the two necessities.

She wished she could have ordered a retainer or two up there to help her keep her vigil, but it would have been ill-advised, considering that any of her minions might be the object of her hunt.

She also wished she had more cover. Except for a few token walkways and crenellations so small as to be essentially ornamental, the apex of the stalagmite keep was bare of fortifications or even level places to stand. If

Faeryl looked closely, she could see subtle signs that at one time, when the keep had served another purpose, such defenses had existed in abundance, but subsequently, a wizard had melted the ramparts back into the rest of the calcite. It made sense. The Menzoberranyr would see no reason to gift an outsider with any notable capacity to resist a siege.

Faeryl perched on the northeast side of the roof. Outlined in blue, green, or violent phosphorescence, the homes of her wealthier neighbors glowed all around her. Had she looked from a distance, she would have observed her own residence shining in the same way. Fortunately, the luminescence only defined the silhouette of the tower and picked out several spiders sculpted in bas-relief. As long as she stayed away from the images, kept silent, and enjoyed a measure of luck, it shouldn't reveal her presence.

A soft, indefinable sound rose from the northwest. Grateful that she at least still had the brooch that would make her weightless, she scuttled quickly along the sloping pitch of the roof, fearless in the knowledge that even if she lost her footing, she needn't fall.

In a few seconds, she reached the northwest aspect. She peered over the drop and discovered the source of the sound in the plaza below.

Bare to the waist, rapiers in one hand and parrying daggers in the other, two males circled one another. They stood straight and stepped lightly in the manner of well-trained fencers. Their discarded *piwafwis*, mail, and shirts lay where they'd tossed them on the ground along with a pair of empty wineskins. A third male looked on from beneath an overhanging balcony some distance away, where the combatants quite possibly hadn't noticed him.

Faeryl sighed. This little tableau was mildly intriguing, but it clearly had nothing to do with her own situation.

After her frustrating interview with Matron Mother Baenre, she'd realized she had an opponent. Someone who'd traduced her, possibly to keep her from departing Menzoberranzan, though she couldn't imagine why. From that inference, it was a small step to the suspicion that the enemy had an agent inside her household. It was what any intelligent foe would try to arrange, and it arguably explained how Faeryl's intention to go home had been discerned and countered with a word in Triel's ear.

Seething with the need to outwit those who had made a fool of her, Faeryl devised a ruse to unmask the spy. She surprised her retainers with the order to pack. They were slipping out of Menzoberranzan that very night. She thought her loyal vassals would obey, but the traitor would try to sneak away to report the household's imminent flight. Crouched on the roof, Faeryl would spot her when she did.

That was the plan, anyway. The ambassador could think of several reasons why it might fail. The residence had means of egress on all four sides, but she couldn't survey all four at once, not unless she floated well above the roof, and that option presented problems of its own. Most dark elf boots possessed a virtue of silence, and their mantles, one of obscuration. The traitor might even have some more potent means of escaping notice, such as a talisman of invisibility. Were she any higher above the ground, Faeryl might have no hope at all of detecting the spy's surreptitious exit.

Of course, the traitor might also have a means of communicating with her confederates via clairaudience, or a charm of instantaneous transit, in which case the envoy's scheme was doomed no matter what. She'd cling to the roof until someone in authority, a company of Baenre guards, perhaps, showed up to take her and her entourage into custody, but she'd had to try something.

She crawled on. Below and behind her, one of the duelists groaned as his foe's blade plunged through his torso. Magic flickered and sizzled, and the victor dropped as well. The wizard who'd been watching from a distance strolled forward to inspect the steaming corpses.

Faeryl wondered if the three had been siblings, and the wizard was the clever one. She'd had a brother like that once, until an even trickier male turned him to dust and absconded with his wands and grimoires. A minor setback for her House, but interesting to watch.

Overhead, something snapped. She glanced up. Four or five riders on wyvern-back were winging their way east. Above them, projecting from the cavern ceiling, the stalactite castles shone with their own enchantments, a far lovelier sight, in her opinion, than the miniscule monochromatic stars that speckled the night sky of the so-called Lands of Light.

Then, so faintly that she wondered if she'd imagined it, something brushed against something else. The sound had issued from the southwest.

Faeryl scurried over to that part of the roof and peered down. At first glance, nothing appeared changed since the last time she'd checked that way. Perhaps her nerves were playing tricks on her, but she kept on looking anyway.

Octagonal steel grilles protected the round windows cut in the wall below her, but if a drow knew the trick, she could unlatch one and swing it aside for an entrance or exit via levitation. Apparently, someone had, for after a few more moments, Faeryl noticed that one of the web-pattern shields hung ever so slightly ajar. With that sign to guide her, she spotted the shrouded figure skulking toward the mouth of an alleyway.

The noble of Ched Nasad was a fair hand with a crossbow. She might have been able to shoot down the traitor from behind, but that would gain her few answers. She didn't happen to possess a scroll with the spell for interrogating the dead. She needed to catch up with the spy and take the wretch alive.

She read from a scroll she did have, then she stepped away from the top of the tower into empty space.

Except that it wasn't empty for her. The air was as firm as stone beneath her soles. For two paces, she strode on a level surface, and, because she willed it so, the unseen platform dipped into an equally invisible ramp. She sprinted down with no fear of blundering off the edge. Wherever she set her foot, the incline would be there to meet it. That was how the magic worked.

Her progress entirely silent, she dashed unnoticed above the traitor's head, then with a thought dissolved the support beneath her boots. Her crossbow ready, she dropped the last few feet to the ground and landed in front of the spy.

Started, the traitor jumped. Faeryl felt her own pang of surprise, for though she liked to think she maintained a proper suspicion of everyone, in truth, she never could have guessed the pinched, sour face she saw half hidden inside the close-drawn cowl could be the spy's.

"Umrae," the ambassador said, aiming her hand crossbow.

"My lady," the secretary answered, bending with her usual stiffness into an obeisance.

"I know all about it, traitor. I'm not actually planning to leave tonight. My pretending so was a trick to see who would slip away to play informer."

"I don't know what you mean. I just wanted to buy some items for the journey. I thought that if I hurried over to the Bazaar, I could find one of those merchants who stays open late and be back before anyone missed me."

"Do you think I haven't realized I have an enemy here in Menzoberranzan, someone with access to Matron Baenre? Two tendays ago, Triel considered me loyal. She approved of me. She granted a good deal of what I asked on behalf of our people. Now, she doubts me, because someone has persuaded her to question my true intentions. What did my foe offer to lure you to her side? Don't you realize that in betraying me, you betray Ched Nasad itself?"

The scribe hesitated, then said, "Matron Baenre has people watching the residence. Someone is watching us right now."

"Perhaps," Faeryl replied.

Umrae swallowed. "So you can't harm me. Or they'll harm you."

Faeryl laughed. "Rubbish. Triel's agents won't reveal their presence just to keep me from disciplining one of my own retainers. They won't see anything odd or detrimental to Menzoberranzan's interests in that. Now, be sensible and surrender."

After another pause, Umrae said, "Give me your word you won't hurt me. That you'll set me free and help me flee the city."

"I promise you nothing except that your insolence is making me angrier by the second, and a quick capitulation is your only hope. Tell me, who turned you, and why? What does anyone hereabouts have to gain by persecuting an envoy, one who stands apart from the feuds and rivalries among the Menzoberranyr Houses?"

"You must understand, I fear to betray them and remain. They'll kill me if I do."

"They won't get the chance. I'm the one pointing a poisoned dart at you. Who are your employers?"

"I won't say, not without your pledge."

"Your friend didn't slander me to Triel until after I started contemplating a return to Ched Nasad. Was that the point of the lie? To keep me from venturing out into the Underdark? Why?"

Umrae shook her head.

"You're mad," Faeryl said. "Why would you condemn yourself to perpetuate someone else's existence? Ah well, you're plainly unfit to live, so I suppose it's for the best."

She made a show of sighting down the length of the crossbow.

"No!" Umrae cried. "Don't! You're right, why should I die?"

"If you answer my questions, perhaps you won't."

"Yes."

Trembling a little, her nerve having been broken, the clerk raised her hand to her face, perhaps to massage her brow. No—to lift a tiny vial to her lips!

Faeryl pulled the trigger and her aim was true, but by the time the quarrel pierced Umrae's stomach, the secretary's form was changing. She grew even thinner, shriveling, but taller as well. Her flesh cooled and stank of corruption, leathery wings sprouted from her shoulder blades, and her eyes sank into her head. Even her garments altered, blurring and splitting into moldering rags. No blood flowed from the wound the poisoned dart had made, and it didn't seem to inconvenience her in the slightest. She didn't even bother to pull the missile out.

Faeryl was furious at herself for allowing Umrae to trick her. Next time, she'd remember that even a dark elf devoid of beauty, grace, and facile wit, seemingly undone by fear, was yet a drow, born to guile and deception.

The potion had temporarily transformed Umrae into some sort of undead, in which form she likely wouldn't suffer at all from her usual clumsiness. Had Lolth not forsaken her priestesses, Faeryl might have controlled the cadaverous thing with her clerical powers, but that was no longer an option. Nor were any of her other retainers likely to notice her plight and dash to her rescue. She had them all too busy packing up the house.

It was unfortunate, because like most undead, except for the lowly corpses and skeletons spellcasters reanimated to serve as mindless thralls, Umrae in winged-ghoul form could probably do grievous harm with any strike that so much as grazed the skin, and Faeryl didn't even have a shield to fend her off. How was she to know the spy would possess such a potent means of defense?

Umrae took a shambling step, then, with a clap of her wings, bounded forward. Faeryl hastily retreated, dropped the useless crossbow, and opened the clasp of her cloak. Pulling the garment off her shoulders with one hand, she unsheathed a little adamantine rod with the other. At a snap of her wrist, the harmless-looking object swelled into Mother's Kiss, the long-hafted, basalt-headed warhammer the females of House Zauvirr had borne since the founding of their line. Perhaps an enchanted weapon would slay Umrae where the envenomed quarrel had failed.

Faeryl would have to hope so. Even if she were willing to stand meekly aside and let the traitor fly away, Umrae, her thoughts perhaps colored by the predatory guise she'd assumed, plainly wanted a fight, and the envoy could see no way to evade her. It would be stupid to evoke darkness and run. In undead form, Umrae would likely manage better in the murk than its maker did. It would be even more pointless to try to levitate or ascend through the use of the air-walking charm when the shapeshifter could simply spread her ragged wings and follow.

Faeryl waved her *piwafwi* back and forth at the end of her extended arm, to confuse Umrae and serve as some semblance of a shield. No one had ever taught Faeryl to fight thusly, but she'd observed warriors practicing the technique, and she tried to believe that if mere males could do it, it would surely present no difficulty to a high priestess.

Umrae lunged, Faeryl lashed the cloak in a horizontal arc. Possibly thanks to luck as much as skill, the garment blocked Umrae's hands. Her talons snagged in the weave.

Surprised, Umrae faltered in the attack and struggled to free her hands. Faeryl stepped through and smashed the pointed stone head of her hammer into the center of the servant's carious brow. Bone crunched, and Umrae's head snapped backward. A goodly portion of her left profile fell off her skull.

Certain the fight was over, Faeryl relaxed, and that was nearly the end of her. Transformed, Umrae could evidently endure more damage than almost any creature with warm flesh and a beating heart. She opened her mouth, exposing long, thin fangs, and what was left of her head shot forward over the top of the cape. The ambassador only barely managed to fling herself back out of the way in time.

The *piwafwi* was stretched taut between the two combatants, as if they were playing tug-of-war. Both yanked on it simultaneously, and Faeryl was the luckier. The cloak tore free of Umrae's grasp, but despite the garment's reinforcing enchantments, it returned to the ambassador with long rips the ghoul's claws had cut. A few more such rendings and it would be useless.

The cape's sudden release also sent Faeryl stumbling backward. With another beat of her festering wings, Umrae hopped and closed the distance. Her clawed hands shot forward.

Crying out in desperation, Faeryl managed to plant her feet and arrest her helpless stagger. She lashed out with the hammer and clipped one of Umrae's hands. The imitation ghoul snatched it back and gave up the attack. Instead, she began to circle. Just as a living creature would, she shook her battered extremity several times as if to dislodge the pain, then lifted it back on guard.

Faeryl turned to keep the foe with her crushed, half-flayed head in view. What is it going to take to stop this thing? the ambassador wondered. *Can I stop it?*

Yes, curse it!

When she was a child, her cousin Merinid, weapons master of House Zauvirr, dead these many years since her mother tired of him, had told her that any opponent could be destroyed. It was just a matter of finding the vulnerable spot.

Umrae lunged. Once again, the ambassador snapped out the folds of her frail, flapping shield. The cloak entangled one of the servant's hands. The other raked, rasping and snagging, across Faeryl's coat of fine adamantine links. The winged ghoul's touch sowed cramping sickness in its wake, but the claws hadn't quite sheared through the sturdy mail, and the sensation only lasted an instant.

Faeryl swung at Umrae's withered chest in its covering of filthy, crumbling cloth. If she couldn't slay the ghoul-thing with a strike to the head, then the heart must be the vulnerable spot, just as with a vampire. Or at least she hoped so.

To her surprise, Umrae denied her the chance to find out one way or the other. It looked as if the traitor had so committed to her attack that she would find it impossible to defend against a riposte. Yet she interposed her withered arm to take the shock of the warhammer, then stooped to claw at Faeryl's unarmored knee.

The envoy avoided that potentially crippling attack with a fast retreat, meanwhile ripping the cloak away from her foul-smelling adversary. The garment was starting to look more like a bunch of ribbons than one coherent piece of silk.

The duelists resumed circling, each looking for an opening. Occasionally Faeryl let the tattered *piwafwi* slip or droop out of line, offering an invitation, but Umrae proved too canny to attack when and how her opponent wished her to.

Faeryl realized she was panting and did the best to control her breathing. She wasn't afraid—she *wasn't*—but she was impressed with her servant's potion-induced prowess. Formidable from the moment she imbibed it, Umrae was truly getting the hang of her borrowed capabilities as the battle progressed.

While still maneuvering and keeping an eye on Umrae, Faeryl nevertheless entered a light trance. With a sense that was neither sight, hearing, nor any faculty comprehensible to those who'd never pledged her service to a deity, she reached into that formless yet somehow jagged place where she had once been accustomed to touch the shadow of the goddess.

The presence of Lolth had absented itself from the meeting ground, leaving a vacancy that somehow throbbed like a diseased tooth. Still, it seemed an appropriate domain in which to pray.

Dread Queen of Spiders, Faeryl silently began, I beg you, reveal yourself to me. Restore my powers, even if only for a moment. Has Menzoberranzan offended you? So be it, but I'm not one of her daughters. I'm from Ched Nasad. Make me as I was, and I'll give you many lives—a slave every day for a year.

Nothing happened.

Umrae sprang in, clawing. Faeryl jerked the part of her spirit that had groped in the void back into her body. Retreating, she blocked the undead creature's claws with her cloak and struck a couple blows with the warhammer. She didn't withdraw quickly enough to take herself completely out of harm's way, nor did she settle into a strong stance and swing as hard as she could have. She wanted the ghoul to feel on the brink of overwhelming her opponent and keep coming. If Umrae grew too eager, she might open herself up for an effective counterattack.

Umrae's talons whizzed through the air, tearing scraps from the sheltering cloak until it was the size of a ragged hand towel. Unexpectedly, the spy beat her riddled wings, hopped in close, and struck at Faeryl's face. The noble recoiled, but even so the claws streaked past a fraction of an inch before her eyes, so close she could feel the malignancy inside them as a pulse of headache.

Still, it was all right, because she thought Umrae was finally open. She sidestepped and swung her stone-headed hammer at the ghoul's rib cage— —to no avail, even though Faeryl had been correct, Umrae couldn't swing her hands around in time to block the blow. Instead, she took another stride, slapped the ambassador with a flick of her wing, and sent her reeling.

Faeryl's head rang, and the world blurred. As she struggled to throw off the stunning effects of the blow, she thought fleetingly how unfair it was that Umrae, who had long ago forsaken combat training as a humiliating exercise in futility, was demolishing a female who still doggedly reported to her captain-of-the-guard for practice once a tenday.

After what seemed a long time, her head cleared. She whirled, certain that Umrae was about to attack her from behind. She wasn't. In fact, the animate corpse was nowhere to be seen.

Plainly, Umrae had taken to the air. Had she finally done the sensible thing and fled? Faeryl couldn't believe it. Umrae hated her. The envoy didn't know why, but she'd seen it in the traitor's eyes. Such being the case, Umrae wouldn't break off when she had every reason to believe she was winning and close to making the kill. No drow would, which meant she was still hovering somewhere overhead, poised to swoop down and, she undoubtedly hoped, catch her mistress by surprise and smash her to the ground.

Her heart pounding, Faeryl peered upward and saw nothing. She listened for the beat of the creature's wings but heard only the eternal muffled whisper of the city as a whole. She wasn't entirely surprised. The undead were famously stealthy when stalking their prey.

A black sliver momentarily cut the line of violet luminescence adorning a spire of the castle of House Vandree. The obstruction had surely been the tip of one of Umrae's wings.

Faeryl stared for another moment, then jumped when she finally spotted Umrae. Her tattered cloak flapping between her wings, the transformed secretary was already hurtling down like a raptor from the World Above diving to plunge its talons into a rodent.

Hoping Umrae hadn't seen her react to the sight of her, Faeryl kept turning and peering. When she felt the disturbance in the air, or perhaps simply the urgent prompting of her instincts, she jumped aside, pivoted, and swung the warhammer in an overhand blow.

Under those circumstances, she had little chance of smashing the thing's heart, but she'd seen that Umrae could suffer pain. Perhaps the initial blow would freeze the undead thing in place for an instant, affording Faeryl the opportunity for what she prayed would be the finishing stroke.

The ambassador had timed the move properly, and the weapon's basalt head smashed into Umrae's flank. Deprived of her victim, unexpectedly battered, the ghoul slammed into the smooth stone surface of the street with a satisfying crash. Scraps of flesh broke away from her raddled body, releasing a fresh puff of stench.

Faeryl marked her target, the place on Umrae's chest beneath which her heart ought to lie, and swung Mother's Kiss back for the follow-up attack. The traitor rolled and scrambled to her knees. Faeryl struck, and Umrae lashed out with a taloned hand. The ghoul caught the warhammer in mid-flight, tore it out of the ambassador's grip, and sent it spinning to clack down on the ground ten feet away.

Faeryl felt a crazy impulse to turn and go after the thing, but she knew Umrae would rip her apart if she tried. She backstepped instead. The inhumanly gaunt spy leaped to her feet—she looked like a pile of sticks spontaneously assembling themselves into a crude facsimile of a person—and pursued.

While retreating, Faeryl started edging around in a looping course that might ultimately bring her to the spot where the hammer lay. Leering, Umrae moved sideways right along with her in a way that demonstrated she knew exactly what her mistress had in mind and would never permit it.

Well, the aristocrat still had one weapon—pitifully inadequate to the situation though it was—a knife hidden in the belt that gathered her light, supple coat of mail at the waist. The gold buckle was the hilt, and when she pulled on it, the stubby adamantine blade would slide free. She started to reach for it, then hesitated.

Against Umrae's talons, long reach, and resistance to harm, the dagger really would be useless . . . unless Faeryl could get in close enough to use it, and unless she attacked by surprise.

But how in the name of the Demonweb was she to accomplish that? Umrae was rapidly closing the distance, snapping her wings every few steps to lengthen a stride, and for three unnerving backward paces, Faeryl's mind was blank.

Then she remembered the cloak, or rather, the remnants of it, still clutched in her off hand. Perhaps she could employ it to conceal her drawing of the knife. The *piwafwi* was just a sad little mass of tatters, and she was no juggler adept at sleight-of-hand, but curse it, if clumsy Umrae had palmed a potion vial without her mistress noticing until it was too late, surely the mistress could do as well.

Faeryl had been reflexively moving the cloak around the whole time, so it shouldn't look suspicious for her to cover her waist with it. At the same time, she hooked the fingers of her weapon hand in the oval hollow at the center of the buckle and pulled. She had never before had occasion to employ this last desperate means of defense, but in the sixteen years since an artisan had made it to her specifications, she had always kept the knife and scabbard oiled, and the blade easily slid free.

She studied Umrae. As far as the envoy could tell, the imitation ghoul hadn't seen her bare the dagger, but she doubted she could keep it hidden for more than a second or two. She had to manufacture a chance for herself quickly if she was to have one at all.

She pretended to stumble. She hoped her unsteadiness looked genuine. Umrae had touched her, after all, so it might seem credible that her strength was failing.

The ghoul took the bait. She leaped forward and seized Faeryl by the forearms. This time, her claws punched through the envoy's layer of mail and jabbed their tips into her flesh. At once, a surge of nausea wracked Faeryl, then another. Retching, she wasn't sure she could still use the knife in any sort of controlled manner. Perhaps she'd just served herself up to her foe like a plate of mushrooms.

Umrae grinned at Faeryl's seeming—or genuine—helplessness. The envoy felt the clerk's fingers tense, preparing to flense the meat from her bones, even as she pulled the noble closer and opened her jaws to bite down on her head.

Fighting the sickness and weakness, Faeryl tried to thrust her hand forward. The effort strained her flesh against the ghoul's talons, tearing her wounds larger and bringing a burst of pain—but then her arm jerked free. The blade rammed into Umrae's withered chest, slipping cleanly between two ribs and plunging in all the way up to Faeryl's knuckles.

Umrae convulsed and threw back her head for a silent scream. The spasms jerked her hands and threatened to rip Faeryl apart even without the traitor's conscious intent. Umrae froze, and toppled backward, carrying her assailant with her.

In contradiction of every tale Faeryl had ever heard, the shapeshifter didn't revert to her original form when true death claimed her. Still horribly sick, the envoy lay for some time in the ghoul's fetid embrace. Eventually, however, she mustered the trembling strength to pull free of the claws embedded in her bleeding limbs, after which she crawled a few feet away from the winged corpse.

Gradually, despite the sting of her punctures and bruises, she started to feel a little better. Physically, anyway. Inside her mind, she was berating herself for an outcome that wasn't really a victory at all.

Given that she needed to learn what Umrae knew, not kill her, she'd bungled their encounter from the beginning. She supposed she should have agreed to the traitor's terms, but she'd been too angry and too proud. She should also have spotted the vial and fought more skillfully. If not for luck, it would be she and not her erstwhile scribe lying dead on the stone.

She wondered if her sojourn in Menzoberranzan had diminished her. Back in Ched Nasad, she had enemies in- and outside House Zauvirr to keep her strong and sharp, but in the City of Spiders none had wished her ill. Had she forgotten the habits that protected her for her first two hundred years of life? If so, she knew she'd better remember them quickly.

The enemy hadn't finished with her. She wasn't so dull and rusty that she didn't recall how these covert wars unfolded. It was like a *sava* game, progressing a step at a time, gradually escalating in ferocity. Her unknown adversary's first move, though she hadn't known it at the time, had been to turn Umrae and lie to Triel. Faeryl's countermove was to capture the spy and remove her from the board. As soon as Umrae missed some pre-arranged rendezvous, the foe would know her pawn had been taken and advance another piece. Perhaps it would be the mother. Perhaps the foe would suggest to Matron Baenre that the time had come to throw Faeryl in a dungeon.

But life wasn't really a *sava* game. Faeryl could cheat and make two moves in a row, which in this instance meant truly fleeing Menzoberranzan as soon as possible, before the enemy learned of her agent's demise.

Light-headed and sour-mouthed from her exertions, Faeryl dragged herself to her feet, trudged in search of Mother's Kiss, and wondered just how she would accomplish that little miracle.

Cloaked in the semblance of a squat, leathery-skinned orc, whose twisted leg manifestly made him unfit for service in a noble or even merchant House, Pharaun took an experimental bite of his sausage and roll. The unidentifiable ground meat inside the casing tasted rank and was gristly, as well as cold at the core.

"By the Demonweb!" he exclaimed.

"What?" Ryld replied.

The weapons master too appeared to be a scurvy, broken-down orc in grubby rags. Unbelievably, he was devouring his vile repast without any overt show of repugnance.

"What?" The Master of Sorcere brandished his sausage. "This travesty. This abomination."

He headed for the culprit's kiosk, a sad little construction of bone poles and sheets of hide, taking care not to walk too quickly. His veil of illusion would make it look as if he were limping, but it wouldn't conceal the anomaly of a lame orc covering ground as quickly as one with two good legs.

The long-armed, flat-faced goblin proprietor produced a cudgel from beneath the counter. Perhaps he was used to complaints.

Pharaun raised a hand and said, "I mean no harm. In fact, I want to help."

The goblin's eyes narrowed. "Help?"

"Yes. I'll even pay another penny for the privilege." he said as he extracted a copper coin from his purse. "I just want to show you something."

The cook hesitated, then held out a dirty-nailed hand and said, "Give. No tricks."

"No tricks."

Pharaun surrendered the coins and to the goblin's surprise, squirmed around the end of the counter and crowded into the miniature kitchen. He wrapped his hand in a fold of his cloak, slid the hot iron grill with its load of meat from its brackets, and set it aside.

"First," Pharaun said, "you spread the coals evenly at the bottom of the brazier." He picked up a poker and demonstrated. "Next, though we don't have time to start from scratch right now, you let them burn to gray. Only then do you start cooking, with the grill positioned here."

He replaced the utensil in a higher set of brackets.

"Sausage take longer to fry," the goblin said.

"Do you have somewhere to go? Now, I'm going to assume you buy these questionable delicacies elsewhere and thus can do nothing about the quality, but you can at least tenderize them with a few whacks from that mallet, poke a few holes with the fork to help them cook on the inside, and sprinkle some of these spices on them." Pharaun grinned. "You've never so much as touched a lot of this stuff, have you? What did you do, murder the real chef and take possession of his enterprise?"

The smaller creature smirked and said, "Don't matter now, do it?"

"I suppose not. One last thing: Roast the sausage when the customer orders it, not hours beforehand. It isn't nearly as appetizing if it's cooked, allowed to cool, then warmed again. Good fortune to you."

He clapped the goblin on the shoulder, then exited the stand.

At some point, Ryld had wandered up to observe the lesson.

"What was the point of that?" the warrior asked.

"I was performing a public service," answered the wizard, "preserving the Braeryn from a plague of dyspepsia."

Pharaun fell in beside his friend, and the two dark elves walked on.

"You were amusing yourself, and it was idiotic. You take the trouble to disguise us, then risk revealing your true identity by playing the gourmet."

"I doubt one small lapse will prove our undoing. It's unlikely that any of our ill-wishers will interview that particular street vendor any time soon or ask the right questions if they do. Remember, we're *well* disguised. Who would imagine this lurching, misshapen creature could possibly be my handsome, elegant self? Though I must admit, your metamorphosis wasn't quite so much of a stretch."

Ryld scowled, then wolfed down his last bite of sausage and bread.

"Why didn't you disguise us from the moment we left Tier Breche?" he asked. "Never mind, I think I know. A fencer doesn't reveal all his capabilities in the initial moments of the bout."

"Something like that. Greyanna and her minions have seen us looking like ourselves, so if we're lucky they won't expect to find us appearing radically different. The trick won't befuddle them forever, but perhaps long enough for us to complete our business and return to our sedate, cloistered lives."

"Does that mean you've figured out something else?"

"Not as such, but you know I'm prone to sudden bursts of inspiration."

The masters entered a crowded section of street outside of what was evidently a popular tavern, with a howling, barking gnoll song shaking the calcite walls. Pharaun had never had occasion to walk incognito among the lower orders. It felt odd weaving, pausing, and twisting to avoid bumps and jostles. Had they known his true identity, his fellow pedestrians would have scurried out of his way.

As the two drow reached the periphery of the crowd, Ryld pivoted and struck a short straight blow with his fist. A hunchbacked, piebald creature—the product of a mating of goblin and orc perhaps—stumbled backward and fell on his rump.

"Cutpurse," the warrior explained. "I hate this place."

"No pangs of nostalgia?"

Ryld glowered. "That isn't funny."

"No? Then I beg your pardon," Pharaun said with a smirk. "I wonder why this precinct always seems so sordid, even on those rare occasions when one finds oneself alone in a plaza or boulevard. Well, the smell, of course. We don't call them the Stenchstreets for nothing, but the buildings, though generally more modest than those encountered elsewhere in the city, still wear the same graceful shapes our ancestors cut from the living rock."

The teachers paused to let a spider with legs as long as broadswords scuttle across the street. The Braeryn notoriously harbored hordes of the sacred creatures. Sacred or not, Pharaun reviewed his mental list of ready spells, but the arachnid ignored the disguised dark elves

"That's a foolish question," said Ryld. "Why does the Braeryn seem foul? The inhabitants!"

"Ah, but did the living refuse of our society generate the atmosphere of the district, or did that malignant spirit exist from the beginning and lure the wretched to its domain?"

"I'm no metaphysician," said Ryld. "All I know is that somebody should clear the scavengers out of here."

Pharaun chuckled. "What if said clearing had occurred when you were a tyke?"

"I don't mean exterminate them—except for the hopeless cases—but why just let them squat here in their dirt like a festering chancre on the city? Why not find something useful for them to do?"

"Ah, but they're already useful. Status is all, is it not? Does it not follow, then, that no Menzoberranyr can find contentment without someone upon whom she can look down."

"We have slaves."

"They won't do. Predicate your claim to self-respect on their existence and you tacitly acknowledge you're only slightly better than a thrall yourself. Happily, here in the Stenchstreets, we find a populace starving, filthy, penniless, riddled with disease, living twenty or thirty to a room, yet nominally free. The humblest commoner in Manyfolk or even Eastmyr can turn up his nose at them and feel smug."

"You really think that's the reason Matron Baenre hasn't ordered the slum scoured clean?"

"Well, if that conjecture seems implausible, here's another: Rumor has it that from time to time, someone meets the goddess herself in the Braeryn. Supposedly she likes to visit here in mortal guise. The matrons may feel that the neighborhood is, in some sense, under her protection."

The wizard hesitated. "Though if Lolth has gone away for good, perhaps they don't need to worry about it anymore."

Ryld shook his head. "It's still so hard to belie—"

Pharaun pointed. "Look."

Ryld turned.

On a curving wall below a dark elf's eye level was a sketch, this time smeared in blue. It consisted of three overlapping ovals, conceivably representing the links of a chain.

"It's a different mark," said Ryld. "Hobgoblin maybe, though I couldn't tell you the tribe."

"Don't be intentionally dim. It's the same peculiar, reckless, pointless crime."

"Fair enough, and it's still irrelevant to our endeavors."

"It's a dull mind that never transcends pragmatics. Two signs, representing two races, implying two specimens of the lesser races demented in precisely the same way? Unlikely, yet why would a single artist daub an emblem not his own?"

"Coincidence?"

"I doubt it, but as yet I can't provide a better answer."

"It's a puzzle for another day, remember?"

"Indeed."

The masters walked on.

"Still," pressed Pharaun, "don't you wonder how many scrawled signs we passed without noticing and exactly what form they took?"

Ignoring the question, Ryld pointed and said, "That's our destination."

The house's limestone door stood open, most likely for ventilation, for the interior radiated a perceptible warmth, the product of a multitude of tenants crammed in together. It also emitted a muddled drone and a thick stink considerably fouler than the unpleasant smell that clung to the Braeryn as a whole.

Ryld had been born in a similar warren, had fought like a demon to escape it, and he felt a strange reluctance to venture in, as if squalor wouldn't let him escape a second time. Unwilling to appear timid and foolish in the eyes of his friend, he hid the feeling behind an impassive warrior's countenance.

Pharaun, however, freely demonstrated his own distaste. The porcine eyes in his illusory orc face watered, and he swallowed, no doubt trying to quell a surge of queasiness.

"Get used to it," said Ryld.

"I'll be all right. I've visited the Braeryn frequently enough to have some notion of what these little hells are like, though I confess I never entered one."

"Then stick close and let me do the talking. Don't stare at anybody, or look anyone in the eye. They're likely to take it as an insult or challenge. Don't touch anyone or anything if you can avoid it. Half the residents are sick and probably contagious."

"Really? And their palace gives off such a salubrious air! Ah, well, lead on."

Ryld did as his friend had asked. Beyond the threshold was the claustrophobic nightmare he remembered. Kobolds, goblins, orcs, gnolls, bugbears, hobgoblins, and a sprinkling of less common creatures squeezed into every available space. Some, the warrior knew, were runaway slaves. Others had entered the service of Menzoberranyr travelers who picked them up in far corners of the world, took them back to the city, and dismissed them without any means of making their way home. The rest were descendants of unfortunate souls in the first two categories.

Wherever they came from, the paupers were trapped in the Braeryn, begging, stealing, scavenging, preying on one another—often in the most literal sense—and hiring on for any dangerous, filthy job anyone cared to give them. It was the only way they could survive.

This particular lot had likewise learned to live packed into the common space without the slightest vestige of privacy. Undercreatures babbled, cooked, ate, drank, tended a still, brawled, twitched and moaned in the throes of sickness, shook and cuffed their shrieking infants, threw dice, fornicated, relieved themselves, and, amazingly, slept, all in plain view of anyone with the ill luck to look in their direction.

As Ryld had expected, within moments of their entrance, a pair of toughs—in this instance bugbears—slouched forward to accost them.

With their coarse, shaggy manes and square, prominent jaws, bugbears were the largest and strongest of the goblin peoples, towering over the rest—and dark elves, too, for that matter. This pair was, by the standards of their destitute household, relatively well-fed and adequately dressed. They likely bullied tribute out of the rest.

"You don't live here," rumbled the taller of the two.

He wore what appeared to be a severed goblin hand strung around his burly neck. Drow occasionally affected similar ornaments, usually mementos of hated enemies, but they sent them to a taxidermist first. It was too bad the bugbear hadn't done the same. It would have prevented the rot and the carrion smell.

"No," Ryld said, tossing the bugbear a shaved coin, paying the toll to pass in and out of the house. "We came to see Smylla Nathos."

The hulking goblinoids just looked at him, as did several others creatures. A scaly, naked little kobold tittered crazily.

Something was wrong, and the Master of Melee-Magthere didn't know what. He felt a sudden tension and exhaled it away. Looking nervous was a bad idea.

"Isn't this Smylla's house?" he asked.

The shorter bugbear, who still loomed nearly as huge as an ogre, laughed and said, "No, not no more, but she still live here . . . kind of."

"Can we see her?" said Ryld.

"What for?" asked the bugbear with the severed goblin hand.

The weapons master hesitated. He'd intended to say that he and Pharaun wished to consult Smylla in her professional capacity as a trader in information. It was essentially the truth, though that didn't matter. What did was that he hadn't expected it to provoke a hostile response.

Pharaun stepped up beside him.

"Smylla sold our sister Iggra the secret of how to break into a merchant's strongroom," the wizard said in a creditably surly Orcish rasp. "How to get around all the traps. . . . Only she left one out, see? It squirted acid on Sis and burned her to death. Slow. Almost got us too. It's Smylla's fault, and we come to 'talk' to her about it."

The smaller bugbear nodded. "You ain't the only ones wantin' that kind of talk. Us, too, but we can't get at the bitch."

Pharaun cocked his head. "How come?"

"A couple tendays ago," said the bugbear with the severed hand necklace, "we decided we was tired of her bossing us and her lamps hurting our eyes. We jumped her, hit her, but she chucked one of those stones that makes a flash of light. It blinded us, and she run up to her room." He nodded toward the head of a twisting staircase. "We can't get through the door. She locked it with magic or somethin'."

Pharaun snorted. "Ain't no door my brother and me can't bust through."

The bugbears exchanged glances. The smaller one, who, Ryld noticed, was missing several of his lower teeth, shrugged.

"You can try," the larger one said. "Only, Smylla belongs to us, too. Hit her, bleed her, slice off a piece of her and eat it, but you can't keep her all to yourself."

"It's a deal," Pharaun said.

"Come on, then."

The bugbears led them through the crowded room and onto the stairs, where they still had to pick their way through lounging paupers. Partway up, the brute wearing the decaying hand put it in his mouth and began slurping and sucking on it.

At the top of the steps were a small landing and a limestone door with a rounded top. Two sentries, an orc and a canine-faced gnoll with sores on his muzzle, sat on the floor looking bored.

The disguised teachers made a show of examining the door.

"Can you knock it down?" Pharaun whispered.

"When the bugbears couldn't? Don't count on it. Can you open it with magic?"

"Probably. It's magically sealed, so a counterspell should suffice, but I don't want our friends to observe me casting it. That really would compromise my disguise. Stand where you obstruct their view and do something distracting."

"Right." Ryld positioned himself in the appropriate spot and glowered up at the two bugbears. "We can open it. What loot is inside?"

The larger bugbear scowled and, the odious object in his mouth garbling his speech a little, said, "We made a deal. It didn't say nothing about no loot."

"Smylla took Sis's treasure," Ryld replied. "We want it back, and extra too, for wergild."

"Hell with that."

The bugbear with the missing teeth reached for the knife tucked through his belt. Ryld could see it was a butcher's tool, not a proper fighting blade, but no doubt it served in the latter capacity well enough.

Ryld rested his hand on the hilt of his short sword, the weapon of choice for these tight quarters, and said, "You want to fight, we'll fight. I'll slice your face off your skull and wear it like a breechcloth, but my brother and I came to kill Smylla, not you. Let's talk. If you never get the door—"

"Open," Pharaun said.

White light shone at Ryld's back, making the bugbears wince. Squinting, the warrior whirled and scrambled for the opening.

"Hey!" yelped the smaller bugbear.

Ryld felt a big hand fumble at his shoulder, trying to grab him, but it was an instant too slow. He followed Pharaun over the threshold and slammed the door.

"You need to hold it shut," the wizard said.

"I can't do it for long."

Leaning forward, Ryld planted his hands on the limestone slab and braced himself.

The door bucked inward. For a split second, the dark elf's feet slid on the calcite floor, then they caught, and he held the barrier in place. Barely.

Meanwhile, Pharaun was peering about. He gave a little cry of satisfaction, picked up a small iron bar, and set it so it overlapped the edge of the door and the jamb about halfway up. When he took his hand away, the charm remained in place.

"This is quite a clever little device," the wizard said. "Oh, and you can let go now."

Pharaun turned the mechanical locks his spell of opening had disengaged, snapping each shut in its turn. It was actually the enchanted length of iron that had up to then kept the goblinoids out, but he thought he and Ryld might as well be as secure as possible. It also seemed the courteous thing to do.

His hostess, however, didn't seem to appreciate the gesture.

"Get out!" she croaked. "Get out, or I'll slay you with my sorcery!"

The masters turned. Smylla Nathos had lit her sparsely furnished room with a pair of slender brass rods, the tips of which emitted a steady magical glow. They protruded from the necks of wax-encrusted wine bottles like tapers sitting in candelabra, which they perhaps were meant to resemble. Maybe Smylla missed the spellcaster's traditional mode of illumination but couldn't obtain it anymore.

She herself lay at the limit of the light, on a cot in the shadows at the far end of the room. Pharaun could just barely make her out.

"Good afternoon, my lady," the wizard said, bowing. "It shames me beyond measure to ignore your request. Yet should this gentleman and I pass through your door a second time, the bugbears and their ilk will rush in, and that, I think, is the very eventuality you sought to forestall."

"Who are you? You don't talk like an orc."

"My lady is a marvel of perspicacity. We are in fact drow lords come to consult you on a matter of some importance."

"Why are you disguised?"

"The usual reason: To confound our enemies. May we approach? It's tedious trying to converse across the length of the room."

Smylla hesitated, then said, "Come."

Pharaun and Ryld started forward. Behind them, the bugbears were cursing, shouting threats and questions, and pounding on the far side of the door.

After four paces, the wizard's stomach turned at yet another stench, this one humid and gangrenous. He'd half expected something of the sort, but that didn't make it any easier to bear. Even the phlegmatic Ryld looked discomfited for an instant.

"Close enough," Smylla said, and Pharaun supposed it was.

He had no desire to come any nearer to that wasted form with its boils and pustules, even though the enchantments bound into his mantle and Ryld's cloak and dwarven armor would probably protect them from infection.

"Can you help us?" asked Ryld.

The sick woman leered. "Will you pay me with the magnificent greatsword you wear across your back?"

Pharaun was somewhat impressed. The illusion of pig-faced orcishness shrouding his friend made Splitter look like a battle-axe, but Smylla's rheumy, sunken eyes had pierced that aspect of the deception.

When he recovered from his surprise, Ryld shook his head. "No, I won't give you the sword. I worked too hard to get it, and I need it to stay alive, but if you want I can use it to clear away the goblinoids outside. My comrade and I are also carrying a fair amount of gold."

Her dry white hair spread about her head, Smylla lay propped against a mound of stained, musty pillows. She struggled to hitch herself up straighter, then abandoned the effort. Apparently it was beyond her strength.

"Gold?" she said. "Do you know who I am, swordsman? Do you know my history?"

"I do," Pharaun said. "The gist of it, anyway. It happened after I more or less withdrew from participation in the affairs of the great Houses."

"What do you know?" she asked.

"An expedition from House Faen Tlabbar," the wizard replied, "ventured up into the Lands of Light to hunt and plunder. When they returned, a lovely human sorceress and clairvoyant accompanied them, not as a newly captured slave but as their guest.

"Why did you want to come? Perhaps you were fleeing some implacable enemy, or were fascinated by the grace and sophistication of my people and the idea of living in the exotic Underdark. My hunch is that you wanted to learn drow magic, but it's pure speculation. No outsider ever knew.

"For that matter, why did the Faen Tlabbar oblige you? That's an even greater mystery. Conceivably someone harbored amorous feelings for you, or you, too, had secrets to teach."

"I had a way of persuading them," Smylla said.

"Obviously. Once you reached Menzoberranzan, you made yourself useful to House Faen Tlabbar as countless minions from the lesser races had done before you. The difference being that you were accorded a certain status, even a degree of familiarity. Matron Ghenni let you dine with the family and attend social functions, where you reportedly acquitted yourself with a drowlike poise and charm."

"I was their pet," said Smylla, sneering at the memory, "a dog dressed in a gown and trained to dance on its hind legs. I just didn't know it at the time."

"I'm sure many saw you that way. Perhaps some saw something else. From all accounts, Matron Ghenni behaved as if she regarded you as a ward, just one notch down from a daughter, and with the mistress of the Fourth House indulging you, few would dare challenge your right to comport yourself like a Menzoberranyr noble. Indeed, no one did, until she turned against you."

"Until I fell ill," said the sorceress.

"Quite. Was it a natural disease, bred, perhaps, by the lack of the searing sunlight that is a natural condition for your kind? Or did an enemy infect you with poison or magic? If so, was the culprit someone inside House Faen Tlabbar, who saw you as a rival for Ghenni's favor, or the agent of an enemy family, depriving their foes of a resource?"

"I was never able to find out. That's funny coming from me, isn't it?"

"Ironic, perhaps. At any rate, several priestesses tried to cure you, but for some reason, the magic failed, whereupon Ghenni summarily expelled you from her citadel."

"Actually," Smylla said, "she sent a couple trolls, slave soldiers, to murder me. I escaped them and the castle, too. Afterward, I tried to offer my services to other Houses, noble and merchant alike, but no door would open to a human who'd lost the favor of Faen Tlabbar."

"My lady," said Pharaun, "if it's any consolation, you were still receiving precisely the same treatment we would have given a member of our own race. No dark elf would abide the presence of anyone afflicted with an incurable malady. The Spider Queen taught us the weak must die, and in any case, what if the sickness was contagious?"

"It's not a consolation."

"Fair enough. To continue the tale: Unwelcome anywhere else, you made your way to the Braeryn. Despite your infirmity, some magic remained within your grasp, and you employed it to cow the residents of this particular warren into providing you with a private space in which to live. I daresay that wasn't easy. Then, using divinatory rituals, your natural psionic gifts, and whatever secrets you'd discovered during your time with House Faen Tlabbar, you set up shop as a broker of knowledge. At first, only the lower orders availed themselves of your services, then gradually, as your reputation grew, even a few of my people started consulting you. We wouldn't let you dwell among us, but some were willing to risk a brief contact if they anticipated sufficient advantage from it."

"I never heard of you," said Ryld, "but within the district, your reputation seems to be considerable. We've been asking questions all day, and more than one suggested we seek you out."

The door banged particularly loudly, and he glanced back to make sure the bugbears weren't breaching it.

"That's all I know of your saga," said Pharaun, "but I infer from the hostility of your cohabitants that a new stanza has begun."

"I suppose I couldn't bluff them forever," Smylla said. "My powers, sorcerous and psionic alike, are all but gone, devoured by my malady. Once I acquired my stock in trade primarily through scrying, divinations, and such. In recent years, I've cajoled my secrets from a web of informers, whom I betray one to the other."

The withered creature smirked.

"Well," said Ryld, "I hope you teased out the one we need."

She coughed. No, it was a laugh. "Even if I did, why would I share it with you, dark elf?"

"I told you," the warrior said, "we can protect you from the bugbears and goblins."

"So can my little iron trinket."

"But eventually, if you simply remain in here, you'll die of hunger and thirst."

"I'm dying anyway. Can't you tell? I'm not an old woman—I'm a baby as you drow measure time!—but I look like an ancient hag. I just don't want to perish at the hands of those miserable undercreatures. I've ruled here for fifteen years, and if I die beyond their reach, I win. Do you see?"

"Well, then, my lady," said Pharaun, "your wish suggests the terms of a bargain. Oblige us, and we'll refrain from admitting the bugbears."

She made a spitting sound and said, "Admit them if you must. I loathe the brutes, but I hate you dark elves more. It was you who made me as I am. I bartered information with you for as long as I had something to gain, but now that the disease is finally killing me, you can all go to the Abyss where your goddess lives, and burn."

Pharaun might have replied that as far as he could tell, Smylla had sealed her own fate on the day she decided to descend into the Underdark, but he doubted it would soften her resolve.

"I don't blame you," he said, making a show of sympathy. It wouldn't have deceived any drow, but even though she'd trafficked with his race for decades, perhaps she still had human instincts. "Sometimes I hate other dark elves myself. I'd certainly despise them if they served me as they've treated you."

She eyed him skeptically. "But you're the one who's different from all the others?"

"I doubt it. I'm a child of the goddess. I follow her ways. But I've visited the Realms that See the Sun, where I learned that other races think and live differently. I understand that by the standards of your own people, we've treated you abominably."

For a moment, she looked up at him as if no one had commiserated with her about anything since that long-lost season when she was the belle, or at least the coveted curiosity, of the revels and balls.

She said, "Do you think a few gentle words will make me want to help you?"

"Of course not. I just don't want your bitterness to get in the way of your good sense. It would be a pity if you turned your back on your salvation."

"What are you saying?"

"I can take away your sickness."

"You're lying. How could you do what the priestesses cannot?"

"Because I'm a wizard." Pharaun snapped his fingers and dissolved his mask of illusion. "My name is Pharaun Mizzrym. You may have heard of me. If not, you've surely heard of the Masters of Sorcere."

She was impressed, though trying not to show it.

"Who aren't healers," she said.

"Who *are* transmuters. I can change you into a drow, or, if you prefer, a member of another race. Whatever we choose, the transformation will purge the sickness from your new body."

"If that's true," she said, "then why do your people fear illness?"

"Because this remedy is inappropriate for them. It's unthinkable for a drow, one of the goddess's chosen people, to permanently assume the form of a lesser creature except as a punishment. Also, most wizards can't cast the spell deftly enough to purge a disease. It requires a certain facility, which happily, I possess."

He grinned.

"And you'll use it to help me?"

"Well, to aid myself, really."

The soothsayer scowled, pondering the offer.

Eventually she said, "What do I have to lose?"

"Exactly."

"But you have to change me first."

"No, first of all, we must establish that you do indeed possess the information my colleague and I require. We're seeking a number of runaway males hailing from noble and humble residences alike."

"We have a handful of drow hiding out in the Braeryn. Some are sick like me. Some are outcast for some other offense. A couple are just taking a long illicit holiday from their responsibilities and female relations. I can tell you where to find most of them."

"I'm sure," said Pharaun, "but I imagine they've resided here for a while, have they not? We're seeking rogues of more recent vintage. Menzoberranzan has suffered a mass migration in recent tendays."

Smylla frowned. From a subtle shift of expression, the mage knew she was deciding whether or not to lie.

"More drow males than usual have visited the Braeryn," she said. "Indulging their most sordid impulses, I assumed, but as far as I know they didn't stay here. If they did, I don't know where."

Ryld sighed. Pharaun knew how he felt. Generally speaking, the wizard relished a baffling, brain-cramping puzzle, but even he was growing impatient at their lack of progress.

Given the lack of any sensible leads, he resolved to follow where intuition led. Still caught up in his role of sympathizer, he dared to step to the cot and pat Smylla on her bony shoulder. She gasped. In all likelihood, no one had touched her for a long while, either.

"Don't abandon hope," Pharaun said. "Perhaps we can still make a trade. Fortunately, my comrade and I are interested in other matters as well. Has anything peculiar occurred in the Braeryn of late?"

The clairvoyant rasped out another painful-sounding laugh.

"You mean aside from the fact that last tenday, the animals rose up against me?"

"I do find that interesting. As you confessed, your magical talents withered away some time ago. Since then, you've dominated the goblins through bluff and force of personality, and it worked until a few days ago. What changed? Where did the undercreatures find the courage to turn against you? Have you noticed anything that might account for it?"

"Well," said Smylla, "it could just be they saw me failing physically, but—" Her cracked lips stretched into a grin. "You're good, Master Mizzrym. You give me a smile, friendly conversation, a soft touch on the arm, and my tongue starts to flap. That's loneliness for you. But I will have my cure before I give up anything of importance."

"Very sensible." Pharaun extracted an empty cocoon from one of his pockets. "What do you wish to become?"

"One of you," she said, leering. "I once heard a philosopher say that everyone becomes the thing he hates."

"He must have been a cheery fellow to have about. Now, brace yourself. This will only take a moment, but it may hurt a little."

Employing greater care than usual, he recited the incantation and used the ridged silken case to write a symbol on the air.

Magic shrilled through the air, and the temperature plummeted. For a moment, the whole room rippled and shimmered, then the distortion concentrated itself on Smylla's shriveled body. Tendons standing out in her neck, she screamed.

Beyond the door, one of the bugbears shouted, "We want to get even, too! We had a bargain!"

Smylla's sores faded away, and her emaciated form filled out into a healthy slimness. Her ashen skin darkened to a gleaming black, her blue eyes turned red, and her ears grew points. Her features became more delicate. Her snowy hair thickened, changing from brittle and lusterless to wavy and glossy.

"The pain went away," she breathed. "I feel stronger."

"Of course," Pharaun said.

She stared at her hands, then sat up, rose from the cot, and tried to walk. At first she moved with an invalid's caution, but gradually, as she proved to herself that she wouldn't fall, that hesitancy passed. After a few seconds, she was striding, jumping, and spinning like an exuberant little girl testing her strength, her grimy nightshirt flapping about her.

"You did it!" she said, and the pure, uncalculated gratitude in her crimson eyes showed that even wearing the flesh of a dark elf maiden, she was still human at the core.

Though it was foreign to his own nature, Pharaun found her appreciation rather gratifying. Still, he hadn't transformed her to bask in her naïve sentimentality but to elicit some answers.

"Now," he said, "please, tell us."

"Right." She took a deep breath to compose herself and said, "I do believe something emboldened the undercreatures in this house. What's more, I think it's affected goblinoids throughout the Braeryn."

"What is it?" asked Ryld.

"I don't know."

The warrior grimaced.

"What led you to infer this agency?" Pharaun asked. "I assume you were housebound even before you barricaded yourself in your room."

"I saw a change in the brutes who live here. They were surly, insolent, and foul-tempered, ready to maim and kill one another at the slightest provocation."

Ryld hitched his shoulders, working stiffness out or shifting Splitter to lie more comfortably across his back.

"How is that different than normal?" asked the weapons master.

Smylla scowled at him and said, "All things are relative. The creatures exhibited those qualities to a greater extent than before, and whenever I heard tidings from beyond these walls, they suggested the entire precinct shared the same truculent humor."

Pharaun nodded. "Did you hear about tribal emblems appearing in the streets?"

"Yes," she said. "That bespeaks a kind of madness, don't you think?"

"Maybe in one or two thralls," said Ryld. "What of it? You promised my friend information. Tell us something we don't already know, and I mean facts, not your impressions."

The clairvoyant smiled. "All right. I was building up to it. Every few nights a drum beats somewhere in the Braeryn, calling the lower orders to some sort of gathering. Many of the occupants of this house clear out. With what little remains of my clairvoyance, I've sensed many others skulking through the streets, all converging on a common destination."

"Nonsense," said Ryld. "Why has no drow patrol heard the signal and come to investigate?"

"Because," said Pharaun, "the city possesses enchantments to mute sound."

"Well, maybe." Ryld turned back to Smylla. "Where do the creatures go, and why?"

"I don't know," she said, "but perhaps, with my health and occult talents restored, I could find out." She beamed at Pharaun. "I'd be happy to try. I fulfilled the letter of our bargain, but I do realize I haven't provided you with all that much in exchange for the priceless gift you gave me."

"That remark touches on the question of your future," the wizard said. "You'd have no difficulty reestablishing your dominion here in the Stench-streets, but why live so meanly? I could use an aide of your caliber. Or, if you prefer, I can arrange your safe repatriation to the World Above."

As he spoke, he surreptitiously contorted the fingers of his left hand, expressing himself in the silent language of the dark elves, a system of gestures as efficient and comprehensive as the spoken word.

"I think—" Smylla began, then her eyes opened wide.

She whimpered. Ryld pulled his short sword out of her back, and she collapsed. Pharaun skipped back to keep her from toppling against him.

"Despite her previous experiences," the lanky wizard said, "she couldn't quite leave off trusting drow. I suppose it shows you can take the human out of the sunshine, but not the sunshine out of the human." He shook his head. "This is the second female I've slain or murdered by proxy in the brief time since our adventure began, and I didn't particularly want to kill either one of them. Do you suspect an underlying metaphysical significance?"

"How would I know? I take it you bade me kill the snitch because she was feeding us lies."

"Oh, no. I'm convinced she was telling the truth. The problem was that I deceived her. Her metamorphosis didn't really purge her disease. It was a bit tricky just suppressing it for a few minutes."

Pharaun stepped back again to keep the spreading pool of blood from staining his boots, and Ryld cleaned the short sword on the dead human's bedding.

"You didn't want to leave her alive and angry to carry tales to Greyanna," the weapons master said.

"It's unlikely they would have found one another, but why take the chance?"

"And you asked Smylla about the marks on the walls. You're just too cursed curious to let the subject go."

Pharaun grinned. "Don't be silly. I'm the very model of single-minded determination, and I was asking to further our mission."

Ryld glanced at the door and the iron bar. They were still holding.

"What does the strange behavior of goblins have to do with the rogue males?" he asked.

"I don't know yet," Pharaun answered, "but we have two oddities occurring at the same time and in the same precinct. Doesn't it make sense to infer a relationship?"

"Not necessarily. Menzoberranzan has scores of plots and conspiracies going on at any given time. They aren't all connected."

"Granted. However, if these two situations are linked, then by inquiring into one, we likewise probe the other. You and I have experienced a depressing lack of success picking up the trail of our runaways. Therefore, we'll investigate the lower orders and see where that path takes us."

"How will we do that?"

"Follow the drum, of course."

The door banged.

"First," said Ryld, "we have to get out of here."

"Easily managed. I'll remove the locking talisman from the door, then use illusion to make us blend with the walls. In a minute or two, the residents will break the door down. When they're busy abusing Smylla's corpse and ransacking her possessions, we'll put on goblin faces and slip out in the confusion."

ELEVEN

Quenthel's patrol had stalked the shadowy, candlelit passages of Arach-Tinilith for hours, until spaces she knew intimately began to seem strange and subtly unreal, and her subordinates' nerves visibly frayed with the waiting. She called a halt to let the underlings rest and collect themselves. They stopped in a small chapel with the images of skulls, daggers, and spiders worked in bas-relief on the walls and the bones of long-dead priestesses interred beneath the floor. Rumor whispered that a cleric had cut her own throat in this sanctuary and her ghost sometimes haunted it, but the Baenre had never seen the apparition, and it wasn't in evidence then.

The priestesses and novices settled on the pews. For a while, no one spoke.

Eventually Jyslin, a second-year student with a heart-shaped face and silver studs in her earlobes, said, "Perhaps nothing will happen."

Quenthel stared coldly at the novice. Like the rest of the party, the younger female cut a warlike figure with her mace, mail, and shield, but her dread showed in her troubled maroon eyes and shiny, sweaty brow.

"We will face another demon tonight," Quenthel said. "I feel it, so it's pointless to hope otherwise. Instead I suggest you concentrate on staying alert and remembering what you've learned."

Jyslin lowered her eyes and whispered, "Yes, Mistress."

"Wishful thinking is for cowards," Quenthel said, "and if you fools are lapsing into it, we've lingered here too long. Up with you."

Reluctantly, someone's links of supple black mail chiming ever so faintly, Quenthel's minions rose. She led them onward.

In light of the two previous intrusions and the obvious uselessness of the wards the mages of Sorcere had created, Quenthel had placed Arach-Tinilith on alert and organized her staff and students into squads of eight. Most of the units would stand watch at set locations, but several would patrol the entire building. The Baenre princess had opted to lead one of the latter.

She'd also decided to throw open the storerooms and armories and dispense all the potent enchanted tools and weapons still deposited there. Even the first-year students bore enchanted arms and talismans worthy of a high priestess.

Not that the gear had done much to bolster Jyslin's morale, nor that of many another novice. Had Quenthel not been suffering her own carefully masked anxieties, their glumness might have amused her. The girls had seen demons throughout their childhoods. They'd even achieved a certain intimacy with them in Arach-Tinilith, but this was the first time such entities had posed a threat to them, and they'd realized they hadn't truly known the ferocious beings at all.

No doubt some of the females had also been perceptive enough to recognize that they themselves had been in comparatively little danger until Quenthel mustered them in what was more or less her personal defense. If so, their resentment, like their uneasiness, was irrelevant. They were her underlings, and it was their duty to serve her.

"It's the wrath of Lolth herself," whispered Minolin Fey-Branche, a fifth-year student who wore her hair in three long braids. Obviously, she didn't intend for her voice to carry to the front of the procession. "First she strips us of our magic, then sends her fiends to kill us."

Quenthel whirled. Sensing her anger, her whip vipers rose, weaving and hissing.

"Shut up!" she snapped. "The Spider Queen may be testing us, eliminating the unfit, but she has not condemned her entire temple. She would not."

Minolin lowered her eyes. "Yes, Mistress," she said tonelessly.

Quenthel noticed that no one else looked reassured, either.

"You disgust me," the Baenre said. "All of you."

"We apologize, Mistress," said Jyslin.

"I remember my training," Quenthel said. "If a novice showed a hint of cowardice or disobedience, my sister Triel would make her fast for a tenday, and eat rancid filth for another after that. I should do the same, but unfortunately, with Arach-Tinilith under siege, I need my people strong. So all right, though it should shame you take it, you can have another rest. You'll fill your bellies, and it had better stiffen your spines. Otherwise, we'll see how many of you I have to flog before the rest cease their cringing and whining. Come."

She led them on to a classroom where the kitchen staff had set a table. She'd ordered them to prepare a cold supper and leave it at various points around the temple, so that the weary sentinels could at least refresh themselves with food, and the cooks had done a decent job of it. On a silver salver lay pink and brown slices of rothé steak steeped in a tawny marinade, their aroma competing with Arach-Tinilith's omnipresent scent of incense. Other trays and bowls held raw mushroom pieces with a creamy dipping sauce and a salad of black, white, and red diced fungus, while the pitchers presumably contained wine, watered as per her command. Quenthel hoped the alcohol would hearten those residents whom Lolth's absence and the incursions of the past two nights had terrified, but she didn't want any of the temple's defenders sloppy drunk and incapacitated.

Some of Quenthel's minions fell to as if they expected this to be their last meal. Others, likely as certain of their fate, seemed too tense to do more than pick at the viands.

The mistress of the Academy supposed that, though she intended to survive the night, in a sense, she belonged to the latter party. Her stomach was somewhat queasy, and the long hours of edgy anticipation had killed her appetite.

Come on, demon, she thought, *let's get this over with. . . .*

The entity failed to respond to her silent plea.

She decided her throat was a little parched, caught Jyslin's eye, and said, "Pour me a cup."

"Yes, Mistress."

The second-year novice performed the service with commendable alacrity. She filled the silver goblet too high for gentility's sake, but Quenthel expected no better from a commoner. The Baenre accepted the cup with a nod and raised it to her lips.

Her whip of fangs hung from her wrist by the wyvern-hide loop that pierced its handle. She felt a thrill of alarm surge across the psionic link she shared with the vipers. At the same instant, the snakes reared and dashed the goblet from her grasp. She stared at them in amazement.

"Poison," Yngoth said, his slit-pupiled eyes glinting in their scaly sockets. "We smelled it."

Quenthel looked around. Her followers had heard the serpent's declaration and were gawking at her and the reptiles in consternation. They appeared to be in perfectly good health, but she trusted the vipers and knew it wouldn't last.

"Purge yourselves," she said. "Now!"

They never got the chance. Almost as one, they succumbed to the toxin, swaying, staggering, and collapsing. Some retched involuntarily as the sickness hit them, but it didn't help. They passed out like the rest.

Quenthel shifted the whip back to her hand, peered in all directions, and bade the vipers do the same. She'd realized her demonic assailants were supposed to suggest the several dominions of the goddess, and therefore an "assassin" of some sort would turn up sooner or later. Still, she foolishly assumed that being would attack in some obvious way just as the "spider" and "darkness" had. She hadn't expected it to employ stealth and attempt to poison her, though in retrospect, that tactic made perfect sense.

The question was, had the demon done all it planned to do, or, since its first ploy had failed, would it strike at her in some other way?

Off to the west, someone screamed, the sound echoing down the stone halls. Quenthel had her answer, and it was the one she'd expected.

Her heart beat faster, her mouth felt drier still, and she realized she wasn't eager to confront this new intruder, certainly not without the support of her personal guards. Yet she was mistress in these halls, and it was unthinkable to turn tail and let an invader make free with her domain.

Besides, if she fled, the cursed thing would probably track her anyway.

Leaving her fallen patrol with their useless magical treasures strewn about them on the floor, she strode toward the noise. She shouted for other underlings to attend her, but no one responded.

In a minute or so, she entered a long gallery, where wall carvings told the history of Lolth as it had occurred and as it was prophesied: her seduction of Corellon Larethian, chief deity of the contemptible elves of the World Above, their union and her first attempt to overthrow him, her discovery of her spider form and her descent into the Abyss, her conquest of the Demonweb and her adoption of the drow as her chosen people, and her future triumph over all other gods and ascendancy over all creation.

A silhouette appeared in the arched entry at the far end of the hall. It changed color and shape—humanoid, quadruped, blob, worm, cluster of spikes—from one instant to the next. Somehow perceiving Quenthel, it let out a cry. Its voice sounded like a wavering, cacophonous jumble of every noise she'd ever heard and some she hadn't. Within the first discordant howl she caught the shrill note of a flute, the grunt of a rothé, a baby crying, water splashing, and fire crackling.

Quenthel recognized the demon for the profound threat it was, but for a moment, she was less concerned for her safety or fired with a fighter's rage than she was surprised. Poison surely suggested an assassin, yet the demon before her was plainly an embodiment of chaos.

The spirit started down the gallery, and the walls bulged, flowed, and changed color around it. Quenthel reached into the leather bag hanging from her belt and brought out a scroll, then something hit her hard in the back of the neck.

Ryld peered about the room. Judging from the sunken arena in the center of the floor, the ruinous place had, in another era, served as a drinking pit—one of those rude establishments where dark elves of every station went to forget about caste and grace for a few hours, guzzle raw spirit, and watch undercreatures slaughter one another in contests that were often set up in such a way as to give them a comical aspect.

In other words, it would have been a crude sort of place by the standards of elegant Menzoberranzan, but it had grown cruder since the goblinoids had taken it over. Scores if not hundreds of them packed into the space, and the mingled stink of their unwashed bodies, each race malodorous in its own particular fashion, was sickening. The loud gabbling in their various harsh and guttural languages was nearly as unpleasant. It all but drowned out the rhythmic thuds that filtered through the ceiling, but of course the shaggy gnoll drummer on the roof wasn't playing for the folk already inside but to guide others still in transit.

To Ryld's surprise, a fair number of the creatures assembling there hailed from outside the Braeryn. He observed plain but relatively clean and intact garments suggestive of Eastmyr, and even liveries, steel collars, shackles, whip marks, and brands—the stigmata of thralls who'd sneaked away from their mistresses' affluent households. Obviously, those who'd come from beyond the district couldn't have heard the drum through the magical buffers. Some runner must have carried word to them.

Still magically disguised as orcs, though not the same ones who'd tricked the two bugbears, the masters of Tier Breche had squeezed into a corner to watch whatever would transpire.

Certain no one would hear him over the ambient din, Ryld leaned his head close to Pharaun's and said, "I think it's just a party."

"Do you see them celebrating?" Pharaun replied. His new porcine face had a broken nose and tusk. "No, not as such. They'd be considerably more boisterous. They're waiting for something, and eagerly, too. Observe those female goblins chattering and passing their bottle back and forth." Pharaun nodded toward a trio of filthy, bandy-legged creatures with flat faces and sloping brows. "They're aquiver with anticipation. If they're still as giddy after the gathering breaks up, we may want to seek solace for our frustrations in their hairy, misshapen arms."

Certain his friend was joking, Ryld snorted . . . then realized he wasn't quite sure after all.

"You'd have relations with a *goblin*?"

"A true scholar always seeks new experiences. Besides, what's the point of being a dark elf, a lord of the Underdark, if you don't exploit the slave races to the utmost?"

"Hmm. I admit they might be no worse than one of those priestesses who demand you grovel and do exactly as you're—"

"Hush!"

The drum had stopped.

"Something's happening," Pharaun added.

Ryld saw that his friend was correct. A stir ran through the crowd and they started to shout, "Prophet! Prophet! Prophet!"

The master of Melee-Magthere didn't know what he expected to see next, but it certainly wasn't the figure in the nondescript cloak and hood whose upper body appeared above the heads of the crowd. Perhaps he'd climbed up on a bench or table, or maybe he'd simply levitated, for this "Prophet," plainly beloved of the lower orders, appeared to be a handsome drow male.

The Prophet let his followers chant and shout for a minute or so, then he raised his slender hands and gradually they subsided. Pharaun leaned close to Ryld again.

"It's possible the fellow's not really one of us," the wizard said. "He's wrapped in a glamour somewhat like ours, but his spell makes every observer perceive him in a favorable light. I imagine the goblins see him as a goblin, the gnolls, as one of their own, and so forth."

"What's inside the illusion?"

"I don't know. The enchantment is peculiar. I've never encountered anything quite like it. I can't see through it, but I suspect we're about to learn his intentions."

"My brothers and sisters," the Prophet said.

His voice sparked another round of cheering, and he waited for it to run its course.

"My brothers and sisters," he repeated. "Since the founding of this city, the Menzoberranyr have held our peoples in bondage or in conditions equally degraded. They work us until we die of exhaustion. They torture and kill us on a whim. They condemn us to starve, sicken, and live in squalor."

The audience growled its agreement.

"You witness our misery everywhere you look," the hooded orator continued. "Yesterday, I walked through Manyfolk. I saw a hobgoblin girl-child, surely no older than five or six, trying to pick up a scrap of mushroom from the street. With her teeth! Her hands wouldn't serve.

Some drow had magically fused them together behind her back so she would live and die a cripple and a freak."

The crowd snarled in outrage, even though their races commonly engaged in tortures equally cruel, albeit far less varied and imaginative.

"I walked through Narbondellyn," the Prophet said. "I saw an orc, paralyzed in some manner, lying on the ground. A dark elf slit his chest, spread the flaps of skin, cut some ribs with a saw, and whistled his riding lizard over to feed on the still-living thrall's organs. The drow told a companion that he gave the reptile one such meal every tenday to make it a faster racer."

The audience howled its wrath. One female orc, transported with fury, gashed her cheeks and brow with a piece of broken glass.

The Prophet's litany of atrocities ran on and on, and Ryld gradually felt a strange emotion overtaking him. He knew it couldn't be guilt—no dark elf experienced that ridiculous condition—but perhaps it was a kind of shame, a disgust at the sheer waste and childishness manifest in Menzoberranzan's abuse of its undercreatures and a desire to rectify the situation if he could.

The feeling was irrational, of course. The goblins and their kin existed only to serve the pleasure of the drow, and if you ruined one, you just caught or bought another. The weapons master gave his head a shake, clearing it, then turned to Pharaun.

Even through his orc mask, the wizard's amusement was apparent.

"Resolved to mend your wicked ways?"

"I gather you feel the influence, too," said Ryld. "What's happening?"

"The Prophet has magic buttressing his oratory, again, in a sort of configuration I don't quite understand."

"Right, but what's the point of all this bellyaching?"

"I assume he'll get around to telling us."

The speaker continued in the same vein a while longer, goading the crowd to the brink of hysteria.

At last he cried, "But it does not have to be that way!"

The undercreatures howled, and for a moment, until he pushed the feelings away, Ryld felt his magically induced disgust blaze up into savage bloodlust.

"We can be avenged! Repay every injury a thousandfold! Cast down the drow to be *our* slaves! We'll wrap ourselves in silks and cloth-of-gold and make them run naked, feast on succulent viands and feed them garbage! We'll sack Menzoberranzan, and afterward those of us who wish it will return to our own peoples laden with treasure, while the rest of us rule the cavern as our own!"

Not likely, thought Ryld. He turned to say as much to Pharaun, then blinked in surprise. The wizard looked as if he was taking this diatribe seriously.

"They're just venting their resentment in the form of a fantasy," the warrior whispered. "They'd never dare, and we'd crush them in a matter of minutes if they did."

"So one would assume," Pharaun replied. "Come on, I want a closer look."

They started working their way forward through the agitated throng. Some of their fellow spectators plainly resented their shoving. Ryld had to toss one hobgoblin down onto the floor of the sunken arena, but no one seemed to think it odd that they wanted to get closer to the charismatic leader. Others were doing the same.

The Prophet continued his oration.

"I thank you for your work and your patience, which soon will reap their reward. Word of our revolt has reached every street and alley. We have warriors everywhere, and each understands what he is to do when he hears the Call. Meanwhile, the drow suspect nothing. Their arrogance makes them complacent. They won't suspect until it's too late, until the Call comes and we rise as one—until we burn them."

Ryld and Pharaun had forced their way close enough to see the Prophet pick up a sandstone rod and anoint the end with an oil from a ceramic bottle. The rod burst into yellow, crackling flame as if it were made of dry wood, that exotic combustible product of the World Above. The master of Melee-Magthere squinted at the sudden flare of light.

"Eyes of the Goddess!" Pharaun exclaimed.

"It's a neat trick," Ryld said, "but surely nothing special by your standards."

"Not the fire, those two bugbears standing behind the Prophet."

"His bodyguards, I imagine. What of them?"

"They're Tluth Melarn and one Alton the cobbler, two of our runaways.

They're wearing veils of illusion, too, but of a simpler nature. I can see past theirs."

"Are you serious? What are drow, even rogues, doing aiding the instigator of a slave revolt?"

"Perhaps we'll find out when we tail the Prophet and his entourage away from here."

"I taught you how to use the fire pots," the orator continued, "and my friends and I have brought plenty of them." He gestured toward several hovering floatchests. "Take them and hide them until the day of reckoning."

The bright notes of a brazen glaur horn blared through the air. For a moment, confused, Ryld thought "the Call"—whatever that was—had arrived, then a thrill of panic, or at least the memory of it, reminded him what the trumpet truly portended. Judging by the goblins' babbling and frantic peering about, they knew, too.

"What is it?" Pharaun asked.

"You're nobly born," said Ryld, hearing a trace of an old bitterness in his voice. "Didn't you ever go hunting through the Braeryn, slaying every wretch you could catch?"

The wizard smiled and said, "Now that you mention it, but it's been a long time. It occurs to me that this is probably Greyanna's doing. Not a bad tactic, really, even though it involves a lot of waste motion. Once I shielded us our hunters couldn't pinpoint our location, but they knew our mission would bring us to the Braeryn so they organized a hunt for a party of nobles. The idea is that all the turmoil is likely to flush us out and send us scrambling frantically through the streets, at which point they'll have a better chance of spotting us."

"What's more," said Ryld, making sure his swords were loose in their scabbards, "your sister gives us the choice of retaining our veils of illusion and being harried by our own kind, or casting them off and facing the wrath of the undercreatures. Either way, someone might do her killing for her."

The Prophet raised his hands for calm, and the undercreatures quieted a little.

"My friends, in a moment we will scatter as we must, for a little while longer, but before you go, take the fire pots. Once the danger is past, share the weapons and news of our gathering with all those who were unable to attend. Remember your part in the plan and wait for the Call. Now, go!"

Some of the rebels bolted without further delay, but at least half lingered long enough to take a jug or two from the hovering boxes. One orc lost his footing in the press, then screamed as other goblinoids trampled him in their haste. Meanwhile, the Prophet and his bodyguards slipped out a door in the back wall.

"Shall we?" said Pharaun, striding after them.

"What of Greyanna and all the hunters?" asked Ryld.

"We'll contend with them as necessary, but I'll be damned if I hide in a hole while two of the boys we worked so hard to find vanish into the night."

The masters stalked out onto the street. The Braeryn already echoed with more trumpeting, the sporting cries of dark elves, and the screams of undercreatures.

The teachers shadowed the Prophet and the rogues for half a block. The trio moved briskly but without any trace of panic. Evidently they were confident of their ability to elude the hunters. Ryld wondered why.

Then the night gave him other things to think about.

He and Pharaun skulked by a house where several shouting goblins pounded on the granite front door. As was the common practice during a hunt, the inhabitants refused to admit them. They wouldn't let in anyone but folk who actually lived there. Otherwise, a rush of terrified refugees flooding into the already crowded warren might trample or crush some of the residents—or the influx might make the house a more provocative target. It had happened before.

Finally Ryld heard the small, long-armed creatures turn away from the structure. They cried out, then broke into a run, their rapid footsteps drumming on the ground.

Ryld had no idea why the goblins were charging him and Pharaun. Perhaps the creatures had mistaken them for tenants of the house that had denied them entry and thus appropriate targets for revenge. Maybe they simply wanted to take their frustrations out on someone.

Not that it mattered. The brutes were no match for masters of Tier Breche. The dark elves would kill them in a trice.

Ryld drew Splitter from its scabbard and came on guard, meanwhile taking in his assailants' pitiful makeshift weaponry and lack of armor. It was pathetic, really, so much so that the next few seconds would almost be a bore.

Two goblins spread out, trying to flank him. He stepped in and swung Splitter left, then right. The undercreatures fell, one dropping its crowbar to clang against the ground and the other keeping hold of its mallet.

The next two bat-eared creatures hesitated. They should have turned and run, because Ryld couldn't stand and wait for them to ponder whether they still wanted to fight. The Prophet and the rogues were getting farther away by the second.

He stepped in and cut downward. A goblin, this one possessed of a short sword—a proper warrior's weapon, and some martial training to go with it—lifted the weapon to parry. It didn't matter. Splitter sheared right through its blade and streaked on into its torso.

Knife in hand, the fourth goblin dodged behind its foe. Sensing its location, Ryld kicked backward. His boot connected solidly, snapping bone, and when he turned the creature lay motionless on the ground, likely dead of a broken back.

Ryld turned to survey the battlefield. His eyes widened in shock and dismay.

Pharaun too was on the ground. Three goblins crouched over him on their bandy legs. One scabrous creature had blood on the iron spike that served it as a poniard.

Ryld bellowed a war cry, sprang at them, and struck them down before they could do any more damage. He kneeled beside his friend. Beneath the elegant *piwafwi*, Pharaun's equally gorgeous robe had two punctures in it, and was dark and wet from breastbone to thighs.

"I heard them coming a moment after you did," the wizard wheezed. "I didn't turn around fast enough."

"Don't worry," said Ryld. "It's going to be all right."

In reality, he wasn't at all sure of that.

"The goblin thrust through the gap between the wings of my cloak. The little bastard hurt me when Greyanna and her followers couldn't. Isn't that silly?"

c h a p t e r

T W E L V E

When Quenthel had decided she must don armor, she had performed the task as methodically as she did everything else. She'd put on a cunningly crafted adamantine gorget, a Baenre heirloom, beneath her chain mail and *piwafwi*, and it was likely that protective collar that saved her life.

Still, the unexpected impact on the nape of her neck knocked her forward and down onto one knee, and the edge of her enchanted buckler clanked against the floor.

For a moment, she was dazed. The whip vipers hissed and clamored to rouse her, their outburst clashing with the jumbled howling of the advancing chaos demon.

She felt something hanging down her back and bade the serpents pull it off. Hsiv reared over her shoulder, tugged the article out of the mail links and cloth with his jaws, and displayed it for her inspection. She recognized it from the armory. It was an enchanted quarrel sized for a two-hand arbalest, and if it, or one like it, so much as pricked a dark elf's skin, it would almost certainly kill.

Quenthel thought her assailant had had just about enough time to reload. If so, the Baenre obviously couldn't trust her cloak and mail to protect her—the first bolt had pierced them easily enough.

Though it meant turning her back on the demon, she wrenched herself around, remaining on one knee to make a smaller target, and did her best to cover herself with her tiny shield.

Just in time. A second quarrel cracked against the armor. A shadowy but recognizably female figure ducked back into an arched doorway, no doubt to ready her weapon again.

Trapped between two foes, Quenthel thought that if she didn't eliminate one of them quickly, they were almost certainly going to kill her. Judging her sister dark elf the easier mark, she leveled a long, thin rod at her.

A glob of seething green vitriol materialized in the air before her, then shot toward her enemy. Quenthel could just see the edge of her opponent's body in the recessed space, and that was what she aimed for. Even if she missed, the magic ought to slow the assassin down.

The green mass clipped her foe's shoulder. It exploded, and the dark figure jumped. The stonework around her was covered in a sticky mass of something like glue. Quenthel smiled, but her foe, apparently unhindered by the entrapping magic, returned to the task of cocking the crossbow. Something, her innate drow resistance to hostile magic, perhaps, had shielded her from harm.

Quenthel glanced over her shoulder as she slipped the rod back into her belt. Though moving at a leisurely pace, the chaos demon had already traversed more than half of the lengthy gallery, and of course its speed could increase at any moment, just as every other aspect of its being altered unpredictably from one second to the next.

But if the Spider Queen favored Quenthel and the entity didn't accelerate, she might have time for another strike at her foe of flesh and blood. Silently directing the vipers to keep an eye on the demon, she turned back, and read from a precious scroll.

When Quenthel pronounced the last syllable, the scroll disappeared in a puff of dust and a brilliant light filled the chamber. The dark elf in the doorway reeled and clutched blindly at the door frame. She touched the slowly-dripping mass of glue and snatched her fingers away, leaving skin behind.

Quenthel started to read another scroll as the air around her stirred, blowing one direction then another. Hot one second and cold the next, the gusts wafted countless smells, pleasant and foul alike. She took it for a sign that the demon had drawn very close, and the vipers' warning confirmed it.

Still, she wanted to finish her lesser adversary off before the girl recovered her sight. She completed the spell, the exquisitely inked characters burning through the parchment like hot coals.

From the elbow down, the enemy female's left arm rippled and swelled, becoming an enormous black spider with green markings on its bristling back. Still attached to the rest of her body, it lunged at her throat and plunged its mandibles in.

Quenthel spun around. Mauve with golden spots, then white, then half red and half blue, the demon loomed over her. Most of the time it looked flat, like a hole into some other luminous, turbulent universe, and an observer had only its inconstant outline from which to infer its shape. Over the course of a couple seconds, it seemed to become an enormous crab claw, a wagon complete with driver, and a whirling dust devil. The length of gallery behind it resembled a tunnel carved from melting rainbow-colored slush except for one little stretch. That section appeared unchanged until Quenthel noticed that the carvings had flipped upside down.

The high priestess scrambled to her feet. As she rooted in her bag for another scroll, her scourge dangled from her wrist. The vipers writhed and twisted.

The chaos demon blinked from ochre to a pattern of black and white stripes, and from the form of a simple isosceles triangle to that of an ogre. Its cry currently a mix of roaring and cawing, it swung its newly acquired club.

Quenthel caught the blow on her buckler. To her surprise, she didn't feel the slightest shock, but the shield turned blue, changed from round to rectangular, and became many times heavier than it had been before.

The unexpected weight dragged her down to the floor again. Resembling a cresting wave, the intruder flowed toward her. She yanked, but her shield arm was caught somehow and wouldn't pull free of the straps.

Rippling from magenta to brown stippled with scarlet, the demon advanced to within inches of her foot. Quenthel's boot evaporated into wisps of vapor, and pain stabbed through the extremity.

Finally her hand jerked out of its restraints, and she flung herself backward, rolling, her mail whispering against the floor.

When she'd put sufficient distance between herself and her foe, she rose, then faltered. For an instant, she couldn't locate the fiend, and her mind struggled to make sense of the scene before her. Green and blue, shaped like an hourglass, the demon was gliding along the ceiling, not the floor. It was still pursuing her. The cursed thing was random in every respect save its doggedly murderous intent.

The entity's howl ceased for a moment, then resumed with a peal of childish laughter. Quenthel snatched and unrolled a scroll, which abruptly turned into a rothé's jawbone. The air took on a sooty tinge, and her next breath seared her lungs.

Choking, she stumbled back out of the cloud. She could breathe, though the stinging heat in her throat and chest persisted. She suspected that, had she inhaled any more of it, the taint might well have killed her. As it was, it had incapacitated and possibly slain the vipers, who hung inert from the butt of the whip.

She tossed away the jawbone, grabbed another scroll, and started reading the powerful spell contained therein. Shaped like some hybrid of dragon and wolf, the demon, back on the floor again, advanced without moving its legs. Though colored the blue and gold of flame, it threw off a bitter chill that threatened to freeze the skin on her face and spoil her recitation with a stammer.

Quenthel thanked the goddess that her own education in Arach-Tinilith had taught her to transcend discomfort. She forced out the words in the proper manner, and a black blade, like a greatsword without a guard, hilt, or tang, shimmered into existence in front of her.

She smiled. The floating weapon was a devastating magic known only to the priestesses of Lolth. Quenthel had never seen any creature resist it. Though the stone floor was still chilly against the sole of her bare foot, the ghastly cold had passed, and she stood her ground, the blade interposed between her and her pursuer.

"Do you know what this is?" she asked it. "It can kill you. It can kill anything."

Certain the demon could hear her thoughts, she sent it the words, *Surrender and tell me who sent you, or I'll slice you to pieces.*

Emitting a sweet scent she'd never encountered before, looking like a giant frog crudely chiseled from mica with rows of wicked fangs in its sparkling jaws, the chaos demon waddled forward.

Fine, the Baenre thought, *be stupid.*

Controlling the black blade with her thoughts, she bade it attack. It hacked a long gash in the top of the frog head and knocked the demon down on its belly. The edges of the wound burned with scarlet fire.

The intruder turned inky black while flowing into a shape that resembled two dozen hands growing on long, leafy stalks. The stems stretching and twisting, the creature grabbed for the sword.

Quenthel let the hands seize hold of it, and as she'd expected, the magically keen double edge cut them to pieces, which dropped away onto the floor. The demon gave a particularly loud cry, which sounded in part like the rhythmic clanging of a hammer beating metal in a forge. Wincing at the noise, the priestess didn't know if the extreme volume equated to a scream of pain, but she hoped so.

The demon turned into a miniature green tower shaped according to the uncouth architectural notions of some inferior race. A force surrounding it tugged at the sword as if the keep were a magnet and the conjured weapon, forged of steel. Quenthel found it easy to compensate for the pull. She slashed away chunks of masonry.

The tower opened lengthwise like a sarcophagus. It lurched forward, swallowed the sword, and closed up again.

The entity had caught Quenthel by surprise, but she didn't see why it should matter. It might even be more effective to cut and stab her foe from the inside. She used the blade to thrust, felt the point bite, and her psionic link with the weapon snapped.

Startled, she nonetheless reflexively reached for another scroll. The demon spread out into a low, squirming red and yellow mass. A hole dilated in the midst of it, and it spat the sword out. The weapon retained its shape but rippled with shifting colors just as the intruder did, and Quenthel still couldn't feel it with her mind.

She backed away, the blade followed, and, rattling and growling, the demon brought up the rear. The sword swept back and forth, up and down, while she ducked and dodged. So far, she was evading it, but it hampered and hurt her simply by being near. Her mail turned to moss and crumbled away. Her flesh throbbed with sudden pains as the demon's power sought to transform it. One leg turned numb and immobile for a second, and she nearly fell. Itchy scales grew on her skin then faded away. Her eyes ached, the world blurred to black, white, and gray, and the colors exploded back into view. Her identity itself was in flux. For one instant, she thought the thoughts and felt the soft, alien emotions of an arthritic human seamstress dwelling somewhere in the World Above.

Somehow, despite all such disconcerting phenomena, she managed to read the spell on the scroll and avoid the radiant blade at the same time.

She wasn't sure how this particular parchment had found its way to Arach-Tinilith. She questioned that a dark elf had scribed it, for it contained a spell that few drow ever cast. Indeed, some priestesses would disdain to cast it, because it invoked a force regarded as anathema to their faith. But Quenthel knew the goddess would want her to use any weapon necessary to vanquish her foe, and it was remotely possible that this magic would prevail where even the supposedly invincible black blade had failed.

Bright, intricate harmonies sang from the empty air. A field of bluish phosphorescence sprang up around her. Within it, she could make out intangible geometric forms revolving around one another in complex symmetrical patterns.

The cool radiance expressed the power of order, of law, the antithesis of chaos. The sword that had become an extension of the demon's will froze inside it like an insect in amber—and the demon was equally still. For a moment, at least. The creature began hitching ever so slightly forward, working itself loose of the restricting magic.

The Mistress of Arach-Tinilith was essentially a creature of chaos as well, but mortal and native to the material plane, and thus the spell had no power over her. She wheeled and dashed to the body lying in the doorway. Only the spider part of it was moving, chewing and slurping on the rest.

The dead girl turned out to be Halavin Symryvvin, who'd had the surprisingly good sense to remove all that gaudy, clinking jewelry before attempting to attack by surprise. The novice had managed the arbalest rather deftly, considering her sore, mutilated hands.

Quenthel stooped to pick up the weapon and the quiver containing the rest of the enchanted quarrels. She moved warily, but the feasting arachnid paid her no mind.

She turned, laid a dart in the channel, and shot. When the shaft hit it, the demon shuddered in its nearly immobile form, but didn't die.

It occurred to her that she could get away from it while it was trapped, muster any loyal minions who hadn't partaken of the poisoned supper, and fight the thing at the head of a company, just as she'd originally intended. After the harrowing events of the past minutes, the idea had a certain appeal.

But after what she'd endured, she wanted to be the one to teach this vermin a lesson about molesting the clergy of Lolth. Besides, the appearance of strength was vital. So she kept shooting as fast as the cocking action of the weapon would allow. The demon inched its way toward her as if it was made of half-cooled magma.

Four bolts left, then three. She pulled the trigger, the dart struck the demon in the middle of its horned, triangular head, and it winked out of existence.

She could still hear its voice, but knew that was just because it had shrieked so long and loudly. She gave her head a shake, trying to quell the phantom sound, then glimpsed yet another shadow watching her from some distance away.

"You!" she shouted, cocking the arbalest to receive the penultimate quarrel. "Come here!"

The other dark elf bolted. Quenthel gave chase, but she was still a little winded from the struggle with the demon, and her quarry outdistanced her and disappeared.

The Baenre stalked on through the labyrinthine chambers and corridors until she rounded a bend and came face to face with three of her minions. The goddess only knew what their true sentiments were, but confronted with her leveled arbalest and the obvious fact that, while her gear was much the worse for wear, she herself was unscathed, they hastily saluted.

"I killed tonight's intruder," she said, "and a homegrown enemy as well. What do you know of our situation? Is anyone else dead?"

"No, Mistress," said a priestess. The lowered visor of her spider-crested helmet completely concealed her features, but from her voice, Quenthel recognized Quave, one of the senior instructors. "Most of those who ate and drank the tainted meal are waking. I think the poisoner only wanted to render us unconscious, not kill us."

"Apparently," said Quenthel, "she was willing to let the demon administer the coup de grâce to me. What of those who encountered the entity before I did?"

Quave hesitated, then said, "When they tried to hinder it, it hurt them, but not to the point of death. They should recover as well."

"Good," Quenthel said, though she took no joy in knowing she was the unknown enemy's sole target.

"What are your orders, Mistress?" asked Quave.

"We'll have to sort out the living from the dead, and deal with each accordingly. We'll also look for the place where the demon got in, and seal it."

These were tasks that would doubtless keep her occupied for the rest of the night, but she knew she had to find a way to stop the intrusions, and pull the fangs of another crisis as well.

It would all for make an arduous day's labor, with the outcome uncertain enough to depress even a high priestess. Still, her mood lifted slightly when her vipers began to stir.

"I have a healing potion," said Ryld. He took a small pewter vial from his pouch, unstoppered it, and held it to Pharaun's lips. The wizard drank the liquid down.

"That might be a little better," Pharaun said after a moment. "But it's still bad. I'm still bleeding. On the inside, too, I think. Do you have any more?"

"No."

"Pity. A wretched little goblin did this. I can't believe it."

"Can you walk?" asked Ryld.

Pharaun would have to move or be moved, somehow. He couldn't just lie in the street, not in the Braeryn, not on a night when the hunt was out. It was far too dangerous.

"Possibly." The mage strained to lift himself up with his hands, then slumped back down. "But apparently not."

"I'll carry you," said Ryld.

He gathered the mage in his arms, and bidding Pharaun do the same, called upon the magic of his House insignia. They floated slowly upward, and swung onto a rooftop.

The view from that vantage point was far from encouraging. Screaming undercreatures ran through the streets and alleys of the Braeryn with whooping riders in pursuit. The dark elves killed the goblins with the thrust of a lance, the slash of a sword, or simply by trampling them under the clawed feet of their lizards. They tended to find intimate mayhem more amusing. Some, however, had no qualms about loosing a quarrel or conjuring a blast of magic.

Still other drow wheeled above the scene on foulwings, wyverns, and other winged mounts. Ryld saw danger on every side.

He hauled Pharaun up against a sort of gable in the hope that it would provide cover against the scrutiny of the flyers.

"It's bad," the swordsman said. "A lot of drow are hunting. There's no clear path out of the district."

The wizard didn't reply.

"Pharaun!"

"Yes," sighed his friend, "I'm still conscious. Barely."

"We'll hide here until the hunt ends. I'll cover us with a patch of darkness."

"That might w—"

Pharaun gasped and thrashed. Ryld held on to him for fear that he'd roll off the roof.

When the seizure ended, the Mizzrym's face seemed gaunt and drawn in a way it hadn't been before. More blood seeped from his wounded stomach.

"This isn't going to work," said Ryld, "not by itself. Unless you have some more healing, you're going to die."

"That would be . . . a profound tragedy . . . but . . ."

"We have plenty of dark elves in the Braeryn tonight. One of them surely brought some restorative magic along. I'll just have to take it from him, or her. Here's that darkness."

Ryld touched the roof and conjured a shadow that covered the Master of Sorcere and not much else. With luck, the effect was localized enough that no one would notice the obscuration itself.

The weapons master rose and raced away. Whenever possible, he ran along the rooftops, bounding from one to the next. Often enough, however, the houses were far enough apart that he had to jump down to the ground and skulk his way through the slaughter.

It was at such a time that he saw another hunting party. Unfortunately, the group was too large to tackle. He had to hide from it instead. Crouched low, he watched a mage on lizard-back lob a yellow spark through the window of one of the houses. Booming, yellow flame exploded through the room beyond. A moment after it died, the screaming began. Ryld winced. As a child of six, he'd survived precisely such a massacre, and, severely blistered, lain trapped for hours beneath a weight of charred, stinking bodies, the luckier ones dead, the live ones whimpering and twitching in their helpless agony.

But it wasn't him burned nor buried tonight, and he spat the unpleasant memory away. He glanced about, checking to see if anyone was looking at him, then broke from cover and floated upward.

He dashed on along a steeply sloping roof engraved with web patterns and defaced, he noticed, with another slave race emblem. He sensed something above and behind him, and pivoted. His boots slipped, and he levitated for an instant while he found his footing amid the carvings.

He looked up and spied a huge black horse galloping through the air as easily as the common equines of the World Above could run across a field. Fire crackled around its hooves and pulsed from its nostrils. The dark elf male on its back held a scimitar, but wasn't making any extraordinary effort to lift it into position for a cut. Apparently he was counting on his demonic steed to make the kill, and why not? What goblinoid could withstand a nightmare?

Ryld froze as if he were such a hapless undercreature paralyzed with fear. Meanwhile, he timed the speed of the nightmare's approach. At the last possible moment, hoping to take the phantom horse and its master by surprise, he whipped Splitter out of its scabbard and cut.

And missed. Somehow the demon arrested its charge, and the blade fell short.

Its fiery hooves churning eighteen inches above the rooftop, the nightmare snorted. Thick, hot, sulfurous smoke streamed from its nostrils, enveloping Ryld, stinging and half blinding him. He heard more than saw the black creature lunging, striking with its reptilian fangs, and he retreated a step. The move saved him, but when he counterattacked, the nightmare too had taken itself out of range.

Through the stinking vapor, he glimpsed the infernal horse circling. It sprang at him again, this time rearing to batter him with its front hooves. He crouched and lifted Splitter. The point took the steed in the chest, and for a moment, he thought he'd disposed of it, but, its legs working frantically, it flew upward, lifting itself off the blade before it could penetrate too deeply.

The next few seconds were difficult. Ryld could barely make out his foes, while the nightmare could apparently see through its own smoke perfectly well. He stood and turned precariously on the crest of the roof, in constant danger of losing his balance, whereas the flying horse could maneuver wherever it pleased. Just to make life even more interesting, the rider started swinging his curved sword. Fortunately, like most denizens of the Underdark, he had little notion of how to fight on horseback, but his clumsy strokes still posed a danger.

Ryld wanted to end the confrontation quickly, before someone discovered Pharaun's hiding place. Unfortunately, in light of all his disadvantages, the weapons master thought the only way of doing that was to take a risk. The next time the demon reared, he let one of the blazing hooves slam him in the chest.

His dwarven breastplate rang but held. The blow hurt cruelly but didn't break any ribs or otherwise incapacitate him. He fell backward, banged down on the east pitch of the roof, and started to tumble. Kicking and scrabbling, negating his weight, he managed to catch himself and twist around into a low fighting stance.

The nightmare was rushing in to finish him off. He swung Splitter, and this time the demon was too committed to the attack to halt its forward momentum. The greatsword slashed through its neck, nearly severing the head with its luminous scarlet eyes. The steed toppled sideways and rolled, leaving a trail of embers. The rider tried to jump free, but he was too slow. The nightmare crushed him on its way to the ground.

Ryld tore open the dead male's purse, then floated down to the demon horse and checked the saddlebags. There were no potions or any other means of mending a wound.

Why, he wondered, should he expect to find such a thing among the noble's effects? The noble had come to the Braeryn for some lighthearted sport. He hadn't believed the goblins couldn't hurt him or that he was in any other danger, so why bring a remedy for grievous harm to the festivities, even if he was lucky enough to possess one?

There were only five hunters who'd come there with a deadly serious purpose, prepared to cross swords with formidable foes: Greyanna and her retainers. They were far more likely to carry healing magic than any other drow whom Ryld might opt to waylay.

Alas, they were likely to prove more trouble as well, but if he wanted to save Pharaun, he'd just have to cope. Pharaun was a useful ally, and Ryld was unwilling to let that carefully nurtured relationship expire easily. He skulked on, ignoring the hunters who obliviously crossed his path, until he finally spied a familiar figure on a rooftop just ahead of him.

Still masked, one of Greyanna's twin warriors was stalking along that eminence. An arrow nocked, he peered down into the street below.

Ryld threw himself down behind a stubby little false minaret on his roof. He peered around it, looking for the rest of the would-be murderers.

He didn't see them. Maybe the band had split up, the better to look for their quarry. They'd have to, wouldn't they, to oversee the entire district.

He ducked back, cocked his hand crossbow and laid a poisoned dart in the channel. He and Pharaun had been reluctant to kill their pursuers, but with the wizard dying, Ryld was no longer overly concerned with a petty retainer's life.

He leaned back around, his finger already tightening on the trigger—and the space where the archer had stood was empty. Ryld cast about, and after a moment spotted the male atop a round, flat-roofed little tower adhering to the main body of the building.

That posed two problems. One was that the warrior was farther away and ten feet higher up, at or beyond the limit of the little crossbow's range. The other was that the male happened to be looking in Ryld's direction. His eyes flew open wide when he spotted his quarry.

Ryld shot, and his dart fell short of the tower. A split second later, the twin pulled back his bowstring and loosed his arrow in one fluid motion. The shaft looked like a gradually swelling dot, which meant it was speeding straight at its target.

Ryld dodged back. The arrow whizzed past, and the archer shouted, "Here! I've got him here!"

The weapons master scowled, feeling the pressure of passing time even more acutely than before. He didn't want to be there when the rest of the enemy arrived, and the only hope of avoiding it was to dispose of his present opponent quickly. The longbow simply had his hand crossbow outclassed. He needed to get in close.

He drew Splitter, sprang out into the open, and strode toward his foe. The archer sent one arrow after another winging his way, and he knocked them out of the air. The defense was considerably more difficult advancing across the irregular surface of the roof than it would have been standing still on the ground.

Ryld began to sweat, and his heart beat faster, but he was managing. There came another shaft, this one aglitter with some form of enchantment, and he swatted it down. Rattling, it rolled on down the pitch of the roof.

He took another step, slapped aside another missile, then heard something—he didn't know what, just an indefinable change in the sounds around him. He remembered that some enchanters created magical weapons capable of more than flying truer and hitting harder.

He spun around. The sparkling arrow had launched itself back into the air and circled around behind him. It was streaking toward its target and was only a few feet from his body.

Ryld wrenched Splitter across in a desperate parry. The edge caught the arrow and split it in two. Spinning through the air, the piece with the point hit his shoulder, but, thanks to his armor, did him no harm.

He lurched back around with barely enough time to deflect the next shaft, then marched on. Four more paces brought him to the end of the roof.

The gap between this house and the next was five yards across. He took a running start, made himself nearly weightless, and jumped. The twin tried to hit when he was in the air, but for a blessed change, his arrow flew wild. Ryld thumped down atop the same structure his opponent occupied. It felt as if it had taken forever to get this far, even though he knew it had really been less than a minute.

Not that he was done running the gauntlet. The arrows kept hurtling at him, including one that gave an eerie scream, filling him with an unnatural fear until he quashed the feeling, and another that turned into a miniature harpy in flight. Yet another struck two paces in front him and exploded into a curtain of fire. Squinting at the glare, he wrapped his *piwafwi* around him and dived through, emerging singed but essentially unscathed.

After that, he was close enough to the tower to cancel most of his weight and leap up to the top. He sprang into the air like a jumping spider and alit on the platform. The twin hastily set down his bow and drew his scimitar.

"Do you have any healing magic?" Ryld asked. "If so, give it to me, and I'll let you go."

The other warrior smiled unpleasantly and said, "My comrades will start arriving any second. Surrender now, tell me where Pharaun is, and perhaps Princess Greyanna will let you live."

"No."

Ryld cut at the warrior's head. The other male jumped back out of range, sidestepped, and slashed at the weapons master's arm. Ryld parried, beat the scimitar aside, and the fight was on.

Over the course of the next few seconds, the Mizzrym warrior gave ground consistently. Twice, he nearly stepped off the flat, round tabletop that was the apex of the tower but on both occasions spun himself away from the edge in time. He was a good duelist, and he was fighting defensively while he waited for reinforcements to arrive. That made him hard to hit. Hard, but not impossible.

Pressing, Ryld feinted high on the inside to draw the parry, swung his greatsword down and around, and cut low on the outside. Splitter sheared into the Mizzrym's torso just below the ribs, and he collapsed in a gush of blood.

Magic trilled and flickered through the air. When Ryld spun around, the other twin and Relonor popped into being on the rooftop below. Obviously, House Mizzrym's mage could teleport on his own, without the aid of the brooch Pharaun had pilfered.

His voluminous sleeves sliding down to his elbows, Relonor lifted his arms and started to cast a spell. The newly arrived twin nocked an arrow and drew back the string of his pale bone bow.

Ryld threw himself down on his stomach. He was ten feet above his adversaries, and he hoped that they couldn't see him. Sure enough, no magic or arrow flew in his direction. He scuttled across the platform—

enchantments in his armor deadening the sound of his footfalls—and grabbed his previous opponent's bow and quiver, then scrambled to his knees.

The twin and the wizard rose above the platform, the former levitating, the latter soaring in an arc that revealed some magical capacity for actual flight. The archer loosed an arrow, and mystical energy flashed from Relonor's fingertips.

The Mizzrym's magic reached its target first. A ghastly shriek stabbed through Ryld's ears and into his brain. He cried out and flailed in agony. The warrior's arrow plunged into his thigh, and the razor-edged point burst from the other side.

After a moment, the screaming stopped. Ryld could feel that it had hurt him, perhaps worse than the arrow had, but had no time or inclination to fret about it. Quickly as few folk save a master of Melee-Magthere could manage, he loosed two shafts of his own.

The first took Relonor in the chest, and the second stabbed into the warrior's belly. They both dropped down out of sight.

Ryld looked at the twin with the sword cut in his flank. The male appeared to be unconscious, which would facilitate searching him. Ryld hobbled over to him to rifle his pockets and the leather satchel he wore on his belt.

Blessedly, he found four silver vials, each marked with the rune for healing. Greyanna had indeed outfitted her agents properly for a martial expedition. It was the twin's misfortune that he hadn't had time to drink of her bounty before going into shock.

His brother and Relonor no doubt carried healing draughts as well, and Ryld had no guarantee that they'd be unable to use them. They might come after him again any second, and he'd just as soon avoid a second round. He needed to beat a hasty—

Enormous wings beat the air. A long-necked, legless beast passed overhead with Greyanna and the other priestess, the skinny one, astride its back. Glaring down at Ryld, Pharaun's sister pulled at the laces securing the mouth of her bag of monsters.

Ryld dumped the remaining arrows out of the quiver, the better to examine them. One was fletched with red feathers while the rest had black.

He'd already seen his first foe shoot one fire arrow. Praying that the red-fletched arrow was another, he drew back his bowstring and sent it hurtling into the air.

The arrow plunged into the sack, and burst into flame. The scarred high priestess reflexively dropped the bag, and it fell, burning as it went. The magic spores combusting inside turned the fire green, then blue, then violet.

Greyanna screamed in fury and sent the foulwing swooping lower. Ryld looked for another magic arrow and found that none were left. He nocked an ordinary one, and his hands began to shake, no doubt an aftereffect of the punishment he'd taken.

For a moment, it seemed to him that he was finished. If he couldn't shoot accurately, he couldn't hit one of the foulwing's vital spots, or the riders on its back, for that matter. Nor was he in any shape to fight them hand to hand.

Then he realized he still had a chance. He surrounded his arrow with a cloud of murky darkness, then shot it upward.

The descending beast was a huge target. Even shooting blind with trembling hands, he had a fair chance of hitting in somewhere, and the foulwing gave a double shriek that told him he'd succeeded.

He watched the mass of darkness he'd created tumble and zigzag drunkenly through the air. Stung, suddenly and inexplicably sightless, the winged mount inside had panicked, and Greyanna was evidently unable to control it. She quite possibly could have dissolved the darkness with some scroll or talisman, but she couldn't see either or lay hands on her equipment easily with the foulwing lurching and swooping about beneath her.

Ryld snapped the head off the arrow in his leg and pulled the offending object out. He gathered up the healing potions, and quickly as he was able, activated the magic in his talisman, floated down off the roof, and limped away.

chapter

T H I R T E E N

As Quenthel skulked down the corridor, it occurred to her that at the same time, Gromph was casting his radiant heat into the base of Narbondel. Even revelers and necromancers were settling in for a rest. She, however, was too busy to do the same. She wouldn't have a chance to relax until late the next night, unless, of course, she wound up resting forever.

Fortunately, one of the Baenre alchemists brewed a stimulant to delay the onset of the aching eyes, fuzzy head, and leaden limbs that lack of rest produced. Quenthel extracted a silver vial of the stuff from one of the pouches on her belt and took a sip of it. She gasped, and her shoulder muscles jumped. Jolted back to alertness, she continued on her way.

In another minute, she reached the door to Drisinil's quarters. In deference to the status of her family, the novice resided in one of Arach-Tinilith's most comfortable student habitations. Quenthel regretted not sticking her in a dank little hole. Perhaps then the girl would have learned her place.

The high priestess inspected the arched limestone panel that was the door. She couldn't see any magical wards.

"Is it safe?" she whispered to the vipers.

"We believe so," Yngoth replied.

How reassuring, Quenthel thought, but it was either trust them or use another precious, irreplaceable scroll to wipe away protections that probably didn't exist.

She activated the power of her brooch. When a novice came to Arach-Tinilith, the enchantments on certain doors were keyed to allow her to enter, based on the unique magical signature of her House insignia, rooms the high priestesses deemed it necessary for her to pass into. Only Quenthel's brooch could unlock them all.

She unlocked Drisinil's door and warily cracked it open. No magic sparked, nor did any mechanical trap jab a blade at her. As quietly as she could, Quenthel crept on into the suite. Sensing her desire for quiet, the snakes hung mute and limp.

She found Drisinil sitting motionless in a chair, her bandaged, mutilated hands in her lap. For a moment, Quenthel, thinking the other female must have a dauntless spirit to enter the Reverie at such a perilous time, rather admired her—then she caught the smell of brandy, and noticed the bottle lying in a puddle of liquor on the floor.

Quenthel stalked toward the novice. It occurred to her that she was doing to Drisinil as the living darkness had done to her. The thought vaguely amused her, perhaps simply because she was finally the predator, not the prey. Smiling, she gently laid the vipers across the other drow's face and upper torso. The snakes hissed and writhed.

Drisinil roused with a cry and a start. She started to rear up, and Quenthel pushed her back down in her chair.

"Sit!" the Baenre snapped, "or the serpents will bite."

Her wide eyes framed by the cool, scaly loops of the vipers, Drisinil stopped struggling.

"Mistress, what's wrong?"

Quenthel smiled and said, "Very good, child, you sound sincere. After your first ploy failed, you should at the very least have rested elsewhere."

"I don't know what you mean."

Drisinil's hand shifted stealthily, no doubt toward a hidden weapon or charm. The vipers struck at the student's face, their fangs missing her sharp-nosed features by a fraction of an inch. She froze.

"Please," Quenthel said. "This will go easier if you don't insult my intelligence. You have spirit, you believe I punished you too harshly, and you're Barrison Del'Armgo, eager to bring down the one House standing between your family and supremacy. Of course you're involved in the plot against me. You're also an idiot if you didn't think I'd realize it."

"Plot?"

Quenthel sighed. "Halavin tried to kill me last night, and she didn't act alone. A single traitor couldn't have drugged all the food and drink set out at various points around the temple. It would have required abandoning her station for long enough that someone would have marked her absence."

"Halavin could have tainted the meal while it was still in the kitchen."

"She was never there."

"Then perhaps the demon poisoned the viands with its magic."

"No. As I'm sure you noted, each spirit represents *one* of the facets of reality over which the goddess holds special dominion. Poison is the weapon of an assassin, while with its continually fluctuating form, last night's assailant was plainly a manifestation of chaos.

"The conspirators," Quenthel continued, "had to contaminate each and every table because they didn't know where I would stop and eat. Many fell unconscious, but you and the other plotters knew not to sample the repast."

Drisinil said, "I had no part in it."

"Novice, you're beginning to irritate me. Admit your guilt, or I'll give you to the vipers and interrogate someone else." The serpents hissed and flicked their tongues.

"All right," said Drisinil, "I was involved. A little. The others talked me into it. Don't kill me."

"I know what your little cabal has done, but I want to understand how you *dared*."

Drisinil swallowed and said, "You . . . you said it yourself. Each demon seeks to kill only you, and each in its own particular way reflects the divine majesty of Lolth. We thought she sent them. We thought we were doing what the goddess wanted."

"Because you're imbeciles. Has no one taught you to look beyond appearances? If Lolth wanted me dead, I couldn't survive her displeasure for a heartbeat, let alone three nights. The attacks resemble her doing because some blasphemous mortal arranged it so, to manipulate you into doing her killing for her. I'd hoped you conspirators knew the trickster's identity, but I see it isn't so."

"No."

"*Curse you all!*" Quenthel exploded. "The goddess favors *me*. How could you possibly doubt it? I'm a Baenre, the Mistress of Arach-Tinilith, and I rose to the rank of high priestess more quickly that any Menzoberranyr ever has!"

"I know . . ." The novice hesitated, then said, "The Mother of Lusts must have some reason for distancing herself from the city, and we . . . speculated."

"Some of you did, I'm sure. Others simply liked the idea of eliminating me. I imagine your Aunt Molvayas would relish seeing me dead. She'd have an excellent chance of becoming mistress in her turn. We Baenre don't have another princess seasoned enough to assume the role."

"It *was* my aunt!" Drisinil exclaimed. "She came up with the idea of helping the demons kill you. I didn't even want to help. I thought it was a stupid idea, but within our family, she holds authority over me."

Quenthel smiled. "It's too bad you weren't more impressed with my authority."

"I'm sorry."

"No doubt that. Now, I need the names of all the conspirators."

Drisinil didn't hesitate an instant. "My aunt, Vlondril Tuin'Tarl . . ."

As ever, Quenthel maintained a calm, knowing expression, but inwardly she was surprised at the number of conspirators. An eighth of the temple! It was unprecedented, but then she was living in unprecedented times.

When Drisinil finished, the Baenre said, "Thank you. Where did you gather to hatch your schemes?"

"One of the unused storerooms in the fifth leg," Drisinil said.

Quenthel shook her head. "That won't do. It's not big enough. Convene the group in Lirdnolu's old classroom. Nobody's used it since she had her throat slit, so it will seem a safe meeting place."

Drisinil blinked. "Convene?"

"Yes. Last night's plot failed, so obviously you must hatch a new one. You've chosen a new chamber for the conference because you suspect the storeroom is no longer safe. Say whatever you need to say to assemble your cabal in four hours' time."

"If I do, will you spare me?"

"Why not? As you've explained, you only participated reluctantly. But you know, it suddenly occurs to me that we have a problem. If I send you forth to perform this task, how do I know you won't simply flee Tier Breche and take refuge in your mother's castle?"

"Mistress, you already explained that such a course could only lead to my death."

"But did you believe me? Do you still? How can I be sure?"

"Mistress . . . I . . ."

"If I had my magic, I could compel you to do as you're told, but in its absence, I must take other measures."

Quenthel raised the whip, sweeping the vipers off Drisinil's face in the process, and slammed the metal butt of the weapon down in the middle of her forehead.

The mistress then took out the silver vial. She pinched the dazed, feebly struggling girl's nostrils closed, poured the stimulant into her open mouth, and forced her to swallow.

The effect was immediate. The younger female bucked and thrashed until her eyes flew open.

The high priestess hopped back down to the floor. "How does it feel? I imagine your heart is hammering."

Drisinil trembled like the string of a viol. Sweat seeped from her pores. "What did you do to me?"

"That should be obvious to an accomplished poisoner like yourself."

"You've poisoned me?"

"It's a slow toxin. Do as I ordered, and I'll give you the antidote."

"I can't cozen the others like this. They'll see something's wrong with me."

"The external signs should ease in a minute or two, though you'll still feel the poison speeding your heart and gnawing at your nerves. You'll just have to put up with that."

"All right," Drisinil said. "Just bring the antidote with you when you come to Lirdnolu's room."

The mistress arched an eyebrow, and Drisinil added, "Please."

Quenthel smiled. Catching her mood, the whip vipers sighed with pleasure.

"How did you know your darkness would madden the beast?" asked Pharaun, lathering his narrow chest.

The night before, after he made way back to Pharaun, the two of them had found they had enough healing potions to cure all the wounds that either had sustained. Still, despite their restoration to full vitality, the next few hours proved exhausting, as they struggled to survive the madness of the hunt and watch out for Greyanna at the same time. At last they'd escaped the Braeryn.

Claiming that while Greyanna was seeking them in the Stenchstreets, they'd be safe in pleasant, prosperous Narbondellyn, Pharaun had insisted that he and Ryld dispense with disguises and celebrate their sundry discoveries and escapes with a visit to one of Menzoberranzan's finest public baths. The warrior had objected to what he saw as reckless bravado, but not too vehemently. Ryld supposed that he and Pharaun would climb beyond their foes' reach soon enough. The prospect made him feel rather wistful.

Over the course of the past few minutes, he'd been enjoying the luxury of scrubbing off the sweat and grime that had accumulated on his person, sitting down, and thinking about nothing in particular. He should have known the peace and quiet couldn't last for long. Pharaun couldn't go long without craving conversation.

"How did you know that, shrouded in darkness or no, the foulwing wouldn't just keep descending, guided by its other senses?" the wizard persisted.

The warrior shrugged and said, "I didn't know, but it seemed like a good guess. The thing's an animal, isn't it?"

Pharaun grinned. "Not really. It's a creature from another plane. Still, your instincts were sound."

Ryld shrugged and replied, "I was lucky to get away from there with my life. Very lucky."

"Fire and glare, you're a master of Tier Breche. You're not supposed to be modest. Are you ready to move?"

They rose from an octagonal pool set in the black marble floor, and, having completed the quotidian business of cleaning themselves, headed for a larger basin where they would luxuriate in steaming, scented mineral water. Later in the day, it would be packed, but it wasn't fashionable to visit the baths so early in the morning. They had it to themselves, which was convenient. They could converse without fear of eavesdroppers.

Ryld walked straight down the steps and sat on the underwater ledge. The warmth felt good on his leg, mended but still a little sore, and he sighed with contentment. Pharaun made a production of immersing himself in stages, an inch at a time, as if the heat were almost more than he could bear.

"I've been thinking about your malaise," the wizard said, once everything but his head was finally submerged. "I have a solution."

"What do you mean?"

"Resign from Melee-Magthere and become the weapons master of a noble House. It will have to be one of the lesser ones, of course, you being a commoner, but that's all right. You may see more excitement that way."

"Why would I do that? It's not a move up. It might not be a loss of rank, depending on the House, but still, what would be the point?"

"You're bored, and it would be a change."

"One that would put me under the thumb of any number of high priestesses. I'd have less autonomy than I do as an instructor."

"I managed to pursue my own objectives while under my mother's supervision. Still, you make a legitimate point. You might find yourself abhorring the tug of the reins. What's the answer, then?"

"Who says there is one? Except, perhaps, further lunatic holidays with you. I admit, this one broke the tedium."

A diminutive female gnome carried a pile of freshly laundered and folded towels out of a doorway on the far wall. Ryld wondered if she was one of the Prophet's followers, and if she had any of the rabble-rouser's duergar firepots stashed somewhere in the bathhouse. It felt strange to think of a humble undercreature that way—wielding stone-burning bombs against its betters.

"You speak of our errand in the past tense," the wizard said.

"Well, once you tell the archmage the runaways are in the Braeryn fomenting a pitiful little goblin uprising, it'll be over, won't it? Gromph will pardon your transgressions. The Council, having failed to stop our inquiries, will, I trust, see no point in continuing to try to kill us. It'll be more to their advantage to let us go on training wizards and soldiers to serve them."

"You're very certain the insurrection will be pitiful. Is it because Greyanna's followers exterminated so many undercreatures last night?"

Ryld scooped up a handful of hot water and splashed it on his neck, which had gotten a little stiff from his exertions.

"No," he said. "The hunters killed plenty of goblins, but they were only a fraction of a fraction of the creatures jammed into every nook and cranny of the district—you saw the interior of Smylla's home. Trust me, you still don't really understand."

"I understand that many other such specimens inhabit the rest of the city as well. Why, then, do you doubt their ability to do some appreciable damage? It can't be for want of spirit. The underfolk are in an excellent humor, enflamed by their Prophet's oratory, painting their racial emblems hither and yon, and murdering potential informers and unbelievers."

"They still lack martial training and proper weapons."

"Some were warriors before the slavers captured them. Some are thrall soldiers still. As for the arms, well, when visiting the World Above, did you ever see a city burn? I did. I had to torch one myself to complete a mission. The destruction and loss of life were impressive, even though the inhabitants knew their buildings could catch fire and had procedures for dealing with it."

"Whereas we don't? Surely you wizards . . . ?"

Pharaun shrugged. "Not really. Why would it occur to us? Perhaps we could improvise something, but if we didn't catch the conflagration early, it might not be entirely effective."

"But you would catch it early. The undercreatures won't rebel all at once, and that will make it possible to quash each little uprising as it begins."

"You're assuming 'the Call,' whatever it is, will pass by word of mouth, or at any rate, that it won't be disseminated rapidly. You could be right. The noise baffles may hinder it, but what if the Prophet has some arcane means of rousing every goblin and bugbear at the exact same instant?"

"Do you know of such a magic?"

"No."

"And you're a Master of Sorcere. So it's reasonable to assume no such power exists."

Pharaun arched an eyebrow. "Indeed? Thank you for your expert opinion."

Ryld made a spitting sound and said, "Look. You think a rebellion could amount to something. I disagree, but say you're right. Isn't that all the more reason to report to Gromph immediately?"

The wizard waved to a goblin slave who was sauntering by. "The difficulty is that I have yet to succeed."

"What?"

"My assignment is to find the runaways. I glimpsed two of them for a matter of minutes, then lost them. Do you think the Baenre will deem that satisfactory?"

Frowning, Ryld said, "Considering that we did uncover something of interest . . ."

"Remember, our great and glorious archmage doesn't hold me in high esteem. He sent me out as a decoy, a target for the priestesses to harass. Knowing him as I do, I'm sure that if I fulfill the letter of our agreement, he'll swallow his dislike and keep his end, but should I fall the least bit short, it will be a different matter."

"You can at least tell him the rogues are in the Braeryn."

"Can I? We sifted through the Stenchstreets as well as any outsiders could. We didn't find the house where the runaways hang their cloaks, and we actually have only the flimsiest of reasons for assuming it's in the Braeryn at all."

"I suppose you're right."

"Of course. When am I not? Now, here's what I intend to do: Find the rogues' hiding place. Discover who the Prophet is and how his wizardry— or whatever it is—works. Learn where the firepots came from, where they're cached around the city, and the master plan for the rebellion. And most importantly of all, determine what the fugitives know about the clergy losing its magic."

"In hopes of coming out of this affair more powerful than you ever were before."

Pharaun grinned. "More powerful than *we* ever were before. That might dispel your boredom for good and all."

"And those are the real reasons you aren't ready to go back to Tier Breche."

"All my motives are genuine, including my wariness of Gromph. I take it you *are* in a frantic hurry to return?"

Ryld sighed. "I'm in no rush. Our excursion has been interesting, and I like to finish what I start, but what if the orcs rebel before we get around to warning our fellow drow?"

"Then we'll make sure never to tell anyone we knew it was coming." The wizard grinned and added, "Actually, the awareness that we race to avert a calamity will make our exploits all the more stimulating."

"And should we lose the race, maybe the rebellion won't kill anyone who matters to the two of us. I suppose I agree. We'll keep on searching."

"Excellent!"

Bearing a silver tray, the goblin bustled to the side of the pool. Bending the knees of his splayed, bristly legs, he brought the salver low enough for the dark elves to take the goblets on top of it.

Pharaun gave the thrall a smile and a wave, dismissing him, then lifted his cup.

"To mystery and glory!"

Ryld sipped from his own cup, acknowledging the toast. The drink was red morel juice, sweet and very cold, a pleasant contrast to the heat of the water.

"So I guess it's back to looking like orcs," said the weapons master.

"I grieve to disappoint you, but the time for that sort of deception has passed."

"What do you mean? If we don't look like undercreatures, how are we going to get into another one of those secret meetings?"

"We don't know that the Prophet will hold another assembly. He's already explained his strategy and distributed his secret weapon. Even if he does, it might not be for several days, during which we'll have Greyanna seeking us relentlessly. We've evaded her so far, but we must acknowledge the possibility that our luck could sour eventually."

"You're right about that."

"Therefore, we need to find the rogues quickly, which means a change of tactics is in order. Why are the boys trying to instigate a goblin revolt?"

"I don't know."

"Nor do I, really. It doesn't appear to make sense. Still, would you agree that the intent, like the act of eloping itself, reflects an antipathy to the established order?"

"Possibly."

"Then let's assume the Prophet or some other ringleader lured the males away from their homes because he knew they were more than ordinarily resentful of their places in the world."

"It's possible. Where does the notion lead?"

The wizard grinned and said, "If we demonstrate that we share their distemper, the rogues may recruit us as well."

"How can we do that? We may not be clerics, but we're Masters of the Academy. We're pillars of the hierarchy, and more to the point, we have a pleasanter lot and thus less reason for discontent than most."

"That doesn't seem to slow you down."

"Even so."

"Here's what you're overlooking. Thanks to my misadventure with the Sarthos demon, I'm a *disgraced* master, likely in line for some ghastly punishment. Whereas you with your dour demeanor and dwarven armor are clearly an iconoclast and malcontent. Moreover, we've been asking everywhere for news of the runaways. They must know of it, even though they didn't see fit to make contact. During that same time, a high priestess from House Mizzrym has tried to murder us. They surely have some cognizance of that as well."

"Yet they still didn't approach us. Why would they do it now?"

Pharaun smiled. "Because we'll provide proof that we do in fact share their perspective."

"How?"

"The priestesses lead regular patrols through the Bazaar. We'll destroy one, repair to the Braeryn, boast of the deed, and await developments. The rogues will seek us out. How can they not? Whatever their ultimate objective, I'm sure they can use the services of two such talented fellows."

"No doubt, but back up. You want to murder a patrol?"

"In as showy a manner as possible. With a bit of planning, it should be easy enough. They won't be as numerous as Greyanna's hunters and they won't be expecting that sort of trouble."

"What happened to not killing anybody, especially clerics, unless we absolutely have to?"

"We do absolutely have to. We're in a race against time, remember, and this is the speediest route to our objective."

"Maybe, but what happens afterward? Won't any number of folk want to punish us for our impudence?"

"We won't confide our involvement to those likely to prove unsympathetic."

"The priestesses will figure it out."

"Ah, but snug and safe in the lair of our friend the Prophet, we won't care. Besides, the Council has already authorized our annihilation, so we really have nothing to lose."

"Perhaps the crime can't worsen our current situation, but what about the long term?"

"In the long term," Pharaun said, "it won't matter. As you yourself observed mere moments ago, we Menzoberranyr are a pragmatic lot. People forgive whatever outrages I committed yesterday if I make myself useful today."

"Greyanna didn't."

The wizard laughed and replied, "Well, of course, we're likewise prone to grudges, vendettas, and blood feuds. It's one of the paradoxes central to our natures. With luck, though, no one of importance will take our little massacre personally. I doubt we'll be murdering any princesses, or anyone of genuine significance to her family."

"I think it's crazy," Ryld said, shaking his head. "You don't know that the rogues will contact us, or if they'll like what they see if they do."

"Then we'll simply hatch another scheme."

Ryld scowled and shook his head again.

"You're mad," the weapons master said, "but I'm with you."

"Splendid! We must toast our homicidal designs with something stronger than juice." Pharaun looked about and spotted the goblin. "May we see the wine list, please?"

Ryld said, "It's the very beginning of the morning."

"Don't be misled by superficial appearances," Pharaun replied. "As neither of us has enjoyed a moment of repose, it must still be night. Do you think they have any of that '53 Barrison Del'Armgo heartwine?"

chapter

FOURTEEN

Until someone murdered her, Lirdnolu had taught her classes in a sort of indoor amphitheater, one of many architectural oddities scattered through Arach-Tinilith, and as the conspirators slunk in, they seated themselves on the C-shaped tiers.

Drisinil wondered what to say to them, how to stall until Quenthel arrived to confront them. The novice's mind was a blank, but she knew she'd have to think of something. Her mouth was dry and tasted of metal. Her armpits were clammy with sweat, and her accelerated pulse pounded in the stumps of her severed fingers. The poison was obviously well on its way to killing her, and she had to please Quenthel Baenre sufficiently to earn the antidote.

Wrinkled old Vlondril Tuin'Tarl leered at Drisinil as if she knew of the student's distress, but all she said was, "I believe most everyone's here. Let's get this done before our colleagues start missing us."

"Uh, yes," Drisinil said, gazing up at the rows of faces staring back down at her. "Well, mothers, sisters, we all know what happened last night. The vipers in the mistress's whip detected the drugs—"

"So they did," said Quenthel.

Startled, Drisinil spun around. A figure shrouded in a cowled *piwafwi* rose from the first row. She lifted her head, pushed the hood back, and stood revealed as the Mistress of Arach-Tinilith. Somehow she'd entered the room without her enemies realizing her identity.

Quenthel pushed back one wing of her cloak, freeing the arm that held her whip. She sauntered to the center of the room. It occurred to Drisinil that at that moment the plotters could have fallen on their target en masse, but they didn't. The mistress cowed them with her unexpected appearance, her contemptuous demeanor, and the simple fact that she was a Baenre princess.

The mistress smiled at Drisinil and said, "You've done well, novice, except for one detail. It's traditional for priestesses to conduct their affairs by candlelight. That's all right, I've taken care of it." She turned toward the door. "Come."

Two teachers marched in carrying silver candelabra. After a moment, Drisinil, squinting, saw they weren't alone. Many of the residents of Arach-Tinilith filed in after them, all well armed and wearing mail.

Quenthel beckoned to the plotters.

"Move down to the lower seats, why don't you? The latecomers won't mind climbing to the top." She waited a beat, then said, "That wasn't a suggestion."

The conspirators hesitated a moment longer, and the show of force convinced them to obey.

"Thank you," Quenthel said, then waited until everyone had taken a seat and the plotters all had armed loyalists at their backs. "Now, let's discuss the matter that concerns you so."

"I don't know what my niece told you about this gathering," said Drisinil's Aunt Molvayas, clad in a gown of a dark and shimmering green that matched her eyes, "but I assure you, its purpose is entirely innocent."

"Its purpose is to contrive your death, Mistress," Vlondril called out. "I know. I've been in on it from the start."

Quenthel nodded to the mad priestess.

"Thank you, Holy Mother. Your candor helps move things along." The Baenre surveyed her enemies and said, "I understand that your excuse for seeking to depose me was the supposition that the goddess desires it. You postulate that she so abhors my rule of Arach-Tinilith that she renounces all Menzoberranzan."

Molvayas drew a deep breath, evidently screwing up her courage. "We do. Do you deny it's possible?"

"Of course," Quenthel replied. "It's a ludicrous notion unsupported by a single shred of evidence . . . though I'm sure it seems plausible to the lieutenant who covets my position."

Drisinil noticed that while the Baenre appeared perfectly at ease, the twisting whip serpents were keeping watch in all directions.

"What of the demons? They reflect the attributes of Lolth—"

"And they come for me. Because one of my mortal enemies sends them in guises intended to stimulate your imaginations."

"What enemy?" Molvayas demanded.

"That has yet to be determined."

"In other words," said Quenthel's second-in-command, "you don't know what's going on any more than we do."

"At least I know what *isn't* happening."

"Do you? What makes your one opinion superior to all of ours?"

"The answer to that is readily apparent to those with some smattering of intelligence."

"Insults won't resolve this matter, Mistress, but I can think of a test that might. Step down for a year, and we'll see what happens."

Quenthel laughed.

"Meekly surrender the Academy to you, Barrison Del'Armgo? Not likely. As it happens, I too have conceived a test to determine who truly enjoys Lolth's favor, your sad little cabal or me."

"What do you mean?" Molvayas asked, wariness in her eyes.

"My test is simplicity itself. We simply ask Lolth whom she prefers, and await her answer."

"That's insane. The Spider Queen no longer speaks to us."

"Perhaps if we petition, she will at least condescend to give us a sign. Are you willing to try?"

"Perhaps," Molvayas said, no doubt aware that with blades at her back, she actually had little choice. "Do you propose to perform some sort of ritual?"

"As we've lost our magic, what would that accomplish? My idea is simpler. We all bide in this room, engaged in silent prayer and meditation, until the Dark Mother reveals her will."

Vlondril snorted. "What if she chooses to ignore us?"

Quenthel shrugged. "I don't believe she's truly abandoned her chosen people or her chosen ministers. My faith is too strong to credit such a calamity. How strong is yours, Barrison Del'Armgo?"

"Strong enough that I have no fear of the goddess preferring you to me," Molvayas spat back. "I just don't see the point of your scheme. Lolth will speak when she wishes, not when we desire it."

"It's not a waste of time if it's keeping you alive. I could have had my loyal followers kill you the moment they entered the chamber. Instead, I'm proposing an honest inquiry into your concerns, for the sake of all the temple. Under the circumstances, what could be more magnanimous than that?"

"All right," Molvayas said. "We'll remain for a time, but if nothing happens, my comrades and I go free. You can't chastise us if the results of the test are inconclusive. That wouldn't be an honest inquiry."

"Agreed," the mistress said.

Drisinil was bewildered and appalled. This strange, passive procedure sounded as if it could take hours. She needed the antidote before her thundering heart tore itself apart, but she could do nothing to speed things along.

Though plainly just as puzzled as she, the company obediently fell quiet. Meditation was a familiar practice to all of them, though frustrating and futile since Lolth had receded beyond their ken.

For what seemed a long while, nothing happened, except that a muscle under Drisinil's eye twitched uncontrollably, and some of those whom she'd betrayed surreptitiously glared at her, wordlessly vowing revenge. A tiny something scurried across the floor. Or perhaps it did. By the time she tried to focus on it, it was gone.

More minutes crawled by. Cloth whispered as someone shifted position. Later, somebody else smothered a little sneeze. Drisinil realized she could just barely smell the ghost of the funereal incense Lirdnolu had burned when teaching necromancy.

Another mite scuttled along. Drisinil saw that this one was a spider. Nothing unusual in that. Arach-Tinilith was full of the sacred creatures.

Still, something about this particular specimen tugged at her despite her sickness and terror. She stared until she discerned that it had a blue shell with red markings.

That was a little odd. This particular species generally spent its time lurking in webs, not roaming about. Still, she didn't see why the anomaly should trigger a twinge of alarm. It must be the poison clawing at her nerves.

Time dragged on. A priestess on the lowest tier sang a hymn under her breath. She was flat. Another novice with mutilated hands surreptitiously checked the knife strapped under her sleeve, making sure the weapon was loose in the sheath. And, Drisinil noticed, more black dots were creeping on the walls and floor. More than were normal for a disused part of the temple? She thought so, and she glanced over at Quenthel, seeking some sign to confirm her formless suspicions. The Baenre stood motionless with head bowed, the very picture of a mystic absorbed in her devotions.

A novice with a gold earring cried out in pain. She dragged on her shirt, baring her right shoulder, and found the spider that was biting her. Her frantic efforts to remove the arachnid without hurting it should have been comical but Drisinil couldn't laugh. Frazzled, addled by the poison, she could only stare at the dark flecks swarming thickly on every side. Some of the other conspirators had started to notice as well. They whispered to one another, and their eyes grew wide.

Something brushed Drisinil's arm. She cried out and spun around. It was one of the Quenthel's vipers that had touched her.

"Stay close," the mistress said.

Once again, the spiders increased in number. Somehow hordes of them were scuttling over the bodies of the conspirators, biting, crawling under their clothing, freckling their skins like the sores of some hideous plague. Shrieking, no longer caring that the creatures were sacrosanct, their victims struggled to crush them and brush them off, but they couldn't get them all. A few of the traitors retained the presence of mind to activate protective talismans, only to discover that the magic didn't help, either.

The one place free of spiders was the upper tiers. Once they realized the creatures weren't going climb up and attack them, the loyalists mocked and jeered at the plight of the traitors. Whenever one of the plotters tried to grope her way into their safe space, a loyalist would knock her back with a casual swat from a mace or whip. Some even shot down with hand cross-bows any conspirator who attempted to stagger for the door.

Drisinil did remain at Quenthel's side, and the spiders crawled over her feet but otherwise took no notice of her. They didn't avoid the Baenre, however. They climbed all over her body without biting, and, laughing, she stooped, picked up more, and poured them over her head until the creatures virtually encrusted her. Her bright red eyes shone from a pebbled, squirming mask.

Finally the shrieking stopped, uncovering the sound of Vlondril ecstatically chanting one of the litanies as the spiders destroyed her. After another moment, that noise ceased as well. Drisinil noticed her aunt's corpse slumped among the carnage, though she only recognized it by the jade gown. Molvayas's face was swollen and bloodied beyond recognition.

Quenthel gazed up at the living and called, "We asked Lolth for a sign, and she gave us one. My foes are dead and I remain, robed in the goddess's sacred spiders. I am the Mistress of Arach-Tinilith, and my minions will question my leadership no more or else die in agony for their effrontery."

The surviving priestesses and novices hastily paid her obeisance.

"Good," the Baenre said. "You are wise, and so I make you a vow. We will put an end to these nightly attacks. We will regain our magic. We will hear Lolth's voice again. We will make our order and our temple greater than ever before. Now, clear away this mess."

The spiders began to disappear, from the room and Quenthel's person as well. Drisinil couldn't quite tell if they were simply scuttling away or teleporting out.

"I did it," the student said. "I brought the traitors together for you. Now, please give me the antidote."

Quenthel smiled and said, "There is none."

"What?"

"I didn't poison you. The liquid was simply a stimulant to combat drowsiness. I gave you enough to make the effect alarming, but it'll wear off."

"You're lying! Playing with me!"

"I would have administered a slow poison had I been carrying one, but as I was not, I had to improvise."

Drisinil felt a surge of bitter humiliation and a need to demonstrate she wasn't entirely a fool.

"Well," she blurted, "then, you've tricked everyone all the way around. I know Lolth didn't control those spiders. You did. You read a scroll or used some sort of charm before you entered the room."

"If so, does it matter?" A yellow arachnid crawled out of Quenthel's snowy hair and onto her shoulder. She paid it no mind. "Lolth teaches that the cunning and strong must master the foolish and weak. However you look at it, this outcome is in accordance with her will. Now, let's talk about your future."

Drisinil swallowed. "You promised to spare me."

"I did, didn't I?" a smiling Quenthel replied. "Unlike some, we Baenre generally keep our word. A reputation for fair dealing facilitates certain transactions. However, I never promised not to punish you."

"I understand. Of course I'll take a flogging or whatever you think appropriate."

"That's quite agreeable of you. How about this, then? We'll nip off the other eight fingers and cut out your tongue as well."

For a moment, Drisinil thought she hadn't heard correctly.

"Now you're joking."

"Oh, no. I firmly believe you engineered the plot against me, and I intend to make sure you don't get up to any more mischief. Ever. If you can't communicate, work magic, or grip a weapon, that should take care of it. Obviously, it won't be possible for you to continue at Arach-Tinilith, and I wouldn't count on the warmest of welcomes when you return home. I doubt Mez'Barris Armgo will have much interest in a grotesquely crippled and thoroughly useless daughter. She may even consider you an embarrassment to be killed or locked away."

Enraged, panicked, Drisinil lunged, but never landed a blow. Powerful hands grabbed her from behind, hauled her back, and something hard and heavy bashed her over the head. Her legs folded beneath her. She would have fallen if not for her captors holding her up.

Quave's voice sounded over Drisinil's shoulder. "We've got her, Mistress."

"Thank you," Quenthel said. "Take her to the penance chamber and secure her."

"Yes, Mistress," said Quave. "I assume you'll do the cutting yourself."

"I'd like to," said the Baenre, "but there's another matter demanding my attention. You can do it. Enjoy yourself. Just mind she doesn't die of it. They can drown in their own blood when you take the tongue."

Pharaun relaxed in the chair, enjoying the feel of the barber's fingers kneading tonic into his scalp. It wasn't as relaxing as a full-body massage, but soothing nonetheless.

The barber chattered away, and the wizard periodically responded with a noncommittal, "Indeed," or a grunt. Like, he suspected, tonsorial customers of all races in all ages of the world, he wasn't actually listening.

The barber's stall, a little box redolent of unguents and pomades, was open at the front, and it was more interesting to gaze out at the sights of the Bazaar. A commoner strode by carrying a clucking chicken, imported from the Lands of Light, in a box. A merchant had probably promised the fellow the fowl would lay for years to come, though in reality, such birds rarely thrived in the Underdark. A portrait painter rendered his subject, the enchantments in the brush enabling him to fill the canvas with astonishing speed. An armorer drove a rapier through a bound, gagged kobold to demonstrate the sharpness of the point.

Cowl up, mantle drawn close around him, and Splitter hidden by the charm of concealment Pharaun had cast on it, Ryld loitered across the way in a tent with the sides folded up. There, games of all sorts were on display. The hulking swordsman stood pondering a *sava* board, where he'd set up a problem with the onyx and carnelian pieces.

A change came over the scene beyond the doorway, and people looked to the north. Some started to squeeze up against the stalls, clearing the center of the lane. A ragged, furtive-looking commoner hurried away in the opposite direction.

Ryld sauntered to the near edge of the tent, glanced where everyone else was peering, then gave Pharaun a subtle nod, confirming what the wizard had already guessed. A patrol was headed their way.

Pharaun wished the guards could have waited just five more minutes, but alas, he would have to go to work before the barber finished with him. A tragedy, but it couldn't be helped.

A moment later the patrol marched by, casting stern glances hither and yon, their tread silent thanks to their enchanted boots. In at least nominal command was a priestess of Arach-Tinilith armed with a polished wooden wand. Assisting her were a teacher from Melee-Magthere and Gelroos Zaphresz, one of Pharaun's junior colleagues in Sorcere. It was unfortunate. Possessed of a store of jokes and comical ditties, Gelroos was congenial company. At least if Pharaun murdered the other mage today, he wouldn't have to worry about Gelroos trying to assassinate him tomorrow.

In addition to its officers, the patrol consisted of a number of warriors-in-training, boys whom Ryld had almost certainly instructed at one time or another. Pharaun wasn't particularly worried about them. His fellow teachers were the real threat.

The Master of Sorcere waited until the guards had marched past then, surprising the barber, he tossed aside the hair-sprinkled cloth covering his chest, stood up, and handed the craftsman a gold coin, a princely over-payment for his services. He touched a finger to his lips in wordless explanation of what he actually wanted to buy. He picked up his *piwafwi*, whose elegance he'd obscured with a minor illusion, swirled it around his shoulders, walked to the doorway of the stall, and peeked out.

The patrol had tramped about twenty yards down the lane. Any farther and they'd turn a corner, so Pharaun had attained as much separation from the enemy as he was going to get. He draped a fold of silk across the lower half of his face, then stepped out into the open, brandished a glass marble and a pinch of rust, and recited an incantation. His half-barbered hair stood on end, and the air around him smelled of ozone. A crackling blue-white spark appeared in the air before him, then shot down the aisle.

When it reached the patrol, the flickering point of radiance exploded, shooting flares of lightning in all directions. Many of the callow young soldiers danced, burned, and fell, as they possessed neither the spiritual strength nor the protective talismans that might have minimized their injuries and kept them on their feet. Unfortunately, the sizzling, jumping arcs of power struck a handful of vendors and shoppers as well. Pharaun hadn't particularly wanted to harm noncombatants, but the aisle was simply too cramped.

The rest of the patrol began to pivot. The captain from Melee-Magthere was smoking, blackened, and blistered, but if he was anything like Ryld, his burns weren't likely to slow him down. Gelroos and the priestess looked as if the lightning hadn't even touched them. The female was spinning around a hair faster than the other two, raising her baton. Thanks to his silver ring, Pharaun could tell it was a spider wand, a weapon capable of entangling him in sticky webbing.

He had no intention of enduring that kind of humiliation. He rattled off a string of magic words and thrust his arm out. Five slivers of arcane force leaped from his fingertips, hurtled across the intervening space, and slammed into the cleric's torso. She stumbled backward and collapsed.

A wiry male with deep-set eyes, and a trace of a scholar's stoop, Gelroos peered up the street and called, "Master Mizzrym!"

"So much for my ability to manufacture a nonmagical disguise," Pharaun answered, grinning, "but then we do know one another fairly well."

"You're allowed to try to kill another Master of Sorcere," said Gelroos. "That's entirely proper. But you overstepped when you struck down these youths. It was pointless and sloppy, and their mothers won't appreciate the waste. They'll reward me for taking you down."

"Does it help if I explain that all I do, I do to deliver Menzoberranzan from twin calamities?" Pharaun asked.

Gelroos raised his hands, preparing to conjure, and the remaining warriors charged.

"Ah. I thought not."

He too began to cast.

Gelroos completed his spell a moment before Pharaun finished his. Crashing and crunching, the surface of the lane spat stone in the air. It was like a geyser, save for the fact that the chunks of rock didn't fall back to earth. Instead, they shifted around one another and fitted together, forming a towering, massive, and vaguely drowlike form, like a heroic statue abandoned when the sculptor had barely begun. Its footsteps shaking the ground, the creature lurched up the corridor between the stalls.

Pharaun was mildly impressed. It wasn't easy to summon and control an essential spirit of the earth—nor easy to fend one off, either—but the manifestation didn't shake his concentration. He continued his recitation without a flub, meanwhile floating up into the air to avoid, if only momentarily, the swords of the onrushing warriors.

He spoke the final syllable of the conjuration. A dagger made of ice flew from his hand. Gelroos dodged it, but the conjured blade exploded, peppering its target with frozen shards. One slashed open the mage's cheek and he stumbled, but Pharaun could tell he wasn't seriously hurt.

Below the Mizzrym, some of the warriors were readying their crossbows. Others began to levitate. By rushing him, they'd drawn even with the game merchant's tent, and Ryld burst from underneath it. Half an hour earlier, he'd purchased a scimitar to use in this particular battle, but it was Splitter, rendered visible by his touch, that he currently clasped in his hands. He must have decided that, since Gelroos had already called out Pharaun's name, it would be pointless to try to conceal his own identity.

The greatsword leaped back and forth, each stroke dropping a foe to the ground. Bellowing for his minions to turn and face the new threat, Ryld's fellow instructor tried to shove his way toward him.

Stone, liquid as magma, flowed upward from the ground into the elemental's body. Most of the rock served to grow the creature bigger and taller, but some of it accumulated in the palm of its hand, forming a spiky sphere that it no doubt intended to hurl at Pharaun.

The wizard snatched a tiny vial of water from one of his pockets. Brandishing it, he chanted. He felt the walls of the cosmos attenuating, and for a moment, sensed an infinite number of Pharauns conjuring in adjacent realities, receding away from him like reflections in a mirror, growing subtly less and less like himself with each step.

A pulse of scarlet light struck him in the chest. Gelroos must have conjured it. The blaze of pain was extraordinary. Pharaun strained to complete the last word of power and final mystic pass without a fumble.

He wasn't sure he'd succeeded until a vacancy, a gap not in matter but in the medium that underlies it, opened under the elemental's feet. The creature cocked back its arm to throw, and the animating force fell out of the body it had created for itself and down the hole. The wound in the fabric of the world contracted and sealed itself. Rumbling and thudding, the huge stone form fell apart.

Pharaun took stock of himself. It didn't look as if the red light had done more than scrape and prick his skin. He grinned down at Gelroos.

"Not quite, colleague."

"This time," the younger wizard said through gritted teeth.

He started casting, and Pharaun did the same.

Force crackled around the outcast Mizzrym but failed to bite into his flesh. His own magic, launched from the same round little mirror he used to check his appearance, made the air surrounding Gelroos tinkle like chiming crystals. The junior wizard screamed, and in the blink of an eye he was transformed into an inert figure made of cool, smooth glass.

Metal rang below Pharaun's feet. He looked down. Ryld appeared as if he might be having a difficult time of it, but a conjured barrage of ice, flung into the midst of the surviving students, turned the tide. Ryld cut down his fellow Master of Melee-Magthere, whirled to do the same to a young spearman, and the fight was over.

Pharaun surveyed the battlefield. Though burned and incapacitated, some of the warriors-in-training were still alive, but that was all right. The important thing had always been to murder his fellow instructors. That was what would impress the rogues.

He floated back down to earth. "That wasn't too difficult. Looking back, it's a pity we didn't slaughter Greyanna and her allies in the same fashion."

Ryld grunted, pulled up the hem of a fallen fighter's cloak, and wiped the blood from Splitter.

"Can you shatter Gelroos before we decamp?" Pharaun asked. "Otherwise, he'll eventually revert to flesh and blood."

"If you like."

Ryld hefted his blade.

c h a p t e r

F I F T E E N

Wrapped in a plain, dark *piwafwi*, the cowl drawn over her head, Quenthel tramped south across the city. The experience was strange, unique in her personal experience. She was on foot, not mounted on a lizard or enthroned on a floating stone disk. She was alone, not accompanied by a column of guards and servants, and most strangely of all, no one paid her any real attention. Oh, slaves scurried out of her path, and males offered her a cursory show of respect, but no one feared her or cringed in awe of her. Indeed, she herself had to offer obeisance to the noble females she encountered along the way, lest their soldiers chastise her for insolence.

It was galling, unsettling, and somehow tempting as well. In her most private thoughts, she'd imagined herself simply running away from the implacable foe who worked so assiduously to kill her. It might be the only way she could survive. If she opted to flee this minute, she was already off to a good start. She'd managed to slip away from Tier Breche with no one, she hoped, the wiser.

Flight was a cowardly notion, though, unworthy of a Baenre, and it angered her when she entertained it even for a moment. Until the attacks began, she never had before. She turned a corner, and Qu'ellarz'orl, came into view. Her destination was nigh, and she focused her thoughts on the task at hand.

Sneaking away from the Academy had been a little complicated. First, she'd had to surreptitiously lay hands on nondescript outerwear that would allow her to pass for a commoner. Such a *piwafwi* certainly hadn't existed among her own garments, all of which were costly and bejeweled, but she'd found it among the effects of one of the kitchen staff. After disposing of the cook lest the missing garment be reported, she had to exit Arach-Tinilith without anyone realizing it was her, including her own watchful sentries. Finally, she needed to skulk to the edge of the plateau and float down to the cavern floor below without the guards at the top of the staircase noticing.

She'd managed it, though, and she was confident of her ability to sneak back into the Academy, even after the plateau had been put on a state of heightened security.

A road ran up the eminence that was Qu'ellarz'orl to the castles of Menzoberranzan's greatest families. It wasn't off limits to commoners. Merchants and supplicants used it all the time, but they were subject to search and interrogation by House Baenre patrols.

Quenthel started up the twisting road and made it better than halfway to the top before she heard the distinctive grunt and hiss of a riding lizard. She scurried off the path into the forest of giant, phosphorescent mushrooms, where she crouched behind a particularly massive specimen.

The patrol, a mounted officer and a dozen foot soldiers, marched by without so much as glancing her way. Hiding from her own troops was another bizarre, almost surreal experience.

When the warriors passed, she hurried on up the slope. In another minute, she reached the top of the rise. Before her rose the most opulent fortresses in the city. At the easternmost end of the expanse, House Baenre towered on the highest ground of all, dwarfing every other structure.

She turned her steps toward the tall, slender spire known as Spelltower Xorlarrin, residence of the Fifth House. Bands of shimmering faerie fire striped the iron walls.

She climbed the steep steps to the gate under the watchful eyes of the sentries on the battlements. Had she not already known it, their vigilance would have shown that she could maintain complete anonymity no longer.

Still, she'd do the best she could.

When a sentry armed with spear and long sword strode over to ask her business, she said, "I'm going to show you something remarkable. Don't let your amazement show."

He looked skeptical. He lived in the Spelltower, after all, and had seen his share of marvels.

"All right, ma'am. Show me, if you will."

She twitched open her *piwafwi*, giving him a glimpse of the Baenre House insignia hanging at her throat.

His eyes widened, but otherwise, he did a fair job of doing as she'd bade him.

"How may I serve you?" he asked softly, the slightest quaver in his voice.

"I want to enter the tower without anyone paying the least attention to me, and I want to talk to your matron alone."

"Please, come with me."

The guard led her through the gate and into a confusion of service passages such as every castle possessed. The corridors eventually brought them into a nicely appointed room with comfortable-looking sandstone chairs, a carnelian-and-obsidian *sava* set awaiting a pair of players, and frescos of some of Lolth's attendant demons adorning the walls.

Her escort departed in search of his mistress, leaving Quenthel to prowl restlessly about the room. Finally the door opened, and Zeerith Q'Zorlarrin slipped through. Her features were plain and nondescript, but she was notable for a dignified bearing and composure that rarely failed her even in the most extreme situations. For a matron, her costume was rather plain and austere.

The two princesses saluted one another, then Zeerith ushered her guest to a seat.

"When Antatlab told me you'd come without a single guard, I wondered if he'd gone mad," the matron remarked.

"Can I trust him not to gossip about my visit?"

"He's discreet enough. Now, may I ask why I'm so unexpectedly enjoying the honor of your company?"

Quenthel related the events of the past three nights.

"If I still possessed my magic," she concluded. "I could deal with this matter easily, but as things stand . . . I need help."

The words galled her, but they had to be said.

"Why have you sought it here?" Zeerith asked.

"The Xorlarrins have always supported the Baenre and profited thereby. Try as I might, I can't think of a compelling reason you'd want me dead, and your House boasts many of the best wizards in Menzoberranzan. So, if I must trust someone, you're a good chance. Will you aid me, Matron?"

Zeerith took her time replying. Quenthel knew the other female was cold-bloodedly pondering whether to help, deny, or betray her. Where did the greatest advantage lie?

"Your plight is an outrage," the Xorlarrin said at last, "an affront to all priestesses. Of course I'll aid you. For ten thousand talents of gold, and your support when my clan's dispute with House Agrach Dyrr becomes public knowledge."

"What dispute?"

"The one I'll be stirring up in a tenday or two. Do we have a bargain?"

Quenthel's mouth tightened. If she'd come to the Spelltower in the full panoply of a Baenre princess, Zeerith would have thought twice about making conditions, but by arriving incognito the mistress had shown her desperation and in so doing, shifted the transaction to another level.

"Yes," she growled, "I agree."

"I thank you for your generosity. What do you require?"

"Every night," said Quenthel, "a new demon comes to kill me, and I fend it off as best I can. If this goes on, a night will come when the entity kills me instead. I need to do more. I need to end the siege, and it's my hope your mages know a way. I confess I don't. I've ransacked every vault, chest, and drawer in Arach-Tinilith and found nothing that will serve."

"So that's why you came in secret. You want a weapon, and you don't want your foe to know about it. Otherwise, he might take counter-measures."

"Correct."

Zeerith rose. "We'll ask Horroodissomoth. He can do it if anyone can, and he'll keep his mouth shut after."

She opened the door and directed Antatlab, who'd been standing watch outside, to go and fetch her patron and House wizard.

Horroodissomoth arrived shortly thereafter. Quenthel felt a little twinge of disgust, for the mage was the antithesis of the typical vital dark elf male. His features were lined and wrinkled, and his posture, bent. Rumor had it that his appearance of decrepitude had resulted not from extreme age but rather some dangerous magical experimentation.

Moving stiffly, all but creaking audibly, Horroodissomoth tendered obeisance then, at Zeerith's invitation, settled in a chair to listen to a reprise of Quenthel's story. At first the wizard's demeanor was impassive, perhaps even utterly disinterested, but a light came into his rheumy eyes when he realized she was asking him to solve a magical problem.

"Hmm," he said, "hmm. I think I might have something that will help. In a way, I regret giving it to you, because as far as I know, it's unique. Even we Xorlarrins don't know how to make another. But on the other hand, I've always been curious to see if it actually works."

Gossip whispered that at some point in the distant past, the females of House Ousstyl had interbred with humans. Naturally the contemporary Ousstyls denied it and would do their meager best to punish anyone they suspected of passing the rumor. Still, as Faeryl gazed across the table at Talindra Ousstyl, Matron Mother of the Fifty-second House, she could readily believe it. Talindra was tall and, for a dark elf, extraordinarily rawboned. Her jaw was too square, and her ears, insufficiently pointed. Most telling of all was the scatter of empty plates before her. She'd annihilated every morsel of her seven-course supper with a lesser being's insatiable voracity.

Talindra finished with a juicy belch.

"Excuse me."

"Of course," Faeryl said. She thought she heard a thump issuing from elsewhere in the ambassadorial residence. Inwardly, she flinched but Talindra didn't seem to notice the sound.

"Well," the matron said, "that was tasty, but I believe you invited my brood to supper and spirited me away to this private room, because you wanted to talk of something more important than cuisine."

Faeryl smiled and said, "You've found me out, and I have a confession to make. I don't always devote myself to the interests of Ched Nasad as a whole. Occasionally I work solely to advance the fortunes of House Zauvirr."

"How could it be otherwise?" Talindra said, raising her golden cup. "Family, always. Family over all."

Faeryl joined the other noble in the toast. She'd always enjoyed the sweet dessert wine, but this time it tasted too sweet, almost sickeningly so. She supposed her nerves were to blame.

The envoy set down her drink and said, "Let us discuss how our two families might be of service to one another. In Ched Nasad, we Zauvirr are allied with House Mylyl. For the immediate future, we must remain so. Yet it's also time for the Mylyls to begin their decline, for their wealth and influence to start passing into our hands. You see the problem."

Talindra grinned and said, "You want to attack the Mylyls without them realizing who's to blame."

"So why not do it through an intermediary?"

Elsewhere, someone let out a thin, little wail. Faeryl tensed, but once again, her guest failed to react. Fortunately, the sounds of pain were reasonably common in dark elf dwellings.

"You want me to lend you some of my males," the matron said, "to make the long, dangerous journey to Ched Nasad to raid and kill for you. It makes sense. The Mylyls would have no idea who they are, nor that they're working for you. But what do I get out of it? Why—?"

A warrior threw open the door, strode to Talindra's side, and raised a steel baton.

The matron was too quick for him. Surging up in her chair, she knocked him cold with a punch to the jaw, drew a long knife from her belt, and pivoted toward Faeryl.

The ambassador snatched up Mother's Kiss, which had been lying under the table all the while. She sprang up, swung the basalt-headed warhammer in an arc and balked the oncoming Talindra for an instant.

For the next few seconds, the two nobles battled, neither able to score; then Talindra used her free hand to clasp a round medallion pinned to her bodice. Red light shone from between her fingers.

If the matron had the capacity to throw a spell, that changed the complexion of the fight considerably. Faeryl needed to end it quickly, perhaps before the first magical effect manifested. She charged her opponent, striking at her head in an all-out attack.

It was a reckless move, and she suffered the consequences. The knife point jabbed painfully into her ribs. Luckily, it failed to penetrate the mail she wore beneath her silken gown. Mother's Kiss slammed into the Menzoberranyr's head and dashed her to the ground. Her hand slipped away from the amulet, and the glow faded.

An instant later, a second guard burst into the room.

"We've secured them all, my lady."

The warrior was a rugged-looking male with a chipped incisor and a broken nose, whom she had on occasion summoned to her bed.

"Good," Faeryl replied. "How many did you have to kill?"

"Only one, but we could slaughter the rest. If I may say so, it seems more sensible and less bother than tying them up."

"It does, but I came here to promote good relations between Menzoberranzan and Ched Nasad. Even though some schemer has rendered my efforts futile, I won't exacerbate the situation by committing any more outrages than necessary. You soldiers will do as I bade you. Strip the Ousstyls, gag them, and tie them up."

Talindra groaned and groped feebly for her knife. Impressed that the matron was still conscious to any degree at all after the blow she'd suffered, Faeryl kicked the blade out of her reach.

"You can't do this," Talindra croaked, "not to House Ousstyl. We are mighty and never forget at affront."

Tense as she was, Faeryl smiled. The matron's arrogance was woefully misplaced. The Ousstyls were so insignificant they hadn't even known the ambassador had lost the good will of Triel Baenre. Otherwise, they would never have accepted an invitation to feast with such a pariah.

Faeryl bashed Talindra again, this time rendering her entirely insensible, then she roamed through the castle, exhorting her minions to make haste. Soon all were wearing the clothing of the Ousstyls. For the first time, Faeryl was grateful that her household was relatively small. Otherwise, they wouldn't have had enough pilfered garments to go around.

She and her lieutenants sported the finery of the Ousstyl dignitaries, while the common soldiers had donned *piwafwis* and mail, and carried the arms of Talindra's bodyguards.

The outlanders stowed provisions beneath their mantles. The quantity was insufficient, for they couldn't conceal all that much. With luck, they'd be able to hunt and forage on the trail. They headed for the mansion's enclosed stable, where Talindra had left her driftdisc.

Faeryl noticed that some of her retainers were sweaty and wide-eyed. Though she was careful not to show it, she still felt just as apprehensive herself. Was she mad to flout Triel Baenre's express command, especially when she and her subordinate priestesses had virtually no magic implements left?

Well, no. It would be lunacy to sit on her rump and do nothing, knowing that Triel would eventually get around to ordering her arrest. Even if Faeryl weren't concerned about her own fate, with every passing hour she grew more anxious to learn what had halted all traffic from Ched Nasad, and not just because the trade was important in its own right. Absurd as it seemed, she couldn't shake the irrational fear that some misfortune had befallen the City of Shimmering Webs itself.

She had to know. Any great event affecting Ched Nasad could conceivably injure House Zauvirr and diminish her own status. Moreover, though she would never admit it to another, she cared about her homeland for its own sake. Not, she assured herself, that she suffered from love, loyalty, or any other soft, un-drowlike emotion. Yet Ched Nasad had shaped her into the person she was. It was a part of her, and anything that harmed the city would trouble her as well.

In any case, having assaulted and robbed her dinner guests, the die was cast.

The pack and riding lizards hissed and grunted when the party entered the stable. Faeryl dearly wished she could take some of the reptiles with her, but since Talindra hadn't brought any such beasts along with her, it was out of the question.

The matron's driftdisc was a round, flat stone with an ivory throne fastened on top, the whole floating about a foot above the floor. The device glowed with a soft white light tinged ever so faintly with green.

Since it was Faeryl who'd appropriated Talindra's attire, she hopped up on the driftdisc, sat in the ornate cushioned chair, and mentally commanded the apparatus to levitate up to the proper dignified height. She endured a bad moment during which nothing happened, and she was sure the Ousstyl had rigged the vehicle in such a way as to keep anyone else from riding it, then the circular platform rose. It was just sluggish, about what you'd expected of the equipment of the Fifty-second House.

Two of Faeryl's soldiers threw open the gates, and the party ventured out into the open, her retainers forming a proper column around her as soon as they had the room.

They marched away from the luminous keep that had been their home for fourteen years, past the alleyway where Umrae had died, and onward. Faeryl couldn't see Triel's watchers, but she could feel their eyes on her. She felt all but certain they would recognize her.

But maybe not. Most people saw what they expected to see. The spies had watched the Ousstyls enter the residence, and just as anticipated, the petty nobles were departing. Why would anyone bother to peer closely when he was sure he already knew what was going on?

That was the theory, anyway. At the moment, it seemed a dubious notion on which to gamble her life.

Her company left the immediate vicinity of the residence without anyone trying to hinder them, which proved nothing. The watchers wouldn't pop out of hiding and confront the fugitives themselves, They'd scurry away to rouse a company of warriors, who'd intercept the daughters and sons of Ched Nasad in the street.

Thus, while her expression conveyed the proper mix of serenity and haughtiness, her muscles were stiff, and her mouth dry as she floated down the avenues. For the moment, she was heading for Narbondellyn, site of the Ousstyls' modest citadel. It was where the spies would expect her to go.

Drow did their best to clear the way for the matron of even a minor House. She was grateful for that. Still, heavily laden carts and the like could only pull aside so quickly. The impostors' progress was necessarily and nerve-rackingly sedate.

Finally, though, they passed Narbondel itself, where the magical glow had climbed three quarters of the way to the top of the great stone column. Faeryl spotted Talindra's fortress and turned her company aside. If they actually approached the place, some guard peering down from the ramparts was bound to penetrate their disguises.

They marched south, still without interference. If someone was chasing them, the ambassador was sure it would have become apparent by then. Faeryl took a deep breath, told herself her ruse had succeeded, and tried to relax. She couldn't, quite. Perhaps when she reached the Bauthwaf, or better still, escaped Menzoberranyr territory altogether . . .

The outlanders' route carried them to the west of the elevation that was Qu'ellarz'orl, its slopes thick with enormous mushrooms. Then, at last, they reached one of the city's hundred gates to the tunnels beyond. The Menzoberranyr defended all of them, but this one at least was a minor exit. It boasted fewer guards than most.

The fugitives approached boldly, as if they had every legitimate expectation of the sentries ushering them through. The guards must have wondered why a high priestess would wear an elegant cloak and gown and ride her ceremonial transport for an excursion into the dirty, dangerous caves beyond the city, but a matron's whim was law in Menzoberranzan. They offered her obeisance, then set about the cumbersome process of unbarring the granite-and-adamantine valves—or most of them did.

One officer eyed Faeryl thoughtfully. He had a foxy, humorous face and was smaller than most males, which apparently didn't hinder him when wielding the heavy broadsword hanging from his baldric. Though he carried the blade of a warrior, he'd eschewed mail—which could disrupt arcane spells—for a cloak and jerkin possessed of the countless telltale pockets of a wizard. Evidently he was fighter and wizard both. When she gazed directly at him, he respectfully lowered his head but resumed his scrutiny as soon as she turned her head.

She pivoted around to face him and asked, "Captain, is it?"

The small male gave her a smart salute.

"Captain Filifar, my lady, at your service."

"Please, come here."

Filifar obeyed. If he betrayed any wariness, it was only in his eyes. The two gigantic spiders graven in the leaves of the gate stirred ever so slightly. Faeryl realized they would emerge from the carving and fight for him if commanded.

"You have the look of an intelligent male," she said, gazing down at him from atop the driftdisc.

"Thank you, my lady."

"Perhaps you received orders," she continued, "to refuse passage to the delegation from Ched Nasad."

"No, my lady."

Filifar's hand twitched ever so slightly. It wanted to reach for either the hilt of his sword or the spell components in one of his pockets.

"Your subordinates were content to receive their instructions and let it go at that, but not a sharp boy like you. Somehow you contrived to find out what the ambassador looks like, thus making sure you'd be able to recognize her if she came this way."

Filifar's mouth tightened. "My lady," he said, "my company is well armed and well trained. You may also have observed the spiders graven—"

She raised her hand. "Don't agitate yourself, Captain. I mean you no harm. We're just two Menzoberranyr idly chatting, passing the time it takes your fellows to open the gate."

"I regret, my lady, that now that I've seen you up close, I can't allow them to do that."

He took two careful steps back, retreating beyond her reach, then pivoted to shout the order.

Faeryl stopped him dead by displaying a gaudy ruby brooch, formerly Talindra's property.

"I said you were an intelligent lad, Captain Filifar, but I don't believe you're a prosperous one. You wear no jewelry, and your clothing is made of common stuff."

"You're right, milady. Fortune hasn't favored me."

"It can."

Faeryl brought out one ornament after another, the jewels her retainers had stolen from the Ousstyls and her own legitimate treasure as well. She filled her lap with them and laid the surplus on the pale, luminous rim of the driftdisc.

"Here's enough wealth to improve your luck and that of your minions as well."

Filifar hesitated before saying, "My lady, I was told that Matron Triel herself wishes you detained. It's no light matter to cross the Baenre."

"Just say the Zauvirr didn't pass through *this* gate, or if they did, you didn't recognize them. No one will know any different."

He jerked his head in a nod. "Right. Why not, curse it?"

He removed his *piwafwi* to use as a makeshift bag and swept the jewelry in. Some of the soldiers noticed what their captain was doing and scurried over to investigate.

Once the gate was well behind her, Faeryl abandoned the driftdisc. The stately conveyance was just too slow. She and her party quick-marched on through the mostly unimproved passages at the fringe of Menzoberranyr territory, past hunters' outposts and adamantine mines, making for the genuine wilderness beyond.

Faeryl realized she was grinning. It was absurd, really. She'd just surrendered a queen's ransom in gems, Triel would send troops after her, and she was all but certain some dire peril lay ahead, but somehow, for the moment, none of it mattered. Faeryl had outwitted her foes and finally, after fourteen years, she was going home.

The fugitives rounded a bend, and dark figures seemed to flow from the tunnel walls just ahead. The Zauvirr turned to run. Somehow, the shadows were behind them as well.

On the fringe of Menzoberranyr territory, Valas Hune could sense the genuine wilderness beyond. He could feel its vast and labyrinthine spaces and hear its pregnant silences. He could smell and taste its variations of rock and imagined himself simply slipping away into that limitless world.

As fancies went, his wasn't entirely absurd. Most dark elves feared to travel the Underdark except in armed convoys, and with good reason. They, however, lacked the abilities he'd spent decades developing, survival skills that made him one of the finest scouts in Menzoberranzan.

Indeed, the small, wiry male in the rugged outdoorsman's garb liked traversing the subterranean world alone. He relished the wonders, the quiet, and the freedom. Sometimes, when he'd idled in camp too long, he felt he preferred it to the striving, conniving existence of his fellow drow, the luxuries of Menzoberranzan notwithstanding. He yearned for an errand that would take him out into the wilderness, and played with the notion of simply running away.

He heard the Zauvirr coming and put the dream aside. Like it or not, his mission this day wasn't to explore the wild. It was to direct his company, fellow mercenaries of Bregan D'aerthe, in the taking of Faeryl Zauvirr and her retainers.

That was the theory, anyway. In point of fact, he didn't have to give any more orders. No doubt the warriors of Ched Nasad were competent fighters in their own right, but when the sellswords swarmed out of hiding, they caught them entirely by surprise, then proceeded to cut them down with murderous efficiency.

Once Valas was certain his band would be victorious, he started searching for Faeryl herself. His smallness and natural agility enabled him to thread his way through the fury of battle without harm.

He found the princess at the center of the carnage. She'd just finished killing one of his command. The dead male's brains and bloody hair adhered to one end of her basalt-headed warhammer.

"Ambassador," Valas called. "I have orders to take you alive, if possible."

She answered with a curse. He didn't blame her for that. In her place, he wouldn't want to be delivered alive to Matron Baenre, either.

He hefted one of his matched pair of kukris—vicious curved daggers—and fingered a little brass ovoid, one of many trinkets adorning his tunic and cloak.

He'd collected the amulets and brooches from races and civilizations across the Underdark. Fashioned according to alien aesthetics, most of the ornaments were ugly and uncouth to dark elf eyes, but he hadn't acquired them for their appearance, nor were they merely souvenirs. Each contained a different enchantment.

Three images, exact facsimiles of himself, flickered into existence around him. He edged toward Faeryl, and the phantoms came with him.

She stared fiercely, obviously trying to pick out the real Valas from the false. It didn't help. When she swung, she struck at the image on his left.

The illusion vanished on contact, and at the same instant, he sprang. She couldn't come back on guard in time to fend him off. He hooked a leg behind her and threw her to the ground, then kicked her repeatedly in the head until she went limp.

c h a p t e r

S I X T E E N

Laughter echoed through the candlelit corridors of Arach-Tinilith. Quenthel frowned. She'd been expecting something to happen, eagerly anticipating it, in fact. What she wasn't expecting was an explosion of mirth, and she couldn't guess what it meant.

She strode forward, and her patrol followed behind. They seemed edgy, but not quite as reluctant as they had the night before. The fate of Drisinil, Molvayas, and the rest of the plotters had convinced the survivors that Quenthel still enjoyed the favor of Lolth, at least to the same dubious extent as the rest of the stricken clergy.

The laughter rang on and on until at last the searchers found the source. Hunched over, her shoulders shaking, a novice knelt before one of the smaller altars of the goddess. Steady despite the paroxysms of glee, her index finger painted lines of graceful calligraphy on the floor. Quenthel couldn't make out what the girl was using for pigment until she lifted her hand to her face like an artist dipping a brush in a paint pot. She'd gouged her eyes out, another seeming handicap that didn't impair her writing.

The mistress stepped close enough to inspect the lines of blood. For all her erudition, she couldn't read the characters, but she could feel the power in them. They pulled at her and repelled her at the same time, as if they might yank her spirit, or a piece of it, out of her body.

She wrenched her eyes away from the symbols and swung her whip. The vipers cracked into the eyeless female's back, their venomous fangs tore into her, and she collapsed, dead or merely insensible. Quenthel didn't particularly care which.

"What was she writing, Mistress?" Jyslin asked.

"I don't know," Quenthel admitted, smearing the glyphs with her toe, "something in one of the secret tongues of the Abyss. Scribing it may have been a way of casting a spell, so I made sure she wouldn't finish."

"What was wrong with her?" Minolin asked.

Quenthel was still surprised that the Fey-Branche had not, as expected, turned out to be one of the traitors.

"I don't know that, either," said the Mistress of Arach-Tinilith. She actually did have an idea, but wasn't sure of it yet. "Let's move on."

Fifteen minutes later, a runner, dispatched from a squad stationed in the third leg of the spider, found Quenthel to report that one of her comrades had gone mad. Quenthel went to see for herself, half expecting more gouged eyes and bloody writing.

But the new dementia took a somewhat different form. The victim had taken shelter, if that was the right word for it, in a small library devoted, for the most part, to musty treatises on warfare in all its aspects. She sat on the floor in the corner defined by two tall sandstone bookshelves, rocking and whimpering to herself.

Quenthel stooped, jammed her fist under the girl's chin and forced up her head.

"Rilrae Zolond! What ails you? What happened?"

Rilrae's face was blank and seemingly devoid of comprehension. Tears flowed down her cheeks. She smelled of mucus, and the breath snuffled in her nose. She didn't answer Quenthel's question, just made a feeble, ineffectual effort to turn her face away.

The mistress sighed and let her go. She'd seen cases like Rilrae before, generally in some dungeon or torture chamber. The junior priestess had experienced something sufficiently unpleasant to drive her deep inside her own mind. Had Quenthel still possessed her Lolth-granted powers, or been carrying the proper equipment, she might have been able to shake Rilrae out of her delirium, but as matters stood, the useless creature wouldn't be providing any information. Annoyed, the mistress nearly vented her frustration by giving Rilrae a stroke from her whip, but she didn't want to appear rattled or upset in the eyes of her followers.

She led the patrol on and eventually found a suicide sprawled in the corridor with froth on her lips and an empty poison bottle still clutched in her hand.

One of the second-year students reeled from a doorway a few yards farther down. Glaring and twitching, she unrolled a parchment, possibly one Quenthel herself had dispensed from the temple armory, and began shouting the words. The Baenre recognized the trigger phrase of a spell intended to summon a certain type of plague demon.

She snatched out her hand crossbow and pulled the trigger. Others did the same. The flurry of poisoned darts punctured the scroll and the novice as well. She fell onto her back, cracking her head against the calcite floor. The spell, still a syllable or two from activation, dissipated its power in a harmless sizzle of red light.

Quenthel reflected that a pattern was becoming clear. Some power struck a female and more or less drove her mad. She then separated herself from her companions, either making an excuse or just running off, the better to manifest her lunacy in one bizarre behavior or another.

It was odd that the girls' companions never even noticed the attack occurring, odd, too, that the demon assaulted only one member of a group and not all—or that it attacked any, given that the previous intruders had only attacked those lesser priestesses who attempted to hinder them.

The unseen demon's search pattern was equally peculiar. The location and sequences of its attacks seemed to indicate that the being was bouncing erratically around from one end of the temple to the other.

"Mistress," said Yngoth, "I know what's happening."

"As do I," Quenthel said. "I've merely been confirming it." She turned to Minolin. "Fey-Branche."

"Yes?" Minolin asked.

"You're in command of these others. You will all evacuate the temple. Get the sane people out, and the mad ones, too, but only if you can do it quickly."

The Fey-Branche princess blinked. "Mistress, we believe in your authority," she said. "We're not afraid to stand with you."

"I'm touched," Quenthel sneered, "but this isn't a test. I want you to go."

"Exalted Mother," Jyslin said, "what's happening? Which demon invaded the temple tonight? The assassin? Did it poison our sisters to make them go insane?"

"No," the Baenre said, "not in the way you mean."

"Then—"

"Go!" Quenthel raged. "Minolin, I told you to take them out of here."

"Yes, Mistress!"

The Fey-Branche hastily formed them up and led them away. The corridor seemed very quiet once they'd disappeared.

"Mistress," said Hsiv, "was it wise to send them away?"

"You question my judgment?" Quenthel asked.

The viper flinched. "No!"

"You sought to protect me, so I'll let it go. This time. I dismissed the girls because they can't help me, and I'd like to have some underlings left when this nonsense is over."

"They might have guarded you from another would-be mortal killer."

"We can hope that if Minolin gets everyone out, there won't be any more. Besides, why in the name of the Demonweb did I create *you*?"

Greenish candlelight rippling on black scales, Yngoth reared and twisted around to look Quenthel in the face.

"Mistress," the viper hissed, "we are rebuked. We'll keep watch. What will you do?"

"Wait, and prepare myself."

She found a classroom possessed of a reasonably comfortable instructor's chair, the high limestone back carved into the stylized shape of a stubby-legged spider. She sat down, laid the whip at her feet, removed a thin shaft of polished white bone from her pouch, and set it in her lap, holding it at either end.

Closing her eyes, she commenced a breathing exercise. Within a heartbeat or two, she slipped into a meditative trance. She thought she would need the utmost clarity to contend with the night's demon, because Jyslin had guessed wrong. The intruder didn't encapsulate the art of the assassin, nor the spirit of the drow race, for that matter. It embodied the concept of evil.

The traitor elves of the World Above professed to hate evil. In reality, Quenthel thought, they feared what they didn't understand. Thanks to the tutelage of Lolth, the drow did, and having understood it, they embraced it.

For evil, like chaos, was one of the fundamental forces of Creation, manifest in both the macrocosm of the wide world and the microcosm of the individual soul. As chaos gave rise to possibility and imagination, so evil engendered strength and will. It made sentient beings aspire to wealth and power. It enabled them to subjugate, kill, rob, and deceive. It allowed them to do whatever was required to better themselves with never a crippling flicker of remorse.

Thus, evil was responsible for the existence of civilization and for every great deed any hero had ever performed. Without it, the peoples of the world would live like animals. It was amazing that so many races, blinded by false religions and philosophies, had lost sight of this self-evident truth. In contrast, the dark elves had based a society on it, and that was one of the points of superiority that served to exalt them above all other races.

Paradoxically, though, a touch of the pure black heart of this darkest of all powers could be deadly, just as the highest expression of comforting warmth was the fire that consumed. Even folk who spent their lives in the adoration of evil generally had no real comprehension of the endless burning sea of it raging below and beyond the material world, and that was just as well. Even a fleeting glimpse could convey secrets too huge and fearsome for the average mind. Its touch could annihilate sanity and even identity. The threat was sufficiently grave that the majority of spellcasters hesitated to regard the force directly. They preferred to treat with evil at one remove, by dealing with the devils and undead that embodied it.

But it appeared that Quenthel's unknown enemy was the exception. He'd dipped right into the virulent fountainhead and drawn forth a power that dwelled therein.

That demon was presently intangible, a creature of pure mind. That was why it seemed to move and act so erratically; it was passing not through physical space, a medium in which it didn't exist, but from consciousness to consciousness, head to head. And simply through that intimate contact it poisoned its hosts, even if it didn't particularly intend to. It suffused them with a darkness too big and too powerful for their little minds to sustain

It was searching for Quenthel all the while, to show her the most profound malevolence of all.

She prayed she could endure the venom for just a second, until she worked the Xorlarrin's magic. She'd have to. Since the demon was invisible and insubstantial, she wouldn't know it hadn't come close enough for the talisman to affect until she felt it infesting herself.

To make sure she would indeed detect it, she sank ever deeper into her trance. She became acutely conscious of the rise and fall of her chest and the air hissing in and out of her lungs. The steady thud of her heartbeat and the surge of blood through her arteries. The pressure of her buttocks and spine against the chair. The feeblest of drafts caressing and cooling her left profile. The vipers shifting restlessly, brushing her feet and ankles, the touch perceptible even through her boots.

Yet none of the sensations was of any particular significance. They presented themselves so vividly only because she'd entered a state of utter dispassionate quietude, and thus receptivity. A condition in which she would be equally cognizant of events within her mind and soul.

She recalled acquiring this capacity when she herself was a novice in Arach-Tinilith. She'd learned every divine art easily. It had been one of the signs that Lolth had chosen her for greatness. But relatively speaking, this particular mastery had come harder than most. According to Vlondril, unwrinkled but showing signs of madness even then, it had been because Quenthel was of too dynamic a character. She had no instinct for passivity.

Abruptly the Baenre realized her thoughts were nudging her out of the desired state. Vlondril had also said that was always the way. The mind didn't like to hush. It wanted to babble. Quenthel took another deep, slow breath, exhaled it through her mouth, and expelled that importunate inner voice along with it.

Time passed. She had no idea how much time, nor, immersed in the meditation, did she care. The temple was utterly silent, which surely meant that most everyone had exited, or perhaps, in one or two instances, perished.

Gradually it dawned on Quenthel that her trance wasn't quite perfect. The dead quiet, proof that all instruction, prayers, and rituals had ceased, irked her just a little, and she doubted she could purge that final hint of emotion. She cared too much about her role of Mistress of Arach-Tinilith. She'd come to the Academy intent on making it grander and more effective than ever before. Thus would she honor Lolth and demonstrate her fitness to one day rule the entire city. Instead, she'd presided over an extended disaster, regular functions disrupted, residents battered or even dead.

It galled her to think how many of her sister nobles would blame her, but she knew it wasn't her fault. It was in large measure the fault of the teachers and students themselves. Most who had perished earned their destruction by dint of their idiotic little mutiny, and actually, that was as it should be. The traitors had violated the precepts of Lolth.

Indeed, when Quenthel thought about it, the real misfortune might be that weaklings like Jyslin and Minolin were still alive. They were cowards and whiners, unfit, but they'd survive merely because the manifestation of evil hadn't passed their way, and because the Baenre herself had sent them to safety. Perhaps that had been a mistake.

Quenthel realized she was ruminating once more. With an effort of will she arrested the internal monologue. For a few seconds.

But as Vlondril had taught her, it was devilishly hard to attain passivity by straining for it. Besides, Quenthel was pondering important matters, new insights that would guide her steps in the days to come.

If preserving even the most worthless specimens of her flock constituted an error, at least it was one she could rectify. She'd already slaughtered the mutineers. How easy, then, it would be to butcher those who lacked even the spirit to rebel. She imagined herself stalking among her underlings, peering into their eyes, swinging the whip whenever she discerned inadequacy. The trance state facilitated visualization, and the fantasy was as vivid as life. She smelled the blood and felt it splatter her face. The muscles of her whip arm clenched and relaxed.

Quenthel could kill *everyone* if necessary. She'd enjoy it, and perhaps when the clergy was pure and strong again, Lolth would condescend to speak.

If not, that might mean that all Menzoberranzan required cleansing, beginning with the First House. Quenthel would usurp pathetic, indecisive

Triel's throne—not in a hundred years but *now*, and preparation be damned. Then, the very next day, she and her kin would wage a war of extermination on the thousands who served the goddess and her chosen prophet with false hearts or insufficient zeal.

How glorious it would be, and it could begin as soon as she ferreted out the first weakling. Her fingers closed on the haft of her whip, or rather they tried and in so doing reminded her that she was in reality holding the thin bone wand.

She'd forgotten all about the magical artifact and the demon as well, and she could only think of one explanation. Despite her vigilance, the spirit had managed to possess her without her realizing it.

For without its influence, those thoughts would never have occurred to her. Destroy her own followers? Try to murder Triel without the vaguest semblance of a strategy, and fight virtually every other House in the city at once?

It wasn't the prospect of wholesale bloodshed that dismayed her—war and torture were her birthright and often her delight—but this was evil without sense, a delirium that would surely destroy her and conceivably even House Baenre along with her.

Yet did it matter? She sensed the ecstasy implicit in letting go. If she permitted it, the demon would exalt her, and even if she perished an hour later, what difference would it make? She'd find more joy in that brief span that in centuries of mundane life.

For what seemed a long while, she wavered, uncertain whether to manipulate the wand or cast it aside, take up her whip, and go hunting. In the end, one consideration enabled her to choose the former. No matter how sweet the temptation to become a pure and transcendent being, doing so would be to surrender to the will of her phantom enemy, allowing the faceless spellcaster to dominate, transform, and ultimately destroy her. Quenthel Baenre could not embrace defeat.

Instead, she snapped the length of bone in two.

An instant later, she felt an extraordinary lightness and clarity in her head, a sign that the demon had departed, as, in fact, her eyes confirmed. Vaguely visible at last, a misshapen shadow without a source, the entity floated in front of her, then, without turning or shifting any of its amorphous limbs, receded quick as a bow shot. It was tiny, a dot, and gone.

Quenthel felt a pang of loss, but it only lasted a moment. Then she smiled.

Gromph sat before one of the enchanted windows in his hidden chamber. He'd crossed his feet atop a hassock and held a crystal goblet of black wine in his hand. He'd thrown the strangely carved ivory casements wide and supposed he must look like the soul of ease awaiting some pleasant entertainment.

Well, that was the hope, but despite himself the Archmage of Menzoberranzan was growing used to disappointment.

He hadn't made any progress in finding the runaway males. His divinations were so oblique and contradictory as to be useless. Apparently some able spellcaster had forestalled his efforts. His genuine spies had turned up nothing, indeed, had managed to get themselves strangled in Eastmyr by parties unknown. The only satisfaction, if one could call it that, was that his decoy was still on the loose, still occupying the priestesses' attention. Why Pharaun Mizzrym had deemed it expedient to slaughter a patrol from the Academy, though, was more than Gromph could comprehend.

The Baenre wizard hadn't yet managed to kill Quenthel, either. For the past few nights, he'd dispatched his conjured minions, then settled before the window to watch them do his bidding. Impossibly, even stripped of her magic, his sister had disposed of the first three spirits and the traitors he'd inspired as well. Like some bungler in a farce, Gromph had only managed to account for a few lesser clerics with whom he had no quarrel, who would otherwise have gone on to contribute to the strength of Menzoberranzan and the House that controlled it. It was maddening!

This night, he prayed, would be different. Quenthel had turned out to be competent at disposing of spirits wearing some semblance of material form, but surely she would prove more vulnerable to an assailant that slipped imperceptibly into her mind.

The enchanted window afforded Gromph a view of the interior of Arach-Tinilith as if he were but a few feet away. He watched his sister and her squad encounter wretches whom the spirit had already overwhelmed with the infusion of an evil more profound than any mortal, even a dark elf, could readily bear. He looked for some sign that Quenthel was growing afraid. The indication would be subtle if she let it slip at all, but perhaps a brother would spot it.

He didn't, and eventually Quenthel ordered her minions to evacuate the building and sat down to meditate.

The archmage frowned. Evidently the imperious bitch had figured out what was going on and had in a sense responded appropriately. But it shouldn't matter. *He'd* withstood contact with the ultimate essence of evil, but he was the greatest wizard in the world and had taken precautions. Quenthel enjoyed neither advantage.

In time, a sublime cruelty twisted her features. Gromph exclaimed in triumph, for the netherspirit plainly had her in its grasp. Evidently she wasn't going to drop dead of an aneurysm or commit suicide, but no matter: she was doomed. Her personality erased, consumed by the compulsion to degrade and destroy, she was bound to provoke someone into killing her.

Then she broke the skinny white wand in two, unleashing a magic that thrust the netherspirit out of her. Gromph, for all his knowledge, had never seen anything quite like it. Taking on just a hint of palpable form, his agent fled the scene.

The Baenre wizard bolted up in his chair and threw his goblet, smashing it against the wall. He cursed foully, and the malignancy in his words, hammering through the black lotus-scented air, made the greenish flames of the everlasting candles gutter.

Struggling for composure, he told himself it didn't matter. He'd get her eventually. He'd throw entity after entity at her until . . .

But what had happened to the netherspirit? Constrained by Gromph's command, it should have kept attacking until either it toppled the pillars of Quenthel's reason or she destroyed it. Instead, it had run away.

The mistress's unfamiliar magic had broken the binding—so much was clear—but where had the creature gone? Back to its own world? Probably, but something—a slight acceleration of his heartbeat or a subtle prickling on the back of his neck, perhaps—made Gromph want to check.

The casement responded to his will. Framed in that rectangular space, the netherspirit, still visible, perhaps as tangible as smoke, half flew, half bounded down one of the labyrinthine corridors of Sorcere. A defensive ward activated, piercing the intruder with crisscrossing shafts of yellow light, but it tore itself free and charged on. A blue-gowned master peered out the door of his sanctum, spotted the wraith, started to conjure, and the intruder stopped him with a sweep of a shadowy paw. The blow didn't rock the wizard backward or leave a mark, but he fell like a block of stone.

Gromph surmised his erstwhile agent was coming after him. Either it was angry over its forced servitude, or Quenthel had done more than merely dissolve his control. She'd wrested it away from him and turned the entity into her own assassin.

Either way, the spirit represented a threat, and unfortunately, Gromph himself didn't know its full capabilities. Still, he had no real reason for concern. His magic was more than a match for any such entity, especially in his stronghold.

He watched the netherspirit flow through the black marble door of his office like water through a sieve. It scrambled over the white bone desk and headed straight for the hidden access to his sanctum. Magic crackled purple and blue around it, but it burst through. It hurtled up the shaft.

Gromph smiled. He had the creature where he wanted it, for he'd created the passage with defense in mind. Simply by focusing his will, he destroyed it.

The shaft wasn't made of matter. Still, a metallic crashing and grinding sounded through the hole in the middle of the floor as the artificial space folded in on itself. If the rebellious spirit screamed, its voice was lost among the din.

Gromph would have enjoyed hearing it squeal, but the important thing was that it was gone. Most likely, the collapse had crushed it to nothing, but even if not, it had surely ejected it, maimed and disoriented, in some remote halfworld. The crisis was over, and the archmage was left only with the annoyance of transporting himself in and out of his hideaway via spell until such time as he invested the six hours necessary to recreate the passage.

However, just to maintain the habit of caution that had balked a thousand enemies, he turned back to the window, then scowled.

The space still framed the spirit, and as far as Gromph could see, the shadowy thing was unharmed. Darting and wheeling through curtains of pale phosphorescence, it was casting about in the bent spaces surrounding the stronghold.

Gromph didn't see how the creature could find him. Nothing could locate a refuge hidden in a haze of scrambled time, not without the tenant in some way guiding it in. Nonetheless, the wizard hurried into one of the protective golden pentacles adorning the marble floor.

An instant later, a different window burst inward, the casements flying from their hinges. The spirit flowed through, in the process resuming the form it had worn before Gromph transformed it into the semblance of a kind of demon. It somewhat resembled a wingless dragon with long, taurine horns sweeping from its head, which also possessed a single globular eye. The archmage couldn't actually see the orb—it was one with the inky shadow of the spirit's body—but he could feel its baleful regard.

Slightly anxious and uncertain, and all the angrier for it, Gromph shouted, "K'rarza'q! I named, summoned, and bound you, and I am your master. By the Prince Who Dreams in the Heart of the Void and by the Word of Naratyr, I command you to kneel!"

The netherspirit released a humid stink that somehow conveyed the essence of scornful laughter, then it bounded forward.

Very well, Gromph thought, have it your way.

He thrust the curved blade of his ritual dagger into his belly.

As he'd expected, the creature floundered in agony, but only for an instant. Anguish erupted in the archmage's own stomach. He yanked the athame out of his flesh an instant before it would have dealt him an actual wound.

K'rarza'q lunged. Ignoring the residual pain in his gut, Gromph recited a brief incantation and thrust out his arm. The air rang like a bell, and a little red ball of fire shot from his hand. It struck the creature and . . . nothing. The missile winked out of existence.

The entity reached the edge of the pentacle. A barrier of azure light sprang up and vanished with a tortured whine as the spirit drove though. The creature dipped its head and jerked it upward, ramming the tip of one of its horns into Gromph's chest.

The spirit was entirely solid. If not for the Robes of the Archmage and his other protections, the long blade of shadow stuff would surely have impaled Gromph. As it was, it picked him up and tossed him across the room. In midair, he strained to throw off the numbing shock and activate the powers of levitation in his House insignia.

The power woke with a sort of sickening pang, but wake it did. He floated down as light as a wisp of spider silk, avoiding what might have been a bone-shattering fall.

As soon as he got his feet under him, he snatched a polished wooden wand from its sheath on his left hip, pointed it, and murmured the trigger word. A bubble of pungent brown acid swelled on the end, then hurtled at the spirit. It plunged into the being's cyclopean mask, but apparently without inflicting any harm.

The spirit charged. Gromph stood in place until his foe was nearly on top of him, then he spoke a single word. A minor teleportation shifted him instantaneously to the other end of the circular room, behind his attacker's back.

K'rarza'q skidded to a halt and cast about in confusion. Gromph had bought himself a second, no more. He quickly dropped the wand of acid, snatched a spiral-cut staff of polished carnelian from its place on a rack of wizard's tools, lifted it over his head, and began to chant. The rod possessed special virtues against beings from other levels of reality. Perhaps with it in his hand, he could finally drive a spell through his foe's defenses.

The netherspirit heard his voice, turned, and hurtled toward him. This time it charged without moving its limbs, simply shifting over the distance with terrifying speed. Preserving the cadence and intonation as only a master wizard could, Gromph picked up the pace of his incantation. He very much wanted to finish before the creature closed with him again.

He succeeded, though only barely. K'rarza'q was nearly within arm's reach when the magic blazed into existence. A lance of dazzling glare plunged into the netherspirit's eye.

The reeking creature dropped to the floor, its substance unraveling into shapeless clumps and tatters. Gromph smiled, and a dozen strands of spirit-stuff reared up at him like the vipers in his cursed sister's whip.

The archmage gripped the scarlet staff with both hands, just as a Master of Melee-Magthere had taught him centuries before, during the six months every student mage was obliged to spend in the warriors' pyramid. Wielding the implement like a common spear, he thrust one end of it into what seemed to be K'rarza'q's ragged, squirming core.

The netherspirit burst into inert flecks of gray-black slime. Gromph's protective enchantments prevented any of the splatter from fouling his own person.

He felt a certain satisfaction at his victory, but it withered quickly because he hadn't killed the object of his hatred, merely preserved himself from the result of another failed attempt, and in the process discovered he'd utterly failed to comprehend Quenthel's resources and capacities.

What was that bone wand? Where had it come from, and how did it work? Had it merely broken his own control, or had it summarily placed his minion under his enemy's dominance?

He glumly concluded that until he knew more, it would be foolish to continue attacking a foe seemingly capable of turning his own potent wizardry against him.

So he'd break off hostilities.

And, he thought, with a sudden pang of uneasiness, hope his sister didn't guess who'd engineered her recent perils.

chapter

S E V E N T E E N

All the undercreatures gawked when Pharaun and Ryld strolled into the cellar, and why not? The mage doubted this foul little drinking pit had ever seen such an elegant figure as himself, an aristocrat of graceful carriage, exquisite ornaments, dress, and coiffure . . . well, he hoped that, after some emergency adjustments, his hair was at least passable.

In any case, it was plain the goblins, orcs, and whatevers had little interest in aesthetic appreciation. They whispered, glowered, and fingered their weapons whenever they thought the two dark elves weren't looking at them, and the fear and hate in the sweltering, low-ceilinged room were palpable. Pharaun supposed that considering what Greyanna and her hunters had wrought in the Braeryn the previous night, a measure of surliness was, if not good form, at least understandable.

He wondered how they'd react if they discovered his sister had slaughtered their fellows by the score merely to create an opportunity to kill him. Perhaps it was a question best left in the realm of the hypothetical.

Knowing that Ryld was watching his back, the Master of Sorcere sauntered to the bar and, with a sweep of his arm, scattered clattering coins across it. The currency was the usual miscellany encountered in Menzoberranzan—rounds, squares, triangles, rings, spiders, and octagons—half of it minted by the dozen or so greatest noble Houses and the rest imported from other lands in the Underdark and even the World Above. It was all silver, platinum, or gold, though, more precious metal than this squalid hole probably saw in a decade.

"Tonight," Pharaun announced, "this company of boon companions drinks at my expense!"

The taverner, a squat orc with a twisted, oozing mouth and a mangy scalp, stared for a heartbeat or two, scooped up the coins, and began dipping some foul-smelling brew from a filthy tub. Cursing and threatening one another, the rest of the undercreatures shoved forward to get it. The wizard noted that no one thanked him.

After looking around for another moment, Pharaun spotted another dark elf slouched in a corner, evidently one of the wretches who'd sunk so low the goblinoids accepted him as one of their own.

"Come here, my friend," the wizard beckoned.

The outcast flinched. "Me?"

"Yes. What's your name?"

The fellow hesitated, then said, "Bruherd, once of House Duskryn."

"Indeed, until your noble kin kicked you out. We have much in common, Bruherd, for I myself am outcast twice over. Now come advise me on a matter of vital importance."

"I'm, uh, all right where I am."

"I know you don't mean to be unsociable," said Pharaun, setting blue sparks dancing on his fingertips.

The Duskryn sighed, and, limping in a manner that betrayed some chronic pain, did as Pharaun had bade him. He was gaunt, and half a dozen boils studded his neck and jaw. He'd evidently parted with his *piwafwi* at some point during his decline, but he still wore a filthy robe that, the Mizzrym noted with mild surprise, had once been a wizard's. With the aid of the silver ring, he could see that the dozens of pockets no longer held the slightest trace of magic.

"They may kill me for this," Bruherd said, subtly indicating the goblins.

"They only tolerate me because they believe me cut off from my own race."

"I'll pray for your welfare," Pharaun said. "Meanwhile, what I need to know is this: Of all the libations laid up in our host's no doubt vast and well-stocked cellar, which is the least vile?"

"Vile?" Bruherd's lip twitched. "You get used to them."

"One hopes not."

Pharaun handed the other drow a gold, hammer-shaped coin minted in some dwarf enclave.

"Tell the barkeep you want the stuff that bubbles," Bruherd advised.

" 'The stuff that bubbles.' Charming. Clearly, I've fallen among connoisseurs."

"It'll do," said Ryld, still unobtrusively studying the crowd. "The important thing is that we toast our victory."

Pharaun waited a beat, then chuckled. "You're supposed to ask him what he's talking about," he said to Bruherd, "thus affording us a graceful way to commence boasting of our triumph."

The lip twitched again. "I don't think much about victories or triumphs anymore."

Pharaun shook his head. "So much bitterness in the world! It weighs on the heart. Would it cheer you to learn I've avenged us in some small measure?"

"Us?" Bruherd grunted.

Across the room, a scuffle erupted between a shaggy hobgoblin and a wolf-faced gnoll. As the combatants rolled about the floor, somebody tossed them a knife, apparently just out of curiosity as to which would manage to grab it first.

"Hark to the glad tidings," said the Master of Sorcere. "I'm Pharaun Mizzrym, expelled first from the Seventh House and now Tier Breche, neither time for any rational cause. Incensed, I chose to take vengeance on the Academy. With the aid of my similarly disgruntled friend Master Argith, I destroyed a patrol in the Bazaar earlier today. You may have heard something about it."

Bruherd stared. The kobold and goblins within earshot did the same.

"It's true," said Ryld.

"That was you?" Bruherd said. "And you're bragging about it? Are you insane? They'll hunt you down!"

Pharaun said, "They were trying anyway." The entire cellar was falling quiet. "I've heard rumors of an agency that will spirit a drow boy away if he's well and truly discontent with his lot in life, as I trust Ryld and I have shown we are."

Bruherd said, "I don't know what you're talking about."

"Well," Pharaun said, "they probably have to think you can be of some use to them, and if you'll forgive my saying so . . ."

He caught a flash of movement from the corner of his eye, and turned just in time to see the taverner fall back in two pieces. Evidently he'd been in the process of climbing silently over the bar with a short sword in hand, and Ryld, sensing him, had pivoted and cut him. The drow warrior spun smoothly back around, Splitter at the ready.

Pharaun turned back as well, just in time to see a mass of undercreatures rushing him. He snatched three smooth gray stones from a pocket and started to recite a spell. Ryld's greatsword flicked across the wizard's field of vision, killing two gnolls that sought to engage him, allowing him to finish the incantation unmolested.

A cloud of vapor boiled into existence in front of him. Those orcs and goblins caught in the fumes collapsed. Others recoiled to avoid their touch.

The fog blinked out of existence a heartbeat later.

"I'm afraid I can't permit you to kill us and sell the corpses to the authorities," Pharaun told the crowd, "and I'm shocked—shocked!—you would even try. Aren't you pleased we massacred a patrol?"

"They don't want the priestesses to find you here," said Bruherd. He hadn't made a move during the skirmish. Perhaps he'd frozen, or maybe he'd figured his best hope of survival lay in passivity. "I don't, either. They're liable to kill us, too."

"How disappointing," Pharaun said. "And here I thought Ryld and I had found a cozy enclave of kindred spirits. But of course we won't force our company on those who lack the rarified sensibility to appreciate it. Neither, however, will we quit this place before we slake our thirst. You goblins and whatnot will have to withdraw. Good evening."

The undercreatures glowered. The mage could tell what they were thinking. They were many, and the intruders only two. Yet they'd seen what those two could do, and after a few seconds, they started trudging out, leaving their unconscious comrades sprawled on the floor.

"You're crazy," Bruherd told the masters. "You need to keep your heads down very low for a few years. Give the matrons and the Academy time to forget."

"Alas," Pharaun said, "I suspect I'm unforgettable. You too may depart if you can bear to tear yourself away."

"Crazy," the outcast repeated.

He limped for the stairs and in a moment was gone like the rest.

Pharaun walked behind the bar. "Now," he said, "to begin drow's eternal search for *the stuff that bubbles*."

Ryld surveyed the slumbering goblins as if pondering whether to stick his sword in them.

"I still think this is a bad idea," the weapons master said.

Careful not to soil his boots, Pharaun stepped around the two bloody pieces of the barkeep and inspected a rack of jugs and bottles.

"You always say that, and you're always mistaken. The goblinoids will carry word of our whereabouts far and wide. The rogues are bound to hear."

"As will your sister and everyone else we've managed to annoy."

Pharaun uncorked a jug. The pungent liquid inside didn't seem to be fizzing, so he moved on.

"Care to make a wager on who'll arrive first?"

"Either way," Ryld snorted, "we wind up dead."

"Had I wished to hear the dreary voice of pessimism, I would have detained our friend Bruherd," the wizard said as he inspected a jar full of cloudy liquid. "Here's a jar of pickled sausages if you care to break your fast, but I won't vouch for the ingredients. I think I see a kobold's horn floating in the brine."

He opened a glass bottle with a long, double-curved neck, and the contents hissed.

"Aha! I've found the draught the Duskryn recommended."

"Someone's here," said Ryld.

The mage turned. Two figures were descending the stairs. They looked like orcs, with coarse, tangled manes and lupine ears, but Pharaun's silver ring revealed that the appearance was an illusion, disguising dark elf males. The wizard saw the masks as translucent veils lying atop the reality.

He conveyed the truth of the situation to Ryld with a rapid flexing and crooking of his fingers.

"Gentlemen," said the mage, "well met! My comrade and I have been looking everywhere for you."

"We know," said the taller of the newcomers, evidently not surprised that a Master of Sorcere had instantly penetrated his disguise. He was Houndaer Tuin'Tarl, one of the highest ranked of the missing males, likewise one of the first to elope, and thus almost certainly one of the ringleaders. Certainly he looked like a princely commander of lesser folk. His rich silk and velvet garments, the magical auras of many of his possessions, and strutting demeanor all proclaimed it. He wore crystals in his thick, flowing hair—a nice effect—had close-set eyes and a prominent jaw, and looked as if he knew how to manage the scimitar hanging at his side. He also looked rather tense

"We've known for a while," said the other stranger, whom Pharaun didn't recognize.

At first glance, he appeared to be a nondescript commoner, with the squint and small hands of a craftsman proficient at fine work. However, the dagger tucked in his sash fairly blazed with potent enchantments, as did an object concealed within his jerkin. Evidently he'd layered one disguise on another.

"Well," said Ryld, "you took your time contacting us. I guess that's understandable."

"I think so," said Houndaer as he and his comrade advanced. A goblin moaned, and the noble kicked the creature silent. "Why were you seeking us?"

"It's our understanding," said Pharaun, stepping from behind the bar, "that you offer a haven for males who find existence under the thumbs of their female relatives uncongenial and who, for whatever reason, aspire neither to the Academy, a merchant clan, nor Bregan D'aerthe. If so, then we wish to join your company."

"But you two already did aspire to the Academy," the aristocrat said. "You rose to high rank there. Some might say that gives my associates and I cause for concern."

The orc mask's tusked mouth perfectly copied the motions of his actual lips. Pharaun couldn't have created a better illusion himself.

"You speak of the dead past," Pharaun said. "You've no doubt heard I'm in disgrace, and Master Argith finds Melee-Magthere stale and tedious." The dark powers knew, his discontented friend shouldn't have much trouble convincing them of that. "We require an alternative way of life."

Houndaer nodded and replied, "I'm glad to hear it, but what assurances can you give that you aren't an agent the matrons sent to find us?"

Pharaun grinned. "My solemn oath?"

Everyone chuckled, even Ryld and the boy with the dagger, who were both quietly, thoughtfully watching their more loquacious companions palaver.

"Seriously," the wizard continued, "if our escapade in the Bazaar failed to convince you of our bona fides, I have no idea what other persuasion we can offer. But it didn't fail, did it? Otherwise, you wouldn't be here. So unless you perceive something in our manner that screams spy . . ."

The faux commoner smiled. "You're right." He turned to Houndaer and added, "They smell all right to me, and if they're not, I doubt a little quizzing in this stinking goblin hole will prove otherwise. Let's get them home before some servant of the clergy comes sniffing for them and finds us. Either way, it'll all get sorted out in the end."

For a moment, as the power of Pharaun's silver ring wavered, the drow's mild, civilized tone became an orc's growl. He even smelled like a dirty undercreature.

The Tuin'Tarl's mouth tightened. Pharaun suspected he didn't much like taking advice from anyone, his companion included.

"I'm just being careful—as should you—but you may have a point." He turned back to the masters and said, "If we take you to our stronghold, there's no going back. You'll aid our cause or die."

Pharaun grinned. "Well spoken, and quite in the spirit of a thousand thousand conspiracies before you. Whisk us away."

"Gladly," the noble said with a mean little smile of his own, "as soon as the two of you surrender your weapons and that cloak of pockets."

The wizard crooked an eyebrow and said, "I thought you'd decided to trust us."

"It's time for you to show a little trust," Houndaer replied.

Pharaun surrendered his *piwafwi*, hand crossbow, and dagger. He was a little worried about Ryld's willingness to do the same. He could easily imagine the warrior deciding that, in preference to entering the dragon's cave unarmed, he'd subdue Houndaer and his companion there and then and wring what information out of them he could.

The problem with that strategy was that the Tuin'Tarl and his nameless companion might not be privy to all the mystic secrets held by the cabal as a whole, and those who were might flee when the two emissaries failed to return. Thus, while the masters would likely succeed in forestalling a goblin revolt, they'd miss acquiring the extraordinary power they sought.

Besides, it would be much more fun to join, and undo the rogues from within.

Apparently Ryld shared Pharaun's perspective, or else he was simply content to follow the wizard's lead, for he handed over Splitter and his other weapons to Houndaer without demur.

The Tuin'Tarl reached into his pouch, extracted a stone, and tossed it. It exploded in a strange, lopsided way, tearing a wound in the air, a gash the size and shape of a sarcophagus standing on end and the color of the light that swims inside closed eyelids.

He gestured to the portal and said, "After you."

Pharaun smiled.

"Thank you."

As easy as that? Pharaun thought. He was experiencing a certain sense of anticlimax, which was absurd, really. It had been astonishingly difficult to get this far.

He stepped into the portal, and experienced none of the spinning vertigo of ordinary teleportation. Save for a split second of blindness, it was just like striding from one room to the next. The only problem was the drider waiting on the other side.

The wizard struggled not to make a sound. Still, the huge creature, half spider, half drow, a bow in its hand and a quiver of arrows slung across its naked back, turned toward him. Pharaun had no fear of a single such aberration, but the goddess only knew just how elaborate this trap actually was. He whirled back toward the magical doorway just as Ryld came through.

Ryld, who'd slain his share of driders in the caverns surrounding Menzoberranzan, knew that this one—a hybrid creature with the head, arms, and torso of a dark elf male married to the body and segmented legs of a colossal spider—was larger than average; a robust example of its species, if species was the proper term. Nature didn't make them, magic did. Sometimes, when the goddess deemed one of her worshipers insufficiently reverent, the punishment was transformation at the hands of a circle of priestesses and a demon called a yochlol.

The Master of Melee-Magthere naturally focused on the venomous aberration as soon as he stepped through the portal, but like every competent warrior—and unlike Pharaun, evidently—he also took in the disposition of the entire area.

The portal had deposited them in a large, unfurnished hall with a number of openings along the wall. It was the sort of central hub used in castles to link the various wings. A couple males were wandering through, and while neither had ventured into the drider's immediate vicinity, they weren't preparing to attack him or flee from him, either. Nor did the creature himself appear on the verge of assaulting anyone, though he regarded the newcomers with a scowl.

Somewhat pleased to be ahead of his clever friend for once, Ryld gripped Pharaun by the shoulder.

"Steady," the swordsman said. "Don't embarrass yourself."

The wizard looked around, then grinned and said, "Right. Our friends didn't trick us into entering a trap. The drider's magically constrained."

"No."

Ryld glanced back to see that the two bogus orcs had stepped through the portal, which dwindled to nothing behind them. It was the bigger and more talkative of the duo who was speaking.

"The driders help us of their own free will."

"Interesting," said Pharaun.

In the blink of an eye, the goblinoids turned into an aristocratic warrior—Houndaer Tuin'Tarl, specifically, whom Ryld had trained—and a craftsman of one sort or another. The prince closed the portal with a wave of his arm.

"Do you still use that second-intention indirect attack?" Ryld asked. "That was a nice move."

For the first time, Houndaer smiled a smile that had neither malice nor suspicion in it.

"You remember that, Master? It's been so long, I'm surprised you even remember me."

"I always remember the ones who truly learn."

"Well, thank you. It's good to have you with us, and you're going to be glad you are. Great things are in store." the noble said. The drider scuttled toward them. "Ah, here comes Tsabrak. You'll see his mind isn't sluggish or otherwise crippled, yet he's on our side nonetheless."

In point of fact, the drider didn't look especially congenial. The length of his legs lifted his head above those of the four dark elves, and he glared down at them with eyes full of madness and hate. Ryld inferred that Tsabrak had entered into a typical Menzoberranyr alliance. He'd thrown in with the runaways to secure some practical advantage, but he still loathed *all* the drow who'd deformed him and cast him out.

"What is this?" the drider snarled, exposing his fangs. They seemed to impede his speech a trifle. "Syrzan said no!"

Syrzan wasn't a typical drow name, but Ryld had no idea to which other race it might belong. He glanced over at Pharaun, who conveyed with a subtle shrug that he didn't know, either.

"Syrzan is my ally, not my superior," said Houndaer, glaring back at the spider-thing. "I make my own decisions, and I've decided these gentlemen can help us. They're masters of Tier Breche—"

"I know who they are!" Tsabrak screamed, flecks of foam, perhaps mixed with venom, flying from his lips. "Do you think me a mindless beast? I studied on Tier Breche the same as anyone!"

"Then you know how useful their talents could be," said the craftsman, "and how unlikely it is they can do us any harm, particularly now that the prince has disarmed them."

"Just point us to Syrzan," Houndaer said. "It will allay your fears."

It? Ryld wondered.

"I can't," the drider said. "It's gone off somewhere."

"Where?" Houndaer asked

"Agitating slaves? Acquiring more magic fire from its secret source? How do I know? You'll just have to sit on these two until it gets back."

"That's all right," the noble said. "Master Argith and I can reminisce about old times. We'll all wait in the room where Syrzan interviewed the other recruits."

"Perhaps you'd care to tag along," the craftsman said, "to make absolutely sure the masters don't cause any trouble."

Pharaun beamed up at the bloodthirsty aberration and asked, "Please? There are half a dozen questions concerning drider existence that have perplexed me for years."

Tsabrak ignored him, instead glowering at Houndaer and the artisan as if he suspected them of playing a trick on him.

Finally, he said, "Yes. I'll go. Somebody with sense needs to be there."

"Fine." Houndaer nodded to Ryld and Pharaun and said, "Come this way."

The masters and their hosts, or captors, set off through a maze of passageways. As promised, Pharaun treated Tsabrak to a barrage of questions, and, when the drider failed to respond, cheerfully answered himself with a gush of scholarly speculation.

Ryld paid little attention. He was too busy studying the rogues' citadel, a forlorn and dusty place where Pharaun's monologue echoed away into the quiet. No servants were in evidence, merely runaway males and driders, who often recognized their former instructors and curiously peered after them. The marks of magical attacks, bursts of lightning and sprays of acid, scarred the walls.

By all appearances, the conspirators were hiding in the seat of a House extinguished by its enemies. No one was supposed to take possession of such a fortress without the Baenre's permission, and few would dare. The vacant castles were supposedly cursed and haunted places, breeding grounds for sickness, insanity, and bad luck. As if to compound the potential for ill fortune, the squatters had broken the copious shrouds of spiderweb wherever they impeded traffic and even in corners where they didn't.

At one point, the masters and their warders passed a row of small octagonal windows. The glass was gone but the molded calcite cames remained. Ryld glanced out and saw mansions shining green and violet far below. The rogues had taken a stalactite castle, hanging from the cavern ceiling, for their hiding place. No doubt the isolation had attracted them.

A minute later, the little procession reached its destination, a chapel with rows of benches, a crooked aisle snaking up the middle to an asymmetrical basalt altar, and murals, agleam with silvery phosphorescence, carved in bas-relief on the walls and ceiling. To Ryld's surprise, these last depicted not the Demonweb but other hells entirely devoid of spiders, yochlols, or the goddess Lolth herself. Apparently the House that once abode here had sacrificed to forbidden deities. Perhaps that transgression had contributed to its downfall.

The dark elves settled themselves in the pews. While Houndaer and the commoner seemed convinced of the masters' claim of estrangement from Tier Breche, they nonetheless retained possession of the newcomers' gear. Tsabrak crouched just inside the door, his legs splayed out on either side of the entrance.

"I admire the decor," Pharaun said. "Without even trying, I noticed images of Cyric, Orcus, Bane, Ghaunadaur, and Vhaeraun. Quite a nice selection of patron powers for the discriminating worshiper."

"We're not looking for a new god," Houndaer spat.

"I'm sure," the wizard said. "Perhaps you'd be kind enough to tell Master Argith and me what your grand and glorious scheme *is* all about. And why now?"

"Why now?" the noble asked.

"Our fellowship has existed for decades," the craftsman cut in, "though it's only recently that we all eloped and took up residence here full time. Formerly we merely gathered for an hour or two every fortnight or so."

"If you're a male," Houndaer said, "and utterly dissatisfied with your place in Menzoberranzan, you need some sort of a refuge, don't you?"

"I quite agree," the wizard said. "Of course, others have opted for a merchant House, the Academy, or Bregan D'aerthe."

Houndaer made a spitting sound. "Those are just places to hide from the matrons. This is a fortress for males who want to turn Menzoberranzan upside down and put ourselves on top. Why not? Aren't our mages and even our warriors as powerful as the clergy?"

Pharaun grinned and said, "They certainly are now that the priestesses have mislaid their magic."

Houndaer blinked. "You know about that?"

"I've inferred it. You obviously know as well. Otherwise, you wouldn't run about breaking spiderwebs simply for the fun of it, to say nothing of putting your master plan into motion. I'd be curious to hear how you found out and if you know why."

"We don't know why," Houndaer said, shaking his head. "We started to figure it out after a couple of us saw priestesses die fighting gricks out in the Bauthwaf. The bitches should've used spells to save themselves, but they didn't, and we guessed it was because they couldn't. After that, we kept our eyes open and waylaid a few clerics to see what they'd do to defend themselves. Everything we learned supported our theory."

Pharaun sighed and said, "Then you aren't in touch with some chatty informant in the realms of the divine. Like me, you merely observed and deduced. What a pity. Aren't you, in your ignorance, apprehensive that Lolth will rekindle the priestesses' magic just when it's least convenient?"

"Maybe the goddess turned against the clergy because it's our turn to rule," said the commoner. "Who's to say? In any case, this is our chance, and we're taking it."

"Your chance to do what?" asked Ryld. "You talk as if you intend to revolt, but instead you're inciting the slaves into an uprising."

Houndaer cursed. "You know that, too?"

"We stumbled on it while looking for you," Pharaun explained. He brushed a stray strand of his coiffure back into place. His white hair shone like ghost flesh in the soft light shining from the carvings. "As Master Argith noted, on first inspection, whipping the undercreatures into a lather would seem irrelevant to your objective."

"Look deeper," the noble said. "We're canny enough to know we can't topple the matriarchy all at once. Even without their spells, our mothers and sisters are too powerful. They have too many talismans, fortresses, and, most importantly, troops and vassals serving out of fear."

"I begin to comprehend, and I apologize for not giving you sufficient credit," Pharaun said. "This is merely the opening gambit in a *sava* game that will last a number of years."

"When fighting engulfs Menzoberranzan," Houndaer said, "and the clerics cast no spells to put down the revolt, their weakness will become apparent to everyone. Meanwhile, our brotherhood will take advantage of the chaos to assassinate those females who pose the greatest obstacles to our ambitions. With luck, the orcs will account for a few more. At the end of the day, our gender's position in the scheme of things will be considerably stronger, and every male in the city will start aspiring to supremacy.

"In the years to come, our cabal will do whatever we can to diminish the females and put ourselves in their place. One day soon, we'll see a noble House commanded by a male and eventually, a master in every House."

He smiled and added, "Needless to say, a master who belongs to this fraternity. I'll enjoy ruling over House Tuin'Tarl, and I imagine that you, Brother of Sorcere, wouldn't say no to primacy over your own family."

Pharaun nodded and said, "You're far too canny to have forgotten we've all gone rogue. . . ."

"Our kin will welcome us back once we've weakened them to the point where they're desperate for reinforcements. We'll concoct tales of travels to the far ends of the Underdark, or something. It won't matter to them when they're desperate enough."

"Indeed, you've plotted everything out so shrewdly that I only see one potential pitfall, Pharaun said. "What if the goblins and gnolls should actually *succeed* in slaughtering us all, or at least inflicting such damage on our city that the devastation breaks our hearts?"

Houndaer stared at the mage for a moment, then laughed. "For a moment, I almost thought you serious."

Pharaun grinned. "Forgive me. I have a perverse fondness for japes at inappropriate moments, as Master Argith will attest."

Houndaer smiled at Ryld and said, "I'd just as soon hear him attest that I mastered all those lessons on strategy he pounded into my skull."

"You did," said Ryld, and perhaps it was true. His instincts told him that this scheme, outlandish as it seemed, might work, and he abruptly realized he didn't know how he felt about the possibility.

He and Pharaun had infiltrated the rogues to betray them, to placate the archmage, and because the Mizzrym wizard had some vague notion that they'd achieve greater status and power and thus a permanent cure for Ryld's formless dissatisfaction, thereby. Yet now the conspirators were offering high rank and a role in a grand adventure. Perhaps, then, the teachers should become in truth the rebels they were pretending to be.

The warrior glanced over at Pharaun. With a flick of his fingers so subtle that no one else would notice, the wizard signed one word in the silent language: *Persevere*.

Ryld took it to mean that his friend, with his usual acuity, had divined what he was thinking and was urging him to hold to their original intent. He gave a tiny nod of assent. He didn't know if Pharaun was making a wise choice, but he did realize he wouldn't even be here listening to this apocalyptic talk if his friend hadn't asked for his aid. When all was said and done, Ryld had descended from Melee-Magthere to help the wizard achieve *his* ends, and that was what he was going to do.

Pharaun turned to Tsabrak and said, "I assume the driders have allied themselves with the conspiracy because the boys promised you a place of honor in the splendid Menzoberranzan to come. Perhaps they even pledged to find a way to transform you back into a drow."

"Something like that," Tsabrak sneered. "Mainly, though, those of us who joined did it for the chance to kill lots and lots of priestesses."

"I can't say I blame you," Pharaun said. "Well, gentlemen, your plans are inspiring to say the least. I'm glad we sought you out."

"So am I," said Ryld.

"The only things I'm still hazy on," the mage continued, "are Syrzan and the Prophet. One and the same? I see by your expressions that they are. Who is . . . *it* really, and what power does it use to so enthrall the goblins?"

"I think you're about to find out," Houndaer said.

An instant later, something droned through the air, almost like a noise, but not. Actually, the sensation existed solely within the mind. Pharaun turned, and Tsabrak scuttled aside to reveal the robed figure in the doorway. Ryld felt a jolt of dismay. Afraid it was already too late, he sprang up from the bench.

chapter

EIGHTEEN

Off to Faeryl's left stood an iron maiden cast in the form of a tubby jester in cap and bells. The bells looked real, and would evidently jingle while a victim writhed inside. The device was open just a crack, not enough to expose the spikes inside.

Straight ahead, a chain and hook dangled from their pulley, fishing for a prisoner to hoist, and a rack waited to stretch one. To the left, a brazier of coals threw off dazzling heat, and a collection of probes, knives, pincers, and pears hung on their pegs. Her nemesis, the small male with all the ugly baubles, lounged in that vicinity in an iron chair with shackles attached to the armrests.

That was about as much as the envoy could see while roped naked to a molded calcite post.

She was hungry, thirsty, and sore from standing for hours in one position. Her bonds chafed her, and her head ached. However, she had yet to endure one of the genuine agonies this stuffy cellar provided, and she thought she knew why. Some messenger had instructed the torturers to wait for Triel to arrive before commencing the festivities.

Faeryl had already attempted to converse with the little male and her jailers and failed to elicit a response from either. She had nothing else to do but struggle to govern her thoughts. She didn't want to imagine all the things the Baenre might do to her, but she herself had presided over enough excruciations that it was difficult not to envision the possibilities. She didn't want to dwell on the massacre of her followers, either, but the memories kept welling up inside her.

Surrounded and outnumbered, the daughters and sons of Ched Nasad had perished one by one. As Faeryl watched the slaughter, her eyes ached with the tears she refused to shed. Naturally, she didn't "love" her minions, but she was used to them, even fond of a few, and she knew that without a retinue she was nothing, just a fallen priestess in a land of enemies, bereft of goddess and home alike.

Then the small male confronted her and used his magic to confound her and knock her out. She woke tied to the stone stake.

A door creaked, and voices murmured. Faeryl's instincts warned her that Triel had come at last. The ambassador closed her eyes, took a deep breath, and let it out slowly, composing herself. She wouldn't show fear. Dignity was all she had left—for a little while longer anyway, until her captors lashed and burned it out of her.

Sure enough, Triel and her draegloth son emerged from the doorway that apparently led to more salubrious precincts of the Great Mound. The Baenre matron was smiling. Fangs bared in a grin, Jeggred bounded along on his caprine legs.

The little male rose and offered obeisance.

"Valas," said Triel. "Well done. Did the Zauvirr give you any trouble?"

"They tried to sneak away in disguise," the male replied. "It almost fooled the lookout, but once he figured out what was what, everything went as planned."

The Baenre proffered a fat pouch that looked too big and heavy for her tiny hand.

"I'll send word when I need Bregan D'aerthe again," she said.

Valas took the pouch, then bowed low. He withdrew, and Triel and her monstrous son turned toward the prisoner.

"Good evening, Matron," Faeryl said, "or is it morning now?"

Fighting hands outstretched, talons at the ready, jaws agape, Jeggred lunged at the prisoner. Despite herself, Faeryl flinched. Both the claws and the pointed teeth stopped less than an inch from her flesh. The draegloth loomed over her, pressing close, almost seeming to embrace her like a lover. He ran a pointed nail across her cheek, then lifted it to his bestial muzzle. He sucked, and a bit of warm, viscous drool, mixed, perhaps, with a trace of her blood, dripped onto her forehead.

"Have a care," the ambassador said with as much nonchalance as she could muster. "If your son kills me quickly, won't that spoil the fun?"

Jeggred made a low, grinding sound. Faeryl couldn't tell if he was growling or laughing.

Triel said, "You underestimate him. True, I've watched him butcher eight prisoners in as many seconds, but I've also seen him spend days picking one little faerie child apart a mote of flesh at a time. It depends on his humor, and, needless to say, my instructions."

"Of course," Faeryl said. The shallow gash in her cheek began to sting. Jeggred traced the edges of her lips with his claw, not quite cutting, not yet. "I hope the traitor whelp appreciated the honor."

"It was hard to tell," she said. "What about you? Will you savor it?"

"Alas, Exalted Mother," Faeryl said, "your daughter can take no pleasure in an honor she didn't earn."

Still stroking the prisoner's features with the claw, Jeggred lifted one of the smaller hands that, save for their dusting of fine hair, looked no different than those of an ordinary dark elf. He caught hold of Faeryl's ear and twisted it, and she gasped at the brutal stab of pain. When he finally let go, the organ kept on throbbing and ringing. She wondered if the draegloth had inflicted permanent damage, though it really didn't matter. In the hours to come, deafness would be the least of her problems.

"I wish you wouldn't deny your guilt," sighed the dainty little Baenre matriarch. "I always find that dull."

"Even when it's true?" Faeryl felt a fresh cut bleeding under her eye. Apparently, when Jeggred had abused her ear, she'd bucked against his claw.

"Don't be tiresome," Triel said. "You were fleeing, and that confirms your guilt."

"All it confirms is my certainty that someone has poisoned your mind against me," Faeryl retorted. Jeggred caught hold of a lock of her hair and gave it a vicious tug. "My aversion to being condemned unjustly."

"Did you think to escape by running back to Ched Nasad?" Triel asked. "My word is law there, too."

"How do you know?" Faeryl asked.

Jeggred slapped her with one of his enormous fighting hands, bashing her head sideways. For a moment, the shock froze her mind. When her senses returned, she tasted blood in her mouth.

The draegloth crouched, placing his bestial face directly in front of her own, and growled, "Respect the chosen of Lolth."

"I mean no disrespect," Faeryl said. "I'm just saying that for all we know, anything could be happening in Ched Nasad. Cloakers could have over-run the city, or it may have drowned in tides of lava. I doubt it, I pray not, but we don't *know*. We need to find out, and that's why I was sneaking away. Not to betray the weakness of Menzoberranzan's clergy to some enemy or other. Mother of Lusts, it's my weakness too! To gather intelligence, to reestablish communication—"

"I told you I have been in communication with Ched Nasad," Triel said.

"To reestablish *trustworthy* communication . . ." Faeryl persisted, "to make myself useful and so demonstrate I'm your loyal vassal, never a traitor."

Triel made a spitting sound, then said, "My loyal servants obey me."

Faeryl wanted to weep, not from fear, though she was experiencing plenty of that, but from sheer frustration. Jeggred ran his claw along her carotid artery.

"Matron," the Zauvirr said, "I beg you. Let me confront the person who traduced me. Give me that one chance to prove my fidelity. Is it so hard to imagine someone telling you a lie? Don't your courtiers slander one an-other all the time as a means of vying for your favor? Is it impossible that someone or something in Ched Nasad is lying to you even now—telling you all is well while days, then tendays, then months go by without a single caravan?"

Triel hesitated, and Faeryl felt a thrill of hope. Then the ruler of Men-zoberranzan said, "You're the liar, and it will do you no good. If you want me to show any mercy at all, tell me whose creature you are. The svirfneblin? The aboleths? Another drow city?"

"I serve only you, Sacred Mother."

Faeryl said the words without hope, for she saw that she would never convince the Baenre of her innocence. It was too hard for Triel to measure up to her predecessor, too hard to rule in these desperate times, too hard to make decisions. She wasn't about to rethink one of the few she'd managed to squeeze out, no matter how foolish it was.

Jeggred slapped Faeryl and kept on slapping until she lost count of the blows. Finally time seemed to skip somehow, and he wasn't hitting her anymore. Why should he bother? He'd already battered all the strength out of her. She would have fallen if not for the ropes holding her up. A broken tooth had lodged under her tongue, and it was all she could do just to spit it out.

"I told you," the draegloth snarled, "*respect!*"

"I am respectful," Faeryl wheezed. "That's why I give the truth even when it might be easier to lie."

Triel peered up at her son and said, "Princess Zauvirr will not distract you from your duties."

Jeggred inclined his head. "No, Mother."

"But at such times as I do not require you," the matron continued, "you may use the spy as you see fit. If she tells you anything of interest, pass it along, but the point of your efforts is chastisement, not interrogation. I doubt she has anything all that important to confide. We already know who our enemies are."

"Yes, Mother." The half-demon crouched, leered into Faeryl's face, and said, "I can make the fun last. You'll see."

He stuck out his long, pointed tongue and licked blood from her face. The member was as rough as a beast's.

The figure in the chapel doorway had a bulbous head with huge, protruding eyes, dry, wrinkled hide, and four wriggling tentacles surrounding and obscuring the mouth. It had gnarled three-fingered hands, a body with contours and proportions different than those of a drow, and an assortment of talismans and amulets burning with strange enchantments.

Syrzan, Pharaun had no doubt, was a member of the psionically gifted species called illithids. Specifically, it was one of the few such creatures to follow the path of wizardry and ultimately transform itself into an undead entity known as an alhoon. The thing was surely prodigiously powerful, immune to the ravages of time, and still entirely capable of reading the masters' minds and discerning the treachery therein.

Like Pharaun, Ryld had sprung up from his bench. The hulking warrior flung himself at Houndaer, no doubt in an attempt to get his weapons back. Pharaun, who thought he needed his spell components just as badly, scrambled after his friend.

The weapons master threw a punch, knocked Houndaer backward off his bench, and snatched up Splitter. He whirled, looking for the next threat, and almost whacked his fellow teacher with the blade.

Pharaun reached for his cloak, then realized Houndaer's unassuming companion was singing a wordless arpeggio.

Had Pharaun already been wearing the *piwafwi* with all its protective enchantments, he might have resisted the song, but instead its power stabbed into his mind. He laughed convulsively, uncontrollably, and staggered backward. Finally, he fell to his knees, his stomach muscles clenching and aching.

He'd suspected the nondescript little male was more than he'd seemed, a formidable combatant employing a bland appearance to throw his adversaries off guard, and he'd been right. The "craftsman" was in reality a bard, a spellcaster who worked his wonders through the medium of music.

Teeth gritted, Pharaun shook off the compulsion to laugh. Gasping, he lifted his head and looked around. The bard was simultaneously drawing his enchanted dagger and starting another song, this time pitched falsetto. Houndaer was on his feet battling Ryld, their swords ringing. At the end of the room, Tsabrak, shifting his eight legs in agitation, aimed an arrow at Pharaun, while in the doorway the alhoon simply stood with only its mouth tentacles moving, seemingly content to let its compatriots do the fighting.

Pharaun threw himself sideways. The arrow missed him and clacked and skipped across the floor. The mage slapped the stone, and a wall of sheltering darkness sprang up between him and the foe. Moving with a practiced, silent grace, he scrambled on.

Something clamped down on Pharaun's mind, smothering his will and robbing him of the ability to move. The undead mind flayer hadn't been idle after all. Syrzan had simply utilized its psionic strength in preference to its wizardry and thus hadn't needed to whirl its three-fingered hands in arcane passes. The wall of shadow no impediment, the Prophet had reached out, found Pharaun's intellect, and struck a crippling blow.

The barricade of darkness disappeared. Syrzan must have employed a bit of countermagic to dispel it and in so doing, afforded Pharaun a view of the space beyond. Rather to his surprise, Houndaer was still alive, perhaps because Tsabrak had discarded his bow, drawn a broadsword, and come to fight alongside him. The two conspirators were trying to catch Ryld between them, generally an effective tactic, but thus far the teacher's *piwafwi*, dwarven armor, and prowess had preserved him from harm.

The Tuin'Tarl made a halfhearted slash, and Ryld, recognizing the feint for what it was, didn't react. The pale phosphorescence of the carvings gleaming on his naked limbs, Tsabrak spat venom onto his blade. The bard brought his shrill singing to a crescendo, crossed his legs, and wrapped his arms tightly around his torso, all but tying himself in knots.

With the aid of his ring, Pharaun saw a glittering pulse of magic fly from the singer to Ryld. He could even tell what it was intended to do. His friend was supposed to contort his own body in helpless imitation of the bard's constrictive posture. But, strong of spirit, Ryld resisted the compulsion without even realizing he was doing it.

The weapons master faked a cut at Houndaer's head, then whirled and dived. He slid between Tsabrak's legs, breaking away from the drider and Houndaer, too, leaped up, and charged Syrzan. He recognized the alhoon as the most dangerous of his foes, even though the illithilich hadn't attacked him yet.

Syrzan reached into a pocket and produced a small ceramic vial. When it swung the bottle from right to left, a dozen orbs of bright flame materialized in its wake. They shot at Ryld in one straight line and exploded one after the other, banging rapidly like some hellish drum roll.

The glare was dazzling. For a moment, Pharaun couldn't see anything, and he made out Ryld through floating blobs of afterimage. His friend appeared unscathed. He was still charging and almost in sword's reach of the alhoon.

Syrzan used its mind flayer talents. Even though the lich hadn't directed the attack at him, Pharaun felt the fringe of it. It was like a sprinkle of hot ash burning his brain. Ryld dropped.

Syrzan gazed down at the warrior for a moment, evidently making sure he was truly incapacitated, then walked over to Pharaun. Despite the long skirt of its robe, there was something noticeably strange about its gait, as if its legs bent in too many places. Up close, it exuded a faint stink not unlike rotten fish. Its garments, once of princely quality, were frayed and stained.

It touched a finger to Pharaun's brow, and they were elsewhere.

chapter

NINETEEN

The Underdark was boundless, its mysteries infinite, and despite centuries of following wherever his curiosity led, Pharaun had never seen an illithid city. Save for a dearth of inhabitants, he thought he'd just stepped into one.

Artisans had carved the walls and columns of the vault into spongiform masses like brain tissue, then covered the convolutions with lines of graven runes. Pools of warm fluid dotted the floor. Redolent of salt, the ponds crawled and throbbed with a mental force that even a non-psionic intelligence dimly sensed as a whisper of alien, incomprehensible thought at the back of the mind.

Pharaun recognized that the cavern was in some sense an illusion, but that didn't make it any less interesting. He would have liked nothing better than to explore every nook and cranny. It was an inclination rooted in a profound sense of well-being, a blithe unconcern no more genuine than the landscape, but seductive all the same. He would have to fight it.

He turned, saw Syrzan standing a few feet away, and cast darts of force, a spell requiring only words of power and a flourish of the hands. Halfway to their target, the streaking shafts of azure radiance stopped dead in the air, fell to the ground, and turned into limbless things like leeches or tadpoles, which, squealing telepathically, slithered toward the nearest pool.

"Your spells won't work here," said Syrzan in the Prophet's rich, compelling tones.

"I suspected as much, but I had to try. Are we inside your mind?"

"More or less."

Syrzan strolled closer. Off to the side, liquid splashed and plopped as the tadpoles wallowed.

"We're conversing in my special haven," the undead mind flayer said, "but we're also still in the heretic's chapel. In that reality I'm rebuking Houndaer for fetching you after I told him it was dangerous, and you're insensible."

"Fascinating," Pharaun said, "and I suppose you spirited me into the dream for a private tête-à-tête."

"Essentially," the alhoon said. Even in this phantasmal domain, it smelled faintly of decaying fish. "This is actually a form of mind-reading. You won't be able to lie."

The Master of Sorcere chuckled. "Some people would say that so handicapped, I won't be able to speak at all."

The mages began stroll along side by side. The atmosphere felt quite congenial.

"How is it," Syrzan asked, "that you came looking for my associates and me?"

Pharaun explained. He didn't see how it could do any harm.

When he was finished, the illithilich said, "You couldn't wield my particular sort of power."

"I understand that now. You enthrall the undercreatures through a deft combination of wizardry and mind flayer arts, and I lack the innate capacity to master the latter. What's more, you conspirators know nothing about the priestesses' difficulties." Pharaun cocked his head. "Or perhaps you do, Master Lich."

"No," said Syrzan, its mouth tentacles coiling and twisting. "Like the others, I know what's happened but not why."

"So none of what I sought was ever here for the finding." Pharaun laughed and said, "My sister Sabal once told me that a clever drow's wits can lead him into follies no dunce would dare to undertake . . . but that's blood down the gutter. What of you? What in the wide world prompted a creature such as yourself to throw in with a band of Menzoberranyr malcontents?"

"You seek information you can use against me."

"Well, partly . . ." Pharaun had to pause for a second when a wave of psionic force from one of the larger pools dizzied him and threatened to wash his own thoughts away. "In the unlikely event I'm ever afforded the chance. Mostly, though, I'm just curious. You're a mage. Surely we share that trait even if little else."

Syrzan shrugged, the narrow shoulders beneath its faded robes hitching higher than would a drow's.

"Well," the alhoon said, "I suppose it can do no harm to enlighten you, and it's been a long while since I've had the opportunity to converse with a colleague of genuine ability. Not that you're my equal—no elf or dwarf could ever be—but you're several cuts above any of Houndaer's allies."

"Your kind words overwhelm me."

The two wizards stepped onto a bridge, a crooked limestone span arching over one of the briny pools.

"Dark elves will abide a lich," the alhoon said, a brooding note entering its musical and almost certainly artificial voice. "Illithids won't. By and large, they hate the idea of sorcery, a foreign discipline as potent as the psionic skills that constitute our birthright. Still, they'll tolerate a limited number of *mortal* mages, those of us drawn to wizardry despite the stigma, for the advantages we bring. But the thought of undying wizards enduring for millennia, amassing arcane power the while, terrifies them."

"So on the day you achieved your immortality," Pharaun said, "you forsook your homeland forever, or at least until the day when you could conquer it."

The two mages stopped at the highest point on the bridge and looked out over an expanse of warm, briny fluid. Pharaun noticed that the stuff rippled and flowed sluggishly, as if it was thicker than water.

"Indeed," Syrzan said. "I hoped to manage my departure circumspectly, but somehow the folk of Oryndoll sensed my metamorphosis. For decades, they hunted me like an animal, and I existed like one in the wilds of the Underdark. Those times were hard. Even the undead crave the comforts of civilization. Finally Oryndoll forgot me or gave up on me. That was an improvement, but still I had no home."

"I've heard," said Pharaun, "that one or two secret enclaves of illith-iliches exist. Didn't you search for one?"

"I searched for ninety years and found one," Syrzan replied, sounding slightly miffed that its prisoner had jumped ahead in the story. "For a time, I dwelled therein but I quarreled with the eldest alhoons, who considered themselves the leaders of the rest. I conducted certain investigations they had, in their ignorance and timidity, forbidden."

The Master of Sorcere laughed and said, "If you can't find it in your heart—assuming an illithilich retains the organ—to consider us equals, you must at least concede we're kindred spirits. You weren't angling for the Sarthos demon, were you?"

"No," said Syrzan curtly. "Suffice it to say that if not for some bad luck, I would have usurped the place of the eldest lich of all, but as matters fell out, I had to flee into the wilderness, a solitary wanderer once more."

"Surely you found someone to enslave."

Pharaun noticed the air in the dream cavern had grown cooler. Perhaps it was responding to its maker's somber reflections.

"I found small encampments," Syrzan said. "A family of goblins here, a dozen troglodytes there. I used them, used them up, each in its turn, but no little hole infested with a handful of brutes could give me what I truly craved. I yearned for a teeming city, full of splendors and luxuries, over which I would rule, and from which I could conquer an empire. But the taking of such exceeded even my powers."

"Or mine," Pharaun said, "hard as that is to credit. So, lusting for what you couldn't have, you spied on the cities of the Underdark, didn't you, or one of them, anyway. You kept your eye on Menzoberranzan."

"Yes," Syrzan said, "I've watched your people for a long while. I discovered the cabal of renegade males some forty years ago. More recently, I observed the priestesses' debility; no mere dark elves could hide such an enormous change from an observer with my talents. I remembered the would-be rebels and arranged for them to make the same discovery, then I emerged from the shadows and offered them my services."

"Why?" Pharaun asked. "Your collaborators are drow, and you're, if you'll pardon my bluntness, a member of an inferior species. Jumped up vermin, really. You don't expect Houndaer and the boys to honor a pact with you once the prize is won? Dark elves don't even keep faith with one another."

"Fortunately, the prize won't be won for decades, and during those years, I'll be subtly working to impose my will on my associates. Long before they assume the rulership of the city, I'll be ruling them."

"I see. The fools have given you your opening, and now that which you could never conquer from the outside you'll subjugate from within, extending the web of compulsion farther and farther, one assumes, until all Menzoberranyr are mind-slaves marching to your drum."

"Obviously, you understand the fundamentals of illithid society," said Syrzan. "You probably also know that we prefer to dine on the brains of lesser sentients and that we share your own race's fondness for torture. Still, some of your folk will fare all right. I can't eat or flay *everyone*, can I?"

"Not unless you want to wind up a king of ghosts and silence. And where, may I ask, do these stone-burning fire bombs come from?"

"Menzoberranzan isn't the only drow city possessed of ambitious males," the illithilich said.

Pharaun was momentarily speechless. Another drow city—

"Now, it's your turn to satisfy my curiosity," Syrzan said, interrupting the drow's reverie.

"I live for the opportunity."

"When Houndaer and the others explained our scheme, did you sincerely consider joining us?"

Pharaun grinned and said, "For about a quarter of a second."

"Why did you reject the idea? You're no more faithful or less ambitious than any other drow."

"Or illithid, I'll hazard. Why then did I remain firm in my resolve to betray you to Gromph?" The slender dark elf spread his hands. "So many reasons. For one, I'm a notable wizard, if I do say so myself, and in Menzoberranzan we mages have our own tacit hierarchy. In recent years, I've channeled my aspirations into that. Should I rise to the top, it will make me a personage nearly as exalted as a high priestess."

Syrzan flipped its tentacles, a gesture that conveyed impatience, and a flake of skin fell off. Unlike the slimy hide of living mind flayers, the lich's flesh was cracked and dry.

"The renegades are trying to place themselves *above* the females," the undead creature said.

"I understand that, but I doubt it'll work out the way they plan, or even the way *you* plan."

"You believe the priestesses are too formidable, even divested of their spells?"

"Oh, they're powerful. They may well extinguish this little cabal. Yet for the moment, I'm more concerned about the undercreatures. Do you realize how many goblins there are, how fervently they hated us even before you maddened them, or how dangerous your stone-consuming fire is? It could be that after they riot, we won't have a Menzoberranzan left for anyone to rule."

"Nonsense. The orcs will have their hour, and your people will butcher them."

Pharaun sighed. "That's what folk keep telling me. I wish your consensus comforted me, but it doesn't. That's one of the drawbacks of knowing yourself shrewder than everybody else."

"I assure you, the orcs cannot prevail."

"At the very least, they'll destroy some of the lovely architecture the founders sculpted from the living rock, and they'll set a defiant example for future generations of thralls. Your scheme will harm not merely the priestesses but Menzoberranzan itself, and I disapprove of that. It's sloppy and inept. Only a fool mars the very treasure he's striving to acquire."

A sneer in its tone, Syrzan said, "I wouldn't have taken you for a patriot."

"Odd, isn't it? I'll tell you something even stranger. In my way, I'm also a devout child of Lolth. Oh, it's never kept me from pursuing my own ends—even past the point of murdering a priestess or two—but though I strive for personal preeminence, I would never seek to topple the entire social order she established. I certainly wouldn't conspire to place her chosen people and city under the rule of a lesser creature."

"Even gods die, drow. Perhaps Lolth is no more. If Menzoberranzan is indeed the mortal realm she loves best, why else would she abandon you?"

"A test? A punishment? A whim? Who can say? But I doubt the Spider Queen is dead. I saw her once, and I don't just mean the manifestation who visited Menzoberranzan during the Time of Troubles. I've gazed upon the Dark Mother in the full majesty of her divinity, and I can't imagine that anything could ever lay her low."

"You have looked upon the Spider Queen?"

"I thought you might be interested in that," said the mage. "It wasn't long after I graduated from Sorcere, returned home to serve my mother, and sided with my sister Sabal against her twin Greyanna. One night, a delegation of priestesses came to our stalactite castle. Triel Baenre herself led the expedition—she was Mistress of Arach-Tinilith in those days—and she'd brought along dignitaries from Houses Xorlarrin, Agrach Dyrr, Barrison Del'Armgo, and other families of note. It was a momentous occasion, especially for me, because all these great ladies had come to arrest me.

"I never did find out if Greyanna instigated the affair. It was the kind of thing she would have done, but it needn't have been her. You'll scarcely credit it, but in those days, I was considered an insolent, uppity scapegrace, a far cry from the meek and modest gentleman you see before you today. A good many clerics may have suspected me of irreverence."

"This is what happened to Tsabrak," Syrzan said. "The priestesses arrested him, turned him into a drider, and drove him forth."

"Sometimes they mete out punishments even fouler," Pharaun said, "but first they examine you to determine your true sentiments. I hoped my mother would intervene. She was one of the great Matrons of Menzoberranzan, and I'd scored a number of coups for House Mizzrym, but she never said a word. Perhaps she believed me a traitor in the making or was reluctant to disagree with the Baenre. Maybe she simply found my predicament amusing. Miz'ri's like that.

"Be that as it may, the priestesses threw me in a dungeon and put me to the question, employing whips and other toys. Somehow I managed to resist the urge to make a spurious confession merely to stop the pain. A fellow wizard cast a mind-reading spell, only to slap up against the defenses most mages erect to protect their thoughts. I imagine an illithid would have smashed right through, but he was unequal to the challenge."

"Then you passed the test?" Syrzan asked.

"Alas, no," Pharaun laughed. "The examiners deemed the results inconclusive and accordingly asked a higher power to make the determination. They laid me on an obsidian altar, performed a dancing, keening, self-mutilating ritual together, and the torture chamber faded away. You'd think I would have been glad of it, wouldn't you, but my new surroundings were no less ominous."

Pharaun's captors had ignored his silver ring, obviously thinking it mere jewelry, if they noticed it at all. As soon as he'd looked at Syrzan, he'd discovered its magic operated even within the confines of the lich's phantasmal creation. He forced an idea into his subconscious and continued to prattle.

"The priestesses had drugged me to prevent my resisting their attentions, then used me with considerable brutality. It took me a while just to lift my battered head and look around. When I did, I perceived that I lay atop an enormous object with the shape of a staff or length of cord made of a substance that gave ever so slightly but was as strong as adamantine nonetheless. Otherwise, it would have disintegrated under its own weight. Far ahead, my perch fused at right angles with another such object, which connected with still others, the pattern spreading out to form, I suddenly realized, a spiderweb of insane complexity, huge enough to make a world. If it was attached to anything, the anchor points were too distant for me to see. Perhaps it just went on and on forever."

"The Demonweb," Syrzan said.

Pharaun surreptitiously examined his captor's talismans, using the magic in the silver ring, trying to figure out which one would allow an illithid to send a psionic "Call" to every orc and goblin in Menzoberranzan.

"Very good," the mage said. "I see you were paying attention when your teachers discoursed on the sundry planes of existence. I was indeed exiled to that layer of the Abyss where Lolth holds sway. I remembered hearing that the strands of the web were hollow and that much of the life of the place existed inside. Well, I certainly couldn't see any source of food or water on the outside, let alone a portal to take me home, so, still dazed and sick from the clerics' attentions, I started crawling and searching for a means of entry.

"Eventually, I might have found one, but I ran out of time. The strand I was traversing began to tremble. I peered about and saw her scuttling toward me."

"Lolth?" Syrzan asked.

"Who else? Her priestesses say she travels her domain in a mobile iron fortress, but she must have left it behind that day. I beheld the goddess herself in the guise of a spider as huge as the Great Mound of the Baenre. She's appeared to others in the same shape only smaller, but she was colossal when she came for me.

"I was terrified, but what was one to do about it? Run? Fight? Either effort would have been equally absurd. I exercised the only sensible option. I huddled atop the thread and covered my eyes.

"Alas, she denied me the comforts of blindness. Her will took hold of me and forced me to look up. She was looming over me, staring down with a circle of luminous ruby orbs.

"I felt as if her gaze was not merely piercing but dissolving me. The sensation was intolerable, I wanted to die, and in a way, she granted my wish.

"Her legs were immense, but they tapered to points at the ends, and, moving with a dainty precision, she used the two front-most members to dissect me. Did the process kill me? I don't know. By all rights, it should have, but if I lost my life, my spirit lingered in my divided flesh, still suffering the horror and pain.

"My soul was conscious, too, of its own destruction. Somehow, as the Spider Queen picked apart my flesh and bones, she was filleting my mind and spirit as well. It irks me that I can't describe how it felt. I hail from a race of torturers and spellcasters, but I still lack the vocabulary. Suffice it to say, it wasn't pleasant.

"In the end, every aspect of my self lay in pieces before her—for inspection, I realize now, though I was in too much agony and dread to work it out at the time. When she'd looked her fill, she put me back together."

Still careful not to betray himself, keeping his mind focused on the story, Pharaun decided it was the triangle that would power the alhoon's Call. The question then was what to do about it. The real brooch hung on the chest of Syrzan's physical body, back in the material world. The one inside his mind was a sort of echo. An analogue. Would depriving Syrzan of it accomplish anything?

Pharaun continued, "Do you think she reconnected every subtle juncture of my intellect and spirit exactly as they'd been before? Over the course of the next few years, I invested a fair amount of time brooding over that particular question, but it's unanswerable, so let it not detain us.

"After the Mother of Lusts cobbled me together, she tossed me back to my native reality, back onto the altar, in fact, thus indicating she found me acceptable. I imagine the clerics were disappointed. I've never known an inquisitor to rejoice in a suspect's acquittal.

"Perhaps they took a bit of solace in the discovery that I'd gone altogether mad. They carted me back to my family, who strapped me to a bed and debated whether it wouldn't be more convenient all around to smother me with a pillow. Sabal was my advocate and guard. She couldn't afford to lose her staunchest ally.

"Let's skip over all the raving and hallucinations, shall we? Eventually my wits returned, and as I reflected on my experiences in the Abyss, I realized that while Lolth was infinitely dreadful and malign, she was transcendently beautiful as well. I'd simply been too distraught to recognize it at the time."

The magic of both the ring and the brooch had accompanied the dreamers into the dream. Otherwise, Pharaun wouldn't be able to see the triangle glowing. So perhaps if he disposed of the talisman in this place, its counterpart in mundane reality would lose its enchantments.

Possibly not, also, but the Master of Sorcere felt he had to take a chance. He doubted he'd get another.

"Certainly she exemplified that supreme power to which all dark elves, particularly we wizards, aspire," the drow rambled on. "I felt inspired that she was our patron. She's worthy of us, as we are worthy of her."

"She impressed you," Syrzan said, its mouth tentacles wriggling, "as even the pettiest deity can overawe a mortal. Still, you're a scholar of the mysteries. You should know there are powers greater than Lolth, entities who, if they saw fit—"

Pharaun snatched the triangular ivory brooch off the undead mind flayer's soiled and shabby robe and slammed it down on the convoluted parapet at the edge of the bridge. The ornament didn't break. In desperation, he pulled back his arm to throw it. Perhaps the illithilich would have difficulty retrieving it from the murky pool below.

A cold, rough hand grabbed him by the collar and wrenched him down. He was powerless to resist. In the reality Syrzan had created for itself, it was as strong as a titan.

The lich ripped the brooch from Pharaun's grasp and thrust it into a pocket. It clutched the dark elf with both hands, leaned its head close, and wrapped its dry, flaking mouth tentacles over the mage's skull. Pharaun knew this was how mind flayers fed. They wormed their members into whatever orifices were most convenient and yanked out their victim's brain.

He wondered what would happen when Syrzan subjected his dream self to such treatment. Would his physical body perish, or would it survive as a living but mindless shell?

"Didn't you like my story?" Pharaun gasped. The lich's grip was squeezing the breath out of him. "You seemed quite engrossed. That was why I dared to hope I could catch you by surprise."

"You put your hands on me! I do not permit that!"

The mellifluous voice of the Prophet was roughening into an ugly combination of hisses and buzzes. The tentacles squeezed tighter

"Technically, these aren't my hands," Pharaun said. Goddess, it felt as if his skull was going to shatter! "Since this is all imaginary."

"You will tell me how you knew which charm to grab."

"My ring. It allows me to see and interpret patterns of magical force. No wizard should be without one."

"You were a fool to try to thwart me here in my private world. Don't you understand that inside this construct, I'm a *god*."

"I'm dead regardless," replied Pharaun, "and when a drow knows his life is forfeit, he bends his thoughts to revenge."

"But you're mistaken." Syrzan loosened the grip of the tentacles and said, "I'm not going to kill you. That would be wasteful. As you observed, my objective is to enslave all Menzoberranzan. Certainly you, with all your talents, will make a useful thrall. Had you not manhandled me, your bondage might have been relatively light, for I enjoy the society of other mages. Now I'm afraid you aren't going to enjoy it in the slightest."

Pain ripped through Pharaun's head. He screamed.

chapter

TWENTY

"Let me do it," Houndaer growled.

His scimitar at the ready, he stalked toward Ryld.

The Master of Melee-Magthere tried and failed to rise. As a student at the Academy and in all the years since, he'd studied techniques for transcending pain, but he'd never felt anything comparable to the invisible blow the undead illithid had struck him. It had been like a spear driving through his mind.

Syrzan emerged from its momentary trance and said, "No."

Houndaer turned. "No?" he asked. "You were right about them. Obviously."

"And I trust," said the lich, its mouth tentacles wriggling, "that you'll remember whose judgment is superior. Now that they're here, however, they might as well serve our cause as you hoped they would. It's just a matter of reshaping their minds."

The bard lifted an eyebrow and asked, "Can you do that?"

"Yes," said Syrzan, "but not instantaneously, and not now. I need my strength to give the Call."

It pulled Pharaun's silver ring off the unconscious drow's finger.

"Lock them up for the time being," the alhoon ordered.

"All right," said Tsabrak. "I hope you're going to fix it so we can all control them."

He too advanced on Ryld.

The weapons master struggled once again to rise. Someone lashed him over the head with the flat of a blade, and all the strength spilled out of him like wine from an overturned cup.

The next few minutes were a blur. Houndaer, Tsabrak, the bard, and another renegade carried their captives to a cell. It had the same grime and air of desolation as much of the rest of the castle, but someone, exhibiting a proper dark elf's sense of priorities, had gone to the trouble to refurbish the locks and restraints.

The rogues divested Ryld of his cloak and armor, then chained him to the wall. As he'd expected, the conspirators took more elaborate precautions with the wizard, even though Pharaun had suffered a violent seizure shortly after Syrzan stunned him, had apparently passed from that into complete unconsciousness, and showed no sign of rousing any time soon. In addition to shackling him, the rogues locked a steel bridle around his head, forcing the bit into his mouth to keep him from enunciating words of power or anything else. They inserted his forearms into the two ends of a hinged metal tube, a sort of muff or double glove that would make it impossible for him to gesture or crook his fingers into a cabalistic sign.

By the time they finished, Ryld's strength had begun to return, enough, at least, to permit him to speak.

"It'll get you, too," he croaked.

Houndaer turned, scowling. "What?"

"The lich. It doesn't want to share power. It's planning to turn every Menzoberranyr, including you, into its mind-slave. That's what illithids do."

"Do you think we trust the beast?" the Tuin'Tarl sneered. "We're not idiots. It'll serve its purpose, and we'll dispose of it."

"So you intend, but what if Syrzan's already working on subjugating you, so subtly you don't even know it? What if, when the time comes—"

Houndaer punched his former teacher in the mouth, dashing his head against the calcite wall.

"Shut up," the noble said. "You fooled me once and made me look like an imbecile. It's not going to happen again."

The rogues made their departure. With his spidery lower body, Tsabrak had to squeeze through the door. The last one out, the bard gave Ryld a wry smile and a shrug. The door slammed shut.

Ryld licked the salty taste of blood from his gashed lower lip.

"Pharaun," he said in a low tone. "Are you truly unconscious, or is it a trick?"

Slumped with the steel harness clamped around his head, the Master of Sorcere didn't respond. If not for the rise and fall of his chest, Ryld would have feared him dead.

The swordsman tried to go to Pharaun, but his chains were too short. He undertook an examination of the shackles. The cuffs fit tightly, and the locks were strong. The links were heavy, well forged, and anchored securely in the wall. Ryld had broken free of bonds a time or two in his turbulent early years, but without tools or a miracle, he wouldn't be sundering these.

Nor, denied the use of his voice and hands, was Pharaun likely to fare any better. Still, Ryld suspected the mage was his only hope. Pharaun was clever. Perhaps he could think of a workable ploy, if only he was conscious.

"*Wake up!*" Ryld roared. "Wake up, curse it. You've got to get us out of here!"

To add to the din, he beat a length of chain against the wall.

To no avail. He shouted until his throat was raw, but Pharaun didn't stir.

"Bleed it!" the weapons master swore.

He hunkered down on the floor and tried to work up some saliva to wash away the dryness in his mouth. As the renegades hadn't bothered to provide a water jug, spit was the best he could do.

"You have to wake up," he said in a softer voice. "Otherwise, they've beaten us, and we've never let anyone do that. Do you remember when we hunted that cloaker lord? We found out too late that it had *sixty-seven* other chasm rays in its raiding party, many more than our little band of third-year students was prepared to confront. But you said, 'It's all right, it just takes the proper spells to even the odds.' First you conjured a wall of fire . . ."

Ryld rambled on for hours, talking his throat raw, recounting their shared experiences as they occurred to him. Perhaps the stories would strike a spark in Pharaun's unconscious mind, and in any case, it was better than just sitting and wondering what life would be like after Syrzan corrupted his mind.

Finally the wizard's chin jerked up off his chest. His eyes were wild, and he tried to cry out. The bit turned the sound into a strangled gurgle even as it cut into the corners of his mouth. Beads of blood blossomed from the wounds.

"It's all right," Ryld said. "Whatever the lich did to you, it's over."

Pharaun took a deep breath and let it out slowly. Rationality returned to his eyes. Ryld got the feeling that if not for the harness, the wizard would have smiled his usual cheery smile. He nodded to the weapons master, thanking him for the reassurance, then he inspected the sheath constraining his hands. He bashed it on the floor a few times to see if he could jolt the catches open. They held with nary a rattle. He shook his head, sat still for several seconds, then closed his eyes and settled back against the wall, no doubt pondering their plight.

After several minutes, the wizard straightened up. He started scraping the heel of one boot against the side of the other.

Ryld felt a stir of excitement. He could only assume his fellow master had a talisman hidden inside the footwear. It was odd the wizard hadn't remembered until then, but perhaps it was a result of the seizure.

Like all drow boots, Pharaun's were high and fit snugly. By the time it slid off the mage's foot, Ryld was avid with curiosity to see . . . nothing. Nothing but trews and a stocking.

Pharaun set to work shoving off the other boot. Ryld wished he knew what his friend had in mind, but knew it would be pointless to ask. With his hands concealed, the spellcaster couldn't answer even in the silent drow sign language.

Eventually the second boot slipped free, whereupon Pharaun pushed off his socks. His bare feet were of a piece with his hands, slender and long, the digits included.

The wizard lifted his right foot, stared at it intently, and started curling and crossing the toes. He fumbled through a sequence of moves, then repeated it. It took Ryld another few moments to comprehend, and he didn't know whether to laugh or cry.

In point of fact, the Underdark abounded in creatures, Syrzan included, whose extremities differed notably from a dark elf's, yet who worked magic nonetheless. So maybe Pharaun had a chance. Maybe he could cast one of those spells that only required movement, not an incantation or material components.

But only if he could shift his feet and toes through the proper patterns, those precise and intricate passes he'd spent years learning to execute with his hands.

When the toes of his right foot grew tired, he started working with those of his left. After that, he shifted his weight back, lifted his legs, and practiced twining them together. Ryld might have found it quite a comical spectacle had his life not depended on the mage's success.

Soon Pharaun began to sweat and occasionally to tremble, which always forced him to stop and rest for a bit. After an hour, he moved on to the next phase of his experiment: putting the elements of the spell together, moving everything at the same time with the proper sequence and timing.

Ryld watched the process intently. He was no wizard, but to his untutored eye, it appeared that after a while, Pharaun was producing exactly the same pattern two times out of three. The rest he fumbled in one way or another.

Finally, breathing hard, he looked at the weapons master and shrugged.

"That's all right," the swordsman replied. "Two out of three is good odds."

Pharaun slumped back and spent the next few minutes resting. When he sat up and, heedless of the fresh blood that started from the corners of his mouth, he growled through the mask. He banged the box encasing his hands twice against the floor, then looked at Ryld.

"I understand," the warrior said. "Make noise. Bring someone."

Pharaun nodded. The cage around his head clinked.

"Ho!" Ryld shouted. "Somebody, come here! I'm a Master of Melee-Magthere. I know secrets about the defenses of the great Houses, secrets you must know for your plans to succeed. I'll trade them for my freedom!"

He continued in the same vein for several minutes, clashing his chains against the wall for emphasis. Meanwhile Pharaun lay motionless, as if he were still unconscious.

Finally, eyes appeared at the little barred window in the door.

"What?" the newcomer snarled. It wasn't a voice Ryld had heard before.

"I need to talk to you," the weapons master said.

"I heard," said the other drow. "You have secrets. The alhoon will rip them out of you, no bargain required."

"Syrzan said it would take time to turn us into mind-slaves," Ryld replied. "I have information you need before you unleash the under-creatures. Their rebellion will do you no good if the weapons masters strike them all dead before they even get started."

"How could the masters-of-arms do that?" asked the rogue.

"A secret," said Ryld, "that we brothers of the pyramid teach to a chosen few."

"I don't believe you."

"We've been studying war for millennia. Do you think we impart all we know to every young dullard who enrolls in the Academy, or is it likely we hold greater, deadlier mysteries in reserve?"

The rogue hesitated.

"All right, tell me. If there's anything to it, I'll set you free."

Ryld shrugged, rattling his fetters. They were already rubbing his wrists raw.

"Shout it through a closed door?" the weapons master asked. "Is that what you really want?"

"Wait."

The contempt in the prisoner's tone had reminded the rogue of a basic principle. It was best to keep information to yourself, at least until you figured out how to reap a benefit from sharing it. This rogue didn't want anyone overhearing what Ryld had to say.

The door clacked as a key turned in the lock. It creaked open, and the renegade stepped through. He was stocky, with a broken nose squashed across an angular face. He'd decorated rather nondescript clothing with gaudy ornaments, including a silver fillet set with garnets. His rapier hung from a baldric, the hilt of a dagger protruded from the top of either boot, and a hand crossbow dangled from his belt.

He stopped just inside the doorway, where he had every right to think himself safe. The cell was large enough, and the prisoners' shackles short enough, that he was beyond their reach. He swung the door shut behind him but didn't permit it to latch.

"All right," he said, "now you can tell me."

"First," said Ryld, "unchain me."

He thought he had to keep the renegade occupied for just a few more seconds, long enough for Pharaun to cast his spell.

The guard just laughed and said, "Don't be absurd."

"Why not?"

"You know why not."

"But you might just listen to the secrets and leave me imprisoned," said Ryld, watching Pharaun from the corner of his eye.

To his dismay, the wizard wasn't conjuring. He wasn't moving at all. Had he passed out again?

"You're caged," said the renegade, "and I'm not. Therefore, *you* will have to trust *me*, not the other way around."

Ryld scowled, meanwhile racking his brains for inspiration. With Pharaun inert, he was going to have to improvise a story to detain the rogue and pray the wizard would make a move before much longer.

"All right, I suppose I have no choice. Not far beyond Bauthwaf lies the entrance to a tunnel leading to the deepest reaches of the Underdark, where even our people do not—"

"What's this got to do with weapons masters killing slaves?" the guard demanded.

"Listen, and you'll find out. At the lower end of the passage is a mineral I've never seen anywhere else . . ." At last Pharaun moved his feet. Now, if only the renegade didn't notice. "When you crush the rock to powder . . ."

"Hey!"

Evidently the guard's peripheral vision was almost as good as Ryld's, for he pivoted toward Pharaun, but not in time. A disembodied hand made of pale yellow light appeared beside his shoulder and gave him a push.

The impetus sent him staggering closer to Ryld. The weapons master grabbed him and smashed his head against the wall until it left a sticky mess on the stone, then he searched the corpse and found a ring of keys clipped to its belt.

He discovered the one that opened his own restraints, and Pharaun's. The wizard flexed his fingers, restoring circulation, produced a silken handkerchief from his sleeve, and dabbed at the blood on the sides of his mouth.

"I think I'll establish a new school of magic," the wizard said. "Pedomancy—the sorcery of the feet."

"Why did you wait so long to throw the spell?" Ryld asked.

"I was looking for our friend's keys. It wouldn't have done any good to attack him had he not been carrying the means to release us from our fetters. His cape was hanging over them, and it took me a minute to spot them."

"I was certain something had gone wrong. Are you ready to get us out of here?"

"Momentarily," Pharaun said as he pulled on his socks and boots. "I think everything's going splendidly, don't you? We've acquired the knowledge we came for, and now we'll escape, just as planned."

"We didn't plan on having to do it without our gear."

"Please, don't harp on the obvious. It makes for a dreary conversation. Where exactly are we, by the way? Where's the nearest exit?"

"I don't know. They gave me a knock on the head before they carried us here. I think we're up inside the cavern ceiling."

"So we won't encounter a window or balcony unless we descend a ways, but we might find a door opening on a tunnel."

Ryld scavenged the dead rogue's weapons and *piwafwi*. The cloak was much too small for him, but would provide some protection nonetheless. The mail shirt, alas, he simply couldn't wear.

"No gear for me?" Pharaun asked.

"I'm the fighter, and I'll be standing in front."

"Well, when you put it that way . . ."

"Let's go."

The masters stood up. Ryld felt dizzy, swayed, but then recovered his balance. They started for the door, and something happened. It was like the blare of a trumpet and a white light, too, but it was neither. The weapons master didn't know what it was, only that it froze him in place until it faded away.

"What just happened?" he asked.

"The Call," Pharaun replied. "This close to the source, one can vaguely sense it even if one isn't a goblin. The slaves are rising."

chapter

TWENTY-ONE

When the instructors rounded the corner, Pharaun saw a rogue about five yards away. Well armed, the conspirator was striding purposefully along, perhaps to join one of the assassination squads that would descend on the city once the goblin rebellion plunged it into chaos.

He had good reflexes. As soon as he spotted the fugitives, he reached for the wall, no doubt to conceal himself behind a curtain of darkness.

Pharaun lifted his hands to cast darts of force—he had two such spells remaining, neither requiring a focal object—but Ryld was quicker. He shot his hand crossbow. The quarrel plunged into the renegade's eye, and he fell.

The masters skulked up to the corpse and crouched down to examine it. Pharaun was hardly surprised yet disappointed to find that the dead warrior hadn't been carrying any spell ingredients.

The Master of Sorcere hadn't lost faith in himself, but he realized that overconfidence coupled with ambition had lured him and Ryld into a desperate situation. They were stuck in the midst of their enemies. Without the proper triggers, most of the wizard's magic was unavailable to him, and the weapons master was feeling the effects of the blow on the head and Syrzan's psionic assault. Most people wouldn't have noticed, but Pharaun, who knew him well, could see subtle indications in the way he moved.

Well, at least Ryld wasn't bored.

Pharaun stole the dead male's hand crossbow, dirk, and *piwafwi*—including the insignia of a lesser House Pharaun assumed was enchanted in the same way as all the others. The mantle wasn't a bad fit but felt strange without the weight of the hidden pockets to which he was accustomed. At least, he hoped, he'd be able to levitate. Ryld exchanged the rapier he'd been wearing for the fallen drow's broadsword.

The Master of Melee-Magthere cocked his crossbow and loaded a fresh shaft in the channel. The fugitives stalked on down the hallway, and the walls screamed. Pharaun and Ryld screwed up their faces at the painful loudness. Blue sparks of discharged magic showered from the walls and ceiling, and a hot, raw stink of power fouled the air.

The screech stopped as suddenly as it had started, though it left echoes sobbing through the citadel.

"Alarm spell?" said Ryld, trotting onward.

"Yes," Pharaun said, racing to catch up. His ears were ringing. "Had I seen it, I would have dispelled it, but—"

"But as it stands, the rogues will be coming for us." Pharaun frowned. "Unless they're too busy getting ready to murder priestesses."

"No, they'll realize they have to catch us at any cost. If a spy slipped away from here and reported their plans to the Council, it would ruin everything for them."

"You're right, curse it."

The masters had been moving stealthily and therefore slowly ever since departing their cell, and they would have to sneak along even more warily, backtracking and detouring whenever they sensed their enemies were near. That would make it easier to get lost. The long-dead nobles had built their fortress according to a defensive strategy still occasionally employed in Menzoberranzan. The place was something of a maze. If a person had grown up there, that wouldn't pose a problem. He'd know every turn and dead end, but outsiders had a difficult time moving about. Outsiders like Pharaun and Ryld, who had yet to find an exit.

Perhaps, the wizard thought, the renegades will have trouble navigating as well.

Though they'd squatted in the castle, they might not know it as well as the original occupants had. It was possible they'd simply familiarized themselves with a few key areas and primary passageways and left the rest of the allegedly cursed and haunted keep pretty much alone.

Still, Pharaun knew it was only a matter of time until the hunters stumbled onto their prey, and he was correct. He and Ryld were traversing a gallery hung with musty phosphorescent tapestries when something rustled behind them. The masters pivoted. Silent in their drow boots, half a dozen warriors had appeared behind them and were leveling their crossbows.

Ryld crouched and lifted a fold of his cloak in front of his face. Pharaun copied the move. Two arrowheads plunged through his makeshift shield, which apparently wasn't as powerfully enchanted as the *piwafwi* Houndaer had taken from him. One quarrel hung up in the weave. The other hurtled right through and grazed the mage's shoulder, stinging him and slicing a shallow cut. He prayed it wasn't poisoned.

Hearing a ragged clatter, Pharaun uncovered his eyes. The rogues had dropped their crossbows and were charging. They'd already dashed too close for him to employ the incantation he would have preferred. Instead he cast darts of light and dropped two renegades. He discharged his crossbow and missed a third.

Ryld bellowed a war cry and sprang forward to meet the foes remaining. The broadsword flashed back and forth, thrusting, cutting, and parrying with the small, precise movements that characterized true mastery. Pharaun edged forward with his dirk in hand but never got a chance to use it. The rogues all died before he could advance into range.

Pharaun took stock of himself and decided he didn't have any venom in his system, but Ryld groaned, made a face, and clutched at his temple.

"What is it?" the wizard asked.

It seemed likely that one of the enemy had scored, but he didn't see any blood slipping between his friend's fingers, and head wounds bled copiously.

"A throbbing headache," said the swordsman. "Left over from Houndaer and Syrzan, I suppose, made worse when my heart started beating harder. I'm all right now."

"I rejoice to hear it." Pharaun turned, right into a second volley of quarrels.

He had no time to raise his cloak, dodge, or do anything else but gawk at the second band of renegades who'd crept up from the other direction. Miraculously, every shaft missed.

One of the newcomers shouted, "They're here!"

The guards charged, and Pharaun brandished a bit of spiderweb, the one spell focus he'd had no difficulty replacing. A mesh of taut, luminous cables appeared around the onrushing renegades. Anchored to the wall, the cables were as strong as rope and as sticky as glue. They snared and held the rogues.

All but the two in front. Either they'd been nimble enough to jump clear before the effect fully materialized, or their innate dark elf resistance to magic had protected them.

Undeterred by the loss of their comrades, the warriors drove onward into sword range. The one who focused on Pharaun had a birthmark staining his left profile.

Pharaun shot. The shaft hit the male square in the chest but glanced off his mail. The ugly male swung his sword in a flank cut. Pharaun twisted aside and commenced an incantation.

He had to dodge two more attacks before he finished. Shafts of light sprang from his fingertips.

Only one such spell left, he thought, and only one more chance to conjure a trap of webbing, too.

The missiles passed through the renegade's mail and sent him reeling backward. Wounded but still alive, the rogue gave his head a shake. Pharaun yanked his new dirk out of his belt and flung himself at the guard. The wizard rammed his point up under the ugly male's chin before the latter had quite recovered his wits.

Pharaun turned. Feinting low and striking high, Ryld whipped his broadsword through his opponent's neck. The renegade fell, his severed head tumbling away. For a moment, Pharaun felt a touch of relief, then he noticed his friend's grimace and the blood on his thigh, and heard the calls of other pursuers drawing near.

"It sounds as if *all* the rogues are hunting us," the wizard said. "What a gracious compliment."

"They heard the fight," Ryld replied. "They have some idea where we are, and thanks to you, this passage has become a cul-de-sac. We have to move—*now*."

"Perhaps you would have preferred me to let the rest of our attackers swarm all over us."

"Just move."

They did, with the prisoners in the web shouting imprecations after them. Pharaun soon discerned that Ryld was making an effort not to limp nor show any sort of distress but couldn't mask his pain completely.

The wizard considered leaving patches of darkness behind to hinder pursuit, but had he done so, he would have been marking his trail. He could only think of one trick he could use to evade the renegades, and hoped it wouldn't be necessary.

Twice, the masters sensed a band of rogues was near and hid in a room until they passed. Finally they found a staircase leading downward. Pharaun hoped their descent to the lower level would throw off the pursuit but soon realized it hadn't. Perhaps it was because the fugitives were leaving a trail of blood. Pharaun's little cut had stopped bleeding, but Ryld's gashed leg had not.

Despite himself, the burly swordsman began taking uneven strides, one shorter than the other. Pharaun heard a murmur of voices coming from behind and out of a side passage as well.

He said, "Stay where you are. I have an idea."

Ryld shrugged.

The wizard advanced a few paces down the corridor. He lifted his wisp of cobweb and chanted. Power groaned through the air, and crisscrossing cables sealed the corridor. The rogues he'd heard were on the other side. So was Ryld.

The swordsman looked at his friend through the interstices and said, "I don't understand."

"And you a master tactician. Truly, I regret this, but I could either stick with you and let your injuries retard my progress or else leave you behind as a rear guard to slow my pursuers. Considering how vulnerable I currently am, the choice was reasonably obvious."

"Damn you! How many times have I saved your life?"

"I've lost count. At any rate, this will make one more, in the course of which you'll finally be rid of your melancholy. Good-bye, old friend."

Pharaun turned and strode away.

He heard a crossbow clack, and flung himself to the side. The quarrel flew past him. Ryld had needed commendable accuracy to avoid snagging the missile in the adhesive mesh.

Pharaun glanced back and said, "Nice shot, but you might want to save your quarrels for the renegades."

He skulked on, and quickened his pace when someone shouted behind him, and metal clashed on metal.

Ryld quickly learned that one of the rogues was a wizard, and a deft one at that. He had no difficulty lobbing spells through the line his comrades had formed across the hall, leaving them unscathed but battering the weapons master with one attack after another.

So far the flares of power had seared and chilled the Master of Melee-Magthere but done no serious harm. He doubted that would last. He needed to put a stop to the magic before the mage slipped an attack through his natural resistance, and that meant breaking through the line

He faked a sidestep to the left, then dodged right. His wounded leg throbbed, and a soreness, the residue of Syrzan's attack, twisted through his mind. The pain slowed him just enough to render the deception ineffective. Urlryn, the long-armed, gap-toothed renegade on the right, another of Ryld's former students and a good one, met him with a wicked thrust to the belly.

As every warrior knows, you can't retreat at the same instant you're advancing. Ryld had no choice but to defend with the blade. He swept his broadsword across his body in a lateral parry. Urlryn tried to dip his point beneath the block, but moved just a hair too slowly. Ryld smashed his adversary's blade aside, loosening his grip in the bargain.

The weapons master started to riposte with a chest cut, then sensed movement on his flank. He pivoted. Hoping to take him unawares, the rogue next to Urlryn was swinging an axe at his knee. It was how warriors fought in a line. You killed the male who was focused on your neighbor.

Ryld leaped over the attack. When he landed, his leg screamed with pain and threatened to buckle beneath him. Shouting, he made it hold and cut at the axeman's belly. The broadsword crunched through mail, and the rogue toppled.

Ryld's blade was still buried in the axeman's guts when Urlryn and the other surviving warrior rushed him. The master floundered backward, dragging the broadsword free. Swords flashed at him, and somehow, even off-balance, he dodged them, but in so doing, fell on his rump.

The rogues scrambled forward to finish him. He surprised the other stranger with a bone-shattering kick to the ankle, knocking him reeling backward, then reared up on one knee, his sword raised in a high guard for what he knew was coming.

Urlryn's blade crashed down on his own, and he felt the jolt all the way to his shoulder. With both feet planted beneath him, the renegade could bring all his strength to bear. Ryld couldn't.

But he was bigger and more powerful than his adversary and was nicely positioned to hamstring other drow. Teeth gritted, he maintained his defense until his enemy faltered, then whipped the broadsword behind the rogue's leg for a drawing cut.

Urlryn let out a shrill cry and staggered sideways. Ryld heaved himself up and turned toward the wizard, only to discover he could no longer see him. Deprived of his wall of warriors, the spellcaster had conjured another defender, a vaguely bearish thing with folded bat wings and luminous crimson eyes, so huge it nearly filled the corridor.

Ryld had watched Pharaun exercise the famous Mizzrym talent for illusion on numerous occasions, and his experiences stood him in good stead. He sensed, though he couldn't say how, that the demon bear was just a phantasm. He limped forward, flicked the broadsword at it, and it popped like a fungus discharging a cloud of spores. It was strange to think that, had he believed in it, it could have torn him to shreds.

The rogue mage turned tail. Ryld didn't want the bastard to reappear and try to kill him again later, so he gave chase. His head and wounded leg seemed to scream in unison, and he had to stop. The sorcerer scuttled round a corner and disappeared.

As Ryld waited for the pain to subside, he realized he couldn't survive many more fights in his present condition. He either had to escape his foes posthaste or shed his disabilities.

Sadly, he had just about come to the conclusion that he was fated to wander through the castle, ducking his enemies the while, until pure luck led him to an exit. That could take hours.

He had reason to hope he wouldn't need nearly as long to revitalize himself, but he'd leave himself vulnerable during the process. He wouldn't be able to sneak in the opposite direction whenever he detected a party of hunters. He'd have to stay in one place. Still, it seemed the better option.

He skulked along the corridor, peering into doorways. One led to a desolate training hall. The target mannequins looked like ghosts in their shrouds of spiderweb.

Near the right-hand wall were tiers of seats, from which spectators could watch the warriors train. If Ryld crouched down behind the structure, no one would see him without making a careful search of the entire room.

Besides, the master thought, going to ground in a salle might bring him luck. The dark powers knew, he needed it.

He limped behind the sculpted seats and sat down on the floor with his legs crossed. He rested his hands on his thighs, closed his eyes, and commenced a breathing exercise.

Spellcasters smugly imagined they were the only folk who truly knew how to meditate. They were mistaken. The brothers of Melee-Magthere had mastered the practice as well. It helped them reach the highest level of martial proficiency.

Spellcasters. The thought reminded him of Pharaun. It brought the shock and anger flooding back.

But at the moment, those feelings were an impediment. He had to relax and empty his mind.

He could heal the wound Syrzan had left inside his head. He could stop his leg bleeding. He could banish pain and fatigue and tap his body's deepest reservoirs of strength.

If only the enemy gave him time.

Pharaun groped his way onward for just a few more minutes, then found another staircase, this one a narrow spiral leading downward. It was almost as if the mysteriously silent Lolth had returned long enough to reward him for his treachery.

If so, he soon had cause to recall that she was a fickle and treacherous entity herself. He reached the bottom of the steps, headed down a hallway with a high, arched ceiling, and heard another band of hunters. It sounded as if they were just about to round the corner dead ahead. Pharaun looked around at the blank walls. The corridor lacked any doorways into which a fugitive might duck.

The wizard could run, but he didn't want to retreat back the way he'd come. He could evoke a curtain of darkness, but that would alert the rogues that someone was hiding behind it. He could throw darts of force, but it would exhaust his offensive magic. He decided to take a chance.

Concentrating on the stolen House insignia, he shed his weight and floated upward to stretch out horizontally, his spine pressed against the crest of the rounded ceiling.

The hunters passed below him, oblivious to his presence. He stared down, looking for a fellow mage. If there was a chance he could obtain new spell foci, he might attack and the odds be damned, but the males were all warriors.

Once they'd gone by, he drifted back down to the ground and skulked onward. He got turned around once more, then unexpectedly found himself before a small service entrance to a stable much like the one in his family's castle. Moldy stone troughs, casks, mounting blocks, and rusty iron-ring hitches defined regular patterns across the floor, while musty, rotting tack hung along the walls. The aerial steeds were long gone, stolen by the conquerors, evidently, as he didn't see any bones. Two rogues stood watch, guarding the huge sliding doors.

Pharaun smiled, threw his last darts of light, and, without waiting to see how much damage they did, broke from cover and sprinted toward the sentries.

One renegade coughed blood and fell. The other appeared unaffected. A nice-looking fellow with a single elegant tendril dangling beside each cheek, he turned, spotted Pharaun, and calmly lifted his crossbow.

The wizard threw himself flat, and the bolt whizzed over his head. Still prone, he shot his own crossbow. The shaft plunged into the renegade's chest.

The rogue snarled, drew his scimitar, and advanced, but only for three steps. He stopped, and his arm fell, his sword clattering against the floor. An astonished look on his face, he dropped to his knees.

Rising, Pharaun noticed that the dying male's garments were as tasteful as his coiffure.

"Who's your tailor?" Pharaun asked, but the renegade merely fell face-down. "Ah, well."

The wizard strode on to one of the outside doors, unbolted it, and shoved it open. Perhaps the casters were magical, for they worked as well as ever. The panel rolled easily and quietly aside.

On the other side was a sheer drop to the glowing palaces a thousand feet below. Silently thanking the dead guard's House, he touched the stolen brooch and sprang over the edge.

chapter

TWENTY-TWO

Pharaun could float down a thousand feet, or he could fall, relying on levitation to slow his descent at the end. The latter course was dangerous. If he waited too long to counteract the pull of gravity, he would break bones or even pulp himself when he landed.

Still, he chose to plummet, because of what he saw beneath him.

He'd lost track of time inside the rogues' citadel, but it was plain that the Call had gone forth around the black death of Narbondel, when most dark elves had gone home for the night. With few drow about to contest them for possession of the streets, the undercreatures had erupted from their kennels to kill, loot, and destroy. Pharaun couldn't make out individuals, but he could see the mobs as great surging, formless masses like the living jellies that infested certain caverns, and he could certainly see the fires they were setting. He could smell the strange, foul smoke of burning stone, and he could hear the goblins shouting.

Perhaps the embattled commoners looked to the noble Houses for succor. If so, they waited in vain. Sorcerous power flashed white and red from the windows and baileys of the stalactite castles as the nobles struggled with their own rebellious slave soldiers. For the time being, at least, the drow were pinned down, unable to brace the marauders outside their own walls.

A house was growing larger and larger beneath Pharaun's boots. He made himself lighter than air but still slammed down hard. The impact knocked the wind and the sense out of him, and when his wits returned, he was bouncing upward again.

Restoring a portion of his weight, he achieved a more graceful landing, flattened himself against the roof, and peered about. The goblins weren't running amok in his immediate vicinity—not yet—so he jumped down onto the street. Glad the Bazaar was just three blocks away, he dashed in that direction.

He'd almost reached his destination when a motley assortment of scaly little kobolds, pig-faced orcs, and shaggy, hulking bugbears surged from an alley. So far, the revolt was going well for them. They'd manage to lay their hands on spears, swords, and axes, and bloody them, too.

Pharaun ran even faster. A javelin flew past him, but the thralls didn't chase him. Evidently they were more interested in other prey.

When the wizard reached the marketplace, he cursed, for the riot had arrived there ahead of him. Undercreatures were looting and burning the stalls, creating patches of dazzling glare. Some of the merchants had fled. Others attempted to defend their wares, unsuccessfully if they relied on goblin underlings for assistance.

Pharaun skirted the edge of the Bazaar, witnessing scenes of carnage as he skulked along. Laughing, a goblin flogged his master's corpse with a scourge. A bugbear used her manacles to strangle a merchant. Trapped in a blazing stone pen, riding lizards hissed and scuttled back and forth in fear.

The first stall Pharaun had hoped to find intact was burning merrily, and the second was crawling with gnolls, growling, whining, and barking as they pawed through the vendor's goods. The Master of Sorcere knew of only one more possibility on the perimeter of the Bazaar. Should that one be lost to him as well, he would either have to venture deeper into the burning, orc-infested maze of stalls or conceive another plan.

Warty, bearded ogres overturned a twelve-wheeled wagon, dumping out the dark elves who'd been making a stand inside. A walking mushroom, taller than any of the brutes, and, with its slender, fluted stem, far more graceful, swung wide to avoid the little massacre.

Pharaun slipped around the slaughter as well. A few more strides brought him to a scene that, after the carnage he'd just witnessed, seemed almost unreal. The westernmost portion of the marketplace was quiet. Some of the merchants had armed themselves and taken up positions outside their tents and kiosks, but they seemed calm and unafraid.

Over the course of an adventurous life, Pharaun had witnessed the same phenomenon before. Under the proper circumstances, it was possible for folk to remain essentially oblivious to a pitched battle raging just a few yards away.

The wizard ran on. Ahead, a luminous green circle scribed on the ground surrounded a commodious stall built of hardened fungus. A heavyset male stood in the doorway with an arbalest in his hand and a toad, his familiar, squatting on his shoulder. He wore a nightshirt, and his feet were bare. The merchant scowled when he spotted Pharaun.

"Stay back," he said, his throaty voice even deeper than Ryld's.

Pharaun halted, took a breath, and wound up coughing, thanks to the smoke fouling the air.

"My dear master Blundyth, is that any way to greet a faithful customer?"

"It's the way to greet the madman who attacked a patrol only yesterday."

That was right, Pharaun thought, it had been only yesterday. So much had happened since, it felt like a year.

"My past indiscretions no longer matter," the Mizzrym said. "Do you have any notion what's going on?"

"You mean the smoke and commotion over yonder?" Blundyth nodded to the east. "I guess a merchant's eliminating the competition. It's nothing to do with me, though I'm ready if trouble spills this way."

"Would that were true," said Pharaun. "Alas, none of us is truly ready for tonight. Have you glanced up over the roof of your shop?"

He pointed to the orange light presently flickering in the east.

"The nobles are up to something," Blundyth said. "Maybe some of the Houses have joined forces to wipe out a common rival. Again, it's nothing to do with me."

"You're mistaken. All across the city, the undercreatures are rebelling."

Blundyth snorted, "You *are* mad."

"Don't you or your neighbors own thralls?"

"Of course. They're off somewhere."

"Indeed. Off preparing to cut your throats."

"Just go away, Master Mizzrym." Blundyth shifted his grip on the staff and added, "We always got along. Don't make me hurt you."

"The orcs pose a considerable threat. I know how to oppose it, but I need your help. I still have credit here, don't I?"

"I don't sell to outlaws. I don't want any trouble with the priestesses."

Pharaun looked into the merchant's eyes and saw that he'd never convince him.

"Too bad. You'll regret this decision. In just a few minutes, most likely, but by then it will be too late."

The master turned and strode away, but once he was out of Blundyth's sight, he circled back around. Creeping through the cramped spaces between the booths, he approached the burly drow's stall from the side. As he skulked along, he listened to hear if the undercreatures were coming closer, but he couldn't tell. He suspected that one of the cursed sound baffles was muffling the noise.

At any rate, he reached the dimpled fungal structure without any orcs attacking him. He swept his hands through a mystic pass and whispered an incantation. The protective circle of light winked out of existence.

Pharaun ran to the stall, floated upward, and swung himself onto the roof. The petrified fungus supported him like stone. Blundyth cursed and came stalking around the side of the stand, his crossbow at the ready. Pharaun thought he'd better make sure the merchant didn't get a chance to use it.

The wizard jumped off the roof onto Blundyth's back. He knew he hadn't executed the move as nimbly as poor Ryld would have, but it worked. It slammed the merchant to his knees. The toad hopped away.

Clinging to his victim, the master drove his dirk repeatedly into the big male's side. Sometimes the blade plunged deep, and sometimes it caught on a rib. Blundyth flailed and bucked for a while, couldn't break free, then tried to aim the arbalest back over his shoulder. Pharaun ducked away from it. Finally the merchant fell sideways, pinning his attacker's knife and hand beneath him.

Pharaun dragged his hand free, but didn't bother with the dirk. He was about to procure a set of vastly superior weapons. He wiped his bloody fingers on Blundyth's clothing, then rose and headed for the entrance to the stall.

Blundyth's neighbors watched him, but didn't interfere. As the dead male might have observed, his murder was nothing to do with them.

The wizard's supply shop was as well-stocked as usual. Jars, bottles, and boxes stood on limestone shelves, and a greenish mirror glowed on a wooden stand in the corner. The air smelled of spices, herbs, bitter incense, and decay.

Blundyth's *piwafwi* lay carelessly draped across a chest, and it was the first item Pharaun appropriated. The cloak fit him like a tent, but it had the customary row upon row of hidden pockets. Next he examined the vials and drawers, finding the magical components that corresponded to the spells he had prepared. With every one he filched, he felt a little better, almost like a cripple regaining the use of his legs.

As he worked his way across the room, he spotted a pair of boots sitting atop a little cupboard. They were plainly special in some way, for the maker had tooled runes into the leather. Without his silver ring, Pharaun lacked the ability to instantly discern what virtues they possessed, but playing a hunch, he decided to take the time to try them on.

The boots squirmed, molding themselves to his feet, then quivered against his flesh like an animal eager to run. He took an experimental step, and the magical footwear kicked off on its own, augmenting the strength of his legs and propelling him all the way across the shop in a single bound.

Not bad, he thought. Not as good as a flying carpet, but helpful nonetheless.

He took a few more strides, getting the feel of the boots, then headed out. Just as he exited the shop, a howling, shrieking cacophony exploded out of the air. An instant later, a horde of undercreatures—orcs, mostly, with a sprinkling of long-armed goblins—came charging out of the stands of stalls and kiosks to the east.

Blundyth's neighbors gaped in utter astonishment. For some, the instant of consternation was fatal. The undercreatures swarmed over them like ants harvesting the carcass of a mouse.

Some of the remaining merchants bolted. Others shot their hand crossbows, or conjured flashes of magic. One optimist sought to cow the rebels with threats, invective, and commands until a scrofulous orc, slopping the liquid out of a tin bucket, threw some of Syrzan's liquid fire on him. The incendiary ignited flesh as easily as stone.

His great blanket of a *piwafwi* flapping around him, Pharaun ran. Each amplified stride bounced him off the ground, but thanks to the virtues of the magic boots, he always landed softly.

A pair of orcs glared at him and hefted their spears. He whispered an incantation, and a ragged blackness, the essence of death itself, danced among the undercreatures. They collapsed, already rotting.

For the moment at least, Pharaun was in the clear. He raced on, while all around him, his city went down in blood and fire.

"You must know some song, some magic, to track an enemy," Houndaer said.

"If I did, I'd be singing it," Omraeth said curtly. "Now be quiet. If the masters hear us coming, they'll do their best to evade us."

"He's right," said Tsabrak, scuttling along on his eight segmented legs. "Shut up, or we'll never get this done."

Houndaer was wearing Ryld Argith's greatsword strapped across his back, and for an instant he fairly quivered with the urge to try it out on his companions. He wasn't used to such insolence, not from other males, and certainly not from a degraded creature like a drider.

Yet he restrained himself, because he needed them. He prayed he'd be the one to catch up with the fugitives, who'd made him look a fool in the eyes of the other renegades, but he knew he couldn't kill both of them by himself.

Tsabrak raised his hand and whispered, "Wait!"

"What is it?" Houndaer asked.

Instead of replying, the half-spider started taking deep breaths. His nostrils flared. He turned this way and that, then crouched down to sniff along the floor. His front legs bent, and his arachnid lower body tilted like a tray to bring his dark elf head down.

"Did you pick up the scent?" Houndaer asked.

He felt an upswelling of excitement, and made a conscious effort to quell it. He didn't doubt that Tsabrak smelled something pertinent, but over the course of the last hour, the brute, whose metamorphosis had evidently altered his perceptions, had picked up the trail several times only to lose it again.

"Follow me," said Tsabrak, nocking an arrow.

The drider led his companions to the arched entrance to a training hall, where target mannequins stood in shrouds of spiderweb and a tally board hung on the left-hand wall. Over the years, the chalk had lost most of its phosphorescence, but Houndaer could still read the score of a fencing bout in faintly gleaming ciphers.

Peer as he might, however, he could see no sign of Masters Argith and Mizzrym. He gave Tsabrak a questioning and somewhat impatient glance. The drider responded by pointing at the floor.

When a proud noble family had held the castle, a workman in their employ had painted the floor with pistes and dueling circles. Like the chalk, the magical enamel still radiated a trace of light. At one spot, a spatter of blood was occluding it.

Houndaer's pulse ticked faster. He looked up at the drider and mouthed, "Where?"

Tsabrak led them toward the tiers of seats on the right. The noble noticed for the first time that a space separated the sculpted calcite risers and the wall.

Elsewhere in the castle, one hunter shouted to another.

Relax, thought Houndaer. It's *my* kill.

He held his breath as he and his underlings—for that they were, even if they, by virtue of belonging to the conspiracy, imagined otherwise—peeked around the edge of the steps. Master Argith was sitting cross-legged a few yards down the aisle.

The Tuin'Tarl instantly pointed his crossbow. Indeed, he nearly pulled the trigger before he took in all the details of the scene. His former teacher sat motionless, his eyes shut. To all appearances, he was unconscious, or in any case oblivious to the advent of his foes. Master Mizzrym was nowhere to be seen.

Ryld's passivity left Houndaer unsure as to the best course of action.

Should he and his minions summarily dispatch the spy or seize the opportunity to take him prisoner? If the weapons master was dead, he couldn't tell them what had become of his partner.

Then the noble realized that while he'd stood pondering the matter, Tsabrak had drawn back his bow string and sighted down the arrow. Houndaer lifted a hand to signal him to desist, then thought better of it. Master Argith was a superb warrior even by the standards of Melee-Magthere. That was why, when a student, the Tuin'Tarl had admired him so, and had been so eager to recruit him. Perhaps it would be wiser to kill him while they had the chance.

Besides, Houndaer was reluctant to risk the vexation of giving Tsabrak an order and having it ignored.

He lifted his hand crossbow. He and the drider took their time aiming, and why not? Ryld was still unaware of them.

Tsabrak released the string, and Houndaer pulled the trigger. The shafts leaped at the still-motionless weapons master. The noble had no doubt the two missiles would suffice. They were flying true, and the heads were poisoned. It was strange and vaguely unsatisfying to dispatch a master of war so easily, as if it was vengeance on the cheap.

Then, when surely it was too late to react, Ryld moved. He twitched himself out of the way of the crossbow quarrel and caught the hurtling arrow in his hand.

Swiftly, yet somehow without the appearance of haste, the weapons master flowed to his feet and advanced. His bloody thigh didn't hinder him in the slightest. His face and eyes were empty, like those of a medium awaiting communion with the dead.

His voice pitched deep, Omraeth sang a quick rhymed couplet. Power glittered through the air. Evidently the spell was supposed to afflict Ryld, but as far as Houndaer could observe, it didn't. The huge male just kept coming. Tsabrak loosed another arrow, and the teacher slapped it out of the air with his broadsword.

Tsabrak and Houndaer dropped their bows and drew their swords. The drider spat poison on his blade. They'd engage Ryld while he was still in the cramped space behind the seats with no room to maneuver. Omraeth took up a position behind his comrades, where he could augment their efforts with bardic magic.

Houndaer felt a pang of fright and willed the feeling away. He had nothing to fear. It was three against one, wasn't it, and the one had no mail. Indeed, by the look of him, he might not even have any wits.

Except that then he proved he did. Ryld touched the vertical surface that was the back of the steps. He summoned darkness, blinding his foes.

Houndaer hacked madly, and sensed Tsabrak doing the same. Darkness or no, when the spy lunged forward, they'd cut him to pieces. Their swords split nothing but air.

After a few seconds, Omraeth shouted, "Come back this way! Now!"

Houndaer and Tsabrak turned and blundered their way toward the sound of their comrade's voice. The drider's envenomed sword bumped the Tuin'Tarl's arm, but fortunately without sufficient force to penetrate his armor and *piwafwi*.

When Houndaer stumbled out of the murk, Master Argith was in the center of the salle. Under the cover of darkness, he'd made it to the top of the steps and bounded down the other side. He had a good chance of reaching the exit unchecked.

He didn't take it, though. Standing in the center of one of the faintly luminous circles, he settled into a fighting stance. He hadn't scrambled over the steps to flee, rather to reach a battleground more to his liking.

Houndaer swallowed away a dryness in his mouth. Ryld hadn't the sense to run? Well, good. Then they'd kill him.

The noble and drider fanned out to come at the Master of Melee-Magthere from opposite sides. Omraeth hung back and commenced another song.

Advancing to meet his adversaries, Master Argith glided through the first of three moves—parry, feint high, slash low—of one of the broadsword katas he'd taught Houndaer back on Tier Breche. The noble discerned an instant too late that the purpose was to distract attention from the crossbow in the weapons master's other hand. The dart plunged into Omraeth's throat, ending his song in an ugly gurgle and dissipating the charged heaviness of arcane force accumulating in the air. The spellsinger fell backward, and it was two to one.

Houndaer told himself it didn't matter. Not when he was wielding Ryld's own greatsword, a weapon that could supposedly shear through anything, and Tsabrak's blade was dripping poison. They only needed to land one light little cut to incapacitate their foe.

Ryld gave ground before them. Houndaer assumed he wanted to put his back against the wall, so neither of his opponents could get behind him, but with an agility astonishing in so massive a fighter, Ryld changed direction. In the blink of an eye, he was driving forward instead of back, plunging at the half-spider on his left.

Startled, Houndaer faltered, then scrambled toward Ryld and the drider. It would take him a few heartbeats to close the distance.

In that time, Ryld charged in on Tsabrak's right, the side opposite the creature's sword arm. A drider's spidery lower half was sufficiently massive that, like a mounted warrior, he had difficulty striking or parrying across his torso.

Tsabrak slashed at the weapons master's head. The stroke was poorly aimed, and Ryld didn't bother to duck or parry, simply concentrated on his own attack.

Tsabrak made a desperate effort to heave himself aside. Still, Ryld's broadsword crunched through the top of one of the drider's chitinous legs. Tsabrak cried out and lurched off-balance.

Stepping, Ryld whirled his weapon around for what would surely be the coup de grâce. Houndaer shouted a war cry, ran a final stride, and swung the greatsword. He wasn't in a proper stance, and the stroke was a clumsy one, but it sufficed to drive the weapons master back. Ryld knew better than anyone how deadly was that enormous blade.

As soon as the stroke whizzed past, the master advanced with a thrust to the chest. Houndaer wrenched the greatsword around for a parry. It should have been impossible to bring such a huge weapon about so quickly, but it seemed to grow as light as a roll of parchment in his hands. Ryld's broadsword caught on one of the hooks just above the leather-girt ricasso.

Ryld retreated, snatching his weapon free. Houndaer shifted the greatsword into a middle guard, and Tsabrak hobbled up beside him. The drider's face twisted in pain, and pungent fluid spattered rhythmically from his wound.

Ryld continued to back away. The rogues spread out again, though not so widely as before. Tsabrak began to make a soft whining sound in the back of his throat.

Then, seemingly without any windup, just a sudden extension of his arm, Ryld threw his sword. Though the weapon wasn't intended for such an action, it streaked through the air as straight and sure as an arrow. The point plunged into Tsabrak's chest.

The drider's eyes widened. He coughed blood, then flopped forward at the waist, dropping his sword. His spider half, slower to die than the upper portion, continued to limp forward.

It was all right, though, because Ryld had no melee weapon save for a dagger, which would surely be of little use against a blade as long as the greatsword. Houndaer rushed in to deliver the finishing stroke.

"*Tuin'Tarl!*" he screamed.

His face still as blank as a zombie's, the weapons master dodged to the side.

Houndaer turned, following the target, and saw that Ryld had ducked behind one of a row of wooden mannequins. Up close, the crudely carved dummies were oddly disquieting figures, smirking identical smiles despite their countless stigmata of dents and gashes.

Ryld stood poised, waiting, and Houndaer discerned the spy's intent. When his adversary lunged around one side of the dummy, the master would circle in the opposite direction, thus maintaining a barrier between them.

Houndaer saw no reason to play that game, not if his new sword was as keen as it was supposed to be. He brought the blade around in a low arc. It tore away the mannequin with scarcely a jolt, depriving Ryld of his pitiful protection.

Unfortunately, the weapons master sprang forward at the very same instant, before Houndaer could pull the greatsword back for another cut. Ryld slashed at the noble's throat.

Houndaer frantically wrenched himself back, interposing his weapon between himself and the spy, before recognizing that the cut had been more of a feint than anything else. Ryld had tricked him into assuming a completely defensive attitude, then seized the opportunity to dash past him. Houndaer cut at the master's back but only managed to tear his billowing cloak.

The Tuin'Tarl gave chase, and Tsabrak, dying or dead but still mindlessly ambulatory, staggered into his path. Houndaer shouted in frustration and cut the drider down.

When the hybrid fell, the noble could see what was happening behind him. Ryld had reached Tsabrak's fallen sword. Heedless of the venom drying on the blade, the teacher slipped his toe under the weapon, flipped it into the air, and caught it neatly by the hilt. His expression as unfathomable as ever, he came on guard and advanced.

I can still kill him, Houndaer thought, I still have the reach on him.

Aloud, he shouted, "Here! I've got one of the masters here!"

Ryld stepped to the verge of the distance, then hovered there. Confident in his ability to defend, he wanted Houndaer to strike at him. A fencer couldn't attack without opening himself up.

At first, the noble declined to oblige. He intended to wait his opponent out. Ryld beat his blade.

The clanging impact startled a response out of him, but at least it was a composed attack. Feint to the chest, feint to the flank, cut low and hack the opponent's legs out from underneath him.

Even as he flowed into the final count, he remembered Ryld teaching him the sequence, and sure enough, the instructor wasn't fooled. He parried the genuine low-line attack, then riposted to Houndaer's wrist. The broadsword bit through his gauntlet and into the flesh beneath.

Ryld pulled his weapon free in a spatter of gore. He drove deeper, cutting at Houndaer's torso. The Tuin'Tarl floundered backward out of the distance, meanwhile heaving the greatsword back into a threatening position.

His bloody wrist throbbed, and the huge blade trembled. It was brutally hard to hold it up, its enchantments notwithstanding. He choked up on it, his weakened hand clutching the ricasso, but that only helped a little. He listened for the sound of another party of rogues rushing to his aid. He didn't hear it.

"Well done, Master Argith!" Houndaer declared. "I declare myself beaten. I yield."

Ryld stalked forward, broadsword at the ready.

"Please!" said the Tuin'Tarl. "We always got along, didn't we? I was one of your most dutiful students, and I can help you get out of here."

The teacher kept coming, and Houndaer saw that his face wasn't empty or expressionless after all. It might be devoid of emotion, but it revealed a preternatural, almost demonic concentration, focused entirely on slaughter.

Houndaer saw his own inescapable death there, and, suffused with a strange calm, he lowered the greatsword. Ryld's blade sheared into his chest an instant later.

The echoing metallic crash startled Quenthel. It was well that she'd spent a lifetime learning self control, for otherwise, she might have cried out in dismay.

She and her squad were patrolling the temple. After the events of the past four nights it would have been mad to relax their vigilance, but as the hours had crept uneventfully by, her troops began to speculate that the siege was over. After all, it was supposed to be. The bone wand had supposedly turned the malignancy of the past night's sending back on she who cast the curse.

Yet Quenthel had found she wasn't quite ready to share in the general optimism. Yes, she'd turned an attack back on its source, but that didn't necessarily mean her faceless enemy had succumbed to the demon's attentions. The spellcaster could have survived, and if so, she could keep right on dispatching her unearthly assassins.

From the sound of it, another such had just broken in, and Quenthel didn't have another little bone wand.

For a moment, the Baenre felt a surge of fear, perhaps even despair, and she swallowed it down.

"Follow me," she snapped.

Perhaps her subordinates would prove of some use for a change.

Their tread silent in their enchanted boots, the priestesses trotted in the direction of the noise. Greenish torchlight splashed their shadows on the walls. Parchment rattled as one novice fumbled open a scroll. Female voices began to shout. Power reddened the air for an instant and brushed a gritty, pricking feeling across the priestesses' skin.

"It's not a demon," said Yngoth, twisting up from the whip handle to place his eyes on a level with Quenthel's own. Her stride made his scaly wedge of a head bob up and down.

"No?" she asked. "Has my enemy come to continue our duel in person?"

She hoped so. With her minions at her back, Quenthel would have a good chance of crushing the arrogant fool.

But alas, it wasn't so. Her course led her to the entry hall with the spider statues. The poor battered valves hung breached and crooked once again. This time the culprit was a huge, disembodied, luminous hand, floating open with fingers up as if signaling someone to halt. A lanky male in a baggy cloak had taken shelter behind the translucent manifestation from the spears and arrows that several priestesses were sending his way.

Quenthel sighed, because she knew the lunatic, and he couldn't possibly be her unknown foe. By all accounts, he'd been too busy down in the city the past few days.

She gestured with the whip, terminating the barrage of missiles.

"Master Mizzrym," she called. "You compound your crimes by breaking in where no male may come unbidden."

Pharaun bent low in obeisance. He looked winded, and, most peculiarly for such a notorious dandy, disheveled.

"Mistress, I beg your pardon, but I must confer with you. Time is of the essence."

"I have little to say to you except to condemn you as the archmage should have done."

"Kill me if you must." The giant hand winked out of existence and he continued, "Given my recent peccadilloes, I half expected it. But hear my message first. The undercreatures are rebelling."

Quenthel narrowed her eyes and asked, "The archmage sent you here with this news?"

"Alas," the mage replied, "I was unable to locate him but knew this was something that must be brought to the attention of the most senior members of the Academy. I realize no one ever dreamed it could happen, but it has. Walk to the verge of the plateau with me, and you'll see."

The Baenre frowned. Pharaun's manner was too presumptuous by half, yet something in it commanded attention.

"Very well," she said, "but if this is some sort of demented jest, you'll suffer for it."

"Mistress," Minolin said, "he may want to lead you into—"

Quenthel silenced the fool with a cold stare, then turned back to Pharaun. "Lead on, Master of Sorcere."

In point of fact, the high priestess didn't have to walk all the way to the drop-off to tell that something was badly wrong in the city below. The wavering yellow glare of firelight and a foul smoky tang in the air alerted her as soon as she stepped outside the spider-shaped temple. Heedless of her dignity, she sprinted for the edge, and Pharaun scrambled to keep up with her.

Below her, portions of Menzoberranzan—portions of the *stone*, how could that be?—were in flames. Impossibly, even the Great Mound of the Baenre sprouted a tuft of flame at its highest point, like a tassel on a hat. Once Quenthel's eyes adjusted to the dazzling brightness, she could vaguely make out the mobs rampaging through the streets and plazas.

"You see," said Pharaun, "that's why I ran halfway across the city, dodging marauders at every turn, to reach you, my lady. If I may say so, the situation's even worse than it may look. By and large, the nobles haven't even begun reclaiming the streets. They're bogged down on their estates fighting their own household goblins. Therefore, I suggest you—"

The mage was smart enough to stop talking at the sight of Quenthel's glare.

"We will mobilize Tier Breche," she said. "Melee-Magthere and Arach-Tinilith can fight. Sorcere will divide its efforts between supporting us and extinguishing the fires. You will either find my brother Gromph or act in his stead."

Pharaun bowed low.

Quenthel turned and saw that her priestesses and novices had followed her out onto the plateau. Something in their manner brought her up short.

"Mistress," said long-eared Viconia Agrach Dyrr, one of the senior instructors, rather diffidently, "it makes perfect sense for Melee-Magthere and Sorcere to descend the stairs, but . . ."

"But you ladies have lost your magic," Pharaun said.

The sisters of the temple gaped at him.

"You know?" Quenthel asked.

"A good many males know," the mage replied, just a hint of impatience peeking through, "so there's no point in killing me for it. I'll explain it all later." He turned back toward the rest of the clerics. "Holy Mothers and Sisters, while you may have lost your spells, you have scrolls, talismans, and the rest of the divine implements your order hoards. You can swing maces, if it comes to that. You can fight."

"But we've lost too many sisters," Viconia said to Quenthel. "The demons killed a couple, and you, Mistress, by summoning the spiders, slew more. We don't dare risk the rest. Someone must endure to preserve the lore and perform the rituals."

"That's far too optimistic," Pharaun said.

Viconia scowled. "What is, boy?"

"The assumption that, should you remain up here, annihilation will pass you by," the wizard replied. "It's more plausible to assume that if the orcs triumph below, they'll climb the stairs to continue their depredations up here. You profess devotion to Arach-Tinilith. Surely it would be more reverent to engage the undercreatures in the vault below and thus deny them the slightest opportunity to profane your shrines and altars. Similarly, it would be better strategy to fight alongside allies than to wait till they perish and you're left to struggle alone."

"You're glib, wizard," the Agrach Dyrr priestess sneered, "but you don't know our efforts are needed. Flame and glare, they're only goblins! I think you're just a scareling."

"Perhaps he is," Quenthel said, "but how dare we seek the Dark Mother's favor if we decline to defend her chosen city in its hour of need? Surely, then, we never would hear her voice again."

"Mistress," said Viconia, spreading her hands, "I know we can find a better way to please her than brawling with vermin in the street."

Quenthel lifted her hand crossbow and shot her lieutenant in the face. Viconia made a choking sound and stumbled backward. The poison was already blackening her face as she collapsed.

"I thought I'd already demonstrated that *I* rule here," the Baenre said. "Does anyone else wish to contest my orders?"

"If so," Pharaun said, "she should be aware that I stand with the mistress, and I have the power to scour the lot of you from the face of the plateau."

Ignoring the boastful wizard, Quenthel surveyed her minions. It appeared that no one else had anything much to say.

"Good," the Baenre said. "Let us rouse the tower and the pyramid."

chapter

TWENTY-THREE

With Quenthel in the lead, the Academy descended from Tier Breche like a great waterfall. Some scholars tramped after her on the staircase, while others floated down the cliff face. A few, possessed of magic that enabled them to fly, flitted about like bats.

"Perhaps Mistress would care to bide a moment," said Pharaun. At some point he had slipped off to his personal quarters long enough to wash his face, comb his hair, and throw on a new set of handsome clothes. He returned alone, still claiming ignorance of Gromph's whereabouts. "This is as good a spot as any to spy out the lay of the land. We're below some of the smoke but still high enough for an aerial inspection."

Since Gromph was still either unavailable or uninterested, the Mizzrym was—with obvious relish—acting in the archmage's stead. It was arguably an affront to House Baenre as much as the archmage, but Quenthel had given the order anyway. Until her brother returned or the crisis abated, she needed someone to speak for Sorcere, and she was sure it would upset Gromph in an amusing way to have this dandy taking his place for so important a task.

She halted, and her minions came to a ragged, jostling stop behind her. The whip vipers reared to survey the cityscape along with her. From the corner of her eye, she saw Pharaun smile briefly as if he found the serpents' behavior comical.

"There," said Quenthel, pointing, "in Manyfolk. It looks as if House Auvryndar may have finished exterminating their own slaves, but a mob keeps them penned within their walls."

"I see it, Blessed Mother," said Malaggar Faen Tlabbar from the step behind her. The First Sword of Melee-Magthere was a merry-looking, round-faced boy with a fondness for green attire and emeralds. "With your permission, that might be a good place to start. We'll lift the siege and add the Auvryndar to our own army."

"So be it," Quenthel said

The residents of the Academy reached the floor of the lower cavern, whereupon the instructors, particularly the warriors of the pyramid, set about the business of forming the scholars into squads, with swordsmen and spearman protecting the spellcasters. Then they had to arrange the units into some semblance of a marching order.

Like every princess of a great House, Quenthel had a working knowledge of military matters, and she watched the attempt to create order with a jaundiced eye.

"I could wish for a proper army," she muttered.

She hadn't meant for anyone to hear, but Pharaun nodded.

"I understand your sentiments, Mistress, but they're all we have, and I'm sure that if we've trained them properly, we have a chance." He coughed. "Against the thralls, anyway."

"Your meaning?"

"The greatest danger of all is this pall of smoke. I think Syrzan, for all its cunning, miscalculated. If the mages we left upstairs don't extinguish the flames, we'll all suffocate, female and male, elf and orc alike, leaving the alhoon a necropolis to rule. Still, I suppose we must concentrate on our task and not fret about the rest."

"What alhoon?" she demanded.

He hesitated. "It really is a long story, Mistress, and not crucial at this moment."

"I will decide what is crucial, mage," she said. "Speak."

Before Pharaun could begin she saw the First Sword approaching, presumably to inform her that the company was ready to set forth.

As they started to march, she listened to the mage's tale of the undead mind flayer and its designs for Menzoberranzan. There was more, she was sure, that he was holding back, but she could always torture it out of him later.

Along the way, the teachers and students found their way littered with mangled dark elf corpses, some headless, some partially devoured, firelight gilding their sightless eyes. The rich smell of blood competed with the acrid foulness of the smoke.

Or course, no drow objected to the spectacle of violent death, but the ubiquity of the ravaged shapes, combined with the glare of the flames and the uncanny sight of burning stone, made it seem as if Menzoberranzan itself had become a sort of hell, and that was, for Quenthel at least, unsettling.

The Mistress of Arach-Tinilith thought that were she a weaker person, she might have felt as if she were moving through a nightmare, or interpreted the carnage as proof positive that Lolth had turned her back on Menzoberranzan for good and all. She consoled herself with the thought that at least this time she was marching against an enemy she could see and smite.

Periodically the scholars saw small groups of undercreatures looting, slaughtering hapless commoners, or even flinging stones and arrows at the column. The younger students sought to attack the thralls, and the teachers bellowed at them to desist. The Academy had to act as a unit and stick to a plan if it hoped to win the day.

Malaggar raised his hand, signaling a stop.

We're close, I think, he reported in the silent drow sign language.

They stood in place until a flying scout, a brother of the pyramid possessed of a cloak that converted into batlike wings, swooped down and gave his report.

Mistress, Malaggar signed, *may I suggest that ten squads keep on straight, and the rest of us circle around that block of houses. We'll take the orcs from two sides.*

Very well, Quenthel replied as she surveyed her army. *All of you from the head of the column to the mouth of that alley, follow me. The rest of you, go with Master Faen Tlabbar. Everyone, quietly as you can.*

Hands lifted at intervals down the column to relay the orders to those who couldn't see her.

The company divided, then Quenthel's troops crept on, toward a clamoring mob that quite possibly outnumbered them. Fortunately, the slaves hadn't noticed the Academy's arrival, and she meant to take full advantage of their ignorance. She quickly arranged her troops in a ragged but serviceable formation, then bade them attack as one.

Power howled and flashed, burning, blasting, and devouring masses of goblins. Darts leaped through the air to pierce orcs and bugbears. Undercreatures fell by the score.

Yet after that first volley, scores remained, and they flung themselves at the scholars in a yammering frenzy. The drow hastily abandoned their crossbows for swords and spears. Hidden behind lines of warriors, mages and priestesses peered, trying to see what was going on in the midst of the savage melee so they could target their spells without harming their own comrades.

Quenthel could have cowered behind her own rank of protectors—perhaps, as high priestess and leader, she should have—but she thought it might stiffen the spines of the first- and second-year students if she led from the front, and in any case, she wanted to kill up close and see the pain and fear in her victims' faces. Her vipers rearing and hissing, she shoved her way to the front.

She slew several goblinoids, and dazzling yellow light flashed and crackled around her. The fire magic did her no harm—her mystical defenses held—but several of the folk around her, drow and undercreature alike, shrieked and fell.

For a moment, everyone, every survivor in the immediate vicinity, was stunned. Then orcs scrambled forward at the gaps the blaze had created in the drow line, and scholars darted forward to fill them. No one paid any heed to the burned comrades beneath their feet, save to curse them if she tripped.

Quenthel stepped back, letting a student warrior from House Despana take her place, then cast about, seeking the source of the burst of flame. She had a vague sense that the magic had plunged down from above, so she looked there first, at the upper stories of the buildings to either side.

She blinked in surprise. Like true arachnids, driders were scuttling about the walls and rooflines. Many such debased creatures retained their spellcasting abilities, and one of them must have conjured the fire.

Quenthel had no idea how the thralls and outcasts could have conspired together, nor did she have time to stop and ponder the question. She had to stop the driders before they destroyed her company from above. She levitated upward through the smoky air, meanwhile looking about for the mage who'd created the flame.

Barbed arrows and bolts of light streaked at her from all directions. She shielded her face with a fold of her *piwafwi*, and the missiles rebounded or dissolved when they encountered her layers of enchanted protection. The impacts stung but did no serious damage.

When she'd ascended to their level, she recognized certain snarling faces even with the fangs, driders whom she herself had helped to make. Perhaps it explained why they'd throw magic at her despite the inevitable damage to the mob of orcs.

She quickly unrolled another scroll and read the trigger phrase therein. Blades appeared, floating among the driders in front of her, then began to revolve around a central point. The razor-sharp slivers of metal sped along so fast they were invisible, and their orbits curved through the bodies of their foes. The blades sliced and pierced the half-spiders without even slowing down, reducing the brutes to scraps of meat and splashes of blood.

Quenthel laughed and started to twist around to face the driders atop the stalagmite buildings on the opposite side of the street. A length of something sticky lashed her and looped tightly about her torso, binding her free hand to her chest.

It was webbing. She knew that some driders could spin the stuff. As they sought to reel her in, she levitated once more, resisting the pull like a fish on a line. Meanwhile, she struggled to reach another scroll despite the constriction of her arm. The vipers bit and chewed at the cable.

Pharaun levitated into view, and sizzling white lightning leaped from his fingertips. It stabbed one drider, then leaped to the next, then another, until the twisting, dazzling power linked all the half-spiders like beads on a chain. They danced spasmodically until the magic ended, then instantly collapsed. Stinking smoke rose from the remains.

Pharaun smiled at Quenthel and said, "I've often wondered why the goddess doesn't transform our misfits into something harmless," he said. "I suppose driders are another tool for culling the weak."

Ignoring his blather, Quenthel peered down to see what was transpiring on the battlefield.

Malaggar's contingent had arrived and was tearing into the enemy's flank. At virtually the same instant, the Auvryndar threw open their gates, and, mounted on their lizards, charged forth in a sortie.

Teeth gritted, Quenthel pulled the gummy web off her person and floated down to rejoin her troops on the ground. Contemptuous of the enemies' arrows, Pharaun continued to hang above the warriors' heads from which point it was no doubt easier to aim his magic.

The scholars only had to fight for a few more minutes then, hammered on three sides, the mass of goblins collapsed in on itself, the implosion laying a carpet of corpses in its wake.

Quenthel allowed her troops only a few minutes to collect themselves, then she formed them up and marched them on toward the next of the goddess only knew how many battles.

"Out!" Greyanna shouted. "*Now!*"

The canoe maker gawked at her and sputtered, "Wh-what about my stock?"

The items in question sat about the floor of the workroom or hung cradled in straps hooked to the ceiling.

"The goblins will destroy them," the scar-faced princess said. "Like this." She smashed a half-finished kayak, a fragile-looking construction of curved bone ribs and hide, with a sweep of her mace. "Afterward, you'll make more, but only if you live. Now get moving, or I'll kill you myself."

The craftsman scrambled off his stool, and she chivvied him out the door. Up and down the street, her half dozen minions were rousting out the occupants of other manufactories and shops.

A mob of hairy hobgoblins, all well-armed and many a head taller than the average dark elf, slouched around a corner onto the thoroughfare. They spotted the drow, bellowed their uncouth battle cries, and charged.

After the disastrous encounter with Ryld Argith, one of the twins was dead. The other, and Relonor, lay grievously wounded, as they still did in House Mizzrym. There they would live or die without recourse to further doses of healing magic, since Miz'ri declined to squander the House's limited resources on such incompetents. Greyanna had entirely agreed.

After taking the wounded home, Greyanna, with the questionable aid of Aunrae, had selected five new males to join her in the hunt. This time, they'd stalk Pharaun on foot, Greyanna having belatedly realized that foulwings weren't lucky for her.

She and her band had been wandering the streets seeking word of their quarry when the rebellion erupted. Once she'd grasped the magnitude of the disturbance, she wondered if it was the raid on the Braeryn that she had engineered, that brutal attempt to flush her brother out of hiding, that had inspired the thralls to revolt. In a mad, dark way, the possibility pleased her, but she decided not to share her hypothesis. Few would see the humor.

Most of her thinking, however, was given over to practical considerations. She thought her hunting party could help put down the undercreatures, but only if it could combine forces with a bona fide army. Otherwise, the larger mobs would overwhelm it.

In those first minutes of slaughter and destruction, she watched for some noble clan to ride forth from their castle and drive the goblins before them. To her consternation, none did, at least not in her immediate vicinity. Her little troop was on its own.

Life then became an infuriating business of running and hiding from orcs of all things, of watching beasts no better than rothé destroy beauty and sophistication they couldn't even perceive. Occasionally, she and her companions slew a small group of goblinoids wandering on their own, but it meant nothing, would do nothing to arrest the dissolution of all that was finest in the world.

Where was the Spider Queen? Perhaps she was bored with her toy Menzoberranzan, magnificent though it was. Perhaps she intended to break it to make space for a new one.

In time, Greyanna's dodging and backtracking brought her to a street she recognized, a double row of prosperous shops—to be precise, establishments owned by tradesmen under the patronage of House Mizzrym. She herself had called hereabouts, collecting rents and fees, occasionally chastising a fool who was late paying on a loan or had otherwise displeased Matron Mother Miz'ri.

It occurred to Greyanna that if the merchants perished, they'd contribute no more gold to Mizzrym coffers. Whereas if she conducted them to safety, she might curry some favor with her mother. Miz'ri had grown impatient with her continuing failure to kill Pharaun and had even hinted that another might carry the mantle of First Daughter with more grace.

At the very least, preserving Mizzrym assets would feel more constructive and less frustrating than simply skulking about, and so Greyanna instructed her followers to extract the frightened traders and artisans from their homes.

She loosed a crossbow bolt at the hobgoblins, and her soldiers did the same. Her wizard conjured a cold, towering shadow like the silhouette of a mantis, which mangled several thralls in its oversized pincers before melting out of existence. In all, at least a dozen brutes fell, but others shambled forth from the smoke and fiery glare to take their place.

Voices of torment, she thought, how many undercreatures were there in Menzoberranzan?

Until that day, Greyanna had never really noticed. She guessed no one else had, either.

The hobgoblins charged.

The Mizzrym princess shouted, "Dark wall!"

Three of her retainers, those closest to the onrushing thralls, stooped and touched the ground, conjuring a curtain of shadow between themselves and the undercreatures, then fell back.

One of the Mizzrym warriors herded the shopkeepers farther from the threat. The rest, Greyanna included, scrambled to form a line at a narrow place three yards behind the intangible barrier. The princess pulled a little silver vial from her belt pouch and guzzled the bitter, lukewarm contents down. She shuddered and doubled over as her muscles cramped, and the discomfort gave way to a tingling warmth.

Hobgoblins strode from the darkness. They'd dwelled among dark elves too long for the trick to deter them more than a few seconds.

At least the blinding veil precluded their advancing in anything resembling a coherent formation. They screamed and charged in a gapped and formless wave, which looked murderous even so.

The first hobgoblin to lunge at Greyanna was particularly large and, in marked contrast to his fellows, hairless from the shoulders up. A mistress or master had depilated the slave to prepare the canvas for a work of art, hundreds of tiny round burn scars arranged in a complex swirling pattern.

The thrall cut at Greyanna's head. Under other circumstances, she would have retreated out of range, but that would break the line. Wishing she'd brought a shield to the revel, she lifted her mace in a high parry. The hobgoblin's broadsword rang against the stone haft of the war club and skipped off.

At once she riposted with a strike to the flank, and the undercreature whipped his targe around to block. The blow bashed a dent in the round steel shield and knocked the hobgoblin reeling back, his slanted eyes wide with surprise. He didn't know about the potion that had lent her an ogre's strength.

Greyanna struck to the side, slaying the slave who was menacing her neighbor, then her own bald adversary came edging back. He hovered a second, then feinted to the flank and finished with a cut to the chest. Discerning the true threat, she half-stepped inside the arc of the attack and swung at his jaw. The blow crunched home, and he toppled backward with a shattered, bloody chin and a broken neck.

She killed two more hobgoblins, then something prodded her shin, a thrust that failed to penetrate her boot. She looked down, and it was a kobold, armed with a fireplace poker, who had apparently been scurrying about the feet of the larger slaves. Greyanna killed the reptilian imp with a roundhouse kick.

She cast about for her next adversary. She didn't seem to have one. The fight was over, and the few surviving hobgoblins were running away.

"Form up!" she shouted. "I want a column with the traders in the middle. Fast!"

Once the procession was under way, Aunrae, striding along at Greyanna's side, asked, "May I know where we're going? An ally's castle?"

"No," Greyanna replied. "I suspect we couldn't get in. We're going to hide our charges in Bauthwaf."

The column crept past corpses and burning stone, and as they made their way to the cavern wall, other commoners came running out of their homes to join the procession. Greyanna's first impulse was to turn away those without ties to House Mizzrym, but she thought better of it. Many of the newcomers carried swords, and she could press the dolts into martial service if needed.

Occasionally someone collapsed, coughing feebly, poisoned by the stinging smoke. The rest stepped over her and pressed on.

Someone gave a thin, high cry, as if at an unexpected pain. Greyanna spun around. The goblins weren't attacking. Her client the canoe maker had simply seized his opportunity to knife another male in the back.

"A competitor," the craftsman explained.

The labyrinthine fortress known as the Great Mound contained a number of magically sealed areas. Unbelievably, the rebellious slave troops penetrated everywhere else. The Baenre fought the goblinoids in the stalagmite towers, across the aerial bridges that connected them, and through the tunnels beneath them, even along the balconies and skywalks of the stalactite bastions, reclaiming their domain a bloody inch at a time.

The thralls made their final stand in the courtyard, a spacious area surrounded by a weblike iron fence. The barrier was a potent magical defense, and, as the Baenre had just discovered, of no use whatsoever if one's foe was already inside the compound.

Triel floated down from the battlements above to take a hand in the last of the fighting. Jeggred, who'd stood beside her since the battle commenced, drifted down as well. Both mother and demidemon son wore a copious spattering of blood, none of it their own.

In truth, Triel could have left the task of clearing the yard to her warriors, but she was enjoying herself. Partly, it was simple drow bloodlust, but she'd also found a directness, a simplicity, in slaughtering goblins that was sadly lacking in the complex task of ruling the city. For the first time since ascending to her mother's throne, she felt she knew what she was doing.

Half a dozen minotaurs, formidable brutes she had often employed as her own personal guards, chanted, "Freedom! Freedom!" as they swung their axes or crouched to gore an enemy with their horns. Triel read the last line of runes from a scroll that, when the rebellion commenced, had contained seven spells.

Dazzling flame blazed up from the ground beneath the minotaurs' hooves. Four of the huge beasts fell down screaming and thrashing. The other two leaped clear of the conflagration. They didn't escape harm entirely. The fire burned away patches of their shaggy fur and seared the flesh beneath, but the injuries didn't slow them down. They bellowed and charged.

A minotaur towered over a drow of normal stature, and made Triel look like a tiny sprite. Still, she smiled as she stepped forward to meet the foe. One of the slaves focused on her and the other, on Jeggred.

The matron mother knew a minotaur liked to overwhelm an opponent with the momentum of its initial rush. She waited until the creature was nearly on top of her, then sidestepped. He was lumbering too fast to stop or compensate, and she smashed his knee with her mace as he plunged by.

The slave fell on his face, and she robbed him of the use of his limbs with a bone-breaking strike to the spine. Meanwhile, Jeggred simultaneously chewed on his own opponent's neck and ripped at the brute's torso, hooking the guts out.

After that, Triel and the draegloth killed several gnolls before running out of foes. Panting, the Baenre strode to the foot of a wall and floated upward again, high enough to peer beyond the eminence of Qu'ellarz'orl to the burning city beyond. Jeggred followed.

Earlier, when she'd first discerned that slaves throughout Menzoberranzan were rebelling, she'd used a certain magical diamond to call the males of Bregan D'aerthe from their secret lair. The sellswords were at their work.

One neighborhood in the south of the city was thick with goblins. Even from the Great Mound, she could make out the boil of motion in the streets. Then, over the course of just a few seconds, that agitation ceased, as the creatures apparently fell dead all at once.

It was an extraordinary feat of mass assassination, but the mercenaries had only cleared one small part of Menzoberranzan. They couldn't reclaim the entire city by themselves, if, in fact, the job could be done at all.

Triel shouted down into the yard, to any officer within earshot, "Assemble my troops. We're marching out."

Jeggred couldn't speak for joy. This had already been the best night of his admittedly young life, and he was drunk on slaughter. He'd killed and killed and killed and killed again, an ecstasy that put his sport with Faeryl Zauvirr to shame.

And his mother said it wasn't over! They were going to descend into the city to gorge on murder, and Jeggred would know a fiend's transcendent bliss. The only hard part would be remembering not to kill dark elves, just everyone else.

He squeezed Triel's shoulder with a quivering hand, one of the smaller ones.

Valas Hune skulked around the corner, then blinked. A keep blocked the street, where no bastion should be—then the huge thing moved.

No, not a keep after all, but the biggest stone giant he'd ever seen. The scout knew that some Houses kept giant slaves as well as the more common goblinoids and ogres, and, gray in the firelight, with a long head and black, sunken eyes, this specimen still wore iron bracelets dangling lengths of broken chain. From somewhere it had procured a greataxe sized for a creature of its immensity, and was using it to pulp any drow it noticed scurrying about.

Valas had gotten separated from his comrades sometime back. That was all right. He was used to traversing wild places by himself, though in truth, he'd never explored any tunnel as perilous and unpredictable as Menzoberranzan had become this night.

He'd been killing orcs and gnolls, first with his shortbow, and, after the arrows ran out, close in with his kukris. He'd thought he was making some genuine progress until he encountered this.

It was a daunting sight, but someone would have to kill the big under-creatures as well as the little ones, if Menzoberranzan was to survive and Bregan D'aerthe was to be paid for its services.

Valas touched a fingertip to a nine-pointed tin star pinned to his shirt, and murmured a word in a language of a race few Menzoberranyr had ever even heard of. In the blink of an eye he was crouched on the stone giant's shoulder.

The surface was smooth and rounded. He started to slip off, but, reacting like the accomplished rock climber he was, negated his weight and caught himself. He clambered within reach of the giant's neck and started hacking at the arteries within the behemoth's neck with both kukris.

To no avail. Perched somewhat precariously, Valas couldn't use his strength and weight to full advantage, and his first stroke skipped harm-lessly off the giant's rocklike hide.

The behemoth did feel the impact, though. Its head snapped around, the chin nearly brushing Valas away. The giant glared down at him, and he struck, this time with greater success. With a crackle of lightning, the enchanted weapon split the slave's lower lip.

Crying out in pain and anger, a deep sound Valas felt in his bones, the stone giant flinched its head away. A huge gray hand rose up to catch the drow, who scrambled forward and cut at the colossus's neck.

Dark, thick blood leaped forth and washed Valas into space. He fell hard onto a rooftop and watched the giant stumble about, clutching at its throat. After a few steps, the huge thrall fell backward, crushing some un-lucky hobgoblins that were wandering by.

Gromph was in a vile humor as he floated up the cliff face. He'd cast light into the foot of Narbondel the same as always, and the world ex-ploded into madness. Orcs lunged out of nowhere and attacked his guards. His own ogre litter-bearers summarily dumped his luxurious con-veyance on the ground and joined in the uprising.

The archmage had sought to strike the undercreatures dead with a spell, but nothing happened. Someone had conjured a magical dead zone around him. Either one of the orcs was a shaman powerful enough to create such an effect, or, more likely, one of the brutes had stolen a talisman from his owner.

However they'd managed it, the beasts were charging, and the spells in Gromph's memory were just odd little rhymes, his robe and cloak, mere flimsy cloth, and his weapons, inert sticks and ornaments. Well, probably not all of them, but he wasn't reckless enough to stand and experiment while the orcs assailed him with their pilfered blades. Forfeiting his dignity, he turned and ran. The exertion made his chest throb where K'rarza'q had gored him.

When he reached the edge of the plaza, he thought he must have exited the dead zone. He'd better have, because he could hear the grunting ogres with their long legs catching up behind him. He turned, pointed a wand, and snarled the trigger word.

A drop of liquid shot from the tip of the rod. It struck the belly of the lead ogre and burst into a copious splash of acid.

With his magic restored, Gromph obliterated every attacker who lacked the sense to run away. His dark elf attendants were already dead, leaving him to make his way back to Tier Breche alone.

As it turned out, the slave rebellion was pandemic, and the trek wasn't altogether easy. He considered going to ground in some castle or house, but when he saw the flames gnawing stone, he knew he had to get back.

Dirty, sore, and coughing, he eventually made it home, and when he rose to the top of the limestone wall, he saw something that lifted his spirits, albeit only a little.

Eight Masters of Sorcere stood in the open air, chanting, gesturing, attempting a ritual, while an equal number of apprentices looked on. The wizards had fetched much of the proper equipment out of the tower. That was something, Gromph supposed, but the incantation was a useless mess.

The Baenre reached out and hauled himself onto solid ground and his hands and knees, another irksome affront to his dignity.

He rose and shouted, "Enough!"

The teachers and students twisted around to gawk at him. The chanting died.

"Archmage!" cried Guldor Melarn. He was supposedly without peer in the realm of elemental magic, though it couldn't be proved by his performance thus far that night. "We were worried about you!"

"I'm sure," said Gromph, striding closer. "I noticed all the search parties you sent out looking for me."

Guldor hesitated. "Sir, the mistress of the Academy commanded—"

"Shut up," said Gromph. He'd come close enough to see that the teachers were standing in a complex pentacle, written in red phosphorescence on the ground. "Pitiful."

He extended his index finger and wrote on the air. The magic words and sigils reshaped themselves.

"My lord Archmage," said Master Godeep. "We drew this circle to extinguish the fires below. If you break it—"

"I'm not breaking it," said Gromph, "I'm fixing it." He turned his gaze on one of the apprentices, some commoner youth, and the dolt flinched. "Fetch me a bit of fur, an amber rod, and one of the little bronze gongs the cooks use to summon us to supper. *Run!*"

"Archmage," said Guldor, "you see we already have all the necessary foci for fire magic." He gestured to a brazier of ruddy coals. "I'm whispering to the flames below, commanding them to dwindle."

"And making more smoke in the process. That's just what we need." Gromph kicked the brazier over, scattering embers across the rock. "Your approach isn't working, elementalist. I should exile you to the Realms that See the Sun for a few decades, then you might figure out what it takes to extinguish a fire of this magnitude."

The male came sprinting back with the articles Gromph had requested. The Baenre whispered a word of power, and the pentacle changed from red to blue.

"Right, then," he said to the wizards. "I assume you can tell where you're meant to stand, so do it and we'll begin. I'll say a line, you repeat it. Copy my passes if you're up to it."

For a properly schooled wizard, magic was generally easy. He relied on an armamentarium of spells, many devised by his predecessors, a few, perhaps, invented by himself. In either case, they were perfected spells that he thoroughly understood. He knew he could cast them properly, and what would happen when he did.

An extemporaneous ritual was a different matter. Relying on their arcane knowledge and natural ability, a circle of mages tried to generate a new effect on the fly. Often, nothing happened. When it did, the power often turned on those who had raised it or discharged itself in some other manner contrary to their intent. Yet occasionally such a ceremony worked, and with his station, his wealth, and his homeland at stake, Gromph was resolved to make this one of those times.

After the mages chanted for fifteen minutes, power began to whisper and sting through the air. The archmage tapped the beater to the gong, sounding a clashing, shivering tone. At once a vaster note answered and obscured the first, a booming, grinding, deafening roar. Gromph's subordinates flinched, but the Baenre smiled in satisfaction, because the noise was thunder.

Perched high in the side cavern, the residents of Sorcere had an excellent view of what transpired next. The air at the top of the great vault, already thick with smoke, grew denser still as masses of vapor materialized. The shapeless shadows flickered like great translucent dragons with fire leaping in their bellies. Following each flash, they bellowed that godlike hammering blast, as if the flames pained them.

Gromph knew that many of the folk in the city below had no idea what was occurring—it was possible that even some of his erudite colleagues didn't know—but whether they understood or not, clouds, lightning, and weather were paying a call on the hitherto changeless depths of the Underdark.

As one, the clouds dropped torrents of water to fall in frigid veils. The Baenre could hear the sizzling sound as it pounded the cavern wall.

"That's impressive," said Guldor, "but are you sure it will put out the flames? The fire's magical, after all."

Gromph's bruise gave him a twinge.

"Yes, instructor," he growled, "because I'm not an incompetent from a House of no account. I'm a Baenre and the Archmage of Menzoberranzan . . . and I'm *sure*."

Before it was over, Pharaun lost track of how many battles he and his comrades had fought. He only knew they kept winning them, through superior tactics more than anything else, and that despite their losses, their numbers kept growing, swelled by garrisons that had fought their way out of their castles.

Occasionally the ragtag army came upon a section of the city that had already been pacified, and though he never caught so much of a glimpse of them, Pharaun knew Bregan D'aerthe was fighting in concert with his own company. It was as much a comfort as anything could be on this fierce and desperate night.

Finally the army from Tier Breche encountered an equally impressive force under Matron Baenre's command. The two companies united and marched on Narbondellyn, where several bugbears with some degree of martial experience had striven to organize thousands of their fellow under-creatures into a force capable of withstanding their masters' wrath.

The great stone pillar of Narbondel shone above fighting that was wild and chaotic. Miraculously, partway through, the upper reaches of the cavern began to storm, allaying Pharaun's greatest fear. An hour later, the drow swept in and annihilated the opposing force, and thus they took their homeland back.

In the aftermath, the wizard walked through the downpour, looking this way and that. Strands of wet hair clung to his forehead, and his boots squelched. As a mage, he had to concede the storm was a glorious achievement, to say nothing of the salvation of Menzoberranzan, but it was a pity his colleagues couldn't have accomplished the same thing without wreaking havoc on everyone's appearance and chilling them to the bone.

The Mizzrym grinned. Neither Quenthel nor Triel was anywhere around. He'd taken direction from them all night, willingly enough, but he wanted to command the finale of this extraordinary affair himself, and their absence gave him an excuse to proceed without consulting them.

He cast about once more and spied Welverin Freth. The capable weapons master of the Nineteenth House, Welverin excelled at combat despite the seeming impediment of a prosthetic silver leg, and had fought in tandem with Pharaun several times during the night. Currently he was huddled in a doorway conferring with two of his lieutenants.

"Weapons Master!" Pharaun called.

Welverin looked up and gave him a nod. "How can I help you, Master Mizzrym?"

"How would you like to help me kill the creature responsible for this insurrection?"

The warrior's eyes narrowed and he said, "Is this another of your jokes?"

"By no means. But if we're going to do this, we'd better do it quickly, before our quarry slinks away into the Underdark. I trust that you and your troops can ride aerial mounts?"

Pharaun gestured to the giant bats, created by some enchanter, penned in a nearby latticework dome. It seemed a petty miracle they'd survived the rebellion unsuffocated and unburned.

"Where do they keep the tack?" Welverin asked, peering at the cage.

T W E N T Y - F O U R

Water dripping from the hem of his cloak, Pharaun found that the layout of the renegades' fortress wasn't quite so perplexing when he wasn't dodging hunters and suffering the brain-jangling aftereffects of a psionic assault. The empty, echoing rooms and corridors still seemed just as ominous, however, just as fitting an abode for wraiths and maledictions.

The Mizzrym watched Welverin and the other warriors of House Freth to see if the place was unsettling them. It didn't look like it. Perhaps they were too brave. Or perhaps the fresh, butchered corpses littering the floor turned their thoughts from shadowy terrors to the commonplace violence that was their profession.

They found the bodies, often cut in two or more pieces, lying here and there about the castle. Pharaun was astonished at the quantity. Apparently poor wounded Ryld had had a nice long homicidal run of it before the conspirators slew him. Perhaps it had even required Syrzan to do the job.

In retrospect, Pharaun wondered why the alhoon hadn't joined the search for the escaped prisoners right from the start. Maybe giving the Call had temporarily depleted its strength.

The Master of Sorcere led the soldiers into a long, spacious hall with a large dais at the far end. there, no doubt, a matron mother had held court and also dined, judging by the benches and trestle tables stacked in an alcove. Carved and painted spiders crawled everywhere, a sort of mask, Pharaun supposed, given that the former tenants of the keep had petitioned other deities in private. Sheets of genuine spiderweb veiled the artwork.

Welverin said, "Look."

Pharaun turned his head, then caught his breath in surprise. Ryld Argith had just stepped from the mouth of a servants' passage midway up the left-hand wall.

The weapons master's strides were even and sure despite his wounded leg. He was noticeably thinner, as if his body was burning fuel at a prodigious rate, and somehow he'd recovered Splitter.

The soldiers aimed their crossbows.

"No!" Pharaun said. Not yet, anyway.

Ryld pivoted toward the newcomers and stalked forward. His eyes were intent yet somehow empty, his face, expressionless, and he seemed indifferent to the weapons leveled at his burly frame. One warrior muttered uneasily, as if he'd mistaken the Master of Melee-Magthere for a ghost. Pharaun knew better; he recognized a deep trance when he saw one. Evidently his friend had utilized some esoteric martial discipline to keep himself alive.

"Ryld!" Pharaun said. "Well met! I knew you could defeat Houndaer and the rest of those buffoons. Otherwise I never would have left you."

The lie sounded thin even to the liar.

Certainly it didn't impress Ryld. Perhaps in his altered statue of consciousness, he hadn't even heard it or recognized his fellow master, either. He just kept coming.

"Wake up!" the wizard said. "It's me, Pharaun, your friend. I came back to rescue you. These boys hail from House Freth, and they're our allies."

Ryld took another gliding swordsman's advance, still directly toward the Master of Sorcere.

I'm sorry, Pharaun thought, but this time you bring it on yourself. He drew breath to give the order to shoot, and shapes surged through the three tall arched doorways at the rear of the dais.

In the lead capered several human-sized creatures wrapped in lengths of clattering chain. They were kytons, malign spirits whom mages could summon and control. Behind the devils strode the surviving conspirators, and Syrzan in its decaying robes.

Ryld wheeled and oriented on the conspirators. The rogues shot a flight of whistling quarrels, and the Freth warriors responded in kind. The renegades had the advantage of their elevated platform, and the soldiers, of numerical superiority, but neither volley dropped more than a smattering of its targets. The combatants were too well armored, by metal, magic, or both.

Eager to see if swords would serve where the darts had failed, the Freth soldiers howled a battle cry and charged. Most of them, anyway. In his deep, booming voice, Welverin ordered some of the troops back outside to find their way around to the entrances the traitors had used and attack them from the rear. Not a bad idea, but Pharaun thought the warriors had a good chance of getting lost instead

Whirling loose lengths of chain, eight kytons, each a match for a dozen ordinary fighters, leaped down off the stage to meet the oncoming foe. The rogues remained on the platform with Syrzan, where they started reloading their crossbows with the obvious intention of shooting down into the melee.

Pharaun decided he wouldn't allow that. He levitated above his comrades, thus obtaining a clear shot at the dais.

He felt a twinge in the center of his forehead, but only for a second. As he'd expected, Syrzan had attacked first with a psionic thrust, not realizing its foe had warded himself against such effects with apposite talismans and spells.

This time, the Mizzrym thought, you'll have to fight me charm to charm and spell to spell.

To his surprise, he received an answer, a telepathic voice grating and buzzing inside his mind.

So be it, mammal, the alhoon said. *Either way, I'll have revenge on the wretch who condemned me to exile yet again.*

Even as he attended to Syrzan's threat, Pharaun was murmuring an incantation and manipulating a little steel tube. A bright pellet of flame hurtled from the open end, expanding into a skull-sized orb as it flew. It smashed into one of the renegades on the dais, rebounded, and struck another. It bounced and slashed back and forth across the platform, sowing a zigzag trail of sparks and afterimage in its wake, striking everyone. Before it winked out of existence, it killed a good many of the rogues or turned them into reeling, flailing living torches, whom their own allies had to slay lest they ignite them as well. Syrzan, however, was unaffected.

Below his feet, Pharaun glimpsed the clash of stabbing, cutting blades and spinning chains. As they flailed at their adversaries, the kytons, who resembled oozing, festering corpses within their coiled armor of chains, altered their features. The devils had the capacity to take on the appearance of a deceased intimate from an enemy's past. Supposedly svirfneblin and their ilk found this deeply distressing, but it was only slightly discomfiting to representatives of a race that did not love.

Ryld was at the forefront of the fighting, sweeping Splitter about with all his accustomed strength and skill. Pharaun was glad to see that his friend was only striking at the demons.

Mouth tentacles writhing, bulbous eyes glaring, Syrzan lifted its three-fingered hands to conjure. Around it, many of the rogues who still survived jumped off the dais. Evidently they'd rather fight the Freth warriors on the floor than stand near the alhoon while Pharaun threw spells at it.

The Master of Sorcere was surprised that so few of the traitors simply tried to run away. Certainly loyalty—that alien conceit—didn't hold them there. They must have known that with their schemes thwarted, their conspiracy revealed, they were outlaws, outcast from all they coveted and cherished. Perhaps their plight filled them with such rage that they prized vengeance above survival.

As Syrzan wove magic, its dark elf counterpart was hastily doing the same. The lich finished first. A blaze of lightning, kin to those still twisting and forking through the open air outside, leaped from its parched, scaling hand, crackled entirely through Pharaun's torso, and burned a black spot on the ceiling.

Pharaun's muscles clenched, and his hair lifted away from his head, but his protections averted any real harm. Indeed, the attack didn't even disrupt his own conjuring. On the final word, he thrust out his hand, releasing a wave of cold, fluttering shadows like ghostly bats.

Screeching and chattering, the phantoms swooped and whirled about the alhoon, slashing at it with their claws. The mind flayer growled a word in some infernal tongue, and a jagged crack snaked up one of the walls. Pharaun's illusory minions vanished.

The Mizzrym extracted five glass marbles from one of his pockets, rolled them dexterously in his palm, and rattled off a brief tercet. A quintet of luminous spheres appeared in the air and shot toward Syrzan, attacking it with fire, sound, cold, acid, and lightning simultaneously. Surely at least one of those forces would pierce its defenses.

Syrzan gave a rasping, clacking shriek and swept its hand through the air. In an instant, the orbs reversed their courses, streaking back at their source as fast as they'd sped away.

Caught by surprise, Pharaun nonetheless attempted to dodge in the only manner possible. He restored his weight and dropped toward the floor like a stone. Two of the radiant projectiles streaked past him to explode against the ceiling. Two more simply vanished when they came into contact with his *piwafwi*. The fifth ghosted into his chest.

The loudest scream he'd ever heard shook his bones, jabbed agony through his ears, and smashed his thoughts to pieces. Stunned, he kept plummeting until he smashed down in the midst of the melee.

For a moment he simply lay amidst scores of shifting, stamping feet, then his mind focused, and he realized he needed to get off the floor before somebody trampled him. He started to scramble up, and a swinging length of chain struck him on the temple.

It was just a glancing blow, but it knocked him back down. A kyton loomed over him, whirling its flexible weapons around for another attack. The spirit had Sabal's face.

Pharaun pointed his finger and rattled off a spell, realizing partway through that he couldn't hear himself—or anything else. Seconds before, the battle had been a hammering cacophony, but it had fallen silent.

Luckily he didn't need to hear his voice to recite a spell. Power blazed from his fingertip into the devil's body. In a heartbeat, the kyton's flesh shriveled within its wrapping of chain. The links sliding and flopping around it, the fiend collapsed.

A hand gripped Pharaun's shoulder and hauled him up. He turned and saw Welverin. The officer's mouth moved, but the wizard had no idea what he was saying. He shook his head and pointed to his ears, which, though useless, were far from numb. They throbbed and bled. His insides hurt as well, and the pain made him want to destroy Syrzan all the more.

Pharaun levitated, only to find himself mere feet from something the illithilich must have conjured while its fellow mage was floundering about below. It was a huge, phosphorescent, disembodied illithid head, with mouth tentacles longer than the drow was tall. The members writhing, the squidlike construct flew forward. Up close, it smelled fishy.

Pharaun snatched a white leather glove and a chip of clear crystal from his cloak and commenced a spell. A tapered tentacle tip whipped around his forearm, tugged, and nearly spoiled the final manipulation, but he pulled free and completed the pass successfully.

An immense hand made of ice appeared beside the mind flayer's head. It wrapped its fingers around it, dug its talons in, and held the thing immobile.

The only problem was that the phantom illithid head was still blocking Pharaun's view. He simultaneously wove a spell and bobbed lower until he saw Syrzan.

On the final word of the incantation, white fire erupted from the alhoon's desiccated flesh . . . fire that died a second later. The magic should have transformed the undead wizard into an inanimate corpse, but the only effect had been to singe its shabby robe a little. Pharaun reflected that despite several attempts, he had yet to injure or even jostle his adversary. If the dark elf hadn't known better, he might have wondered if Syrzan was not in fact the better arcanist.

Much as the Mizzrym disliked hand-to-hand combat, perhaps a change of tactics was in order. He snatched a delicate little bone, dissected from a petty demon he'd killed in a classroom demonstration, and started to conjure.

Syrzan swung its arm and hurled a dozen flaming arrows. They missed, bumped off course by their target's protective enchantments. Pharaun completed his incantation and so inflicted a hundred stabbing pains upon himself.

His body grew as large as an ogre's, and his hide thickened into scaly armor. His teeth lengthened into tusks, and his nails into talons, while long, curved horns erupted from his brow. A hairless tail sprouted from the base of his spine, and a whip appeared in his hand.

The transformation only took a moment, and the discomfort was gone.

With a beat of his leathery new wings, Pharaun hurled himself at his foe.

The wizard raised his monstrous arms high and bellowed an incantation. Pharaun felt a surge of churning vertigo. The scene before him seemed to spin and twist, and despite himself, he veered off course. He smashed down on the dais, and time skipped. When he came to his senses, he'd reverted to his natural form and felt as weak and sick as Smylla Nathos.

The lich was staring down at him.

"What an idiot you were to return," Syrzan said. "You knew you were no match for me."

Pharaun realized he could hear again, albeit through a jangling in his ears. He wouldn't die deaf, for whatever that was worth.

"Stop preening," said the Master of Sorcere. "You look ridiculous. This isn't your pathetic dream world. This is reality, where I'm a prince of a great city and you're just a sort of mollusk, and a dead, putrid one at that."

As he taunted the creature, he groped for the strength to cast a final spell. No doubt the attack would fail like all the others.

So why, he thought, bother to attack? Try something else instead. Shaking with effort, he cast a spell off the side of the platform. Blue scintilla of power glittered briefly in the air.

"You call *me* pathetic?" Syrzan sneered. "What was that supposed to be?"

If you were wearing the ring you stole, Pharaun thought, you'd know, but I doubt it would fit on your bloated fingers.

The alhoon hoisted him off the ground, then wrapped dry, flaking tentacles around his head.

You're still going to serve me, Syrzan said directly into the mage's mind, holding up one gnarled finger to reveal the silver ring. *When I devour your brain, I'll learn all your secrets.*

"Perhaps the infusion would even cure your stupidity," Pharaun wheezed, "but I fear we'll never know. Look around."

The lich turned, and he felt it jerk with surprise.

The lens of illusion he'd formed in front of the dais made Syrzan look exactly like a certain witty Master of Sorcere, and Pharaun himself resemble yet another humble orc. Once the Mizzrym created it, he'd willed the hand of ice to release the illithid's head, and there came the construct, swooping straight at its originator.

Syrzan threw Pharaun down and faced its creation. No doubt if left unmolested, it could have averted the construct somehow, but Pharaun found the strength for one more spell. His labored incantation shattered the floor of the dais, staggering the alhoon and breaking its concentration.

The huge tentacles scooped Syrzan up and conveyed it to the maw behind them, whereupon the strangely shaped mouth began to suck and chew. The alhoon's own magic mangled him as Pharaun's never had. The lich faded for a moment, then became opaque and solid again. It was trying to shift to another plane of existence but couldn't focus past the agony.

After a time, the enormous head blinked out of existence. Its passing dumped inert chunks of mummified mind flayer on the floor.

Pharaun's strength began to trickle back. He rummaged through the alhoon's stinking remains until he found his silver ring, then turned his magic on the renegades, though it wasn't really necessary. Ryld, Welverin, and their cohorts already had the upper hand.

When the last rogue lay dead, the entranced Master of Melee-Magthere sat down cross-legged on the floor. His chin drooped down onto his chest, and he started to snore. Silver leg rattling as if a blow had loosened the components, Welverin limped over to check him and, Pharaun supposed, tend him as needed.

The Mizzrym thought he ought to take a look as well but when he tried to stand, his head spun, and he had to flop back down.

Triel stood on the balcony gazing down at the city below. It was virtually the same view she'd surveyed on the night of the slave uprising, the burning spectacle that showed her all Menzoberranzan was in turmoil.

The fires were gone. In their place, cold pools of standing water dotted the streets and hindered traffic. The rain had flooded cellars and dungeons as well, and it would take time to get rid of it. No one had anticipated a downpour, not with miles of rock between the City of Spiders and the open sky, and in consequence, no builder had made much provision for drainage.

Someone coughed a discreet little cough. Triel turned. Standing in the doorway, Gromph inclined his head.

"Matron."

She felt a thrill of pleasure—relief, actually—at the sight of her brother, who'd come to her so quickly once she'd given him leave. She took care to mask the feeling.

"Archmage," she said. "Join me."

"Of course."

Gromph walked somewhat stiffly toward the balustrade.

In one corner of the terrace, Jeggred slouched on a chair too small for him and gnawed a raw haunch of rothé. He looked entirely engrossed in his snack, but Triel was confident he was watching her sibling's progress. That was his task, after all, to ward her from all potential enemies, including her own kin. *Especially* her own kin.

Gromph looked out at the city's domes and spires. Some had lost their luminescence, as if his rain had washed it away, and many had flowed and twisted in the fire's embrace, warping the spider carvings into crippled shapes or effacing them entirely. The wizard's mouth twisted.

"It could have been worse," Triel said. "The stoneworkers can repair the damage."

"They have their work cut out for them, especially without slaves to help."

"We have some. A few undercreatures declined to revolt or were captured instead of slain. We'll drive them hard and buy and capture more."

"Still, does anyone remember precisely how every rampart and sculpture looked? Can anyone recreate Menzoberranzan exactly as it was? No. We're changed, scarred, and—"

He winced and rubbed his chest.

"Forgive me," the archmage continued. "I didn't come to lament but to perform my function as your advisor, to share my thoughts on how to meet the challenges to come."

Triel rested her hand atop the cool, polished stone of the rail and asked, "How do you see those challenges?"

"It's obvious, isn't it? We've just experienced what promises to be the first in a series of calamities. By dint of observing you in combat, every Menzoberranyr with half a brain now knows you priestesses have lost your power. Rest assured, no matter what measures the Council takes, the word will spread beyond our borders. Perhaps some escaped thrall is proclaiming it even now. Soon, one or another enemy will march on us, or, if our luck is really bad, they might all unite in a grand alliance."

Triel swallowed. "None of our foes dares even to dream of taking Menzoberranzan."

"This Syrzan did. When its kin, and others, find out we've lost our divine magic, a significant fraction of our drow warriors, and virtually all our slave troops, it may inspire them to optimism. And they're not even the greatest threat."

"We ourselves are," Triel sighed.

"Exactly. We always have our share of feuds and assassinations. Occasionally one House exterminates another outright, and that's as it should be. It's our way, it makes us strong. But we can't endure constant, flagrant warfare. That would be too much . . . chaos. It would tear Menzoberranzan to shreds. Up to now, fear of the Spider Queen and her clergy has kept the lid on, but it won't anymore." He spat. "It's a pity our new heroes didn't die heroic deaths in their homeland's defense."

"You refer to Quenthel and the outcast Mizzrym?"

"Who else? Do you imagine them any less ambitious than the rest of us? They championed the established order yesterday, but, inspired by the knowledge that many would rally to their banners, may themselves seek to topple it tomorrow. Quenthel may try to seize your throne, not in a hundred years but now. Pharaun may strike for the Robes of the Archmage—by the Six Hundred and Sixty-six Layers, he all but did, having spent no effort in finding me before scurrying to your side. What a disaster that would be! Aside from any personal inconvenience to you and me, the city in its weakened state can't withstand that sort of disruption."

"I suppose they could be planning just that," Triel said, frowning. "Perhaps we should have followed through and at least killed Master Pharaun."

"If we execute one of the saviors of Menzoberranzan—damn his miserable little hide—it would have made House Baenre look frightened and weak." The archmage smiled a crooked smile. "Which we are, at the moment, but we don't dare give the appearance."

"What, then, do you recommend?"

Below the balcony, a lizard hissed and wheels creaked as a cart rolled by.

"Use them in a way that simultaneously benefits us and neutralizes the threat they represent," said Gromph. "Surely you and I agree that the present situation can't continue. We must find a way to restore the priesthood's magic."

Triel nodded, looking away from her battered city.

"I propose that as a first step," the archmage continued, "we send agents to another city—likely Ched Nasad—to find out if their divines are similarly afflicted, and if so, whether they know why. You can assign Quenthel to lead the expedition. After all, it concerns Arach-Tinilith perhaps most of all. I'll be delighted to loan you the services of Master Pharaun. If the story I heard was correct, that weapons master friend of his should go as well, if for no other reason than it'll make Pharaun squirm."

"Ched Nasad . . ." Triel whispered.

"The three of them ought to be more than capable of surviving a trek as far as Ched Nasad," continued Gromph, "and they can't very well try to overthrow us while they're leagues away from the city, can they? Who knows, perhaps Lolth will return before they do, and in any case, with time, their notoriety will fade."

His suggestion left Triel feeling a little sheepish. She hid it as best she could by pretending to consider his plan.

"Faeryl Zauvirr proposed an expedition to Ched Nasad. She claimed to be concerned because the caravans have stopped."

Gromph cocked his head. "Really? Well, our representatives can sort that out as well. You know, it's good that the ambassador is already keen to go. She'll make a valuable addition and a more than adequate cover for the whole enterprise."

"Waerva told me Faeryl was a spy," said Triel, "and sought to depart the city in order to report our weakness to her confederates. So I forbade her to leave."

"What proof did Waerva offer?"

"She told me she learned of Faeryl's treachery from one of her informants."

Gromph waited a moment as if expecting something more.

"And that's it?" he asked at length. "With respect, Matron, may I point out that if you haven't spoken with the informer yourself, if you haven't probed the matter any further, then you really only have Waerva's word for it that the envoy is a traitor."

"I can't handle everything personally," Triel scowled. "That's why we

have retainers in the first place. I have not entirely lost touch with my—
our interests in Ched Nasad, though their explanations and excuses do
wear thin."

"Of course, Matron," Gromph said quickly. "I quite understand. I have
the same problem with my own retainers, and I only have Menzoberranzan's wizards to oversee, not an entire city."

"Why would Waerva lie?"

"I don't know, but I've had some dealings with Faeryl Zauvirr. She never
struck me as stupid enough to cross the Baenre. Waerva, on the other
hand, is reckless and discontented enough for any game. Accordingly, I
think it might be worthwhile to inquire into this matter ourselves."

Triel hesitated before saying, "That could prove difficult. Despite my
orders, the Zauvirr tried to flee Menzoberranzan. I hired some agents of
Bregan D'aerthe, led by Valas Hune—do you know him?"

"I've heard the name mentioned," Gromph replied.

"He would make a fair addition to your little band of explorers," Triel
said. "He's known to be more than passingly familiar with the wilds of the
Underdark—a guide of some accomplishment, in fact."

Gromph bowed his agreement.

"Be that as it may, it was Valas Hune I hired to fetch Faeryl back. He
completed his task well, and I gave the ambassador to Jeggred."

The wizard rounded on the draegloth.

"What's the prisoner's condition?" he asked the creature. "Is she alive?"

"Yes," said Jeggred through a mouthful of bloody meat. "I was taking
my time, to prove I can. But you can't have her. Mother gave her to me.
She just told you."

Gromph stared up into the half-demon's eyes.

"Nephew," he said, "I'm sore, frustrated, and in a foul mood generally.
Right now I don't give a leaky sack of rat droppings whether you're a sacred
being or not. Show some respect, lead me to this prisoner forthwith, or I'll
blight you where you sit."

Clutching the rothé bone like a club, Jeggred sprang upward from his
seat.

Triel said, "Do as the archmage bade you. I wish it as well."

The draegloth lowered his makeshift weapon.

"Yes, Mother," he sighed.

T W E N T Y - F I V E

Her pack weighting her shoulders, her heart pounding, Waerva turned and peered about. The cave stretched out before her and behind, with stalactites stabbing down from the ceiling and stalagmites jutting up from the uneven floor. Nothing moved.

What, then, had she heard? As if in response to her unspoken question, a drop of falling water plopped somewhere in the passages ahead. It was one of the most common sounds of the Underdark, and scarcely a harbinger of peril.

Waerva wiped sweat from her brow and scowled at her own jumpiness. She had good reason to be edgy, though. Everyone said it was suicide to travel the subterranean wilderness alone.

Sadly, thanks to the cursed goblin rebellion, she had little choice. Because of the desperate fighting all across the city, the clergy's incapacity was no great secret anymore. Certainly Gromph had discerned it, which meant Triel no longer had anything to hide from him. Surely, then, she would seek his counsel once more.

Waerva had been confident she could manipulate the frazzled matron mother, but she very much doubted she could fool the canny archmage. Accordingly, she'd cleared out of the Great Mound and Menzoberranzan itself before her kinsman could start asking questions, and there she was, a solitary wayfarer hiking through a perilous wilderness.

But she was strong and cunning, and she'd survive. She'd make her way to her secret allies, and everything would be all right.

She took four more strides, then heard another little sound, and this one wasn't falling water. It sounded more like a stealthy footstep brushing stone, and it came from behind her.

She whirled and saw no one, then something stung her arm. She pivoted. At her feet lay the pebble someone had thrown. Soft, sibilant laughter rippled through the air. From the sound of it, the merrymakers were all around her.

Why, then, couldn't she see them?

Adamantine mace at the ready, one wing of her *piwafwi* tossed back to facilitate the action of her weapon arm, Waerva advanced in the direction from which the rock had come. Weaving her way through the stalagmites, she reached the cavern wall without so much as glimpsing her attacker. She caught a whiff of a familiar reptilian musk, though, and she knew.

Kobolds. The horned, scaly undercreatures were small enough that it was relatively easy for them to hide amid the calcite bumps and spikes.

She turned once more, and despite herself, gave a start. Evidently the kobolds lacked the patience to play their skulking game for very long, because they were done hiding. While her back was turned, they'd crept out into the open and there formed a ragged **C**-shaped line to pen her against the wall.

The brutes were Menzoberranyr thralls. House brands and whip scars gave that fact away. Indeed, a couple still wore broken shackles. Waerva plainly wasn't the only one who'd fled the city.

She glared at the kobolds and said, "I'm a Baenre. You know what that means. Make way, or I'll strike you dead."

The undercreatures stared back at her for a moment, then lowered their eyes. The line broke in the middle, making an exit.

Sneering, head held high, Waerva started for the opening. For a moment, all was silent, then the reptiles laughed, screeched, and rushed her.

Bellowing a battle cry, she swung her mace, and every stroke smashed the life from a thrall. But for every one she killed, there were dozens more hacking and beating at her legs.

Her knee screamed with pain, and she fell. The kobolds swarmed over her and pounded her until she just couldn't struggle any more.

With some difficulty, they divested her of her armor and clothing, and went to work on her. Amazingly for such a bestial race, they seemed to understand anatomy as thoroughly as her dear Tluth, but their ministrations were nothing like massage.

Faeryl had learned to court unconsciousness. It brought surcease from the lingering pains of past tortures. Unfortunately, it couldn't avert new ones. When Jeggred found her so, he simply waved a bottle of pungent smelling salts beneath her nose until it jolted her awake.

She could hear him coming. So could the jailers, who scurried to the back of the dungeon to give him privacy. Shivering, she struggled to compose herself. Perhaps she could deny him the satisfaction of a scream—at least for a while—or even provoke him into killing her. That would be wonderful.

The draegloth appeared in the doorway, stooping to pass through. Despite herself, Faeryl flinched, then saw he was not alone. Dainty little Triel accompanied him. So did her harsh-featured brother, clad as usual in the Robes of the Archmage.

"My . . . salutations, Matron," the Zauvirr croaked.

"Hush," said Gromph, "and all will be well." He looked up at the glowering half-demon. "Free her, and be gentle about it."

Jeggred strode to Faeryl. This time, she managed not to cringe. The draegloth supported her weight with his smaller hands while cutting her bonds with the claws of the larger ones, then scooped her up in his arms. She passed out.

Next came a blur of hours or days, during which she would wake for a few muddled seconds, then lapse into unconsciousness again. She lay on a soft divan, where servants salved and bandaged her wounds and sometimes spooned broth into her mouth. Priestesses read scrolls of healing, and Gromph appeared periodically to cast his own spells over her. She noticed Mother's Kiss lying on a little table beside her, and when she felt strong enough, stretched out her trembling arm and touched it.

Finally she opened her eyes to find her thoughts clear and vitality tingling in her limbs. The servants helped her don new raiment. They said it was for a meeting with Triel.

Faeryl considered taking her warhammer along, then thought better of it. If her rehabilitation was an elaborate prank, if the Baenre was summoning her to further torment, the weapon wouldn't save her.

Her legs still the least bit unsteady, she followed a male through the endless corridors of the Great Mound. Eventually he opened the door to a small but lavishly decorated room.

Triel sat at the table in the center of the space, with two bodyguards standing against the wall behind her. Faeryl inferred that this was a chamber the matron used when she wished to palaver away from the formal trappings of her court.

The Baenre rose and took her prisoner's hands.

"My child," Triel said, "I rejoice to see you. Some folk said you wouldn't recover, but I never doubted it. I knew you were strong, a true drow princess favored of Lolth."

"Thank you, Matron," said Faeryl, thoroughly perplexed.

Triel conducted her a chair.

"You'll be glad to know we caught them," the matron said.

"Them?"

"The brigands who waylaid you and murdered your followers, who left you for dead in that place where my servant Valas found you. I supervised the executions myself."

Faeryl was beginning to comprehend her situation. For some reason, Triel had forgiven her her disobedience. The Zauvirr could go free, her honor and rank restored, but there was a catch. Henceforth, she would have to endorse the fiction that Triel was in no way responsible for any of her misfortunes. For after all, the sovereign of Menzoberranzan was a perfect being, whom the Spider Queen herself had exalted above all others. How, then, could she possibly make a mistake?

It rankled a little, but Faeryl was more than willing to embrace the lie to avoid a return to the dungeon.

"Thank you, Matron," she said. "Thank you with all my heart."

Triel waved her hand, and a servant brought wine.

"Do you still want to go home?" the Baenre asked.

Pharaun had been summoned to a good many audiences in the course of his checkered career, and it had been his experience that no matter how urgent the occasion, one generally wound up parked in an antechamber for a while. Matron Baenre's waiting area was considerably more lavish than most, and in ordinary circumstances, he would have amused himself by passing esthetic judgment on the décor. Instead he had to address another matter, for when he arrived, Ryld was sitting on a chair in the corner, half hidden behind a marble statue.

The carving depicted a beautiful female doing something unpleasant to a deep gnome, for the greater glory of the Dread Queen of Spiders, one assumed.

The Mizzrym hadn't spoken to his friend since the slaughter of the renegades. He supposed the time had come. But first he paid his respects to Quenthel, who, much to her annoyance, was being kept waiting as well. The mage then bowed to a stern-faced drow male, looking ill at ease and out of place in rough outdoorsman's clothes and ugly trinkets. Pharaun didn't know him.

"Valas Hune," the warrior said, "of Bregan D'aerthe."

Pharaun introduced himself, then strolled toward the Master of Melee-Magthere.

"Ryld!" the wizard said. "Good afternoon! Have you any idea why the Council summoned us?"

The burly swordsman rose and said, "No."

"To shower us with honors, one assumes. How are you?"

"Alive."

"I rejoice to hear it. I was concerned because I could tell that warrior's trance strained even your constitution."

For a moment, the two masters regarded one another in silence.

"My friend," Pharaun said, having lowered his voice. "I truly regret what happened."

"What you did was tactically sound," said Ryld. "It was what any sensible drow would have done. I hold no grudge."

The wizard looked into weapons master's eyes and realized that for the first time, he couldn't read him.

Perhaps Ryld meant what he was saying, but it was just as likely he was lying, lulling his betrayer's suspicions to facilitate some eventual revenge. Thus, while Pharaun might continue to observe the forms of their long friendship, he could never trust his fellow master again.

For a moment he felt a pang of loss, but he quashed the sensation. Friendship and trust were for lesser races. They weakened a dark elf, and he was better off without them.

Pharaun gave Ryld an affectionate clap on the shoulder, just as he had a thousand times before.

When the tall doors opened, all eight Matrons of the Council sat enthroned and illuminated on an eight-tiered pyramid of a dais, with Triel of course set higher than the others, and a span of radiant marble webbing arching overhead. Quenthel stalked in proudly, ahead of Pharaun and the other males, and why not? She was Mistress of Arach-Tinilith and a Baenre.

Truth to tell, a miniscule part of her, a part she loathed and repudiated, hadn't wanted to come in, because her unknown enemy was very likely in the room

The matriarchs weren't the only folk in the vicinity of the platform. A symbol of the goddess's favor and a source of practical protection, Jeggred loomed behind Triel's chair. Servants scurried about the steps to do the great ladies' bidding. Gromph stood on the highest riser, a place of ultimate honor for a male.

When she, the mage, the weapons master, and the mercenary reached the foot of the dais, Triel began to praise them for their efforts against the illithilich and its pawns. At first the oration was pretty much what Quenthel had expected, but soon it took an unexpected turn.

She herself would lead an expedition to Ched Nasad to find out why no travelers came from that direction, and what the priestesses of the vassal city might know concerning the silence of Lolth. Ryld Argith, Pharaun Mizzrym, and Valas Hune would serve as her lieutenants, accompanying the ambassador, Faeryl Zauvirr.

Upon hearing the news, the hulking warrior in the dwarven breastplate simply inclined his head in acquiescence. The wizard grinned, and the scout smiled. At first the envoy, who was standing nearby, looked equally pleased.

Then Triel said, "Finally, dear sister, I lend you my own son Jeggred for your journey. A draegloth carries the blessing of the Dark Mother, and you may need his strength."

For an instant, it looked as if Faeryl would protest, and Jeggred leered down at her. Plainly, something had once transpired between them, an unpleasantness that made the ambassador loathe and mistrust him.

Gromph shifted his weight as well and Quenthel thought he looked surprised, even a bit put out. Perhaps he hadn't thought Triel had sense enough to want her own special agent on the mission, a minion devoted to her particular interests alone.

A thousand arguments against her being sent away at so uncertain a time for Menzoberranzan, the faith, House Baenre . . . came to Quenthel in a rush. Ultimately, however, she said nothing.

The assembly discussed the practicalities of their scheme for an hour or so, and Triel dismissed her newly appointed emissaries. Pharaun caught up with Quenthel in the antechamber. He bowed to her, and she waved her hand, giving him permission to speak.

"I assume, Mistress, that you know why they picked us?" he murmured.

"I understand better than you," she said.

Pharaun arched an eyebrow and asked, "Indeed. Will you elucidate?"

She hesitated, but why not state at least the obvious? He had come to her, after all, when the slave revolt began. He was a true drow—ambitious and ruthless enough that she could always trust him to do what was to his advantage. Gromph had made him a decoy and a target, perhaps someday she would make him Archmage of Menzoberranzan.

"My brother and sister send us both forth because they fear our ambitions."

"I daresay that's very sensible of them," Pharaun said. "Does this mean you undertake our errand reluctantly?"

"By no means. Whatever my siblings' motives, the plan has merit, and I would go anywhere and do anything to restore my bond with Lolth and save Menzoberranzan; it is of course the same thing."

In fact, she was eager to distance herself from them until such time as she recovered her magic, provided she could do it without a loss of status, and surprisingly, it seemed she could. The matter of the demonic assassins had still not been settled, too, and she wondered if her leaving the city would bring her unknown assailant into the open.

She looked her foppish companion up and down.

"What of you?" she asked the wizard. "You're brave enough—I've seen the proof—but still, are you eager to march across the Underdark?"

"You mean, can an exquisite specimen such as myself bear to dispense with warm, scented baths, succulent meals, and delicate, freshly laundered attire?" Pharaun asked with a grin. "It will be excruciating, but under the circumstances, I'll manage. I enjoy unraveling mysteries, particularly when I suspect I might enhance my personal power thereby."

"Perhaps you will," Quenthel said, "but I recommend you keep your hands off any prize your leader covets for herself."

"Of course, Mistress, of course."

The Master of Sorcere bowed low.

Pharaun cast a spell, then slipped through the closed door like a ghost. On the other side was a drab, stale-smelling little room. Wrapped in a blanket like an invalid, her scarred face a mask of bitterness, Greyanna sat in the only chair.

For an instant, she stared at him stupidly, then started to throw off the cover, presumably with the intent of jumping up. He lifted his hands as if to cast a spell, and the threat froze her in place.

"What a dreary habitation," he said. "It was Sabal's, wasn't it, when her fortunes were at their nadir. Mother has a good memory and a charming sense of irony as well."

"And she'll kill you, outcast, for breaking into the castle."

"I always assumed so. That's one reason I never paid you a visit hitherto. But our circumstances have changed. The Council needs me to help determine what's become of the Spider Queen, and you, dear sib, are no longer a person of any importance. As Miz'ri's demoted you for your repeated failures to kill me, I doubt she'll make an issue of your extinction, even if she's certain I'm responsible. She *smiled* at me this afternoon when I saw her in House Baenre, can you believe it? She must have decided she'd like me to resign from Sorcere and rejoin the family someday. Evidently she's just realizing how powerful I've become in the decades since you chased me out the door."

"I'm surprised you still want to kill me," Greyanna said. "You've already defeated and ruined me. Death may prove a mercy."

"I considered that, but I'm going on a journey into the unknown, a quest fraught with peril and adversity to be sure, and I need something special to hearten me, a memory fraught with spectacle and drama to cheer me on the trail."

"I suppose I understand," the priestess said, "but I wonder why it's come to this. All these years, I've never truly understood the basis for our feud. If I'm to die, will you at least tell me why you chose Sabal over me? Was it fondness? Was it lust?"

"Neither," Pharaun chuckled. "My choice had nothing whatever to do with personalities. How could it, when you twins were so alike? I threw in with Sabal simply because she was dangling from the bottom rung of the Mizzrym ladder. I thought it would be an amusing challenge to lift her to the top."

"Thank you for explaining," Greyanna said. "Now die."

Pharaun's own living rapier leaped from beneath the blanket. Obviously Greyanna had not only claimed the fallen weapon but figured out how to control it. No doubt she'd been wearing it in its steel-ring form when he entered the room. Knowing how he loved to talk, she'd lulled him with conversation and took him by surprise.

The long, thin-bladed sword hurtled across the room toward Pharaun's chest. He frantically shifted to the side, and the point plunged into his left forearm instead. For a second, he couldn't feel the puncture, and it flared with pain.

He had to immobilize the weapon or it would pull itself free and attack again. He grabbed hold of the blade with his right hand, and it sliced into his palm. A rapier was made for thrusting, but it had sharp edges even so. Sharp enough, anyway.

At the same instant, Greyanna cast off the blanket and snatched a mace from behind her chair. She jumped up and charged.

Pharaun narrowly dodged her first swing, then threw himself against her, ramming her with his shoulder. The impact knocked her stumbling backward.

It didn't hurt her, though. She laughed and advanced on him again.

He knew why she was so exhilarated. She thought that with his left hand dangling at the end of a spastic arm and the right busy gripping the rapier, he wouldn't be able to cast any appropriate spells to fend her off.

And she was right.

Edging away from Greyanna, his hand dripping blood, he let go of the living sword and started to conjure, rapidly as only a master could.

His sister rushed him. The rapier jerked itself out of his wound, hurting him anew. It pivoted in the air and aimed itself at his heart.

Five darts of azure force shot from his right hand into Greyanna's body. She made a sighing sound and collapsed, her mace clanking against the floor.

At once the rapier became inert, and fell clattering to the floor.

He studied Greyanna, making sure she was truly dead, then examined his own wounds. They were unpleasant, but a healing potion or two would mend them.

"Thank you, sister," he said, "for a most inspiring interlude. When I sally forth to save our beloved Menzoberranzan, it will be with a heart full of joy."